RAGNEKAI

STORMS

BOOK THREE OF THE OLD WOUNDS TRILOGY
AN URAMI WORLD NOVEL

PETER BUCKMASTER

RAGNEKAI STORMS
This paperback edition 2019
Peter Buckmaster asserts the moral right to be identified as the author
of this work.
ISBN-13: 9781081418991

This novel is entirely a work of fiction.
The names, characters and incidents in it are the work of the author's
imagination. Any resemblance to actual persons, living or dead,
events or localities is entirely coincidental.

Copyright © 2019 by Peter Buckmaster (www.buckmasterbooks.com)
Printed by Kindle Direct Publishing
First Printing, 2019

For Eriko, Haruki & Tomoki

You are the three pillars that hold me up

RAGNEKAI

STORMS

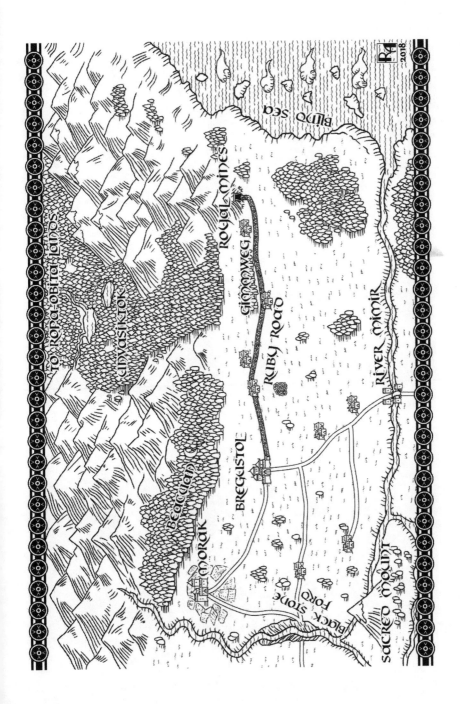

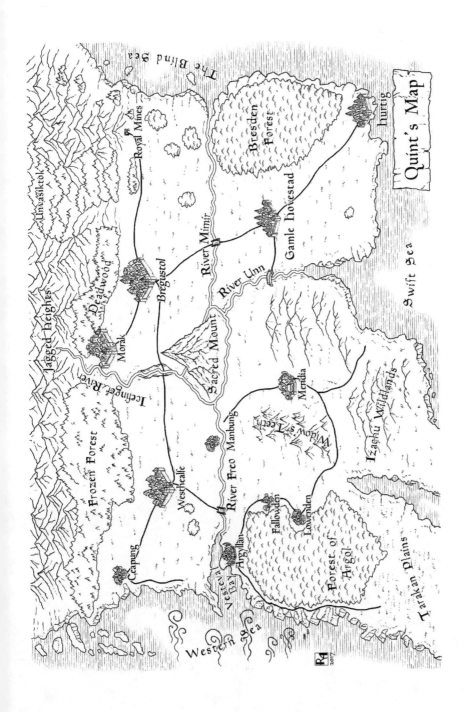

Events since Sedmund's death

25th Day of Aprus	Death of High King Sedmund
2nd Day of Maia	Meridian soldiers arrive in Argyllan
5th Day of Maia	City of Meridia falls to Helligan forces
9th Day of Maia	Brother Eswic disappears
11th Day of Maia	City of Morak falls to Duthka and Unvasik
13th Day of Maia	Battle for Argyllan
15th Day of Maia	Battle at the Black Stone Ford
19th Day of Maia	Unvasik attack the Royal Mines and the village of Gimmweg

PROLOGUE (19ᵀᴴ MAIA)

It had been almost a whole day since the harsh clanging of bells had been heard in every corner of Gamle Hovestad, telling the Helligan people their ruler, Lord Orben, was dead. And it had been a month now since Lorken had left. He had gone west to Meridia, marching as a Helligan soldier, and hadn't come back. The assassination of Orben had frightened Jenna, but her husband's death had already devastated her.

The Helligan widow's heart ached endlessly in ebbs and flows. At times, the great waves of anguish made her legs weak and compelled her to sit for a while as she remembered her husband. She wanted to be strong for their three children, Darl, Torg, and Eira, but half of her being was no longer here. The half of her being that could make her smile when there was less food on the table than usual; the half that made her feel young again as hands roamed over her body and whispers floated to her ears telling her how she was more beautiful than a sunrise over Bresden Forest; and the half that gave her confidence her three children would grow into fine adults.

That half was gone. Lorken was dead.

I can't do this without you, Lorkie. I need you.

Jenna could hear Darl and Torg chopping wood outside as she list-lessly washed the breakfast crockery. The two of them had not slacked in their work in the slightest; if anything, they had taken on more work than was perhaps sensible. Jenna believed they were keeping themselves busy not just to keep their minds away from their father's death, but also because they felt a deep obligation to continue his work and keep all the customers satisfied.

Lorken, if only you could see them now. You'd be so proud...

The Helligan widow realised she had stopped washing the plates and was now just standing at the bowl, her fingers hanging in the tepid water. Her daily routine, that had previously been carried out without a thought, had now become a chain of tasks—tasks to which she some-times felt there was no point. Without Lorken, the future was a glaring white expanse, barren and desolate. Gone were the images she would conjure up of Darl and Torg standing shoulder to shoulder with their father in the district hall, their names being etched into the walls. Gone was the gentle picture in her mind of Lorken and herself making the trip to the southern port of Hurtig, a journey he had always promised. And gone was the joy of the day when Eira would speak her first words to her father.

Her eyes watered, and she shook her head as a sob began to rise within her. *First Warrior, why? Tell me why Lorken was taken! Our future has been stolen...*

A knock at the door startled her. She blinked, thinking she had imagined it, until it came again. A gentle *ton-ton* on the oak door. Jen-na hurriedly dried her hands.

"A moment, please," she called out. She hoped it wasn't a carpentry customer. She inhaled deeply, wiped away at the streaks upon her face where tears had traced lines in their fall, and walked to the door. When she opened it, she was surprised to see a woman.

"Can I help you?" she asked politely.

The woman looked uncomfortable, unsure of herself. "Sorry to bother you. Erm..." She shifted her weight from left to right, then back again. She was roughly the same height and build as Lorken had been, with muscular arms bared to the elements as she wore a leather vest. Blue ink swirls patterned these, and Jenna noticed more than one scar on her left arm and around her neck. Her chestnut hair was tied back, and her dark eyes darted from side to side, seemingly trying to avoid looking at Jenna directly.

She cleared her throat and spoke again. "The First Ranger asked that I visit you, Miss Jenna."

A friend of Svard's then.

Jenna's eyes widened. She suddenly had an impossible notion that there had been a mistake and Lorken was still alive, and this had been the kind of nightmare one wakes from.

The next words shattered this brief feeling of euphoria.

"I was with your husband when he…"

Their eyes met and Jenna saw sorrow mixed with guilt there.

"Come in. Please."

The woman hesitated, her body turning away slightly. Jenna opened the door wider and the woman stepped over the threshold, head hung.

"Please sit," said Jenna, gesturing toward the eating table. The woman dithered momentarily, then sat, her eyes looking anywhere but Jenna. Lorken's widow quickly retrieved two clay cups and a pitcher of barley tea from the larder. She set them on the table and pulled out a chair for herself.

The sound of the tea sloshing into the cups was loud within the silence, neither having any words. The woman dipped her head in thanks, picked up the cup and drank deeply, as if she was parched.

"Please tell me your name," said Jenna gently.

She looked up. "Freda. It's Freda…and I…I'm so sorry, Miss Jenna, I was there but I wasn't worthy enough to save him." The words began to tumble. "We didn't expect any cavalry. It was chaos. Geir and I tried to keep Lorken safe, but we failed…I failed."

Jenna battled the emotion surging upward from her heart, gathering in her throat and enticing yet more tears from the eyes. She breathed slowly, trying to regain control.

"When the Dark Raven flies over our heads, none are safe." She paused, again mustering the strength to speak without breaking down. "I thank you, Freda, for risking your own life in trying to protect my husband. Would that the First Warrior had stood with you all that day."

Freda nodded, and Jenna saw that expressing herself through the Dark Raven and the First Warrior touched this soldier more deeply. The woman looked up and offered a smile.

"He spoke of you and the children every night at the campfire."

Freda had probably thought this would delight Jenna, but it had the exact opposite effect. Her defences crumbled and she let out a sob, her mind seeing her beloved husband speak of them with warm words. Not only was he gone but the love he bore for his family had been taken also, cast into the void between life and death, hanging in limbo.

"F-forgive me," stammered Freda. "I did not...mean to bring sadness."

Jenna waved a hand dismissively but couldn't raise her eyes, blinded as they were by hot tears.

At that moment, the back door opened. Jenna lifted her head and saw her elder son, Darl. His expression changed from confusion to anger.

"Mother?"

He then addressed Freda. "Who are you?"

His tone was less than polite, and this brought Jenna back to the here and now.

"Darl, you forget your manners!" she scolded him. "This is Freda. She stood with your father at the battle." She took one of her son's hands as he approached. "We were not the only ones to lose someone that day. Remember that."

Lorken's elder son hung his head for a moment, then raised it and looked at Freda.

"I'm sorry. That was rude of me." He swallowed and then spoke again. "It was a terrible day." He looked embarrassed and Jenna sensed he had wanted to say something worthwhile to a valiant soldier who had been there when Lorken had died. But there were no words that could make sense of war.

Freda nodded and smiled gently at the lad. Jenna saw she was an attractive woman under a rough exterior. Darl blushed and she wondered if he was taken in by the combination of a pretty face coupled with the brave nature of those who fought battles. She patted his arm.

"Let me speak with Freda some more. Take out this tea and make sure Torg is drinking. The sun is hot today."

Darl picked up the jug and turned to go. He hesitated and then refilled Freda's cup before hurrying out the back again. Jenna couldn't help but chuckle.

"I think you charmed my son somewhat."

Freda looked almost horrified. "Me?! I'm an ugly, messed up soldier who speaks with a tongue that was born in the gutter!"

"Maybe to yourself. But to some, perhaps like my son there, you possess a fierce beauty and a strength that I myself envy."

Freda looked nothing short of amazed. Her head titled to one side and a smile formed on her lips.

"You are the lady Lorken spoke of. I thought he was just missing his wife and remembering only the good times because he'd had a few ales." She shook her head. "But you really are all he said."

Jenna's heart rose and this time it was a joyous emotion. Lorken had loved her as much as she had loved him. And now her love for him swelled as Freda's words told her he had let others know of this love.

"Thank you," she murmured and reached out to place a hand on Freda's forearm. It was hard with muscle the way Lorken's had been. The Helligan soldier seemed embarrassed by the gesture but did not move her arm away.

"So, how old is your son?" asked Freda, seemingly suddenly very interested.

Jenna's eyes widened as she imagined this handsome woman stealing her son away. Freda's serious expression fell away and she laughed.

"I'm jesting!"

Jenna breathed a laugh herself and felt her body relax. Freda chuckled and shrugged her shoulders.

"He'll have his pick of the ladies though, I reckon. Handsome and strong. Polite with it. More than can be said for my worthless husband."

Jenna's eyebrows rose in interest. "You're married?"

"Yeah, wasn't exactly the usual year of courtship and then him kissing my old man's arse." Jenna smiled, seeing Freda was over any initial awkwardness now and speaking as she would to a friend. "Both of us got wrecked on some cheap rum one night out on the rolling waves, got a fair bit of chafing from the ropes up on deck, declared our undying love for each other, and the ship's captain married us the next day. Back on land, things were rougher though." Freda cackled a mischievous laugh. "But what can you do?"

Jenna found herself warming to this woman who lived a life she would never know. She blurted out a question and quickly regretted it.

"Do you have children?"

Freda's face clouded.

"We tried for a while. Maybe a year or so. No luck. Not sure if I'm barren or he has no seed, don't really care anymore. First Warrior perhaps figured we wouldn't make the best parents so guided us to another life."

"I'm sorry," was all Jenna could think to say.

"No need to be sorry. I'd be a terrible mother. Out to sea much of the year, blind drunk the rest of the time." Freda looked around her. "You've got a good home for your children here, Miss Jenna."

"Please, just Jenna. I'm no lady!"

"You're a queen compared to the likes of me, Jenna!" Freda laughed again, and Jenna couldn't help but join her. She realised this was the first time she had felt any kind of mirth since Svard had come to their house that day, bearing the crushing news. It felt good but was tinged with a slight guilt. She knew Lorken would want her to laugh again, but she wanted to finish each spell of merriment with words, to anyone who would listen, that she hadn't forgotten her sorrow and loss. It felt odd, but she knew mourning manifested itself in strange ways.

"So, the son who likes me…" Freda winked. "He's the eldest then?"

"Yes, Darl is sixteen and Torg thirteen. Then there is Eira, our daughter, who is the baby of the family."

Freda turned her head this way and that, searching the room. She looked at Jenna questioningly.

"Oh, she's not here." Jenna sighed. "Since Lorken died, she has been out of sorts. I'm not sure she really understands he is gone. She keeps running off to play Raven knows where. The first few times we spent the mornings searching the district for her to no avail. But she always comes back around the middle of the afternoon. I worry about where she's going but I think it might just be her way of dealing with her father not being here anymore."

"Wish I had some advice for you." Freda blew out a breath. "But I wouldn't know where to begin with children. The thought of being responsible for what kind of adult they become scares me. You've got to guide them, right? Teach them right and wrong. How do you know what to do?"

Jenna smiled. "You don't know. Nobody does. It's all a case of doing what you feel is best. Lorken and I always talk about…" She trailed off, realising she was speaking as if her husband were still alive.

She sighed and squeezed her eyes against the tears. Freda's hand touched her arm gently.

"If you ever doubt anything, just ask yourself what Lorken would have said. It's what I do. My mother was the wisest soul I knew. If things get hard, I ask myself what she would say in this moment." Freda let out a throaty laugh. "Only trouble is I'm shit at taking advice… Sorry, didn't mean to curse. But you know Lorken better than anyone. You know what he'd say or do, whatever the Dark Raven throws at you. Ask him and you'll have your answer." She shrugged.

Jenna found herself nodding. The lady sitting before her was right. Lorken still lived within Jenna, and so she could still guide their children in a way that would honour the man he had been.

Freda coughed. "I'm sorry, Jenna. But I must head off now. Orders have been flying since Lord Orben's death yesterday. My boat crew and others are heading down to Hurtig, leaving at noon. Lady Ulla wants us patrolling the southern coast. Worried Orben's murder was some Xerin-thian plot, I think."

Jenna tensed at these words. Was her home in danger? Freda contin-ued talking, a frown upon her face.

"My friend, Geir, who also stood with your husband that day, left days ago. Before the Dark Raven visited Orben." The marine scratched the shorn sides of her head. "Not sure anyone knows what is going on." She rose from her chair. "But orders are orders."

Jenna pushed back her chair also.

"Thank you for coming, Freda." She paused. "Will you come again? Maybe join us for lunch one day?"

Jenna was surprised at how Freda's face lit up.

"You serious?! You want me to eat with you? My manners aren't the best…"

"You'd be welcome here. Lorken would say so too."

Freda nodded vigorously, a beaming smile lighting up her face.

"I'd be honoured. Thank you. I'll be away a ten-day at sea so when I get back?"

"Of course. And please bring your husband with y—"

Freda burst into laughter, shaking her head left and right frantically. "Trust me, you don't want that drunken oaf anywhere near your table! His arse makes more conversation than he does."

Jenna's mind spun with images of a rough and ready sailor, long in his cups, with terrible flatulence.

"Anyway," said Freda, leaning in, "I won't be able to flirt with your son if my man's watching." She grinned at Jenna's wide eyes.

Then Jenna moved in and hugged this beautiful sea storm of a woman. Freda's body stiffened, then relaxed.

Jenna whispered in her ear. "Thank you, Freda. You've given me the strength to stand today."

She let her go. Freda looked embarrassed by the show of emotion, but her eyes were a well of friendship waiting to be drawn from.

The Helligan soldier took a step back, turned to go, but then cocked her head. "So, does your son drink yet? Got some good grog I can bring along."

Jenna made a shooing motion with her hand. "Away with you, sea siren!"

Freda grinned and stepped outside. Jenna followed.

"May the First Warrior guide your sails!" Jenna called as Freda waved good-bye.

She watched as the soldier jogged away.

Jenna went back into the house and sat down. She ran her hands over the table, her fingers finding the glyphs the boys had carved. And for the first time since Svard had brought her the devastating news, she felt she could live.

And then her mind turned to Eira.

Where does she run off to?

PART ONE

CHAPTER 1

KAPVIK

19th Day of Maia, After The Battle In The Sacred Mount

"We have climbed high."

Kapvik paused and took a breath. He looked up at Siorraidh, now resting upon a shadow of rocky outcrop. He made the three steps it took to reach her and raised his eyes to the darkening sky.

She spoke again, her voice something he had known for only a matter of days, yet it was as familiar to him as any song praising Tatkret The Watcher. Like the wind that swirled around them, her voice was free, boundless and breath-taking.

"This is like your home I think, Kapvik. This fresh air and bracing wind."

Home…

The Unvasik warrior gave a small nod. The Duthka woman had set a punishing pace for their trek up the mountain, and the dull, orange glow of dusk was now drawing in, the last of the daylight slipping away in the west beyond this mighty behemoth of nature. They were only halfway up, on the north face, but the exhilaration he felt with each breath made him wonder if he would be satisfied living in the green lowlands after all. Siorraidh had the truth of it; feeling the wind up here reminded him of the Unvasik tribelands. His home. There was a bite to the gusts that gently buffeted him. Nothing as harsh as the northern plateaus where his people resided, but enough to induce some reflection by the giant warrior.

I feel more alive up here. The wind is forever calling me.

Kapvik did ruefully admit, though, that it wasn't just the mountain air that was affecting his spirit; being with the Duthka lady had sparked something within him. She was in total control when with her people, issuing orders that were obeyed without question, but gentle and inquisitive when they were alone. And Kapvik couldn't shake the feeling that she possessed a great power within her, or at least knowledge that was as beyond his understanding as the stars were beyond his reach. She was no witch but Kapvik was convinced she was somehow more than just a young lady.

"The lowlands are crowded. And the air makes me drowsy," he muttered, wishing he could express his thoughts in a more impressive fashion.

"Qaneq illit daku Unvasik wa-um ni untok, Kapvik?"

Kapvik raised his eyebrows and couldn't help but grin. Her language skills were impressive.

"Yes," he replied in the Unvasik tongue, "speaking in my words would be good."

He looked at her, the setting sun behind her creating a majestic silhouette and her lack of hair defining the shape of her head: an oval of perfect symmetry. She turned slightly and his breath caught in his chest, those high cheekbones under her upturned eyes telling Kapvik she was surely blessed by Tatkret the Watcher's first wife, Kahdlu. This was a woman who shone even at night, stood strong against fierce and frigid winds, and would blind lesser men as she rose within a storm. Kapvik realised he was staring and sniffed.

"How do you come to speak so many words of so many people?" he mumbled, lowering his eyes to break her spell.

Siorraidh laughed and shrugged. "I have always had a gift for learning new things, especially language. And I listen. Most people *hear* what others are saying but they do not truly *listen*. They merely wait for the flow of others' words to stop so they can listen to their own voice." She raised her hands to his face. Kapvik had to dip his head, as she was almost two feet shorter than him. Her fingers ran through his beard and he felt a surge in his chest.

Tatkret, give me the strength to resist this wonderful creation of the gods!

"Come, let us build a fire before we lose all the sun's light," she said, still using his language, and still leading the way in all they did. "There is a small cave there that will shelter us."

Kapvik got to work. After they had retreated from the heart of the mountain, after the skirmish within, she had sent the surviving Duthka away to carry out whatever was next in Seolta's plan, several hefting the sacks of the harvested fungus. Then she had retrieved various belongings from a hollow tree that had fallen: a sack of cut wood, full water-skins, a bag of dried meat and other provisions, and two rolled-up blankets. His first reaction had been one of weariness, imagining they would be camping longer in the woodlands at the foot of the mountain and waiting for orders from her lord. But then she had turned to the gargantuan summit, a seductive smile upon her lips.

"Are you coming?" she had asked, as if there were nothing unusual in all her actions. He had followed her of course, finding it difficult to resist her charm and almost fearing to part from her. He did feel some unease though. The Duthka, and Siorraidh in particular, seemed to have everything planned out, and Kapvik reckoned the Unvasik were being led forward, rather than marching in unison with these moon worshippers. The Unvasik had shown their strength in Morak but the city had already been felled by the hand of the Duthka, truth be told. Kapvik felt his people were being used as a blunt instrument, a cudgel to club the stubborn ones.

Perhaps that is all we are good for…

He returned his attention to the task Siorraidh had set him and soon had the fire going. He found he was grateful for the light more than the warmth. For in the flickering glow of the flames her face shimmered, the ink swirls on her shorn head alive, and her smile an almost mischievous mystery.

"So tell me why we are climbing this mountain," he said when they were seated side-by-side, in the mouth of the cave. The flames licked the evening air before them and sparks burst forth as tiny globs of resin caught fire. "What is up here that you want so badly?"

She leaned in and squeezed his thick bicep.

"I cannot be sure we will find it, but I believe there is something at the summit that I desire. Something from a past age, before those down there came over the waters," she said, sweeping her arm across the vista, now submerged in dark blue shadows.

Those who came over the waters… The Plague From The Sea.

Kapvik grunted at the thought but followed her hand with his gaze. Stretching out before them, now lost to the deepening darkness, was the north of Marrh. The pale blue of the Icefinger River had been visible during the day, coming down from between the Beacuan and Abhaile forests, the Jagged Heights a silent presence behind them. The city of Bregustol could also be seen when the sun had graced the sky. The view had been impressive and Kapvik had realised that this was the first time he had taken a moment to appreciate the beauty of the world around him.

I am becoming one of these weak lowlanders…

Kapvik brought his thoughts back to their conversation, wondering what could possibly be at the top of this mountain.

"What is this thing?"

Siorraidh smiled cryptically. "Please forgive me if I keep that to myself for now. If it is not there, I would prefer that only one of us be disappointed."

He huffed lightly. There was a crack and a snap as some wood succumbed to the flames, rupturing and falling deep into the tiny inferno. Kapvik stared into the fire and grinned. He didn't really care if they found this thing or not. Being with her was reward enough for this climb.

"Maybe we will feel it the closer we get. I believe the birds do," she said softly.

Kapvik snorted a laugh. "You make no sense, mystical lady of the moon."

She leaned up and kissed him. His very nature seemed to protest at the power of her seduction. He was a mighty warrior and yet with her, he was a foolish boy. He put his arm around her and pulled her in toward him.

"Vorga would have my head if he could see me now," Kapvik grumbled.

"Seolta and Vorga are far too busy to concern themselves with us right now." She turned her head. "You know why your lord sent you with me, I presume?"

Kapvik frowned. "I was surprised he ordered me to go with you. I am his Fist and should be by his side."

"You are his most trusted warrior," Siorraidh commented. Kapvik nodded slowly, his thoughts jumbled.

"So, he trusts you with whatever he deems most important," she continued.

Vorga thinks Siorraidh is up to something...

He turned to face her and saw she wore an expression that seemed to say Kapvik had the answers already. The Unvasik warrior thought back to Vorga's order.

"Do not let her out of your sight."

"Vorga believes you are doing more than just gathering that fungus?" he proposed, thinking aloud.

"And who gives me orders?" she asked, grinning.

Kapvik saw it then. He pulled away from her, his body angling to face the Duthka woman.

"Vorga does not trust Seolta. Vorga thinks your lord is hiding something from him." Kapvik looked up sharply. "So, we are climbing this damn mountain to find something your lord would hide from mine?" His voice rose like a wave coming to shore.

Siorraidh held up her hands, palms outward, then put them together in front of her. Kapvik waited as she took a deep breath.

"Seolta does not know we are climbing the Sacred Mount now. He is unaware I am seeking this thing."

Kapvik clenched his teeth. This woman was full of riddles and confused him as much as enchanted him with each word that danced out from between her lips.

"Why do you hide this from your lord?" he asked, his eyes narrow with suspicion.

Siorraidh sighed. "Vorga is wise not to trust Seolta completely."

This sat poorly with the Unvasik warrior. Would Seolta betray them?

"What do you mean?" he asked slowly.

"I mean that Seolta is like any other man. He yearns for power so he can rule. But like any man, he will become drunk on the power and end up crushing what he desires to control. Forgive me for saying so, Kapvik, but men have a tendency to destroy. Women have ever sought to protect."

The Unvasik tribesman, Vorga's Fist, let her words swirl within his mind. He couldn't deny that a woman's natural instinct was to protect the young while the man sought to kill any that threatened his people. But the man was defending his own, so he too was keeping the children safe. He voiced his thoughts to Siorraidh.

"You are not wrong, Kapvik, but what is it that the man defends? It is his territory, his home, and his property, and that property includes his wife, I would suggest. In a sense, all that a man protects is his own pride."

Kapvik shook his head. She was wrong. Kapvik fought hard to protect his people. He fought hard so Tatkret the Watcher would see him and…

See me and praise me.

Siorraidh shuffled over to him and pushed her body against his. "Do not be angry with my observations. I am not saying men are all worthless, with all their ambitions cascading into catastrophe. I simply believe that some men are arrogant and putting too much power in such a man's hands is dangerous, especially if he has nobody he cares for. No love in his life."

Kapvik's frustration was boiling over. There was truth in what she said but reckless love could also be dangerous and drive men to commit unspeakable acts.

"Seolta has nobody?" he asked, his eyes avoiding hers.

"No. He does not. He has only ever looked to his own future. And that is why I fear, if he possessed great power, he would destroy everything in his quest to rule. A king of ashes, a lord of bones. Power must be shared, Kapvik." She squeezed his hand with her own. "And I would share whatever power is up there…" she said, pointing above them.

With you.

Kapvik jumped in his own skin. Her voice had sounded within his head. He pulled away from her once more and stared.

"How…how did you do that? I heard your voice in here!" he gasped, tapping his temple.

Siorraidh smiled. "I didn't mean to startle you, Kapvik."

I only wanted to show you a gift I have.

Kapvik reeled. Was this indeed a witch before him? Did she practice dark arts? How could she be within his head?

I can share my words with you, my thoughts flowing.

"It is a gift, not a curse," she said aloud.

Her head dropped and she spoke quietly.

"Though some have claimed I am cursed."

Kapvik's doubts crumbled as he saw her pain. He grabbed her and hugged her tightly, kissing her shaven head.

"You are not cursed, Siorraidh." He struggled to find words. "It is a gift. It must be." Then Kapvik remembered the first night they had lain together.

"That night. You were speaking in someone's mind?"

She looked up at him and offered half a smile. "I believe she was speaking in my mind. Somehow, she found me. I don't know why but she is very…"

Her voice trailed off and Kapvik sensed an anxiety in Siorraidh. That alone troubled him.

The Unvasik warrior's thoughts stumbled over one another.

Too many riddles. Too much that I cannot see with my own eyes.

Kapvik gently pushed her back and went to put more wood on their little fire. He again felt his mind being suffocated. In Unvasiktok, his life had been simple, clear, and he understood all that happened. Now he had entered a world in which nothing made sense, and all was ever changing.

He turned back to her. "Can you see my thoughts?"

She let out a small laugh. "No more than anyone can." She raised an eyebrow. "Test me. Think something and I will try to divine what it is!" she said, her tone light.

Kapvik gazed at her beauty in the warm glow of the fire.

You are a goddess walking among us.

She shook her head, her mouth twitching at the corners. "You were thinking something nice about me."

Kapvik stared, his eyes wide and his jaw dropping.

Siorraidh burst out laughing. "Kapvik, I didn't see your thoughts. I looked at your face and saw it there."

He relaxed, feeling slightly foolish.

"Do not think about me. Think about anything but me," she chided.

He closed his eyes and cleared his mind. Then he pushed through the fog of the present and traced back into deep memories, peering through the snow-storms of Sila to see his past, a clear but pale blue lake.

Jakpa was such a skilled fighter, yet I beat him at the Tratok to become Vorga's Fist. I will never forget that day.

Siorraidh squinted and Kapvik began to feel she was teasing him.

"You are wondering again why you are climbing this mountain with me?"

He grinned, despite himself. Maybe she was lying but he didn't think so. She was perceptive, not drenched in sorcery. How she put her words in his head, he didn't know, but it didn't seem an evil gift. Kapvik had heard stories of humans communicating with animals in ages now lost to the murkiness of myth. Perhaps there was truth in them. Maybe some did possess the power to speak without moving their lips.

Too many wonders have I witnessed of late.

"Come and keep me warm," she whispered, and pulled him into the cave, where the furs waited. Kapvik was powerless to resist.

They made love and Kapvik felt dizzy at times with the ecstasy. Her eyes seduced him, her lips comforted him, her tongue teased him, and her body obliterated his willpower.

When their lust for each other was sated, they lay in a warm embrace despite the mountain chill, Siorraidh's head upon his chest. Kapvik yearned for this moment to stretch into eternity. *I'm happy* he thought to himself and wondered at the feeling. Laughter and rage were what he had known; now he felt desire and peace. Kapvik began to dream of the two of them sailing far away to an island where it would be only them.

"Your heart beats faster," she whispered.

Kapvik took a deep breath and tried to calm himself, pushing away these fantasies. He cast his mind to Vorga and his lord's iron will. And the trust Vorga bestowed upon his Fist. Guilt surged and he realised then he was walking a path laden with risk. Siorraidh was gently enticing him toward a road that Kapvik was certain Vorga would smash to rubble if he knew of it. The Unvasik warrior tried to focus on recent events. Part of him wanted to find an error in Siorraidh's judgment, something that would tell him Seolta and Vorga were to be trusted and obeyed without doubt. He shifted his arm under her and rolled onto his side so he could see her eyes.

"What happened in the mountain?" he asked. "Why did you say the battle was lost? Who was that man?"

At his third question, he felt her body tense.

She knew him, that much is certain.

"So many questions..." she said.

He said nothing, his silence hopefully sending a message.

She let out a breath and smiled sadly. "I called you back because I feared you would be slai—"

"I have never been bested in combat!" he protested.

Siorraidh seemed about to respond but her mouth closed, her lips drawing into a thin line.

He waited.

"I was worried," she said flatly. "And yes, I knew that man. His name is Corann. He leads the Duthka to the west of the Icefinger River and is no friend of Seolta. You must have seen his skill with those blades. He cut down many of my kin with ease."

"He had help," interjected Kapvik. "I would have taken his head if the battle had continued."

Siorraidh's voice rose with frustration. "Yes, yes, I am sure you would have killed him, Kapvik. Does that ease your mind?"

Anger grew within him at the sting in her words. He suddenly wondered why it had seemed so important a few moments ago to make this point. Kapvik huffed and turned his head to the dark shadows that concealed the rocky roof of their tiny refuge.

"Kapvik." Her voice was like the gentle lapping of water at the lake's edge as spring came and the ice melted. Tranquil but full of life. Her hand turned his face back to hers.

"Is it so strange that I fear for you, Kapvik? We may know little about each other, but I feel we share something. And I would share more. I do not want you to throw your life away because you yearn for glory in battle. Can you understand this?"

Kapvik could understand the words she was saying but did not feel them deep within his core. Suddenly, her voice was inside his head again, strangely un-invasive in nature.

Walk with me on this path, Kapvik. Share in the wonders we will find.
A pause.
And warm my body once more, my gentle giant.

Her hand ran down his chest and came to rest in his groin, applying a pressure that was at once beguiling and firm in its desire. He groaned, his rational mind crumbling into a chasm of carnal emotions.

Kapvik woke and was momentarily disorientated. His hand touched cold stone and there was a frigid wind lashing his face. He shook the sleep from his head and raised himself up on one elbow. Siorraidh sat with her back to him at the mouth of the cave, the still flickering fire making her seem a wraith of the night.

A beautiful wraith though.

She was swaying slightly, and he could hear a shallow murmur. She didn't seem to have noticed he was awake. He watched her in silence. It looked like she was once again communicating with someone who was not physically here. He took in the chilly mountain air in slow, deep breaths and waited.

"Yes, I am here. Is this your home?"

A pause.

"You are sad? Why?"

Another pause.

"Oh, little one. I know, I know. I too lost my father."

Kapvik waited for more.

"I'm sorry, but I cannot come now. I will though, I promise. I will take away your sadness." Siorraidh began to hum. Its sound was soothing and Kapvik sensed she was trying to comfort whoever she was connecting with. It must be some child, he reasoned.

She says little one *and speaks to it as an Unvasik mother would to their baby.*

Siorraidh spoke again. "Will you show me some more of your gift? I would like to see m—" A gasp. "How…how is that possible?"

Kapvik shifted uneasily. Siorraidh could put her words into his head, she could communicate with a child perhaps far away, and now this child had some *gift* that surprised his lover.

He fought the notion Siorraidh was a witch, but too many truths were gathering before him that pointed to her dabbling in some kind of sorcery. Kapvik had seen how Seolta had turned a man into a mindless beast with only a powder; such tampering with the natural order of the world seemed akin to practicing dark arts.

And she seeks some power from a past age up this damn mountain…

Kapvik stared into the darkness of the cave. He knew he was a fool, but he was beginning to question the wisdom of being content with this.

CHAPTER 2

SVARD

19th Day of Maia, The Night Gimmweg Was Attacked

The Helligan First Ranger lay back on the cot and gazed up at the rafters in the hospice. The oak beams were old, splintering in places, and Svard wondered how many more years this building had left in it. He didn't plan to lie around long enough to find out though. This sisterhood of healers in grey robes had quite possibly saved his life but done so in a shockingly brutal manner. One of them had killed a True Son who had come in, looking for *the Helligan spy*. Svard was grateful but thought it a bit extreme to have killed the poor fellow. A few lies could have sent him on his way. Was there some kind of rivalry between the True Sons and Grey Sisters?

Sons versus sisters? Religion? Politics maybe?

Whatever it was, he didn't have time to investigate. Nor did he have any reason to do so, besides curiosity. He had to focus on turning this pig's arse of a situation into something resembling success.

The mission Orben had sent him on was a sham, his real objective he now knew being the assassination of Brother Eswic, rather than just abducting the holy man. But his murder had been carried out by parties unknown to even the royal chamberlain, Worsteth. Svard had a gut feeling that a rival within the church had sent Eswic into eternal slumber, and that this rival was now the leader of their holy movement. The bastard in question had seen to the execution of Stigr and Erland. Svard's captains, Svard's friends. If he could exact his revenge on that religious zealot, he would take immense pleasure in doing so.

He suddenly tensed, his ears picking up something.

"Hnn…, hmm…ahhh…"

What was that?

A muffled sound, a voice, had drifted through the night. Svard listened hard but the hospice was again silent. Possibly someone dreaming, thought the First Ranger. He returned to his ruminations and regrets. He'd failed to keep Lorken from danger and now his closest friend was dead. Two captains of the Helligan Rangers had been killed on his watch, and that was a huge and utterly tragic failure. His lord had lied to him and seemed to be taking the Helligan nation down a path of dark dealings and clandestine murder. And now he was alone. He hoped Cuyler had left the city. Svard had not made the rendezvous as planned, so his captain should now be on his way to Barleywick, where he would regroup with Gudbrand and Stian.

His ears caught another sound.

There it was again!

Svard could definitely hear something now. It was a low moan. A patient in pain maybe. But the sound was not coming from this dormitory where the sick and injured lay. Svard quietly slipped out of the bed and put on his boots. The strange noise was a good distraction from all his troubles, and he needed to stretch his legs anyway.

He padded softly to the archway that led out of the sleeping chamber and looked into the corridor beyond. Candles in glass tubes were mounted on the wall, spilling light into a small pool around each lantern but leaving larger inky patches of darkness. Svard peered into the gloom and waited for the next murmur in the night. It soon came.

One of the nuns doing some strange incantation?

Svard's curiosity had been tickled and he found himself eager to know what kind of god or gods these women worshipped. The moaning chant came again. Except, now that he was closer to the source, it didn't sound much like a holy prayer.

It sounds like…

He stopped in his tracks. Passion was what it sounded like. A voice was moaning in passion! Svard frowned. He hadn't expected to hear that kind of sound in a holy house run by women. Was there a pious father here who persuaded the sisters he was doing *the Ever-Father's work?* Svard snorted a laugh and decided to see what kind of man was being so very saintly.

He crept along the passageway, pausing every few yards to listen. As he advanced, the moans suddenly stopped, and he heard a voice. It sounded like someone was speaking to another but Svard could only hear the one voice. It was female. He didn't recognise the language but he felt like he'd heard it before somewhere. Svard shrugged.

A nun telling the holy father how big and manly he is, in an ancient tongue? Or possibly just someone talking to themselves?

A door was slightly ajar, and it was clear the moaning and muttering had come from within. Svard heard a giggle and his curiosity swelled. He carefully peeked in.

What he saw surprised him in no small measure. There was a bed in the room with a naked woman lying on it, but there was no man thrusting away. Instead a second woman had her head in between the first woman's legs and the cause of the moans was quite apparent.

Raven's wings!

If they hadn't both been stark naked, Svard might have thought he was looking at two men. Their heads were shorn of all hair and inkings were visible under the stubble. But their lithe forms and ample breasts told Svard the truth of the matter. He knew he should turn away, but he couldn't tear his eyes off them.

The one on the receiving end of her lover's tongue was in a blissful state. It was a magnificent sight, two beautiful creatures in the throes of ecstasy. Svard felt himself harden and a spark of shame lit within him.

This act of voyeurism was at best impolite, looking upon two lovers without their knowledge, and at worst, was disrespectful to his fallen captains, Erland and Stigr. He had more important things to do here than get cheap thrills.

Time to get my head back in the right place.

Svard turned away from the two lovers and quietly headed back to the dormitory to retrieve his belongings. He picked up his sword, knives, and the cloak he'd use to conceal the weapons, and then tightened the various buckles that kept them all secure on his body. The moans drifted after him and he fought down the urge to have one more look before he departed. The front door was before him and Svard was relieved to see it was not only unlocked but wasn't even fully closed.

Maybe they are nocturnal creatures, and come and go in the night, these rather glorious ladies in grey.

He slipped out into the street and began making his way to the rendezvous point, his heart kindling a small hope Cuyler would have ignored his orders, but his mind telling him this wouldn't be the case. His captains prided themselves on sticking to the plan and following commands to the letter, if that were possible.

Svard took in his surroundings, not entirely sure where he had ended up after his panicked escape from the True Sons. The streets were deathly quiet and Svard began to feel uneasy.

Where is everyone?

It was perhaps the darkest breath of the night, a time when the Dark Raven flew low over the lands and delivered death and sorrow, according to Helligan legend. Svard prayed to the First Warrior to hide him from those beady eyes that were forever searching for fresh souls. The First Ranger still saw no one. He felt as though he were walking through a strange dream that ends with a slip, and jolts the dreamer awake.

Then a *ting-ting* sound came to him. One smith was still working. Svard doubted it was the one who had got in his way and taken him down. Cuyler's arrow should have put pay to that man wielding a hammer for a while.

Svard heard voices and relaxed somewhat. Bregustol, a city that never slept, had seemed for a moment there to be a city of the dead. He shook his head to dispel that ghoulish thought and casually rounded the corner, expecting to see some fellows on their way home from one too many ales.

"You there!"

Svard stopped abruptly. *Raven's arse!*

"What are you doing out at this hour?" Two city guards, by the look of their uniform, were moving toward him, lanterns held high and cudgels hanging at their sides.

Svard decided that running was not a good idea this time. If they had whistles, they could wake up the whole city in moments, and then Svard would really be in a deep pit. The First Ranger held up his hands but stumbled a bit to give them the impression he was drunk.

"Jus' on my way 'ome, good shirs," he slurred. "Bit of a long night."

The two guards were less than two yards from him now. "When a curfew is in place, breaking it carries a one-month sentence, you drunken fool!" one of them growled.

Curfew?! Shit upon the Dark Raven! Must have been ordered this afternoon while I was hiding...

Svard recovered as best he could. "Ish'zat the time? All-Father bless my soul, I've had too many tonight."

A sudden hostility filled their eyes. "*All*-Father? Don't you mean *Ever*-Father?"

Damn...

Svard gave up the pretence. "Ah, you have me there, good men of the guard," he said, straightening to his full height. "What say I slip you both a silver each and then I'll be on my way?" He gave them a sly grin, loosening the coin bag at his waist.

The cudgels were rising but Svard kept his gaze on the their eyes. The First Ranger knew that more often than not, a man's eyes gave away his next move.

"Alright, I guess the money idea is off the table." Svard sighed, letting his hands fall to his hips, the bag of coins in his right hand. He prayed they were not too perceptive. "Truth is I am Meridian, a Velox rider of Lord Rencarro. With the Helligan scum having taken our city in the south, I am here on a mission to request aid from Bregustol."

The two exchanged a look, then turned back to him. "Horse shit!" *Oh well…*

Svard let his instincts and experience take over. He was the Helligan First Ranger and had faced far worse than a couple of city guards. He hurled the silver at the guard on the left. The bag struck him squarely on the nose and elicited a cry of pain. The fellow's lantern dropped to the street and was snuffed out with the impact.

Svard's sword was only half-drawn as a cudgel swung at him. He arched back and it missed his own nose by an inch. Grabbing the guard's wrist with his left hand, he yanked, pulling the man to him. Then crashed the pommel of his now-freed sword into the guard's head. A strangled cry erupted from his mouth and he crumpled to the street. His lamp stayed lit.

Svard barely had time to lower his blade to parry an overhead swing, the other guard having quickly recovered from that stinging smack of coinage to the face. The cudgel crashed down onto the sword and stuck, the force of the blow coupled with the sharpness of the blade resulting in the two men locked together. Svard barrelled into him, snarling into his face. The guard was not to be cowed though; he gritted his teeth and growled right back at the Helligan First Ranger.

"Bloody bastard spy! You'll hang like the others!"

That was probably the worst thing the guard could have said. It ignited the rage within Svard and with a surge forward, he twisted his blade, pushing it down toward the man's head. The man had been courageous to face up to a trained Helligan soldier so far, but the look in his eyes said he valued his life more than his duty.

The guard stumbled backwards, tripping over his own feet and crashing to the cobblestones. His motion yanked the cudgel from Svard's blade. The club fell and made a horribly loud, wooden clatter as it hit the street. Svard stood above the defenceless man.

"Mercy!" he whimpered.

Svard wasn't about to kill the poor fool but leaving him conscious wasn't a good idea either. The Helligan First Ranger stepped forward to give the man a similar blow as he had dealt his companion.

A whistle sounded.

Svard whirled around to see two more of the city-watch rushing his way.

Luck was with the Dark Raven. He had to run. Svard broke into a dash, heading down the main street, then turned into the first side street that looked wide enough not to be a dead-end. Two and three-storey houses lined the alley, all manner of objects hanging from windows and more than one raised voice evidence that not all the residents of Bregustol were peacefully resting. Svard heard more whistles from behind and knew he would have to hide somewhere.

Raven's arse, why didn't I just stay in that warm bed?

He slowed his pace and kept to the shadows. He could not hear any pursuit and reasoned he would remain undetected if he kept his movements to a creep, stayed out of the glow of the street lanterns, and found himself somewhere he could hole up for the rest of the night. When dawn came, he would need to have another meeting with Worsteth. He'd climb the ministry whilst it was still dark, then drop down to the chamberlain's balcony when the sun broke past the city walls.

Svard stopped in his tracks as he realised Cuyler had the rope. *Raven's claws!* And he had just thrown away the last of his silver, so buying more rope was now not an option. He groaned.

First Warrior, send me something this night!

Svard began moving again, stopping every few yards to listen. He heard another couple of whistles, but they sounded a few streets away now. He neared the end of this narrow side-street and carefully poked his head out, taking in the wider area. He grinned as he spotted the unmistakable shape of the Holy Sepulchre, a dark hulk blotting out the waning crescent of the moon behind. He knew roughly where he was now and could reach the ministry. But how to get in?

Could always knock on the front door...

Dawn had arrived but its warmth was yet to reach the Helligan First Ranger. He had mentally kicked himself a thousand times for leaving the hospice at night. If he had stayed in that warm bed, he would not have bumped into the guards maintaining a curfew, he would still have silver, and he wouldn't be so damn cold.

Damn fool.

The sun was rising and the city was waking up. A mist had settled during the night, but it was now lifting from the streets as folks moved here and there. Svard joined the morning bustle, his cloak wrapped around him tightly and his weapons concealed. There didn't seem to be a greater presence of city patrols this morning, so Svard hoped he could enter the ministry without any trouble. He fell in behind a couple of tanners, judging by the smell. They were jabbering away so Svard strained his ears to hear the gossip.

"I don't disagree with you, Ben, but I'm not sure anywhere is safe right now. At least we have walls here. Big ones, if you hadn't noticed."

"Yeah, yeah, I know we're better off here than in Barleywick or Rumbleton, or any of the other smaller settlements if the Helligans come north. But sounds like something happened in Morak."

"Rumours, nothing more. Folk saw the King's Shield to the west and quickly, but wrongly, concluded he had come to kick Worsteth in the arse. It was Cyneburg who went north, or so I heard."

"Well, even if all is well in Morak, you can't deny things are getting a bit tense here with the True Sons. Reckon their new leader was the one who killed Eswic. Look at how those holy lunatics are arming themselves now. They were quiet as mice under Eswic. Something has shifted."

"Is a bit worrying seeing monks with clubs, I'll grant you that. Just be sure to slip an extra copper into the offering box tomorrow!"

They both laughed at this, and Svard peeled off as they were heading off in the wrong direction for the ministry.

Morak? What happened up there?

Svard kept his head down and hurried on his way. The ministry was soon before him and he took a moment to survey the surrounding area and who was where. There were guards out front but not city watch. Their uniforms were far too upmarket.

Here goes nothing…

Svard pushed back his hood, hoped his stubble wasn't too scruffy, and strolled to the main entrance with a confidence he didn't feel deep down. There, he hailed the sentries.

"Good day to you, sirs. This is the Royal Ministry, is it not?"

The two sentries stared straight ahead, ignoring him.

"Excellent, excellent," commented Svard. "General Torbal told me the guards at the ministry were the best in Bregustol. Why, not even a little urchin could sneak past you."

As soon as the words were out his mouth, he cursed himself inwardly. *Why can't I resist making these kinds of digs?*

One guard's eyes slid to the left and looked at him, the jaw clenching beneath.

Svard quickly continued. "Indeed, I am here to see the chamberlain himself. Be so kind as to inform him that a friendly *bat* is here. He will wish to speak with me and without a moment's delay, good men of the guard."

Svard wished he had Erland with him. He knew his talent with accents was limited and his acting skills even worse.

The guard who had eyed him, frowned. "A bat?"

"Yes. Trust me, the chamberlain will understand, but I do urge you to hurry. I have news that cannot wait."

The guard looked less than convinced but turned back to beckon to someone inside the building. A young boy came out of the shadows and the guard whispered to him. The servant ran off.

"That some kind of password?" he asked, weighing up Svard with suspicion written all over his face.

The First Ranger prayed the servant had fast legs; being out on the street was making Svard feel extremely vulnerable. All it would take would be for a patrol of the city guard to see him, a visitor to the ministry, and decide he was worth a look. Especially if those two lads had been crying about their ordeal last night.

"Not a password. More of a reminder to the chamberlain. He will definitely want to see me."

The guard grunted. "And what makes you so important?"

Svard sighed. He pretended to look bored and turned his head from the ministry doorman.

Shit!

Strolling down the street in their direction was indeed a patrol, four in number. They weren't hurrying so were just doing their rounds. But they would soon see Svard waiting at the ministry's front door.

First Warrior, hurry up!

"Not sure Chamberlain Worsteth would want me divulging sensitive information to just anyone," Svard replied with as much mystery as he could muster in his voice. The doorman smirked.

Raven's beak, I need my captains...

Svard casually shot a glance back to where the patrol had been and saw that they were less than thirty yards away now. Svard tensed, weighing up the odds here. If he made a break for it now, he should be able to outrun the city guards. But that would mean losing all hope of ever getting into the ministry without some more rope. On the other hand, if he held his nerve a bit longer, the servant would return and he would surely be let in. Worsteth would definitely want to speak to him again.

Come on, young man, pick up those feet!

Svard looked up in the sky as if he were admiring the morning, then let his gaze roam around. He cast his eyes to the side and saw the guards approaching. Swiftly. They were going to check out the cloaked figure hanging outside the Royal Ministry. He turned back to face the entrance, his body ready to move.

First Warrior, give that lad wings!

He heard the sound of running feet.

"Oi, you there! Stop!"

CHAPTER 3

KAPVIK

20th Day of Maia, The Day After Gimmweg Was Attacked

The air was noticeably thinner but Kapvik found it bearable. He was surprised that Siorraidh seemed to have no trouble with the height they had climbed to, but then again, she was not a normal lowlander. She seemed to possess gifts that Kapvik felt bordered on arcane sorcery, and a physical strength that belied her size. He had insisted on carrying the bulk of their supplies, but he sensed she had let him win that argument to satisfy him, rather than to save her any strenuous effort. He had held her naked form, she was muscular and lithe. Kapvik felt himself hardening and pushed carnal images from his mind.

She is a witch! A beautiful witch...

He smiled as he trudged up the mountain. After he had woken and silently watched her talk to someone across the wind, he had gone back to sleep and had a restful slumber, despite his numerous misgivings. This morning he had awoken feeling fresh, free of most doubts, and almost detached from the realm far below. The brilliant white of the sun had cast away the morning mist from the lowlands and also struck down his gloomy thoughts. The boundless azure blue sky above caused him to ponder.

Maybe there is more to this life than feasting and fighting…

Their path was steep, but they could progress on two feet. A few hundred yards before, they had been forced to climb on all fours, clambering over outcrops of rugged stone, the cold mountain air no longer held at bay by their exertion. He turned to see how Siorraidh was coping now and couldn't help but grin. She was looking up at him, head cocked to one side.

Cease your worrying, my gentle giant. I have climbed the Jagged Heights!

The voice in his head shocked him no longer; it was almost comforting. But her admission was surprising. The Jagged Heights were cruel beasts of nature, a mountain range that prevented full-scale war between the Unvasik and Ropa-Obita. The passes saw skirmish after skirmish, but neither side could ever have marched in vast numbers to stage an invasion. Vorga had told Kapvik the previous year that it was an eternal struggle that neither could afford to lose. The passes had to be guarded at either end by both peoples.

Kapvik had fought the Ropa-Obita more than once, their squat stature a contrast to the large Unvasik frames. What they lacked in height, though, they made up for in ferocity and near suicidal courage. They lived underground, praying to Sila and His sons. It was said they mined so much gold that they ate off golden plates. Kapvik fancied that was just some tale though, cooked up to give Unvasik warriors something to dream about.

The Unvasik warrior had climbed the Jagged Heights himself and the memory remained: one tribesman had begged for a merciful death after his toes blackened with frostbite, and two more comrades had lost their footing, plunging into an abyss that was inches away from each step they took.

Here on the Sacred Mount, the climb was not so treacherous. They reached a shelf of smooth stone and Kapvik stopped to catch his breath. He inhaled slowly, allowing the cold, thin air to fill his lungs gradually. Siorraidh was soon beside him, doing likewise. Kapvik cast his gaze out from the mountain and his eyes widened. It was an incredible sight. They were now facing east according to Siorraidh, having followed the only accessible path.

Siorraidh stretched her arm wide and spoke with her back to him, her voice barely audible over the wind. "Look at the beauty! This is why we must retake the land. The servants of the Ever-Father and the war-mongering Helligans will keep building stone monstrosities upon this land, defiling it."

Kapvik could see the dark grey areas that he knew to be towns and cities. They were ugly, but a stone hall was warmer than the Unvasik wooden longhouses, and so probably a nicer place to drink mead. The Unvasik would do well to learn the ways of these lowlanders, he mused. Although, it would be quicker to simply storm their towers and cities and take up residence within them, he thought with a shrug.

The Unvasik warrior surveyed the landscape below, his eyes roaming over vast miles that were mere inches at this height. He stared at the dark green, almost black of a huge forest. He ran his eyes farther still and saw an endless bank of white cloud that seemed far too low in the sky. He pointed at it and looked questioningly at Siorraidh.

The Blind Sea, Kapvik. Thick fog lies upon it and does not move.

"What is beyond it?" he asked, taking a deep breath as he did.

Nobody knows.

She looked up at him and gave one of those smiles he had become accustomed to.

"But you suspect."

She stretched her arms around him and hugged tightly. She couldn't quite reach all the way round his bulky frame, but she gave a firm squeeze even so.

Yes, I do. I believe there are many other lands out there. Waiting to be discovered!

Once again, Kapvik felt excitement surge within him and the doubts he had felt the previous day seemed like those of another man. Siorraidh offered so much. The ambitions of Seolta and Vorga were beginning to pale in comparison.

They promise this realm, yet she promises me the whole world!

Kapvik felt that if he walked the same path as Siorraidh, he would see wonders beyond the dreams of even the most crazed of his fellow tribesmen, and possess power that Vorga himself would envy.

"I still think you are a witch," he teased.

She pulled his head down and kissed him. "And I think you are an enigma yourself."

"A what?" Kapvik didn't know the word.

"Something that is not so easy to understand. A mystery."

Kapvik frowned, the wind beginning to whistle around them, like a wraith who was lost and afraid. "I am no mystery, Siorraidh. I am a warrior. I fight, I feast, and I pray to Tatkret the Watcher. Where is the mystery there?" he huffed.

Siorraidh released him from their embrace and started clambering up the rocky incline again. Kapvik rolled his eyes, expecting the lack of answer to mean he was right. He was as simple as the snow in the Unvasiktok tribelands.

"The mystery is how I have charmed such a mighty mountain of a man," her voice called back.

Kapvik grinned. This enchantress at the very least had a tongue laced with sorcery. She always seemed to know which words in any moment would pierce his chest and envelop his heart. Kapvik hurried after her, forgetting how lethal the terrain could be. One boot slipped and he fell forward. His body crashed down against a large boulder. The rock dislodged, and Kapvik found himself tumbling sideways, the mountain appearing to crumble under him.

"Kapvik!" came Siorraidh's cry.

He flailed his arms, desperate to stop his slithering down the rocky terrain, but his bulk worked against him. The speed of his uncontrolled descent increased. Showers of small rocks cascaded around him, dust filled his nose and mouth, and his hands could find nothing to grab. He grunted as his body slammed into a hard slab of rock jutting upward—but still he did not stop; his momentum rolled him right over it, and for a terrifying instant he was in the air, the vast expanse of the realm suddenly filling his vision.

His eyes shut and true fear swallowed him.

Kapvik hit the mountainside again with bone-rattling impact, slid off an edge, then finally jerked to a stop, a fierce pressure on his chest. He couldn't comprehend what had happened. His legs were dangling in the air, his breath was ragged, his body was wracked with pain but he wasn't falling. Something had stopped him.

How…

Siorraidh! She used sorcery!

He tried to turn his head, but it was as if he was hanging from something. He again felt pressure at his chest and looked down. The strap of his pack was straining against his muscles and he realised this was what was stopping him from continuing his terrifying descent.

"Kapvik!" he heard her voice again, and the scrabbling of feet. She was coming to him. "Don't move! Wait till I reach you."

The Unvasik warrior tried to remain calm, but the sensation of being in the air with nothing beneath him for maybe a hundred feet and an abyss yawning before his eyes was searing into his consciousness. He had never known fear when facing an opponent in combat, but moments ago he had had absolutely no control over his fate, and death had been rushing to greet him.

Siorraidh was close now. "Keep still!" she urged.

Kapvik almost laughed. His fear was paralysing his body; keeping still was not something that required any effort. He heard Siorraidh doing something close behind him, but he couldn't turn his head. He gazed out at Marrh and he imagined Qimmiq, his slain fellow, asking why in Tatkret's name he was up a huge mountain with a mysterious woman he hardly knew. He was now closer to death than when they had faced the soldiers of Morak at that ford.

"Here," came her voice. "Grab the rope but don't move your body."

A rope flopped down over his left shoulder and he slowly moved his right hand to grip it. But the straps of his pack restricted his movement. He jerked his arm to gain some slack and small rocks cascaded around him.

"No!" cried Siorraidh. "Make no sudden moves! I am sure you don't need to be told your life is hanging by a thread."

Her tone of voice relaxed Kapvik in a strange way. She was in control of his fate now and he somehow knew he would not fall, not while Siorraidh was with him.

"Try your other hand but stop if you can't reach the rope."

Kapvik carefully raised his left hand to the rope and was able to grasp it.

"Good," she said. "Now wait while I secure the other end."

He waited and began to smile. How he could smile when all that prevented him plunging to his death was a leather strap and this rope was a mystery.

Ah, maybe I am a…whatever that word was.

"Now grip the rope as tight as you can. I am going to cut the strap at your right shoulder."

The image of cutting what was his lifeline seemed a bad idea, but Kapvik was sure Siorraidh knew what she was doing. He gripped the rope with his left hand until his knuckles went pale. He slowly pulled downwards and could feel she had fastened the other end to something solid that did not move.

A knife and her hand came into view over his right shoulder. It slid under the pack strap and very gently began sawing.

"Hold tight. This will suddenly sever."

As the last word left her mouth, the strap broke apart and Kapvik felt himself slip. His stomach lurched but he held fast to the rope, bringing his now freed right hand around to grip the line. His sack hung loosely from his left shoulder. He slowly twisted around and saw Siorraidh looking down at him, her jaw set but tears in her eyes.

In that moment, he felt his world tumble, but it wasn't a fall from the mountain. The Unvasik people did not talk about love openly but Kapvik knew this was what it must feel like. He gazed up at her again and this time she looked angry.

"You foolish ox! You almost died. Watch your footing! I have said that a thousand times already…"

She continued admonishing him, but he wasn't listening. He gripped the rope tightly and climbed up, regaining a strong purchase on the mountain with his boots. He reached out and took her hand.

"Forgive me, Siorraidh," he said.

She stopped her fussing and squeezed his hand.

"Maybe one day I will," she said with half a smile. "But not today, my clumsy giant."

He grinned and the two of them carefully picked their way back to where he had begun his tumble, then continued their ascent.

Tatkret, guide my steps!

The wind grew stronger as they neared the summit, and Kapvik found himself leaning in toward the mountainside to keep his balance. He noticed Siorraidh was almost flat against the rock, being of much less weight than himself. The air was thin at this height, to the point where Kapvik found himself having to suck in as much as he could every few steps. Where they had spent the night, there had been no snow, but up here it hadn't yet entirely melted.

They were almost to the top, but they were now advancing very slowly, and Kapvik couldn't help but feel the mountain did not want them here. Fresh in his mind were the images of his fall. The Hall of Bones had rattled for him; of that he was certain. He didn't want to doubt his Duthka lover but this was beginning to feel like a fool's quest.

I owe her my life, but she still may be the death of me, he grumbled inwardly.

Before him Siorraidh suddenly stopped and raised her right hand. Kapvik carefully brought himself up behind her, the wind now beginning to howl.

"What is it?" he shouted.

"Can you feel it?" she called over her shoulder. "We are close!"

Kapvik had no idea what she was talking about. He was cold and feeling ever more anxious about the precarious nature of the mountaintop. Kapvik assumed she felt something more than that.

Maybe she can connect to the mountain itsel—

Kapvik felt a tingle in his left hand, which was pressed against the mountainside. He took his hand away and then replaced it, leaning in with his weight. There it was again. Something hummed within the rock. Siorraidh had begun moving again so he followed her. And he felt something in the air.

Tatkret! What is this?

His thoughts were interrupted by her voice sounding inside his head.

We are so close now. I know it is here.

Kapvik didn't bother asking what was here. He hadn't got an answer to that question the dozen other times he had asked it, so he doubted she would tell him now they were apparently so close.

"There!" she cried, pointing. He followed her finger and saw an opening in the mountain ahead. Kapvik wondered if they were about to see more of those strange blue worms that had been writhing around in the heart of the mountain.

No, it has to be something else.

They approached the cave, almost staggering against the fierce wind. Siorraidh entered and Kapvik followed. Instantly, the cry of the wind lessened, and the icy chill lost its bite. But Kapvik felt a strong buzz in the air. Something was here. He surveyed the gloom of the cave, taking a step forward.

Something crunched under his boot. He looked down.

Bones?!

Bones they were, crushed under his feet, but they were small. He leaned down to pick one up. They looked like they came from birds. He peered at the stone floor around him and saw the cave was littered with them, some small, some larger, but all from birds it seemed. He tensed as he imagined this cave was the lair of some mountain predator and jumped when Siorraidh slapped his arm.

"What?"

"Look over there," she said, a tremble in her voice.

Sila's cold breath!

Toward the back of the cave lay two skeletons, which in life had most definitely not been birds. They were the remains of two humans, the bones discoloured where their clothing had decomposed and their deaths surely a tale of many years ago. They looked to be in some kind of struggle, both skeletal hands gripping something, a short pole of sorts, curved slightly like a crescent moon.

The cave abruptly lit up. Siorraidh had sparked a torch, sending shadows racing along the walls. The flames illuminated the two dead ones and Kapvik saw some of their bones were blackened as if burnt. He then noticed more scorch marks on the walls beyond.

He gestured to the skeletons. "This is what you're looking for?"

Yes, oh yes, Kapvik, we have found it!

The two of them stepped carefully over to the long-dead ones, the bones of birds collapsing in tiny explosions as they moved. Kapvik presumed Siorraidh sought the pole gripped by the skeletal hands, so he leant down to pry it free.

"Stop!" she cried.

He straightened and looked at her.

"Do not touch it with your hand. Their fates should be a warning."

Kapvik was growing weary of all the riddles. He watched as she removed a strange glove from her sack. At least it looked like a glove; it didn't seem to be made of cloth. Kapvik stared at the yellowish colour and strange texture.

Siorraidh put the glove on her right hand and reached down. Kapvik held his breath, wondering if the pole was hot or something. He tensed as she hesitated a handspan away from the thing. Kapvik was about to tell her to let him bash it free with his axe when she shot forth her hand and grabbed it.

Nothing happened.

We came all this way for a trinket?!

Siorraidh tugged it from the skeletal hands and held it aloft, a huge grin on her face and eyes wide with something Kapvik had not seen before.

"I have it!" she breathed. Her eyes closed and it looked like she was in ecstasy.

"In Tatkret's name, what is that thing?" he said, anger tainting his voice.

"Calm yourself, my gentle giant. This is power! A power from a past age." She raised the curved thing closer to his eyes. "Don't touch it," she whispered.

Her quiet voice made him aware that the buzzing in the air had stopped. Kapvik felt uneasy.

Sorcery?

The Unvasik warrior studied the object as Siorraidh held it up. It was about a foot in length, the same girth as a staff and pure black in colour. *Obsidian?* Faint silver symbols were etched into the surface, seemingly all over. He had no idea what power this tiny thing could possibly possess. It certainly wouldn't help much in a fight, being only as long as a hunting knife.

A tiny white flash suddenly ran across its surface.

"What was that?" he gasped, his body tensing.

Siorraidh smiled. Kapvik looked at her closely and felt a moment of anxiety. There was something new within her eyes, an excitement that bordered on abandon.

"Are you well?" he asked, his voice stern.

She blinked and nodded, turning away from him.

"I am well, Kapvik. I am just relieved to find this after searching for so long."

Relieved? Thrilled, it seems.

"And Seolta does not know you have been searching for this thing?"

She seemed to intentionally ignore him, bending down to examine the skeletons. She didn't put down the tool or whatever it was, instead clutching it tightly with her right, while sifting through their ragged clothes and bags with her left. Kapvik shrugged and decided to help her.

There was nothing much there though. Some strange coins with holes in their centres and curious symbols etched upon them. Also, other coins that had some king or lord engraved on one side. He held one up to her.

"Who is this? The king who died?"

Siorraidh shook her head and went back to searching. She spoke as she picked up seemingly useless possessions that were scattered around.

"I believe that is Orben's father on the coin."

"Orben?" queried Kapvik.

"The Helligan lord."

The Unvasik warrior shrugged, then picked up one of the coins with the hole in. "And this?"

Siorraidh stopped her rummaging and looked at the coin. She stared at it, studying it and Kapvik saw something in her eyes. Recognition?

Then she shrugged. "I don't know. I have never seen its like before. Not in Marrh anyway."

Kapvik frowned, not entirely believing her, then tossed the coins on the floor. Years ago he might have pocketed them, but he was becoming weary of this *quest* he had followed her on. They had the strange pole-thing now, and it seemed to hold light or a spark maybe. Kapvik wondered if it could power some device, perhaps giving warmth to those nearby. Whatever it was, the days were moving on. It was time to return to their lords. He pulled her sleeve and gestured for them to leave the cave.

Soon they were outside again, and the wind lashed at them fiercely. Kapvik sensed an anger within the gusts, as if some god was angry at the theft of that rod. The Unvasik warrior hoped Tatkret was not watching him at this moment.

Siorraidh grabbed his arm and raised her voice above the screeching winds. "Do you trust me?"

He hesitated. He wanted to say yes and kiss her, but there was so much beyond his understanding. Kapvik was beginning to question his own judgment. Why had he come up this mountain with her? Why hadn't he returned to Vorga and taken his place at his chief's side, just as a Fist should? Why was Siorraidh seeming to place such importance on some relic when the realm was ready to be retaken?

Will you let me show you something?

He frowned at her, feeling that she spoke inside his head when she wanted to persuade him of something or cast aside his doubts.

"Show me whatever you need to, then let us return to our people," he responded, making no attempt to keep the agitation from his voice. She held his eyes for a long moment, then turned around to face the wide realm, her hands by her side, the rod still gripped in her right. The wind buffeted her, but she stood strong.

Kapvik waited, having no idea what she could possibly show him.

He felt a tingle in the air. His body tensed, his senses becoming alert. Something was happening. Kapvik heard a buzz. He cast his eyes to the rod and saw the white flicker again. Then another. A crackle rode over the sound of the wind.

Siorraidh thrust her right arm into the air and cried out.

"Ao chaak!"

A brilliant flash blinded Kapvik, instantly followed by a bang.

The Unvasik warrior stumbled backwards, blinking to clear his vision.

Tatkret, what is this?!

Again, Siorraidh punched the air with the rod and a second flash of what could only be lightning streaked through the air before her.

"Stop!" roared Kapvik.

She turned to face him, her eyes dancing and her voice tumbling over a wild laughter.

"This is power, Kapvik!" she cried. "True power! This can harness the power of the world itself. With it, *I* can control the coming storms. Ride with me, Kapvik, ride with me!"

Kapvik felt like he was standing on a thin ledge, a blinding light ahead and a pitch-black abyss of madness to either side. He was enthralled yet terrified. Before him was not a witch nor a queen, but a goddess. A goddess of power or a goddess of death, he couldn't tell. He felt a tingle within him, an excitement mixed with fear.

Tatkret, am I to wield this storm with her?

Siorraidh seemed to have grown, and he felt himself diminished.

Or am I to be destroyed by it?

CHAPTER 4

SVARD

20ᵗʰ Day of Maia, The Day After Gimmweg Was Attacked

"I said stop!"

Svard's gut tightened as the patrol marched up. His legs tensed, poised to make a run for it.

"The chamberlain says to let him in and be quick about it, sir!" panted the young lad as he ran out of the shadows within.

The ministry guards turned sharply to give Svard a corridor on entry. He took two swift steps and was in. He turned on his heel and shot off a quick grin at the city guards. The door shut upon angry protests.

Thank you, First Warrior!

Svard inhaled deeply through his teeth and hurried after the servant. The shouts from outside soon faded away.

They were at Worsteth's office after three sets of stairs, two long hallways and an odd chamber with a huge stone ring at its centre. The lad came to a door guarded by men in the same uniform as those manning the door and knocked an intricate combination of single and double taps.

Clever little chap.

The rather stately door swung inwards with a strangely dignified creak. Svard found himself looking at a man a few fingers shorter than the door itself, a bushy moustache under stern eyes, dressed in a dark blue uniform buttoned tightly at the neck.

"Thank you, Moggy," came Worsteth's voice, presumably addressing the young servant and not this grumpy arse stood before Svard. The chamberlain approached and ushered the First Ranger in. Worsteth then turned to the grim-faced soldier. "This man has some very sensitive information for me, Captain Eahlstan, so please ensure we are not disturbed."

The captain nodded, no sign of emotion in his face.

Once the door was closed, Worsteth gestured to a bottle of wine. A cup was beside it.

"Have a drink, Sir Bat."

There was no humour in the chamberlain's voice. He sounded tired and on edge.

Svard helped himself to a generous measure of the red, drank it in one go, shaking his head as it went down, and then poured another. He turned to face the Rihtgellen Royal Chamberlain, theoretically the highest authority in Bregustol now, despite possible conflicting opinions in the camp of the True Sons.

"I'm sorry for the loss of your men," said Worsteth solemnly. Svard sensed the sentiment was genuine. "The True Sons have become more than a nuisance. A danger to the city I would say."

Svard nodded. "I can't argue with that."

"Please sit," said the chamberlain, gesturing to a low sofa.

Svard sank down onto it and felt the weariness in his body cry out. He looked at Worsteth and reckoned the chamberlain had not slept well either.

"Things getting worse?" asked Svard.

Worsteth sighed, sat down behind his desk and drummed his fingers. "Things were bad, they got worse and now they are rather awful," he muttered. "And that is putting it mildly." A hint of fear touched his voice.

Svard waited, sensing the chamberlain needed to vent his troubles. Svard was theoretically the man's enemy but the chaotic path that Ragnekai now walked on, had perhaps turned the Helligan First Ranger into a priest for the chamberlain, one to whom he could confess and confide.

"Sedmund died and blasted Ulla encouraged Torbal to take the throne. Eswic and I believed that not to be in the best interests of the realm, so I persuaded the general to leave the capital. Next, word comes to me that your lord had decided to take advantage of the lack of a High King and annex Meridia."

Svard stayed silent. The chamberlain was definitely not giving him the whole truth here but Svard reckoned he wasn't telling outright falsehoods.

"Eswic then disappears, only to turn up dead!" he cried, looking up at the ceiling and wringing his hands. Worsteth lowered his gaze to the First Ranger. "And before I have a chance to even breathe, you come through my window, scaring me half to death…"

Svard shrugged.

"And it becomes clear that there is a lot more going on in Bregustol than even my network of eyes and ears knew," he lamented, shaking his head.

"And then my men were executed by that holy lunatic," added Svard, not bothering to disguise the accusation in his voice.

Worsteth put up his hands, palms out in a defensive gesture. "When I said I was sorry for the loss of your men, I meant it. I had nothing to do with their deaths," he said. Svard detected no lie. "Though I do have some information regarding their capture."

The First Ranger tensed. "Which is?"

"It was curious. I heard from a reliable source that the True Sons identified your men because of something one of them was wearing. I would have thought all of you would have been careful to remove anything that could mark you as Helligan, so this surprised me somewhat."

Svard's mind stretched back to when he had seen his two captains alive last. All of them had worn non-descript leather hosen and jerkins, long-coats while in the city, and woollen robes when they had entered. Nothing unusual, all very dull. He shook his head.

"I can't remember anything that would have served as a sign to them. These True Sons are perhaps more organised than you know," he suggested. This shred of information also hinted at there being knowledge Helligan Rangers were in the capital. That stank of treachery somewhere along the line.

Worsteth was rambling on.

"I have no information as to the extent of their spy network, if that is what caught your men, but I can tell you they are gathering their strength. And have begun to carry weapons. Eswic may have been a holy hypocrite but he wasn't foolish enough to start arming his flock. Their new leader, Magen, seems more the militant kind."

Svard recalled Orben speaking of Eswic as a holy crusader who wanted to turn the entire realm into the Ever-Father's house of worship. He wondered now if his lord had been exaggerating the threat posed by the deceased servant of the Rihtgellen god. Whatever the case, this new fellow was clearly a far more dangerous proposition.

"And then Morak."

Svard looked up, remembering the two tanners mentioning the city in their gossip. "Morak?"

Worsteth rubbed his temples. "Of course, you probably haven't heard."

Raven's beak, what happened there?

"Over a week ago, Morak was attacked by Unvasik tribesmen."

Svard stared at the chamberlain. He had been surprised more than once in recent days, but this seemed like a rumour too wild to be taken seriously.

"I know," said Worsteth, "Hard to believe, isn't it?"

"Unvasik raiding the Ruby Road I could quite easily take as truth. But assaulting a city? The Unvasik are wild mountain men, not trained soldiers."

Worsteth threw up his hands in a show of helplessness. "The whole realm seems to be going mad. I have heard little from Morak itself but received word that Torbal sent a force of Westhealfe soldiers up there to deal with those barbarians."

Svard frowned. "Aren't you sending any men? Bregustol has two legions garrisoned here if memory serves me well. If Unvasik warriors have attacked Morak, shouldn't you be assisting in some way?"

Worsteth raised an eyebrow. "If I didn't know better, I'd say you were trying to get me to leave the capital under-manned..."

Svard couldn't help but laugh. "Trust me, I am as much in the dark here as you. Orben's plan was to secure the south, then negotiate with you to have the entire west united against Torbal. I assure you, no Helligan forces are coming this way anytime soon. Orben is cunning but he isn't a fool."

This seemed to satisfy the chamberlain. He huffed. "Something happened at the Black Stone Ford as well."

First Warrior, what is happening in the realm?

"A skirmish of some kind. The flow of information has slowed considerably, and I can't help thinking that Torbal is hiding something from me."

Svard cursed under his breath. He really didn't have the head to unravel this sort of political intrigue mixed with mysterious murders and unforeseen attacks.

"What in the name of the Dark Raven is going on?" Svard muttered aloud.

Worsteth steepled his fingers and spoke, his voice once again betraying the fact that he was scared. "There is trouble all over the realm. My first impression was that Sedmund's death ignited a power struggle, but I fear there is something more sinister at work. How could so much happen within a relatively short period of time?" he put to Svard.

The Helligan ranger gave the only answer that made sense. "It was planned."

"Yes. Planned, coordinated, and set in motion. You were sent here to abduct Eswic, correct?"

Svard calculated he had nothing to lose by revealing more to Worsteth, so he gave a quick nod and offered a few more details. "When we learned Eswic was dead though, one of my men revealed to me that Orben had given orders to assassinate the holy brother. An order I found distasteful for what it's worth."

"But someone else beat you to it."

Svard nodded.

"Someone is pulling the strings."

"Who?" asked Svard, baffled.

"I believe it is nobody we know. Much as I suspect Ulla wants Torbal to take the rule of the realm, with her by his side, the King's Shield is not one to instigate chaos. It would be a poor strategy in the long-term." The chamberlain shook his head. "And Orben making some pact with the Unvasik? Unlikely when considering the longer game. It would be unwise to bring those mountain men down into the realm intentionally." Worsteth narrowed his eyes. "No, someone else is lighting fires here and there."

"This new leader of the True Sons?" suggested Svard.

"A possibility," mused the chamberlain. "But I would be surprised if Magen is connected with agents across the entire realm. The man is a holy fanatic by all accounts, and not someone with the kind of patience such a grand plan would require."

Svard stood up. "Well, chamberlain, shall we reconvene again in a few days? I have a couple of theories I want to investigate. Another exchange of information?"

"I am open to mutually beneficial information sharing, if it will shed light on this whole affair." He raised a finger. "But people will ask questions if you come knocking on the front door again. Why in Oblivion's name did you do that anyway?"

"No rope."

Worsteth huffed. "Then get some more."

"No money."

The chamberlain wrung his hands. "Ever-Father, is this some kind of test?!" he cried. "Eswic's revenge for all the arguments I won?"

Worsteth moved behind his desk and opened a drawer. He pulled out a small bag and tossed it at Svard. The First Ranger caught it and was satisfied at its weight and the clink it made as his fingers felt around the shapes of the coins inside.

"I'll have Moggy show you out through the kitchens," the chamberlain muttered.

"Much obliged, Chamberlain," said Svard with a grin.

I'll get a decent meal and a bath before I buy some more rope. A warm bed wouldn't go amiss either.

CHAPTER 5

WULFNER

21st Day of Maia, Two Days After Gimmweg Was Attacked

The clip-clop of hooves was kind to the ears as they journeyed toward the Black Stone Ford, although there was nothing so gentle about being in the saddle for a second day. Wulfner's back-side ached and he reckoned his legs would be bow-shaped when they finally reached their destination.

The stretch of road they travelled on was stone-paved, wide enough for two carts to pass each other, so the big northerner had let his horse plod on without fear of getting lost, falling foul of a pot-hole or snagging a troublesome root. The fields they passed were still full of the glory of spring but also sang with the warmth of the coming summer. Wulfner saw a rabbit in the undergrowth. It froze and stared at him.

Fear not, little one. We are not looking for a meal. We ate very well in Hurtig before we left and brought more than enough provisions for the journey.

Wulfner grinned, then remembered their last meal at the Merry Mount inn had been rabbit stew. He coughed into his hand. The rabbit leapt away into a copse of trees, maybe ash or buckthorn, he always got them confused. The big man continued to cast his eyes left and right as they rode on, taking in the scenery and wishing Emiren were here to tell him the names of the trees and plants. And if Lunyai were with them, Wulfner was sure he'd be doing a better job in the saddle. How the Tarakan girl calmed any horse she rode was a wonder. He missed both the girls.

Travelling with Corann was a very different kind of journey than the one he had had with Emiren and Lunyai, or Tacet for that matter. Much quieter for one thing. There was a strange and terrible bond between them. One that was identical in its grief but was etched into the opposite sides of a coin. Wulfner's wife and daughter had been murdered by Duthka, and Corann was Duthka; Corann's wife and son had been executed by Rihtgellen soldiers, and Wulfner had been in the Morak garrison himself. It was a ragged, ugly thread that connected them; ragged but one that could not be cut. And there was something that tugged at this thread now. They had not spoken another word about it since the Sacred Mount, but Wulfner had thought about Corann's daughter many times since. The northerner imagined his Duthka companion had dwelt on nothing else. It had been a quiet journey indeed.

His own daughter his enemy…

Wulfner couldn't begin to imagine the conflict raging within the brooding, icy blue-eyed figure riding beside him. He was sure that was the reason the woman had revealed herself at that moment. It had been a shock of epic proportions to Corann and as a result he had frozen, and lost the will to act. Thus, his daughter and that Unvasik giant had escaped, along with the Duthka who had deserted the cavern before battle began. Fled with sacks of the poisonous fungus. Wulfner shook his head and turned his thoughts back to Emiren and Lunyai.

Hope the girls get home safely. Tacet is with them. And Moryn.

Wulfner hadn't wanted to part from them. Emiren and Lunyai were like family to him now and it had made his heart ache to bid them farewell in Manbung. But he knew he must walk a different path. Or ride, as was the case. Corann seemed more at ease in the saddle than himself, and Wulfner suspected the Duthka had noticed and slowed his own mount.

At least Olwyn was alive and looked set to recover. The blue worms had not actually healed the wound, but they had kept it from worsening. The bleeding had stopped and there was no sign of infection when they reached the inn. A physician had tended to her and she was now letting the body do its own marvellous job of healing.

Turi was with her in Manbung, at the Merry Mount inn, and Wulfner knew they would be cared for there. His body had wanted to stay there another week, in a warm bed, the decent food and glorious ale filling his stomach; a respite from the shadows that seemed to be lurking in all corners of the realm. But they couldn't afford to linger now. Their tidings could not wait.

We go now to inform the King's Shield that Seolta will without doubt turn the rest of Morak's people into beasts.

And tell him Nerian is dead…

The Westhealfe soldier had become a friend in the brief time they had journeyed together. Then the Unvasik warrior had brutally cut him down. Wulfner regretted his inability to have done more in the battle. He wasn't the soldier he had been twenty years ago, and he certainly couldn't wield the hammer as he used to. The big northerner suddenly wondered if it was time to put aside that heavy weapon and pick up a lighter mace or something.

Forgive me, Nerian. You asked for my help and I wasn't up to the task.

"Wulfner."

He started, the sound of Corann's deep voice something that he hadn't heard for half a day. He looked at his companion, but the man was staring at the road ahead as their horses plodded on.

"What did I do wrong?"

Wulfner was confused. *Is he talking about the battle inside the Sacred Mount?*

"Why did my daughter choose the path of vengeance?"

Wulfner took a deep breath, was about to speak, but found the words did not come. Why had Corann's daughter turned down a road that was drowned in blood? Because Barghest murdered her brother and mother. It was the natural desire for vengeance. She wanted the realm to pay for that crime. Wulfner was about to offer these thoughts but Corann asked another question.

"Did you seek revenge? Did you kill Duthka after your family were murdered?"

Wulfner felt a pressure in his chest. Corann's questions were bringing back bitter memories and reigniting an internal debate he had thought long ago settled. Wulfner had chosen to walk away from more bloodshed. He knew it was what his wife Rowena would have wanted, and he was almost certain he had been right to follow this path. Almost. His thoughts swirled in a murky fog as the horses ate up the yards.

"I vowed to kill every single Duthka," he said finally. "I hated them with every bone in my body. My mind was set, and I was ready to head into the Deadwood by myself and bludgeon any woman or child I found. I wanted the Duthka men to feel the same pain as I. The same loss."

Corann closed his eyes and nodded slowly. "I understand."

Silence held between them for a while, as if sound itself were retreating from the two men, wary of their dark thoughts and bitter memories. The clip-clop of their mounts' hooves upon the road provided a strange beat within this dome of quiet, an almost eerie clattering.

Wulfner found his voice again. "But when I went back to our home, to get my hammer, there was a moment when the rage fell away. Being in our home brought my grief to the surface. I broke down and cried for how long, only the Winds know. I reached out and touched Rowena's shawl. I could smell her scent. I picked up Sunniva's wooden rabbit and saw her smile. And it was as if I could hear my wife's voice, telling me to be still, telling me not to kill, not to do unto others what had been done to me. To us."

Wulfner was surprised no tears fell now. He found himself able to speak over the emotion, almost as if the anguish he shared with Corann was being diluted by their common loss.

"I am glad the memory of your wife reached you in that moment, Wulfner. For your sake. And for the sake of any who would have suffered your wrath," Corann added pointedly. Wulfner couldn't disagree.

How many would I have murdered? What kind of a monster would I have become?

"And you?" asked Wulfner. "Did you not seek revenge?"

Corann shook his head. "I had Idelisa."

Wulfner frowned. "Your daughter?"

He nodded. "Yes, my daughter. I still had a daughter and knew I had to take her away from the cycle of violence. I wanted her to live in the Abhaile with me and look ahead to a different future. But Seolta…"

Wulfner began to see how the story unfolded. "He preached vengeance?"

Corann's jaw clenched. "Many of us thought him a fool. And when he stopped raging at gatherings, became quieter, I believed he would just retreat into the forests as we had, and the Duthka would be forgotten by the rest of the realm."

"But he didn't go quietly into the night, did he?"

"No. No, he did not. We heard some years later that he had become the leader of those who dwelt east of the Icefinger. I…" Corann inhaled sharply and shook his head. "I foolishly visited Seolta and the people there with him. I wanted to find out what kind of man he had become. I wanted to be sure he was creating a future of peace for those Duthka. And if this wasn't the case, which of course it wasn't, I thought I could reason with him, show him a different path."

Wulfner's brow furrowed. "Why was that foolish of you? You had to try."

Corann turned in his saddle and smiled sadly. "I was a fool because I took Idelisa with me."

The picture once again sharpened for Wulfner. Idelisa had obviously been exposed to Seolta's influence and his ideology. Corann continued speaking.

"Back in our own village, Idelisa and I argued constantly. She was convinced Seolta spoke in truth when he said the realm was ours by right, as was vengeance. I tried to change her mind, but she remembered all too vividly seeing her mother and brother die at the hands of Barghest. She left a year later. She had carved a message into the wall of our home. It said, *I love you father, but you are wrong.*"

Wulfner found it hard to take everything in as Corann spoke now. The tale was simple enough, but its ramifications and deeper context set the northerner's mind whirling.

I was one of the soldiers who hounded the Duthka.

Wulfner felt history rising to become a mirror held to his face, reflecting the ugly truth of the past. The Duthka lived in the realm before his ancestors. He was descended from a people that had come from across the sea, and his people had taken the realm by force. Where there had been resistance, it had been met with vicious retribution. Wulfner felt a bitterness within, knowing he had played a part in stoking Seolta's twisted hatred. And so, he was in some way responsible for Corann's daughter stepping onto the path of revenge.

"I'm sorry," he muttered.

Corann ignored his sentiment. "I did try to bring her back. I went to Seolta's settlement, but he claimed she had not come to him. Now I can see he was lying. Back then, though, I assumed Idelisa had headed farther north, to get as far away from the Rihtgellen soldiers as possible. I hoped she'd found peace..."

Peace was definitely not what his daughter had found. Wulfner winced inwardly, imagining the turmoil within Corann now. Guilt, sorrow, anger and a sickening feeling of dread at what might come to pass.

Am I the more fortunate here, with Rowena and Sunniva in their eternal sleep?

Wulfner heard the sounds of soldiers before they came into view. Word had come to Manbung that General Torbal was at the Black Stone Ford, and Wulfner hoped that was still the case. If the King's Shield had moved on to the capital, they would never be able to relay their tidings in person.

"Do you think Torbal will be here?" enquired Corann, echoing his thoughts.

Wulfner shrugged. "Let's hope so. I'd rather deliver the news to his face and I don't think I'll survive another day in this saddle."

Corann said nothing in response.

They kicked their horses into a quicker pace as the camp came into view. Tents of deep red and blue could be seen beyond a neat wall of wooden stakes. Wulfner doubted there was any threat from this side of the ford, but who knew where danger lay in these troubled times?

"Halt!" came a shout. "Stay your mounts and raise your hands."

They obeyed the command with weary sighs.

A column of maybe twenty soldiers jogged alongside them, made a neat turn, and Wulfner suddenly found himself looking at a bristle of spear-points.

"Steady lads, we are friends," said Wulfner in a steady tone, though he felt nervous. The fight within the Sacred Mount had shaken him more than he realised.

"I'll be the judge of that," said a sergeant, approaching slowly on horse-back. "Who are you?"

"I am Wulfner, formerly a soldier under Beornoth of Westhealfe." The sergeant squinted his eyes at Wulfner, as if this would help him discern the truth of that statement. "And this is Corann. General Torbal knows us, knows our business, and if he is here, he will be anxious to see us." Wulfner raised his eyebrows. "Without delay."

The sergeant scowled.

Got a stick jammed right up his arse, this one.

"I find it unlikely you know the King's Shield personally. A couple of fellows who look less than at ease in the saddle. Travelling rogues, I wou—"

"Listen, you foolish oaf of a man!" cried Corann, his eyes ablaze with fury. "We are returned from the Sacred Mount, where one of your men died fighting Unvasik. We have news that concerns the beast-men you fought at this very ford. If Torbal is here, you waste precious time with your doubts and witlessness!"

A silence followed. Accompanied by the sergeant's jaw dropping, eyes darkening, and a deep intake of breath.

Wulfner leaned forward in his saddle before the man's anger

could erupt. "I get the feeling General Torbal is indeed here. Just be quick and tell him Wulfner and Corann are back."

The sergeant looked to be in a quandary, one that Wulfner had experienced himself more than once. Believe the stranger and possibly find yourself facing the wrath of your commanding officer for being so gullible. Or stand in even deeper shit later when it becomes clear you delayed something important getting through to those higher up.

"Follow me," he finally said, his face a grimace. The man clipped off a few orders to his unit and they fell into a square around Wulfner and Corann.

The northerner cast a glance at his Duthka comrade and could almost feel the rage simmering within him. Wulfner couldn't escape the thought that Corann's anger yearned to be set free so it could rampage across the lands in search of the enemy. But the harsh truth was that the enemy was his daughter. The northerner worried that his Duthka comrade would lose control now that this fight had become so personal, be unable to see clearly through the red haze that fell upon the best of folk when in anguish.

They were escorted to the inner camp, passing more soldiers than Wulfner had seen in one place in many years. Torbal appeared to be ready to launch the full wrath of the west upon the Unvasik and Duthka who had taken Morak. And slaughtered so many Bradlastax. Wulfner figured that if Torbal were indeed here, his sister Cyneburg would be too. A passing company of about twenty female soldiers, axes strapped to backs, single and double braids visible, confirmed his thought.

She seeks revenge even more than Torbal. But any battle in Morak will be against the people of that city, albeit in beast-form, and not on those whom she seeks revenge.

Wulfner spied the King's Shield up ahead, and next to him Lady Cyneburg. They were in some kind of heated conversation, Torbal seeming to be trying to calm his sister, hands moving in a placating manner.

The sergeant who had confronted Wulfner and Corann hurried to his lord, spoke briefly, then looked back to where they sat upon their mounts. Torbal slapped the sergeant on the back and the man smiled.

Wulfner nodded. *You judged well, my friend.*

Torbal's face began to lose its enthusiasm as he approached. Wulfner dismounted, Corann following suit while muttering something under his breath. Wulfner saw Torbal looking past them, his face a mask of puzzlement.

Damn the Winds. And damn that Unvasik giant!

"Wulfner, Corann, I am glad to see you again. Where are the others? Where is Nerian?"

Wulfner exchanged a glance with Corann, feeling the weight of the terrible news. Torbal noticed.

"No..." he said, his voice a whisper.

"My lord, I am truly sorry. Nerian was killed in battle."

The general's face hardened, then reddened as blood came to his visage, twisting into an expression of pure rage.

"Damn them! They have stolen so much of our blood!" he growled. His head lifted to the sky and he cried out an oath. "I will bring death. I will wipe them out. Extinguish their existence from the realm!"

Wulfner was taken aback. He didn't know Torbal personally, but the general's reputation and the little he had seen of him spoke of a noble leader who ruled with mercy and patience. The man before them now was akin to a bloodthirsty bandit-lord.

He doesn't even know yet how Nerian died...

The King's Shield was losing control over his emotions, jumping to conclusions, and seemed to be succumbing to the rage ravaging the realm.

"My lord, there is much to tell," began Wulfner. He looked to Corann and saw his companion was fighting to hold back his own fury.

"Perhaps we can speak somewhere?" said Wulfner, desperately trying to quell the fires that seemed to be erupting within those around him.

Torbal held Wulfner's eyes and the northerner's worry deepened. It was if he were peering into the future of the realm and that future was one of conflict. A moment passed, Wulfner wishing he could calm humans as Lunyai did horses. And then Torbal huffed out a weary breath.

"Yes, yes." The general gestured to what had to be the command tent, the red and blue cloth of the tent complemented by lighter blue and silver flags out front.

Wulfner and Corann followed Torbal. Lady Cyneburg nodded greetings to them both and fell in beside her brother. A tall soldier, clearly of rank, came up behind them all, and was then joined by a stocky soldier, again a captain or someone of high standing, judging by the way he followed without a word to Torbal and Cyneburg.

They entered the tent and Wulfner was surprised to see how spacious it was within. He had never been inside a command tent before and his curiosity was aroused. He scanned the interior, seeing a large table with a map as expected, chairs at the sides of the pavilion, and a long trestle upon which was arranged food and drink. Nothing of luxury though. Very functional.

"Will you sit?" asked Torbal.

Wulfner was about to answer but Corann cut in with a curt response.

"We will stand."

Wulfner felt the tension ramp up a notch.

The general raised one eye-brow. "As you will." He looked at Wulfner. "What happened?"

Wulfner proceeded to relate the events of the last few days: finding an opening at the base of the Sacred Mount, entering, the blue worms, the lake and the Duthka already there. And finally, the Unvasik warrior who cut down Nerian.

At the mention of the brute, Cyneburg cursed. "Unvasik bastards! They will pay with their own blood ten times over."

It was at that moment that Wulfner saw Corann's mind, saw the reason for his companion's taut posture. Torbal and Cyneburg seemed ready to slaughter the Unvasik and Duthka. Corann had already seen this and knew where this bloody road would lead. The Duthka whom Corann led were not the enemy, but they were *Duthka*. Would Westhealfe and the Rihtgellen kingdom invade both the Deadwood and Frozen Forest? The cycle of violence and vengeance would begin again, if it had ever really ended. A slumbering beast of bloodshed was stirring once more.

The Winds now blow fiercely. Terrible storms are coming…

Wulfner took a deep breath and related the discovery of the fungus and Emiren's theory that it was what was being used to turn men into crazed animals. And their belief that enough had been harvested to turn an entire city.

"Where is the girl now?" demanded Torbal.

"Hopefully back with her parents," replied Wulfner, slightly taken aback, wondering where else she should be.

"We need her," muttered the general.

Wulfner was about to protest but Cyneburg broke his thought.

"They plan to curse all those who are still within Morak?" questioned Torbal's sister, her voice laced with disgust.

Wulfner nodded slowly. "I fear so, my lady." He knew he had no bearing here but felt he at least had to make a plea for restraint. "If you plan to retake the city by force, my lady, those poor souls will be the first to die."

This brought a collective silence to the tent. Wulfner knew a terrible decision was upon Torbal and Cyneburg. They couldn't just leave Morak to an unknown fate. But marching upon the city with the intention of a full-scale assault would mean these soldiers being forced to kill their own kin.

The taller man who had entered the tent with them spoke. "General, Lady Cyneburg, if we move quickly, we may able to stop this nightmare before it begins."

Torbal nodded. He gestured to the man and addressed Wulfner and Corann.

"This is Wyman, Forwost of the Bladesung legion." Torbal paused. "He knew Nerian as well as I did," the general added quietly.

Wyman stood straighter, the soldier in him pushing down the emotion rising within, Wulfner guessed. Part of him wished he still possessed that kind of discipline. And was still the fighter he had been once.

Forgive me, Nerian.

Torbal looked to Cyneburg, who nodded, then pinched the bridge of his nose, sighing. His hands fell to his sides, balling into fists.

"We ride at dawn. The Bladesung and those Bradlastax warriors who are now with us. They deserve their vengeance. The Heoroth legion will stay here and man the ford." He raised a finger and addressed the Forwost Wyman. "We will need a company of sappers. The walls of Morak are high."

Corann abruptly turned and strode out of the tent, pushing past the two Forwosts. They grunted their displeasure but let him go. Torbal looked at Wulfner.

"Can he be trusted?" he asked, gesturing after the departing Duthka.

Wulfner felt his own anger rise. He tried to speak calmly but couldn't keep the edge from his voice.

"My lord, Corann killed a number of Duthka, his own kin, within the Sacred Mount. Were it not for him, I would not be here to bring you this news. He lost his wife and son to Barghest's merciless hunting of the Duthka all those years ago and yet he has helped us. With respect, my lord, I'd say he deserves a little more of *our* respect!"

Wulfner found he was shaking and sought to steady himself. Torbal held his eyes and Wulfner could see the King's Shield was less than happy. After an agonising moment of silence, Torbal spoke.

"I do not like your tone, Wulfner. Remember whom you address."

Wulfner lowered his gaze and wished he was back in Ceapung, quaffing ale with Balther and tossing Trob strips of meat.

"But I concede Corann is not our enemy. This Seolta is our enemy—the enemy of the entire realm — and we must destroy him and his alliance with the Unvasik." The general turned to the stockier Forwost. "Doecga, take Wulfner to the mess tent and make sure he is well fed. Corann too, if you can find him."

Wulfner dipped his head in respect to Torbal and Cyneburg, then let himself be led out of the tent by Doecga. Once outside, the Heoroth Forwost spoke.

"Think I must have missed the calm before the storm," he said, raising an eyebrow and puffing out a breath.

Wulfner replied. "Clear skies above but the realm rages." He winced. "I let my temper get the better of me in there," he said, shaking his head in disbelief. "I was giving mouth to the King's Shield of all people!"

Doecga chuckled. "Must say you have some stones on you, friend," he said as they wound their way through tents, spear-racks, and soldiers marching by. "I've never known the general to let a man just walk away after letting his mouth run. You were lucky! I have seen the general in all his glorious fury and I can tell you, it will put the fear of the Old Gods in any man."

Wulfner felt his stomach roll and then couldn't stop breaking wind.

"Yeah, exactly," muttered Doecga.

Wulfner saw Corann ahead and turned to the Heoroth Forwost.

"Thank you, Forwost. My friend is there, so just point me in the direction of the food and I'm sure my nose will take me the rest of the way."

"Ha! Not unless somebody has taught Coula and his lads how to cook! His stew reeks like a pond that's being used by drunken farmers to relieve themselves." Doecga clapped Wulfner on the back. "Luck to you, friend."

Wulfner thanked the Forwost once more and headed over to where Corann was standing, tending to their horses.

Corann looked up as he approached. "Do you see now, Wulfner, why my people hid in the Abhaile? Torbal is beyond reason. I see the rage in his eyes. There is no hope. He hates Duthka, he hates Unvasik. As does Cyneburg. It has begun again. They will keep killing now until fatigue and the sheer number of corpses bring an end to the violence. That was how it began before, and that was how it ended over a hundred years ago. History repeats itself. You know this."

Wulfner couldn't argue with the Duthka leader.

"My people are in danger, Wulfner. I must return and take them deeper into the forest."

"You are leaving?" blurted Wulfner. "We need your help."

Corann shook his head sadly. "No, that time is past. The powers in the realm are now well and truly marching down the path of war, and the end of that road is only death. I am turning off this road now, and I urge you to do the same. Return to Ceapung and pray that the war fades before it reaches your people there."

Wulfner knew that would be the sensible thing to do. He was no young soldier anymore. What more could he offer these people now, especially as they were so driven by revenge? Battle and killing were all that lay before Lord Torbal and Lady Cyneburg. He should get as far away as possible. If the conflict did indeed reach Ceapung, then it meant the whole realm was on fire and nobody was safe.

Wulfner placed a hand on Corann's shoulder. "May the Winds blow kindly on your journey, Corann. I hope one day we will meet once more, but perhaps it would be better if we never see each other again," he said, smiling sadly.

Corann raised his hand to Wulfner's shoulder and nodded. "I see the wisdom in your words," he said, offering a slight smile. Corann then hauled himself up onto his horse. He looked down at Wulfner and repeated his advice.

"Return to Ceapung, Wulfner, and wait out the coming storm."

The northerner chuckled. "I'll think on it," he replied, despite already knowing what he would do. Ceapung would have to wait.

Corann kicked his mount into motion and trotted away from Wulfner, the former soldier, then trader, now accidental player in this terrible drama. The Duthka picked up pace as he cleared the outer defences. *Definitely was going slow for my benefit…*

Wulfner turned back and headed to the mess tent. He felt horribly alone after having been with others for the past few weeks and reckoned some food would ease the emptiness. He sniffed the air and caught a whiff of something.

Either that is the latrine trench or Doecga wasn't joking about the food here…

CHAPTER 6

SYLVANUS

21st Day of Maia, Two Days After Gimmweg Was Attacked

Sylvanus was glad to be away from Helligan lands. He was also now farther away from Meridia, which meant there was less chance of him being captured or lynched. The truth of his betrayal of the city was surely out by now; a betrayal deep and long in its forging, but a necessary path. The Duthka must reclaim the realm, take it back from the foreign invaders. And Sylvanus was Duthka.

Rencarro's former Second and secret ally to Lord Orben checked his nocturnal surroundings once more. He had made camp in the sparser woodlands north of the Mimir River and was now seated upon a weathered log within the border of the trees. He could see the shadow of the Gjallag Bridge to the southwest, its towers proud and erect, and was looking forward to watching the drama that should unfold come morning.

Every day brings Seolta a step closer to reshaping the realm. And me a step closer to becoming what I truly am.

Sylvanus uncorked a bottle and let the deep red flow into a silver goblet he had stolen from Orben's solar. The wine, also snatched, was from Ulla's cellar. He took a sip, let it sit within his mouth for a moment, then swallowed. He took another and smiled as the earthy flavour swirled upon his tongue.

Think I prefer this to Meridian wine, truth be told.

Ulla's vineyard was something to be proud of, he mused. Sylvanus was confident the Helligan Lady would never again over-see production of the claret, however. She should be dead by now, beaten to death by her wild, deranged brother. Hopefully Orben had been killed by either Kailen or a guard. If that hadn't happened, then the lord would be as good as dead anyway, poisoned by the fungus. The two leaders of the Helligan nation were no longer in play and thus unable to stop that which had been set in motion. And with the three captains now each unwittingly carrying out one thread of Sylvanus' design, the Helligan nation was dancing to an enchanting tune indeed.

Sylvanus would have liked to see how the poison altered Orben, but that would have been a foolish indulgence. Idelisa had assured him it worked. His thoughts turned to the young Duthka lady and her stories of his people and their home within the forests. His own memories were vague. He had been born within the trees but all he could remember was his mother's face.

Mother, please know that I do this to set right the wrongs done to you and our people.

Sylvanus sniffed and cast his eyes upward, the image of his mother at her end, seared into his mind. He cuffed the tears from his eyes and emptied the goblet. He coughed as the wine coursed down into his belly.

All are guilty by their indifference to what was done to us.

The Meridian wondered if Kailen had also been killed by the turned Orben. If not, Sylvanus had taken certain measures to ensure their plans would go unhindered. There was a strange irony to it all. Sylvanus had found his last conversation with Orben's messenger strangely satisfying, detecting a hint of guilt in the young lady as he pointed out she would never be responsible for a soldier's death.

Death comes to us all.

And it had come to Rencarro's son, Marcus, sooner than anyone could have anticipated, Sylvanus included. The arrogant young man should be now in Lowenden, getting bored and nursing his malcontent. But the local village-boy sneaking about in the forest had twisted fate, so to speak. It had presented an opportunity for Sylvanus to remove an unpredictable piece from the board, a piece he personally had loathed for the last ten years. A man who spit out slurs every single day. A man who was not fit to serve, let alone lead. How Marcus had become such a poor excuse for a human, Sylvanus couldn't fathom. The father was not so.

Rencarro was a decent man. Sylvanus felt remorse over his betrayal to the Meridian lord but had lost no sleep over Marcus' demise.

Damn that girl!

Sylvanus' eyes should have been the only ones to see the killings but that cursed red-head had stumbled in. Her witnessing the act and then escaping had set in motion a chain of events which had corrupted his plans, twisted their timing and laid bare his deception.

Damn her and her blasted pig-herd lover!

A movement out of the corner of his eye snagged his attention the instant he heard the rustling scrape of something moving past a tree. Sylvanus breathed slowly and did not make any hasty moves. Experience had told him that if somebody was sneaking up on you, and you were aware of their approach, then they were not a trained assassin. Much like that boy he had killed in Argol Forest. That lad had been like a drunken boar in his supposed stealth.

Sylvanus kept his head low, pretending to tend to his cook-fire. More crunching of woodland undergrowth told him there were at least two figures approaching. The Meridian exile took stock of where he was in relation to his probable assailants and mentally went through the paces in his mind, the steps he would take if they were indeed a threat.

"Travelling alone?" a voice inquired. Male, a rough accent, slightly leery in tone.

Sylvanus made an exaggerated startled reaction, one hand to his chest as if in shock. There were three of them. Two stood a few yards from him, both with right hands upon the pommels of what looked like long knives hanging from their belts, rust clear to see. The other stood farther back, a crossbow in his hands, loaded but with the bolt pointing toward the ground at present.

Their attire was ragged, dirty woollen cloaks about their shoulders, mud-caked boots on one, while the second stranger's feet were bare and the third's were obscured.

"You speak the common tongue, friend?" The same voice. The speaker had a mouth full of brown teeth and a particularly scraggly beard. It was clear these three lived in the wild; Sylvanus presumed they were bandits or scavengers.

"I do, yes. You startled me there, coming up behind me so quietly." He made sure to inject a healthy dose of anxiety into his reply.

The speaker grinned, showing more of the interior of his disgusting mouth. His tongue looked black. This filthy man was sick in some way.

"Didn't mean to scare ya, friend. We was just a bit worried about someone travelling alone." He paused and looked around nervously. "You are alone, aren'tcha?"

Sylvanus nodded vigorously. "Yes, yes, just me." He shot looks at the other two, displaying wide eyes to show he was frightened. "W-what do you want?" he stammered.

Bad-Teeth chuckled and took a step closer. His companion, who seemed to have poor eyesight judging by his heavy squinting, also came forward. Squinty seemed ill at ease with the forthcoming robbery though.

"You look like a rich man. Might be you can spare us some coin, us being hungry and such."

Sylvanus put on a show of relief and nodded quickly. "I see. Yes, yes, of course, and then we will say our farewells, I trust."

"We might just say goodbye, yeah." Bad-Teeth gave a twisted smile.

Stupid shit-for-brains! Thinks he's putting on a glorious show of bravado for his friends.

"Good, good," Sylvanus gushed. "Well, I daresay I can spare a few coppers for hungry men. Let me retrieve the coins from my bag there."

He pointed to his sack lying between him and the two closest. The crossbow was still pointed downward.

Bad-Teeth gestured for him to go ahead and Squinty let out an excited belch of laughter. Sylvanus stooped and opened the sack. As he did so, he winced and put a hand to his back.

"Ooh, getting stiff in my old age," he wheezed as his right hand, hidden from their sight, gripped the blade's handle.

"Here we are!" Sylvanus announced, gesturing with his left hand to the bag, where there were no coppers but silver coins instead. Bad-Teeth and Squinty leaned down eagerly, peered into the bag, and whistled at the sight of shining silver. They inched in even closer and Sylvanus judged they were near enough.

He stood, withdrew the blade from the sheath on his back, and slashed Squinty's throat before either saw the gleam of the weapon. A spray of blood spat forth; Squinty grabbed his neck and staggered backwards.

Bad-Teeth gasped in horror and Sylvanus lunged forward, ramming the butt of the knife's handle into the man's forehead. He grunted and staggered. Sylvanus grabbed his tunic and pulled him in front of his own body, one arm going around his neck, and the rather fine dagger bequeathed to him by Orben, at the man's ear.

Squinty collapsed in a heap, his front a dark mess of blood mixed with whatever filth had been there already. The one with the crossbow finally came to his senses and raised the weapon, but his hands were shaking. This robbery had not gone to plan.

"Easy there, lad," cautioned Sylvanus, all the false fear gone from his voice. "We don't want any more accidents."

Bad-Teeth squirmed but the man was weak, perhaps malnourished, and Sylvanus was well-fed and well-rested. His hold on the wretch was secure.

"Let him go!" squeaked the crossbow carrier.

Sylvanus realised that this one was quite young, the grime upon his face hiding the youth underneath.

"Just be careful with that weapon, son," said the older man, his voice gentle and almost fatherly. "Now hold yourself steady and watch."

With that, Sylvanus gripped tightly around the other man's upper torso, then slowly but surely pushed the blade in horizontally to the right side of Bad-Teeth's neck. The bandit jerked but Sylvanus held him tightly. The blade ground against cartilage and bone but eased ever deeper. He then withdrew it, whipping his left arm away before he got covered in the blood Bad-Teeth was now choking on. He grabbed the man's collar to stop the body falling.

Sylvanus held the young man's eyes. He could smell feces but wasn't sure if it was from the dead men or if this young fellow had lost his bowels in fear. The crossbow was raised but his hands were shaking. *Steady now...*

Sylvanus felt a jolt in the dead body he was holding up. For a moment he was puzzled. He twisted Bad-Teeth around and saw a crossbow bolt in the wretch's stomach. Sylvanus let go of the corpse and raised his eyes once more. This lad was feverishly trying to reload the weapon.

"You only get one chance with a crossbow," said Sylvanus as he strode the remaining three yards between them, slapped the weapon aside with his left hand, and then rammed his knife into the man's gut. His eyes went wide with surprise. Sylvanus dragged the blade to the right, then withdrew it. The bandit looked down upon his life flowing out. He made a strange sound that sounded like a cat choking as the former Second of Meridia turned to wipe the knife on Squinty's clothes. Sylvanus heard the body crumple to the forest floor behind him.

"Foolish bastards," he muttered.

Three corpses in his campsite were unsightly and would attract all sorts of nocturnal life. Sylvanus kicked the crossbow bandit in the side in anger.

Damn their filthy lives.

Sylvanus had been born into a life of being hunted. He and his mother had been captured, sold to a criminal network, and been forced into a life of slavery and torment in the capital, Bregustol. He had grown up in filth on the streets, been treated like filth as a child, and been forced to eat all manner of filth to survive. That was why he hated filth so bitterly.

There was nothing else he could do but set up camp elsewhere, which would take time and rob him of a relaxing evening drinking wine. He looked with disgust at the three dead men, then began gathering his belongings. When he had everything, he urinated on his campfire to extinguish it and set off to find another suitable place to camp.

Can't I have one restful night?

Sylvanus checked his surroundings again in the light of morning. There was no sign of anyone around and he was confident he was well concealed, but with a good vantage to watch the bridge. He pulled out the wineskin again, took a swig, then chomped down on sausage. He hated to admit it, but he did miss the spicier sausages of Meridia.

His thoughts turned again to Seolta and Idelisa. Seolta, the man who had searched the realm for Duthka refugees and found Sylvanus some ten years ago, when he was an officer on the rise in Rencarro's forces. Idelisa, a woman who had done more than any other to bring about the rebirth of Marrh.

I owe them so much.

He had seen neither of them since High King Sedmund's death, receiving the powdered fungus from a nameless Duthka one night in an inn of Gamle Hovestad. This powder had ended up in Orben's wine. Sylvanus had watched him drink it, then left to find Ulla and Kailen. The timing had been full of risk, but he was outside the city when the bells rang. He had been successful in his task and Seolta would be pleased.

He slowly exhaled as he fought turmoil within himself. The realm belonged to the Duthka. Of that he was certain. But for the better part of two decades, he had buried his heritage, choosing to become part of Meridia. His rise in rank had helped to push the memories deeper, the respect and wealth he gained proving a shiny distraction. But Seolta had found him. How, Sylvanus had no idea, and Seolta never said. A year of regular meetings though had opened his eyes to the injustice and his own shame at abandoning who he was in favour of false gods and fanfare.

Forgive me, mother. I was wrong to turn my back on our people.

But arguably he had ultimately become much more valuable to Seolta because of his years in Meridia. If he had returned to the Beacuan or Abhaile, he would be little more than a forest-dweller. But as Second to the Lord Rencarro, he had been able to engineer a situation where the south was in chaos and would soon spread fear within the north.

As if in answer to his thoughts, shouts drifted over on the wind. Sylvanus peered out from his concealed location. The Helligans had arrived and were assaulting the Gjallag bridge from the southern side. The Rihtgellen defences were significant and a standard frontal assault on the bridge would be destined to fail. This assault was far from standard, however.

The far side of the bridge was beyond his sight, but he could see a great deal of movement on this side. The soldiers manning the towers and gatehouse should be from highly trained companies and not just commoners being handed a spear. Under normal circumstances the Rihtgellen soldiers could hold their end without suffering heavy losses, but today the Helligan attack was two-fold.

Ah, there you are, Brax. Impressive, most impressive...

Advancing from the west of the bridge, on *this* side of the Mimir River, the northern side and Rihtgellen lands, was a large company of people. From where Sylvanus sat, they looked like farmers or villagers, their clothes bearing no bright colours. He was certain, though, that they were the Helligan Sentinels in the north-east after a night-time crossing with many rafts, and what looked like farming tools were actually something of a more deadly nature. Sylvanus knew the plans in detail. He had made them after all, with Orben in the Helligan lord's solar, away from Ulla's prying eyes.

Sylvanus couldn't help but smile. Before his eyes were the results of years of patience and perseverance. Marrh was rapidly descending into conflict and disorder, and most soldiers were not even fighting their real enemies.

The Rihtgellen soldiers had seen the approaching group and one, probably an officer, was shouting at them, likely telling them to flee from the fighting.

Don't think these lads will retreat to safety.

The Sentinels broke into a run. Sylvanus couldn't see the exact moment the Rihtgellen soldiers realised they had enemies front and back, but it was soon too late. Covers were removed, revealing the glint of blades upon the long poles. The screams of those who felt their touch rang out on an otherwise beautiful day.

These Helligans are well trained, no doubt about that.

Sylvanus took another gulp of wine and leaned back against the tree, a strange feeling of euphoria coursing through his body. It wasn't that the violence particularly thrilled him; it was the fact that Seolta's grand plan continued to take shape.

The Duthka will take back Marrh. Never again will we will be hounded or hunted.

The sun was not yet at its zenith when the Gjallag Bridge was secure and Helligan troops were marching over into the northeast of Ragnekai. The red and white flags were held high and the numbers continued to swell. Sylvanus waited long enough to see siege engines trundle over, carts laden with siege tower sections, ballistae, and rams. Orders had been sent by Orben himself and now there was nobody to rescind those orders. The march of war would continue.

Sylvanus, former Second to the Lord of Meridia, duplicitous ally to a Helligan lord and willing servant to a great Duthka man, gathered his belongings and began his journey northward, casting a glance back at the Helligan soldiers now fortifying their position. Dim-witted bandits aside, Sylvanus would be unlikely to take part in any of the conflict from now. He would soon meet Seolta and he hoped Idelisa too.

Seolta, the realm is bleeding. It is yours.

PART TWO

Chapter 1

Paega

20th Day of Maia, The Day After Gimmweg Was Attacked

Paega's shoulder ached. He narrowed his eyes at the bandage covering the wound made by the arrow, his teeth grinding. How could he work at the anvil when his right arm was unable to wield a hammer? His *brave* decision to try to stop that Helligan spy, or whoever he was, had proved to be a very poor one. Paega had tackled the man, bringing him down, and heard the shouts of people coming to his aid. He had held fast even after receiving a butt to the nose. Paega had wanted to crush the life from the scum-bag. Then his shoulder had suddenly exploded with a burning sensation. Not the heat of the forge but the fire of pain delivered by an arrow. An accomplice. And so, the cur had escaped, while Paega lay on the street in agony, blood staining the cobblestones.

Bastards! May the Ever-Father fill their ears with molten iron and break their bones with the True Smith's hammer...

Paega was being well cared for though. The Ever-Father's True Sons had witnessed his actions and had brought him to one of their houses of worship. His wound had been tended to and he had slept most of yesterday. And he had been fed. If he was honest about it, he had eaten better than ever before. Roast meat, fresh fruit, bread not long out of the oven, and a wine that was supposed to help his body heal. Paega had never before drunk wine in his life, so he had no idea what it should taste like. The wine they gave him was light, tasted like some kind of fruit, and certainly made him drowsy. So, for the moment, he wasn't completely unhappy. But he worried his apprenticeship at the forge would be lost by the time he was strong enough to bend iron to his will again.

I won't go back home...

The notion of going back to his parents in the village of Barleywick was not one that filled him with wistful longing. His father had wanted him to make horseshoes and farming tools for the folk there, but Paega had yearned to be a better smith. He had come to Bregustol to learn how to make armour. And he would have been starting on his first breast-plate next week if he hadn't blocked that spy.

Why didn't I just stand aside, mind my own business, just like everyone else?

He lay back on the cot, a comfier bed than his own, and closed his eyes. The chief smith at the forge had been harsh when Paega began working there a year ago. A practically silent taskmaster, who expected his charges to learn by watching him and the senior smiths. He would put work in front of the apprentices and walk away without saying anything. Nothing needed to be said. When the work was finished, he would examine it, frown and huff if the work was not satisfactory, or emit a single grunt and a quick nod if he deemed the job completed.

Paega had worked hard. He had put the time in, having no family or friends here, and little money for ale. It had been a gruelling twelve months, but his master had given more grunts than frowns at the beginning of this year, which Paega took to be a sign his skill was improving. A couple of the other apprentices had left, apparently fed up with the lack of praise and trust, but Paega had persevered.

Then last week, his master had caught his eye, said nothing but given a curt gesture with his hand. Paega had swiftly walked over to see what was required of him. His master had led him to a workbench, upon which were two breastplates. One was finished in its form, but still to be burnished. The other was yet to be fully hammered into shape. Paega had looked questioningly at his master. The taciturn man had pointed to the latter, given the faintest of smiles, and walked off. Paega's time had come and he had relished the excitement. He had felt his dreams and ambitions coming together and settling before him.

Then he had grappled that spy to the ground. And been rewarded with an arrow in the shoulder.

Ever-Father, please look down on your son now and carry me back to the path I was walking.

Paega opened his eyes and jumped, startled to see a man standing above him.

"At ease, young one. I did not mean to disturb your prayer."

Paega was lost for words. How had this man known he was praying? And who was he? He wore a purple robe that was faded at the shoulders and frayed at the sleeves. He was older than Paega but younger than his father, he reckoned. Nearing forty years perhaps. Hair that was brown like the mouse who scurried around Paega's bunk at night, back in the dormitory where he lodged. A face that was not handsome like the jongleur Paega had watched the other day, singing to the crowd and doing comical somersaults. But neither was this man ugly and scarred like his master at the forge. His face was one Paega would forget in an instant, if not for his eyes. They were opened widely as if the man was fascinated with all he saw. And there was something in them that made Paega unable to hold his gaze—not madness, but a conviction that was slightly unnerving.

"I am Magen."

Paega felt like this name was supposed to mean something to him the way it was announced. He desperately tried to remember who he had met so far in this hospice.

Then it clicked. This man must be the leader of the True Sons, the high priest or whatever the title was. Paega adopted a look of awe, raising his eye-brows and gaping, and hoped it wouldn't be taken for ridicule. Fortunately, it wasn't. The man smiled in the way the priest in Barleywick used to when he stood before the congregation. Not a single doubt in his manner. Paega decide to introduce himself.

"My name is Paega," he said, his throat hoarse.

"You were brave, Paega."

The young smith shrugged. And immediately winced as the pain in his shoulder flared up.

"Rest now. You are a man of might. You must heal so your strength can serve the Ever-Father again," said the holy leader, his voice firm but gentle.

Paega wasn't sure what the man meant by that. He hoped it was just a turn of phrase, meaning Magen wanted him to heal so he could get back to bending iron for the good people who worshipped the Ever-Father.

"I should return to the forge. My master waits for my work to be finished," Paega said quietly.

Magen raised his eyebrows.

"I suspected you were a smith. Which forge?" he asked, his eyes unblinking, forcing to Paega to look down.

"The forge on Cog Street...my lord." Paega wasn't sure how to address this man.

Magen chuckled. "Lord? No. Only those who seek to dominate use such titles. I seek to lead, that is true. But with all of you at my side, leading the way to the Ever-Father's light." The holy leader looked up as he said this and inhaled deeply.

Paega shifted, a little uncomfortable. Was this Magen including him in the collective "you" there? It was starting to feel as if he had already been taken in by the True Sons and was now in debt to them.

Magen's eyes dropped to Paega again and continued. "Cog Street? I know it. Hrodgar is your master then."

Paega blinked, surprised this man would know such things. Magen turned and beckoned over a True Son, the man bulky beneath his brown robes. Whether it was muscle or fat, Paega couldn't be sure.

"Dudda. This noble servant of the Ever-Father works at Hrodgar's forge on Cog Street. Go there immediately and tell the smith his man Paega is here, being cared for. Relate to him how his apprentice stood in the way of a Helligan spy when all others cowered. The True Sons will make amends for Hrodgar's loss. Do you understand?"

"Yes, Magen," he replied. Magen waved him away and Dudda hurried off.

Paega's unease grew. The loss of work or the loss of his apprentice? Paega felt he was being sucked into something and for the moment was powerless to stop it.

Magen smiled at him. "Calm your soul now and tell me the tale of how you stopped the Helligan spies."

Spies? I only stopped one. And he got away anyway.

Magen sat down on Paega's cot and the young man from Barleywick knew he would have to get on with the story. He took a breath and began.

And was finished in less time than it took to put his tools away at the end of a normal working day.

Magen smiled. "Join us in the main hall at noon for lunch, brother."

Before Paega had a chance to say anything, Magen rose and walked over to another man on a cot.

Brother?

Paega shovelled another spoon of pie into his mouth and savoured the rich gravy. The True Sons certainly ate well. He was about to take a gulp of the fruit wine when there was a commotion at the far end of the hall. He peered over and saw a True Son relating something to Magen. The holy lord was on his feet, shaking his fists in the air. It looked a bit dramatic to Paega, but then he remembered the performances of the priest in Barleywick, conjuring up images of Oblivion's deathly touch. Paega kept watching Magen.

Something is going on.

He took a swig of wine but almost choked on it when Magen climbed upon a table and called for quiet, his voice booming out to the high ceiling of the hall.

"Brothers! Lay down your spoons and listen now to my words!"

Hundreds of tiny thuds combined to create an odd drum-roll as spoons were placed upon tables. Then the hall was silent, all the True

Sons looking around anxiously. Paega felt the tension in the air, heavy and ominous like Oblivion's breath. It was clear something was wrong and Paega began to wish he wasn't there. If there was to be another lynching, he'd rather not be a part of it.

Unless it's that rat who got away...

Magen raised his arms in the air and called upon the Ever-Father to give them strength and wisdom before he relayed the news.

"I have just received grave tidings. The rumours concerning Morak are true!" Magen paused, casting his eyes this way and that. "The Unvasik have come!" he cried.

Cries of anger erupted as fists beat against tables. Magen let the rage ride forth for a few moments, then raised his hands once more. The noise quickly died down but Paega could feel a simmering rage all around. He couldn't take it in. The Unvasik were meant to be fearsome giants that lived on the plateaus east of the Jagged Heights.

"The Unvasik were not raiding..."

Paega heard gasps but was unsure himself what the significance of those last words was. *What were they doing then?*

Magen answered his question, crying out in a voice that was almost a scream. "They butchered the citizens of Morak!"

The hall exploded again into a cacophony of noise, True Sons roaring out sharp curses, exclamations of disbelief, and promises of righteous retribution. Magen shouted over the rumbling.

"We have news of dark sorcery being cast upon our brothers and sisters. These Unvasik brutes are in thrall to Oblivion, there can be no doubt!" Magen shook his head and pounded a fist into his palm. "We cannot let this pass."

Growls of defiance rang out. Paega cast his eyes around and saw an almost maniacal ferocity in some of the True Sons.

Ever-Father, calm them with your love.

"Worsteth..." Magen said the name in a tone of utter disgust. Paega did not know who Worsteth was, but he didn't seem very popular judging by the mutters and tutting around him.

"Our most diligent royal chamberlain," continued Magen, his voice dripping with contempt, "does not have the courage to face the enemies of the Ever-Father. He will close the city and have us all hide inside, just as he has done since Brother Eswic's murder. He hates Bregustol and its good people!"

Cries of *coward* and even *traitor* could be heard. Paega felt Magen's words weren't making much sense. If this Worsteth truly hated the people of Bregustol, why would he have them stay here, behind high walls? The True Sons clearly didn't share his doubts.

Paega became increasingly anxious. He had walked away from the crowd watching the execution of the two Helligan spies; a mob eager to witness death was all he saw. This was beginning to feel the same, with Magen whipping up the True Sons into a frenzy. Paega once again wished he were somewhere else. At the forge, conversation was kept to a minimum. The forge itself was noisy and idle chatter could bring distraction, which could lead to burns and more serious injury. Paega found a certain peace within the hisses and *ting-ting* of hammer upon metal.

How do I get away from this?

Magen was continuing to raise the temperature in here, adding more coke to the fires.

"Worsteth will do nothing! We, the True Sons, loyal children of the Ever-Father, must act!"

This assertion was met with a thunderous roar of approval. Paega nodded as enthusiastically as he could, figuring it best not to be the only one in the hall who didn't want to die for the Ever-Father.

I'll just try to slip away quietly...

"I know you are all brave, my brothers! But let us all see what true bravery looks like!"

Oh no...

"Paega, stand!"

Shit...

"Paega, stand and be recognised as the man who stood in the way of Helligan spies, while all around hid and mewled like frightened kittens."

Paega knew he couldn't crawl under the table now, so he slowly got to his feet. The True Sons began to cheer and shout his name.

"Paega! Paega!" they cried, pounding the table.

Ever-Father, is this some kind of punishment?

The chanting of his name continued. He felt a hand upon his shoulder and was startled to see Magen had joined him. The holy leader had a firm smile upon his face, but his eyes spoke of an extreme devotion to the Ever-Father. Magen took his arm and guided him up onto the table-top. When they were both standing on the space where moments ago Paega had been enjoying his food, the volume of voices and pounding fists increased around the hall. Paega felt nauseous.

Oblivion's black heart! What in the Abyss is this madness?

Magen ushered for quiet again. Paega looked around at the faces of the True Sons and saw wide grins, enthusiastic nodding heads, and even staring eyes that spoke of divine glory.

"Paega was a simple smith…"

Paega didn't like the way Magen said *was* instead of *is*.

"…on his way to the forge…"

That's not true!

"And I can only think he was blessed with the strength and love of the Ever-Father in that moment…"

I'm strong because I beat metal all day, damn it!

"He held onto one wicked spy but then Oblivion struck!"

Gasps of awe came forth. Paega lowered his head to hide his expression.

This is a mummer's farce…

"An arrow from a second spy pierced his shoulder but still he held!" cried Magen, his hands swirling theatrically.

Paega frowned. He hadn't held on after the arrow had struck him. No human could have performed such a miracle. But Paega could see that was exactly what Magen was conjuring here: a miracle. The holy man was giving his followers a sign that they were favoured by a higher power. Paega felt a quiet resentment that this Magen was abusing the love of the Ever-Father, twisting it for his own ends.

"May the Ever-Father bless us all with Paega's strength and courage!" screeched Magen, and the hall boomed once again.

Paega began to feel dizzy. His knees buckled but in the instant he began to fall, several hands shot up to support him. They gently guided him down from the table and let him sit.

"See how the love of the Ever-Father can overwhelm even the purist of his servants!"

Please stop this, Ever-Father…

Magen continued his improvised sermon, preaching of a higher calling and the righteousness of their cause. Paega stopped listening and hung his head. His world had stopped spinning, but he didn't want to look upon the awe-struck faces of men who were his equals.

"In four days' time, we will gather in the Holy Sepulchre. Until then, I bid you go out into the streets and spread the word. Let people know the Unvasik are coming! Gather our holy soldiers! Encourage the city watch to join us. And bring them all to me!"

Paega's ears had pricked up at the mention of the Holy Sepulchre, it being a place of wonder to him, a place where he had never set foot. But now it was to become a mustering hall.

Ever-Father, help me get back to my life…

Paega chanced a glance upward and knew for certain his prayer would go unanswered. Magen was looking down at him, a wild smile under eyes that silently screamed.

CHAPTER 2

SONGAA

21st Day of Maia, Two Days After Gimmweg Was Attacked

The singing of the Tarakalo ended and the Tarakans lowered their hands. Imala looked to Songaa to say something. He wished he could pass on the responsibility, but choosing a path forward lay upon his shoulders in this moment. Imala and Naaki were older in years but their role in the tribe had always been as storytellers, guiding the young ones to a better understanding of the world and of each other.

What kind of story can help us to understand this?

Songaa could not answer his own question. They were standing outside the walls of Argyllan, the harbour area a stone's throw away. There were no piles of charred bones here, all the pyres being to the east of the city, but one could not fail to see that a battle had been fought. The grass still bore the dirty, brown stains of death, and here and there broken spears and fragments of shields still waited to be cleared away.

Songaa spoke, letting his thoughts flow. "It will take time for the good people here to recover. And some never will," he added sadly.

More than one of the *dii-tsebi* who had rode with him, hung their heads.

"And I doubt there is one of us who will return to the Plains untouched by what we have been through, what we have done. Some more than others," he said, turning his gaze to rest on Enyeto.

The lad had killed several Throskaur raiders with his arrows as they fought in the market square, and it was clear this sat heavily upon his young shoulders. His cousin Choondei had tried to talk with him but Enyeto had been a well of silence since the battle.

"I do not today regret my decision to add our bows to this battle, but I fear it may come back to haunt the Tarakan people in the future. I pray to Yaai and Her Brother that I am wrong."

"Not even the All-Mother knows where each fork in the road leads," commented Imala's sister, Naaki. "We must always do what we think right in the moment. Do not bear the weight of your decision alone, Songaa. And Enyeto," she said, turning to him, "do not keep the darkness inside. Let it out into the light where it will fade."

Enyeto raised his eyes and gave a small nod. Songaa felt it was a good sign.

Lunyai's father clapped his hands to dispel the sombre mood. "Now, I ask you all to be about your tasks today. See to your mounts first, be sure they are watered and can breathe fresh air. Then gather in the market square at midday to eat and during the afternoon, we will help where we can. You will return to the Plains tomorrow, so do all you can today for the people of Argyllan."

The group broke up and the Tarakans headed off to the where their horses had been stabled. Imala shared a word with her sister, then approached Songaa.

"I notice you said *you* will return, not *we*. You intend to wait here for Lunyai?"

Songaa held his arms to his chest and nodded. "Of course. She was in Westhealfe and alive. Captain Lucetta told us she was journeying to the Sacred Mount with others to search for something. She was sparing with details but assures me Lunyai was well. And Lunyai knows I am here. She will come soon."

Imala smiled gently and he knew she could see his words lacked belief.

Please come back, my daughter. The realm has become too dangerous for you to roam.

"I told Lunyai she was a restless imp, when we were halfway up the Sacred Mount," Imala told Songaa. "Seems I was right." She chuckled.

Songaa breathed a laugh himself. "Lunyai always was a little bit too full of curiosity. I knew she would become more so after having glimpsed the wider realm, but I did not expect her to run off, trying to see it all!" he said, shaking his head.

"She shines with Tlenaii's light, your daughter. I believe when she has absorbed more of Yaai's warmth, she will find balance and become a true leader of our people."

Songaa couldn't see that future yet. His daughter was still so young to his eyes but perhaps she had grown in many ways during her strange journey. He hoped her spirit was not diminished.

Lunyai, please hurry back to me. And then we will return to the Plains and your mother.

Imala cocked her head. Songaa heard it too. Shouting from the east side of the city. The two of them shared a look that was laden with fear. Were there still Throskaur out there? Had new enemies come? Songaa unslung his bow and began walking, his pace quickening.

Choondei suddenly appeared at the corner of the north wall. He was waving his arms to Songaa and looked to be laughing.

Imala was behind Songaa. "Hurry! I believe the All-Mother has blessed us this day."

Songaa's breath quickened. He whipped his bow back onto his shoulder and broke into a dash, speeding toward Choondei. His friend gave him a huge grin as he flew past and rounded the wall.

Yaai be praised!

Four figures on three horses were approaching on the road that led to the eastern gate. They were still some two hundred yards away, but Songaa knew one of them was Lunyai. He felt it within him, as if the All-Mother herself was assuring him this was no mirage.

"Lunyai!" he shouted.

His daughter almost fell off the horse in her hurry to dismount. As soon as her feet touched the ground, she was running. Songaa came to a halt and waited, his arms wide.

And then his daughter was in them, crushing herself to his body, laughter peppering her sobbing.

"Lunyai, thanks be to the All-Mother you are back with me. I have been so worried."

He squeezed her tightly and it was as if he had released a breath that had been held tight since the moment Yana had told him Lunyai was missing. His body relaxed like a bow string being slowly released from its tension.

"Where have you been, young one?" he whispered as he hugged her.

"I'm sorry, Father. I have been caught up in a storm," she told him, her voice ragged with emotion.

"Thank Yaai and Tlenaii you have returned," he whispered, stroking her hair.

Songaa became aware of one of Lunyai's companions passing them, still mounted. The man was somewhere between Lunyai and himself in age, dark hair tied back, a week's growth of beard upon his handsome face and a tale of a hard journey in his eyes. The man leaned down as he trotted past.

"Your daughter is a fierce one," he said, grinning. His gaze turned to Lunyai. "And a survivor." The grin disappeared and a look of respect, perhaps, replaced it.

Lunyai let out a small laugh and Songaa wondered what his daughter had been through out there in the wider realm.

The man was past them, raising his hand in greeting to someone.

"That was Tacet," Lunyai told him. "We are friends."

Songaa nodded but then Lunyai added with a sigh, "Now."

He was going to ask what she meant but was interrupted by a voice calling out.

"Emiren! Bless the Spirits!"

Camran, the Argyllan quartermaster, was rushing past them toward the girl who had been on the horse with Lunyai. Songaa looked up at her but saw a girl in terror.

The redhead seemed to be frozen with fear, her eyes staring beyond them to where the man had just ridden. The city gates.

Lunyai tensed in his arms. Her head swung around as she slipped from her father's embrace. Confused, he followed her gaze. Standing at the eastern wall was Lord Rencarro, the Meridian who had led the defence of Argyllan.

"What is it?" he asked, feeling there were tales within shadows within yet more tales.

Lunyai turned back to her friend. Camran was now hugging the girl. Lunyai relaxed. She shook her head.

"So much has happened, Father. And I think we have difficult times ahead. Out there," she said, her arm gesturing in an arc to the north and west, "and here," she finished, looking at the city.

The voice Songaa heard was almost unrecognisable. There was a pain etched within it, yet also a maturity he had never known in his daughter. Again, his mind raced, trying to imagine what had happened to her since she disappeared from Argyllan.

With that thought, the news borne by Yana, one of the Tarakan young ones on the pilgrimage, came back to him. She had said Lunyai attacked a Meridian lord. Songaa's eyes widened.

"You attacked...Rencarro?" he asked, not quite believing this could be true.

Lunyai looked up at him and she was once again his daughter, the young girl so full of adventure and incapable of letting her mind rest. She seemed sheepish.

"It will take some time to tell the whole tale."

Songaa nodded.

"And here is the restless imp!" Imala had quietly approached and was smiling at them.

Lunyai let out a cry and rushed into the elder's arms, babbling a string of apologies and rambling explanations.

"Hush, child," soothed Imala. "You are here now, and we will have time to talk later. Now you must eat and rest your mind. Tlenaii will not show His face for some time so I believe Yaai will have a chance to calm you," she said, giving Lunyai a motherly hug and giving Songaa a curious look over his daughter's shoulder.

She knew what happened with Lunyai and Rencarro.

He shook his head but smiled. Sometimes it was better to let those involved tell the tale themselves.

Songaa looked back to see Camran leading the girl and their horse to the city. Beyond them the last rider who had been with Lunyai stayed where he was. He seemed terribly alone.

"Your friend, Lunyai. Let us bring him into the city."

"All-Mother, forgive me! Moryn has nobody to welcome him," Lunyai chastised herself.

With Imala, they walked over to the man. He was slight in build and looked very weary.

"Moryn, my father and Imala-Shi. This is Moryn of the Duthka people. He saved my life!"

Songaa felt awe swamp his being once again. He raised a hand to the man, and they shook. "You have my eternal thanks," Songaa said, his voice breaking with emotion. "Please come and eat with us."

The man seemed not to hear them. He was looking around him, his eyes full of anguish.

Songaa spoke. "Argyllan had its darkest day but now sees the light again. We are safe here," he added, wondering if this Moryn was fearful of danger close at hand, and hoping he was speaking the truth about there being no immediate threat.

Lunyai took the man's hand and gently pulled, encouraging him to dismount. "Come, Moryn. Let us find food."

The man looked as if he wanted to flee. His eyes flicked this way and that, then found the piles of blackened bones. He gasped. "So many dead..." he whispered.

Songaa nodded. "Fortunately, those are the remains of the Throskaur raiders. The dead of Argyllan and Meridia are buried to the south of the city."

"Buried?" said the young man, his voice hoarse. He looked to be on the verge of bolting, like a shy colt who had been spooked by the Thunder Rider's hooves.

"Throskaur…" he said, his stance tensing. "Are there any still alive?"

Songaa shook his head and felt a strange sorrow. "No, I believe Captain Lucetta and her company made sure all were found…and killed." Much as Songaa felt a burning anger toward the pirates, he could not smile upon a path that showed no mercy.

Yet I put them down, one by one.

He clenched his jaw.

Is it kill or be killed?

Songaa felt an overwhelming anguish that the realm south of the Sacred Mount had descended into chaotic war and worse still was that the Tarakans were now a part of this turmoil. He felt Lunyai take his hand and turned to her.

All-Mother, thank You and Your children for bringing Lunyai back to me.

The four of them followed Camran and the girl into Argyllan.

"And she is Camran's family?" he asked, pointing ahead.

"Emiren. She is my…friend," replied Lunyai, turning her head away as she said this.

Songaa wondered at the hesitation. His daughter was friends *now* with the man who greeted Lord Rencarro and seemed unsure about her friendship with the redhead. He felt there was much to tell but reminded himself of something Chenoa, his wife, used to say.

"Do not blow away answers with your tornado of questions, especially with Lunyai. Our daughter will tell you everything if you are patient."

Songaa saw the wisdom in Chenoa's words, but he felt anxious that events in the realm would rob them all of the time to wait for answers.

And perhaps we should not wait to say the things that matter…

CHAPTER 3

RENCARRO

21st Day of Maia, Two Days After Gimmweg Was Attacked

The once lord of Meridia sat in the simple lodgings he had occupied since arriving in Argyllan what seemed a life-time ago. Arriving in Argyllan with Meridian soldiers, under the pretext that he was protecting the south in a time of unrest. Since he had been here, he had received news his eldest son was dead and his city had fallen to the Helligan nation. The rumour his Velox Riders had spun had become a cruel reality: the Throskaur had sailed into Argyllan harbour. Rencarro had lost many good men fighting the raiders, including his loyal captain, Julius. He swirled the amber rum in its glass and felt empty, as if the Void itself had been born again within him.

Keeper, are You there?

There was no answer. Rencarro knew there wouldn't be. He took a healthy gulp of the rum and turned his thoughts to the newcomers who had arrived that morning. He tried to decide what was the best way to handle the situation with Camran's niece and the Tarakan girl, who just happened to be the daughter of the leader of the Tarakans who had come to their aid in the battle.

The Widow's web is heavily laden with raindrops of the darkest humour.

He had almost killed Camran's niece and the Tarakan had almost killed him. All three were still alive so objectively it was a case of all being well that ends well, but he sensed the two young ladies would not be so practical in their outlook. Rencarro had seen Emiren staring at him as he stood at the wall hailing Tacet. He wasn't sure but it had seemed she'd been petrified. And he wouldn't blame her if that had been the case.

With that in mind, a direct approach and a shake of hands was unlikely to bear fruit. The Meridian lord decided he would relay some words through Camran. The quartermaster trusted him, knew what he had done for Argyllan, and knew why he had almost run her through with a spear. He would probably be explaining all this to her already.

It had been a great relief to see Tacet again, a man he thought may have been killed in whatever unrest had taken the north. The Velox rider had given his report as soon as they were alone, and Rencarro had been taken aback, to put it mildly. The young Meridian was now refreshing himself at the bathhouse and Rencarro had had time to reflect on all he had been told. His Velox rider's journey had been a strange and dangerous one, and he had been witness to various matters that were now shaping the future of Ragnekai. The realm was indeed in peril, that much was clear. And Sylvanus' treachery was possibly connected to the trouble in the north.

The Void take him and his ambitions, whatever they may be...

Rencarro said a silent prayer to the Keeper. He began by asking for strength, but he found himself wondering yet again why he was bothering to seek divine help. He had given everything in the battle, everything except his life. And so many Meridians had died. He took a sip of rum and tried to keep images of the Widow from his mind, and the screech of her laugh from his ears. His own ambition was responsible for their deaths, and his inability to see treachery before his very eyes had cost him his son.

Sylvanus...

The name had become something of a curse in his mind, a word that signified deceit and treachery. And failure. Where was his former Second now? Was he in Gamle Hovestad with the Helligan lord, Orben, being congratulated for his cunning? Rencarro tried to find a motive behind it all, other than the rule of Meridia. If that had been his goal, why had he not simply killed Rencarro himself? The Meridian lord had written a will stating that Sylvanus would govern Meridia for a period of ten years after his death, and had confided his intentions to his Second. Sylvanus could have killed Rencarro, made it look like an accident, then consolidated his power over the next decade. Did High King Sedmund's death spark a new design?

No, he has been in league with Orben for a long time.

Orben had radically changed Sylvanus somehow, promised him more than just Meridia maybe. The entire south-west? Maybe murdering Marcus was more an act of hate. The two had never been on particularly friendly terms.

I lost my city and you took my son from me, Widow's spawn!

Rencarro knocked back the rest of the rum and reached for the bottle. Hurried footsteps and a violent banging on the door stayed that hand and had his other whipping out a dagger as he leapt to his feet.

"Lord Rencarro, are you within?"

Tacet.

He re-sheathed the blade and called out, "Come in."

Tacet entered, looking refreshed, with excitement written all over his face. "We have a guest, my lord!" he blurted, and moved aside to allow a man dressed as a minstrel to enter.

"Salterio! By the Keeper!" exclaimed Rencarro. He moved forward and grabbed Tacet's fellow Velox Rider, embracing him and feeling for a moment that the Keeper had not abandoned him entirely. "It is good to see you," he said, pulling back but still gripping the man's shoulders.

"The Keeper has answered at least one prayer this day," Salterio replied, grinning widely.

He was handsome in a boyish fashion, soft features under bronze curls and deep brown, doe eyes. Like Tacet, he had been a minstrel to the people of Meridia but an agent of Rencarro, gathering information from all over the south of Ragnekai, and his looks had allowed him to loosen many lips.

Tacet clapped his comrade on the back and shook his head. "So many days of late, I thought I'd never see you, Umbran, or Mercutio ever again." He turned to Rencarro. "My lord, Salterio has ridden hard from Meridia, and I believe he has news for us."

Rencarro nodded and ushered the weary rider to a chair. "Sit down and rest, man. You look exhausted. Tacet, there is wine and food over there. I have not eaten my lunch yet. Bring it over and we can talk."

Tacet quickly brought a bottle of wine over with three glasses and poured. It was a white wine. Normally Rencarro would drink red but Camran had been introducing him to some of the local produce.

As the three of them raised their glasses, the reality of recent times hit Rencarro. He took a deep breath and nodded. "To absent friends."

"To absent friends," the Velox riders said as one.

They clinked glasses and knocked back a mouthful. It was a good wine, one that Rencarro had shared with the Argyllan quartermaster the day before, but in this moment now, it tasted bitter.

Tacet turned back to gather the bread, cheese, sausage and grapes that had been brought to Rencarro for his lunch. Salterio refilled his lord's glass, then Tacet's, and then his own. He hung his head and rubbed his eyes. A thought struck Rencarro like a cold slap from the Widow.

"Eligius! Does he live?" he demanded urgently.

Salterio looked up and smiled.

"Yes, my lord. Your son lives and is unharmed."

Rencarro slumped back in his seat, relief flooding through his body. At least the Widow had not taken everything from him. He gestured for Salterio to eat some of the food Tacet had delivered. The Velox rider dove in hungrily.

"You must have indeed ridden hard, old friend," commented Tacet. "Your horse was lathered!"

Salterio nodded, his mouth full of sausage. He chewed and swallowed. "When Meridia settled, an opportunity to leave the city arose." He looked at Rencarro. "Was surprised when a Tarakan offered to look after my horse. We'd heard rumours of the battle here, but it has been difficult to know what is true and what is not."

Rencarro noted the emphasis at the end there. He suspected he would learn much from Salterio. The man was clearly tired and famished though.

"Tacet, perhaps you can tell your story to Salterio, give him a chance to eat. Then I will relate my part in this nightmare, and then we will listen to what you have to say," he said, pointing at the Velox rider, now on his second sausage and third glass of wine.

Rencarro sat back and listened to Tacet's tale for the second time. It took a while for the Velox Rider to relate all that had happened to Rowan the Rhymer and all that he had heard on his journey north. Rencarro tried to imagine the realm from far above, noting what had occurred in each region.

So much and within such a short span of time.

Salterio nearly choked on his wine when Tacet told him of the wonders and horrors within the Sacred Mount. Despite having heard it all that very morning, it still boggled Rencarro's own mind.

I would look upon those sights before I die.

Tacet finished his tale and there was silence. Salterio blew out a breath and shook his head in disbelief.

"By the Widow, we are in a deep pit full of shit!"

Rencarro nodded grimly. "Duthka allied with Unvasik, men becoming beasts, and the north in chaos it seems. We are in strange times indeed."

He then proceeded to give Salterio his account of Sylvanus' treachery and the Throskaur attack on Argyllan. They raised a glass to Julius and the one hundred and twenty-seven Meridian soldiers who had perished. And Rencarro bade them say a prayer for Loranna and the citizens of Argyllan who had been cut down.

"Thank the Keeper for the Tarakans," commented Salterio.

Rencarro raised his eyes to the ceiling. "Whilst I still pray to the Keeper and curse the Widow, my faith in a higher power has been more than shaken by recent events," he said, pushing his glass toward Tacet, who obligingly refilled it.

Tacet agreed. "I believe the Keeper is out there somewhere but I'm not sure His eyes are upon us all the time."

Rencarro gestured to the newly arrived Velox rider. "Well, Salterio, now it is time for you to tell your tale. I sense that you carry little in the way of good tidings."

The Velox rider pursed his lips, then spoke. "I have nothing that will give us hope, I'm afraid, my lord. Mercutio is still in Meridia. I told him to stay there and wait for my return. I have heard nothing from Umbran…" He let it hang.

Rencarro had sent Umbran after Sylvanus. The fact his Velox Rider had not returned could mean only one thing. He gave Salterio a small nod. Salterio shared a look with Tacet, then moved on to news of the city.

"Meridia is under Helligan rule and the people have accepted their new masters. After the taking of the city, which was mercifully brief due to the rapid capture of your son, the—"

"How was he captured so quickly?" demanded Rencarro. "Was he not taken to the keep?"

Salterio nodded vigorously. "He was, my lord, but a company of Helligans scaled the south wall, infiltrated the city, and captured Lord Eligius while the main Helligan force was assaulting the eastern wall. They knew he would be there."

Rencarro slammed his fist on the table, startling both Tacet and Salterio.

"Sylvanus," he muttered. "He gave them all they needed and took everything from me."

"It did mean the battle was over relatively quickly though, my lord. Lord Eligius ordered the Meridian city guard to lay down their arms and surrendered the city," offered Salterio.

Rencarro sighed and motioned for him to carry on.

"So," continued Salterio, "the city is now under Helligan rule but not much has changed for the common folk. I have been playing every night at The Golden Lyre and custom has returned after the uncertainty that immediately followed the battle. There has been discontent and obviously anger from those who lost loved ones in the fighting, but the Helligan occupying force has dealt with all this very deftly, if you'll forgive my saying so, my lord. They are camped outside the city walls but are present in the city patrolling and spending their coin."

Rencarro knew he should be happy to hear there had been a fairly peaceful transition of rule, but it ate away inside him. He had lost his city and also it seemed, the loyalty of his people.

"Lord Eligius has been instrumental in keeping everything running smoothly," Salterio added.

"I suppose I should be proud," said Rencarro bitterly. "And grateful in a perverse sense that it was not Marcus who had been left in charge of the city. He would have fought on and the blood-shed would have been far greater."

"The cavalry charge, my lord..."

Rencarro sat up straight. "Yes?"

"A few of our cavalry survived the battle, although were injured. They were treated by our physicians and have been treated very well by the Helligans. I managed to speak to them, in the guise of Lucian of the Lute, and it is clear Sylvanus deceived them in a hideous fashion."

Rencarro clenched his fist.

"He led them to Meridia, saying the city was in danger and only they could save it. One rider told me Sylvanus painted a heroic image of a brave charge that would smash the enemy lines and turn the tide of the battle. A valiant effort of which songs would be sung. It was only after the battle that the survivors realised Sylvanus had slowed his mount, hung back, then must have turned and ridden away. He led them to their deaths and deserted them, Widow take his soul!"

Rencarro hurled his glass into the corner of the room, where it shattered into tiny shards, threw his head back, and let out a roar of rage. The blood of so many Meridians was on the hands of Sylvanus.

"I will kill him!" he shouted.

Rencarro slammed the table with both fists, the other two glasses toppling and sending the wine spilling everywhere. He felt a strong grip on his left arm. He stared at the hand, then at Tacet. His body tensed and for an instant he was ready to strike the Velox rider. The grip squeezed once, then began to release.

"Breathe, my lord, breathe."

Rencarro closed his eyes and took a deep breath. Then another.

He opened his eyes again and looked at the two men sadly.

"What do I have left? My son is dead, my younger son is perhaps better off now. I have lost my city and its people." He paused. "And Shansu is gone."

Both Velox riders hung their heads and were silent. He didn't blame their lack of response. What could they say?

"All I have left is my vengeance."

Tacet and Salterio looked up, the former shaking his head.

"My lord, you cannot be thinking to bring Sylvanus to justice now. He must be in Gamle Hovestad. We have no army capable of marching even on Meridia."

Rencarro held up a hand to halt further protests. "I do not seek to bring him back. I desire to kill him. And I do not plan on inflicting any more bloodshed upon the Meridian soldiers here. They should stay in Argyllan and make a new life for themselves."

Salterio frowned. "You plan to hunt him alone, my lord?"

Tacet coughed somewhat dramatically. "Alone? Quite risky. One or two allies might be of use…" he said, with a hint of a smile.

Rencarro leaned forward, shook his head and held up a hand.

"I hear the Helligan ladies are fond of the lute," commented Salterio with a grin, ignoring his lord's gesture.

"They prefer the fiddle, I think you'll find," retorted Tacet.

The once Lord of Meridia couldn't help but laugh. "Ha! So, you two fools will follow the biggest fool?"

The two Velox riders extended their hands. Rencarro gripped each in turn.

"Let us spit in the Widow's face!"

Rencarro had decided to leave as soon as possible and without any announcement. When he came back, he would make amends with Magnus or whoever took command of the troops, but the last thing he wanted was for Meridian soldiers to pledge themselves to what was a foolhardy quest for revenge.

But there was one person he had to share a last word with.

The two of them sat in the quartermaster's office, a bottle of rum on the table as always, and the skilfully wrought square glasses of his brother, Emiren's father.

Strange times we live in.

"Camran, you have become a good friend in a short time and have fought with me. I hear your words, but I cannot heed them. Sylvanus must pay for the death of my son and the betrayal of Meridia." Rencarro sighed. "And I believe your niece would like the boy's killer brought to justice, yes?"

Camran nodded, rubbing his left thumb. "Anton…" he whispered. Then the quartermaster looked up. "Do you seek justice though? Or vengeance?"

Rencarro smiled sadly. "Vengeance, my friend. Most definitely vengeance."

"A man who seeks vengeance…finds only torment," he said, one finger raised.

Rencarro raised his eyebrows. "Something your mother told you?"

"No," he replied with a crooked smile, "just made it up." He closed his eyes for a moment. "I just fear you will succumb to rage if you find him and he will get the better of you. He has no anger. He will be cold and calm."

Rencarro was impressed with Camran's perceptiveness. He shrugged all the same.

"Tacet and Salterio will be with me. I will not face him alone. And he will die. Not me."

Camran poured out more rum, the measures noticeably larger since the battle. Rencarro took his glass and sipped again.

"Fine rum."

"It is," Camran said softly.

The room fell silent.

Rencarro took another sip, studying his friend, whose head was hung.

"By the Keeper, Camran, don't be so morbid! I will return and then I propose you and I get in a boat and take a trip to the Radiant Isles!" he said, slapping the table.

Rencarro was pleased to see Camran's face brighten.

"Well…" he began, "I will need more rum soon."

"Ha! And I hear the ladies of the Isles are more beautiful than you can imagine! We can find you a woman, Camran. Bring her back here and make an honest man out of you!"

Camran laughed. "Alright, alright, just so long as we leave those two handsome friends of yours here. I'd never get so much as a smile directed my way if they were flashing their charm this way and that!"

Rencarro joined him in mirth, pleased to see the cloud lifting from his friend's spirit. "I'll order them to cover your duties in Argyllan while we sip rum and you taste sweet fruits!"

Camran choked on a mouthful of rum, erupting in a coughing fit. Rencarro slapped him on the back a few times.

"Will you not taste the sweetness too?" he asked, eyes wide and grinning.

Rencarro tapped his fingers on the table and looked up. "No," he whispered. Then more loudly. "Shansu has my heart and always will. When I stand before the Keeper, I will see Shansu and Marcus just beyond Him. If the Keeper lets me pass, I will rekindle the love we shared."

His jaw clenched.

"While Sylvanus suffers eternal torment at the hands of the Widow."

CHAPTER 4

KAILEN

21st Day of Maia, Two Days After Gimmweg Was Attacked

"Where are Brax and Rorthal?"

"Milady?" stammered the junior officer.

"The Helligan First Sentinel? The Helligan Battle-Sergeant? Your superior officers? Raven's wings, just tell me where they are!" cried Kailen, her patience at an end after a hard ride from Gamle Hovestad to Meridia.

"Lord Brax? But—"

Kailen let out a curse and pushed past him. She had no time for younger soldiers wondering whether or not to bother their commanders.

"Milady!" the officer called after her. She ignored him and stormed through the Helligan camp, leaving her escort of ten riders behind. They were also tired no doubt, so she left them to water the horses and quench their own thirsts. Kailen was amongst Helligan soldiers now, which meant her personal safety was not an issue. Many knew her by sight, and she carried Ulla's seal if she was challenged.

Not Orben's seal.

Her lord was dead, killed by her own hand. She shook her head to clear the guilt-ridden thoughts that had plagued her since. Ulla had been witness to her brother's death and did not blame Kailen, but it didn't change the fact she had ended his life.

"Kailen!" came a hearty roar from her left. She whirled to see Rorthal, the burly battle-sergeant striding toward her with a huge grin on his face. His head was freshly shaved judging by the way it caught the sun and he had tied his forked beard into two tight braids. He appeared to be in good health. Kailen wished she had better news.

"Have you come to check up on us?"

She gripped his beefy forearm in greeting. "No. I need to talk."

"Command tent is ahead. Let's go have a beer!"

The two of them walked through what was a remarkably orderly camp. It was practically a village to Kailen's eyes, a settlement bathed in the red and white colours of the Helligan nation. A hiss sounded and she turned her head to see a smithy plunging a blade into a barrel of water.

"Kjeld, make sure it's as sharp as Kailen's wit!" shouted Rorthal to the man.

The smith looked up, saw Rorthal and then Kailen. The eruption of a huge smile on his face would have cheered the lady another day.

"You ask the impossible, sir!" he called back, grinning at Kailen.

They waved and carried on. A unit of soldiers marched their way, spears resting upon their shoulders, the rim of the shields on their backs visible.

"Keep it tight, lads! Kailen has come to whip some of your sorry arses!"

Kailen couldn't help but snort laughter this time as the soldiers jerked almost as one, and marched past them so stiffly they could have been stone golems.

They were soon at the command tent and Rorthal held open the flap to let Kailen in. Upon entering the tent, he moved to pour some ale for Kailen from a waiting keg. He passed the mug over and she took it gratefully. Her throat parched, the beer was gone in moments. Kailen held out the mug.

"Another please!"

"I don't think so, Kailen," replied Rorthal, all humour gone from his face.

"What?"

Kailen sensed movement behind her and whirled round. Two soldiers had entered the tent and their expressions were bleak as winter in Bresden Forest.

"What is this, Rorthal?" demanded Kailen, a sinking feeling dragging down in her stomach.

"I think you know," he said, his tone grim. "Lads."

Kailen felt a firm hand on her right shoulder. Instinct took over and she dipped her left shoulder to avoid the other soldier, then grabbed the first hand and twisted it. The soldier let out a yelp, then a grunt as Kailen jabbed him under the arm. Using his prone bulk, she grabbed his tunic and swung herself around him, landing a kick in the second soldier's back. He sprawled forward as Kailen landed on two feet.

Where she found her nose mere inches from the spike on the top of Rorthal's mace.

"Raven's arse, you two! Can't you even arrest someone a head shorter than the both of you?"

Kailen's heart raced. Despite her guilt being all too real, she couldn't believe what was happening.

"Now don't so much as twitch, Kailen."

Rorthal's voice was hard and Kailen didn't want to test if he felt any conflict about arresting her.

"Jens, bind her hands quickly, for the love of the First Warrior. Stam, pick up your spear and rest the point against her back."

Kailen wanted to scream. This was Rorthal, someone she thought she could trust, Svard's friend of many years, someone she had met with once a week as Orben gave out his commands. She struggled to gain a foothold on the situation.

"Rorthal, what is going on? Damn it, if this is some kind of jape, I'll pay you back ten-fold!" she snarled.

Rorthal looked at her and Kailen saw a sadness in his eyes. This was no jape and Kailen knew what was coming.

"Kailen Jacobson, you are under arrest for the murder of Lord Orben."

First Warrior, no...

"By order of the Lady Hulda, *widow* of Lord Orben."

Kailen stared at the Helligan battle-sergeant as Jens bound her wrists behind her back with rope. She felt Stam's spear point in her back, but the man wasn't pushing it in. Kailen hoped these two were unsure of what was unfolding here.

"Rorthal, please listen to me. I didn't do it! By the First Warrior, you know me. Am I a killer?"

Her words conflicted with the truth she and Ulla knew. Kailen continued, desperate to claw back some control.

"Sylvanus murdered Orben!" she cried.

"Who?"

"Sylvanus, the Meridian traitor!"

Rorthal frowned. "What are you talking about?" he growled, his eyes alight with suspicion.

Kailen then saw it, how perfectly Sylvanus had played them. Orben had met the Meridian in secret. Svard, Brax, and Rorthal had all left before even Ulla had met him. Nobody knew who he was and the only man who could have laid bare the treachery was dead, killed by her own hand.

First Warrior, help me, I beg you!

"Rorthal, Ulla knows it wasn't me. She was there when..."

She realised what she was saying too late. She was spouting lies on top of a truth and that truth was wheedling its way to the light.

"Ulla was there too? She watched you kill her brother?" Rorthal's voice was a storm of anger crashing through sorrow.

"This is madness, Rorthal. Listen to what you are saying! Why would I murder my own lord?"

Rorthal grabbed her tunic with one ham-sized fist and hauled her up to his face. She was on tiptoes and knew the battle-sergeant had the strength to physically lift her clear off the ground, and then throw her body through the air if he so desired.

"You did it because Ulla ordered you to do it. Ulla did it because she was in bed with Torbal. They planned to usurp the rule of the realm. Don't you think it strange that Ulla fled Bregustol so soon after Sedmund died?"

He let go and she stumbled back, Jens and Stam grabbing her before she fell over completely.

"Ulla poisoned Sedmund, Kailen. She and Torbal were riding upon the Raven's wings," he muttered with disgust.

Kailen's mind reeled. Ulla and Torbal were in a relationship? Ulla murdered the High King? It couldn't be true. This had to be more manipulation by Sylvanus.

Kailen sunk to her knees, the weight of everything bearing down upon her, the Raven's claws on her shoulders.

Ulla!

"Wait, Ulla has been arrested too?"

Rorthal shrugged. "I imagine so. Orders were sent out, signed by Hulda herself. I received the message last night."

"Rorthal, open your eyes! This is all part of some grand scheme. Don't you see? Svard was sent to the capital to assassinate Eswic, you and Brax came west…"

Something occurred to her.

"Rorthal, where is Brax?"

The battle-sergeant looked at her with a stony face and said nothing. Kailen wanted to scream in fury and cry with helplessness. Sylvanus had created a devious path for them all to walk down and they had all done so, never once realising something was off, that something was not quite right, and they were marching to the tune of someone else's flute. She tried to think of something she could say to convince Rorthal, but she knew it was useless. He had orders from Hulda and had no reason to question them.

"Damn you, Rorthal!" she seethed. "Sylvanus poisoned Orben with something, turned him into a wild animal. He attacked Ulla."

Rorthal raised an eyebrow and Kailen saw the utter futility of this, how crazy she sounded.

"Raven's beak, Kailen, enough! I'll have you gagged as well if you don't shut up with your ravings." Kailen saw the hulking battle-sergeant battling with emotion.

"Damn you..." he whispered, then turned his back on her. "Take her to my tent and secure her to something that doesn't move," he said, issuing the order over his shoulder. "Be quiet about it."

Jens and Stam acknowledged the command and dragged Kailen to her feet. She felt a glimmer of hope. Out of Rorthal's sight, and hopefully away from other prying eyes, she could cut the ropes with a tiny blade she carried in her boot. She was quite the contortionist so escape should be possible. She put her head down and let the two soldiers take her. As they exited the tent, Rorthal gave one more order.

"And be sure to secure her with iron shackles, not rope!"

Shit...

Kailen was soon sitting on her arse in Rorthal's sleeping quarters, a canvas tent not much bigger than the standard one used by soldiers. She was chained to the central pole that held the structure upright. The pole was wood but driven deep into the earth, and the chains were iron as per Rorthal's command. She was well and truly stuck. At least her hands were in front of her now, manacled but resting comfortably in her lap.

What in the Raven's stinking shit has happened to me? To us all!

Kailen tried to calm herself, using the breathing techniques her sister swore by. She inhaled long through her nose, let the air go deep down into her body, then slowly let it out through pursed lips. She repeated this several times and found herself focusing. She tried to imagine the scene in Gamle Hovestad.

She had left the city on the nineteenth day of this month, the ringing bells a horrible clanging noise as her company of riders headed out. Ulla had told her to make haste to Meridia and deliver orders to Rorthal and Brax that they were to return to Gamle Hovestad, as the lady suspected a Xerinthian invasion was imminent. It had been chaotic and rushed but both Ulla and Kailen had agreed the priority was to fortify the city with the Helligan army.

But Sylvanus had pre-empted so much. He had sent Ulla and Kailen to Orben's solar, knowing the changed Orben would attack. Possibly he thought Orben would kill them both, but the manipulation of Hulda to issue an order to capture Kailen was a back-up plan if that failed. Why did Orben's widow no longer believe Ulla's account of events? Was Sylvanus still in the city and spreading rumours? There was too much unknown. All that was true in this moment was that Kailen had accidentally killed Orben and now she was under arrest for the crime.

Her thoughts turned to Svard and she wondered if he was faring any better than her. She prayed he hadn't been caught for the murder of Eswic, if the First Ranger had indeed assassinated the holy leader. At least he had his Rangers with him. Kailen was totally alone here in this tent. She took in her surroundings, searching for something that would give her even the faintest hope of escape. There was nothing. Rorthal was a simple man, judging by the contents of his tent. She closed her eyes.

First Warrior, give me a sign. Show me something. The Helligan nation will fall if the lies of Sylvanus are allowed to stand.

She opened her eyes again and unfortunately did not see some young soldier whom she had bedded in the past, ready to set her free in the name of love. Her sister enjoyed stories like that but Kailen had always been more realistic in her expectations.

Damn, damn, damn…

Kailen woke with a start. She was stiff from having nodded off secured to a pole with her hands shackled. She rolled her neck and flexed her muscles as much as the restraints would allow. It was night but flaming torches outside the tent illuminated some of the interior, shadows dancing back and forth around her.

She gasped.

Dark Raven!

One shadow was moving of its own accord. It rose from where it had been sitting and approached the Helligan lady. Kailen stiffened. Was this a final ploy by Sylvanus and she had been followed by an as-sassin, the killer waiting for an opportunity? This certainly was such a chance, with her being tied up and unable to defend herself. She slowly strained against her bonds, but they were iron, unbreakable by all save the First Warrior Himself.

The shadow stopped and seemed to be studying her. Kailen heard steady breathing so knew at least this shadow was human and not a servant of the Helligan deity of death. It stepped forward and a man's face came into view in the soft glow coming from outside. Young, no soldier by the looks of it, and definitely no friend judging by the lack of smile or grin that Kailen would have expected upon the face of a rescuer. Her body tensed to the point of breaking.

Is this some coward who thinks he can use my body?

Kailen would bite chunks out of him with her teeth, she would be sure her knee connected firmly with his stones, and she would fight him with every last ounce of life she had. Her jaw clenched, waiting for him to say something that would give away his intentions.

"Kailen Jacobson?"

Hearing her full name spoken was not what she expected. She frowned but made no attempt to confirm or deny her identity. Who was this man?

He stepped closer to her and lowered himself to a crouch, bringing his face to the same level as hers. He was younger than Svard, looked in need of more meat at dinner, and his hair was a dark mess of unkempt straggles.

"You are Kailen Jacobson, Lord Orben's messenger, are you not?"

The voice lacked warmth, but neither was it cold nor calculating. The man sounded like a clerk at a guild, going through the daily motions that were his job. Kailen decided to venture forth and see where this encounter led.

"Yes, I am Kailen Jacobson. May I enquire as to your name?" She fixed him with a glare. "And your intentions."

He didn't seem to notice the tone of her voice or her hard stare.

"I thought so. Interesting," he said, but the way he uttered the word made it sound like he was anything but intrigued by who sat before him.

"Your name?" Kailen pressed.

He cocked his head, as if her question was foolish and the answer obvious.

"I am Eligius, son of Lord Rencarro."

What?! What's he doing here?

"And administrator of Meridia, it would seem. Funny, really," he finished, but again the tone of voice seemed at odds with the words chosen.

Kailen let herself relax. Eligius was not here to assault her or kill her, of that much she was certain. He knew who she was so he must have heard of her arrest from a source, possibly a Meridian network of informants. He had come here because he wanted something.

"I regret I can't greet you properly with a bow or a curtsey. I find myself in less than glamourous accommodation."

She looked up to see his reaction to her sarcasm.

Not so much as a damn smile. Orben was right about this one.

Eligius clucked his tongue as if considering something. "Lord Orben is dead, is that correct?"

Kailen did not feel like she was being interrogated by a frightening enemy officer, more like she was engaging in conversation with someone whose mind was elsewhere and was barely paying any attention.

First Warrior, you test me in strange ways…

"That is correct."

He nodded. "And you did not kill him. Correct?"

"In a manner of speaking," she replied.

He frowned. Then shrugged. "Do you know if my father lives?"

"I have heard nothing to say he is dead."

One eyebrow was raised.

Damn it, this one is strange!

"And do you know where Sylvanus is?"

Kailen froze. What did that imply? Was Eligius in league with Sylvanus? Was he part of a sinister design that would give him rule of Meridia under Helligan law? She breathed slowly, feeling she was treading carefully on thin ice.

"I believe he is no longer in Gamle Hovestad," she told him, her eyes probing his face for any reaction.

Sorrow.

Kailen saw sorrow in the dim light. Eligius' shoulders had sagged, his eyes had closed, and his head dipped.

"So, it is true," he whispered.

Kailen felt sympathy for the lad. She had just confirmed his suspicion that Sylvanus had betrayed Meridia to the Helligan nation. Defeat in battle was something the Helligans accepted without regret, as it meant they had faced a mightier opponent. But betrayal was a bitter drink to swallow.

"He is responsible for Orben's death. He betrayed your city, and now he has betrayed my people too."

Eligius looked at her and Kailen could almost hear his mind working. His frown became intense and his eyes began to roam this way and that, finally coming back to her with a small nod.

"So, Sylvanus has another master. Who, I wonder?"

Kailen felt that whilst they weren't exactly allies in this moment, they were not enemies. She decided to push for some knowledge from the Meridian.

"Is it possible he is a Xerinthian agent? Meridia has lost many of its fighting men, the Helligan leadership is dead or absent, and its forces spread. If there is to be another invasion, it would seem the groundwork has been well laid."

Kailen was surprised when Eligius went from his crouch to sitting down on the earth, his legs crossing and his elbows resting on his knees, while his chin found a place in his palms. She wondered if he was even aware that she was shackled, as the lad seemed to be settling in for a chat with a friend.

Curious man...

"I have reason to believe that this is not the prelude to a second Xerinthian incursion to our lands." He turned his face to her. "But I cannot give you more detail than that."

Great...

"I would say that Sylvanus is in league with another power that is already here within the realm of Ragnekai. I have a few suspicions but would need to study certain areas of history before I made even an educated guess."

Kailen felt a wave of relief. Why she trusted this man's judgment so much she had no idea. There was something about him though.

Orben had said he was extremely intelligent and knowledgeable, so it was reasonable to take his assumptions as more than just guesswork.

What followed was a strange experience for Kailen. Eligius asked her all manner of questions, some relating to the Helligan annexation, some concerning her conversations with Sylvanus, and some that seemed to have no bearing on anything that was happening now in Ragnekai. Her patience began to wear thin. She was about to ask some questions of her own when he abruptly got to his feet.

"Well, I must get back to my duties now," he said and began walking away.

Kailen felt a wave of despair as he stepped out of the tent. She had hoped he would feel gratitude for relating to him all she knew, and also pity at her plight, and help her in some way.

Raven's arse...

Then Kailen's ears pricked up. Somebody was shouting, not so far away.

"Fire! Awake! Fire!"

First Warrior, please no!

Kailen suddenly lost her faith in Eligius' belief that the Xerinthian Empire was not involved.

They're here...

CHAPTER 5

EMIREN

22nd Day of Maia, Three Days After Gimmweg Was Attacked

The Forest Road was like a kind, old uncle carrying Emiren's small company toward Fallowden. She could imagine one hand holding her up, the other gesturing to Argol, a gentle voice commenting on how the forest was beautiful as ever.

Argol hasn't changed, thought Emiren. But the realm had. Or was it just coming to a point in the circle it had passed through many years ago, a journey that went around and round with no end, history caught in an eternal loop? She wondered how many other young women and men had been caught up in such a nightmare as she had been, forced to flee and witness terrible violence.

Did they all come home?

Fallowden wasn't far now and Emiren's stomach tightened. She had the surely misplaced feeling that her parents would be angry with her. It was the child in her, throwing up memories of running wild in Argol and paying no heed to time, coming home and being scolded by them. It wasn't her fault she had run to Argyllan this time, but she had caused her parents untold worry, and for that she felt remorse. But she also felt less anxious with each yard their horses put behind them upon the road, nearing a place of safety, soon to be with her parents again. She squeezed Lunyai's waist and whispered into her ear.

"Thank you for bringing me home. And thank Neii'Ne too."

Lunyai stroked the horse's mane. "It was kind of Choondei to trust me with her."

For all the horror she had seen, Emiren felt truly grateful she had met the Tarakan people. And she felt blessed to be with Lunyai now.

Spirits, let there be a future for us all.

"There are people ahead," observed Songaa.

Emiren looked over Lunyai's shoulder and saw a caravan of folk approaching.

"Are we in danger?" asked Moryn, a hint of fear lacing his voice.

Emiren squinted, then smiled. "Most definitely not, Moryn."

Lunyai checked her horse as Emiren slid off behind her. The young lady from Fallowden raised a hand and waved. She could see them clearly now.

"Are we going the right way for Fallowden?" she called out.

One of the group let out a yelp and hurried forward, her bustling manner and swaying motion pulling forth a laugh from Emiren's lips. It was good to see Sister Jessa again.

"Spirits, Emiren! Where have you been?"

The two embraced, Jessa squeezing Emiren so hard she gasped. Jessa released her and patted her down as if she were checking for injuries.

"Sorry, sorry, but…oh child, thank the Spirits you have returned!" she said, her voice almost a blabber, then hugged her tightly again. The caravan had caught up now and Emiren's company of Songaa, Lunyai, and Moryn was at her back. The Fallowden villagers looked upon the travellers with wide eyes and almost comically confused faces.

Emiren moved past Jessa and greeted the other villagers from Fallowden, hugging some, grasping hands with others. Anketil, a smith, was there, as was Hame, a wheat farmer. Also with the caravan were Maevy and Rivanon, two sisters who baked the most delicious bread.

"You are going to Argyllan?" asked Emiren.

Jessa nodded.

"We have supplies and will give what help we can. They lost many good folk to those…" Jessa tensed. "Emiren, you were there, in the battle?!"

Emiren shook her head. "I was spared that horror, but Songaa here, he was there," she said, gesturing to the Tarakan on his majestic mount.

Jessa approached him, stroking the horse and jumping slightly when the horse snickered. Songaa patted Ahoni, calming the creature.

"Are you Tarakan?" Jessa asked Songaa, looking up.

"Yes, my daughter and I are from the Tarakan Plains," he replied, gesturing to Lunyai at his side.

Jessa reached up and grasped his hand. "By the Spirits, we thank you! Banseth told us you saved the city of Argyllan," she said, squeezing his hand and shaking her head. "Spirits know those brutes would have come here next."

Songaa smiled down at her sadly. "How is Banseth?"

Jessa shook her head, then turned to Emiren. "Spend time with him, Emiren. He is devastated." She choked back emotion. "As we all are. Loranna, Anton…Fallowden has lost two of its children. I never thought I'd live to see such evil times."

Emiren choked on a sob hearing Anton's name.

Songaa leaned down from his saddle and squeezed Jessa's shoulder. "Nobody does. All we can do is try to give a better tomorrow to our children." Songaa slid his hand away and took his daughter's.

Jessa nodded, her jaw set in a look of determination. Emiren marvelled at how the right words from a stranger could strengthen the resolve of a friend, and how people would help strangers, even at risk to themselves. It reminded her of what her uncle, Camran, had said to her before they left the port-city.

"I know you will never forget what Rencarro almost did, Emiren. But know that he led Argyllan in its defence. He was not a son of Argyllan, but without his courage and words, we would have surely fallen long before help arrived. He lost many of his men that day."

Emiren realised she faced the same difficulty Lunyai had encountered with Tacet. Was it possible to forgive? Some said that to forgive is to forget. She hoped this wasn't the case, as she would never be able to scrub from her mind the image of Rencarro above her, spear ready to plunge down into her chest.

The Fallowden girl worried about her uncle. He had seen more horror and death in half a day than she had seen since witnessing Anton's murder, despite her having roamed far and wide. Camran had seemed to be coping when they talked but Emiren had seen a slight shake to his hand when he picked up his glass of rum. If the glass hadn't been her father's work, she might not have noticed. But there had been a tremble and Emiren had sadly wondered how many of the empty bottles in his room had become so since the Throskaur attack and its after-math.

Spirits, give us the strength to get through the darkness that follows the bloodshed.

Emiren hugged Jessa farewell, promising her she would help in the hospice till her mentor returned. She remounted Lunyai's horse, Neii'Ne, and the two parties carried on their separate ways. She rested her head against her friend's back and tried to hold back her tears.

"We will soon be with your parents, Emiren. Just as Yaai and Tlenaii shine with the All-Mother's love, I know your heart will feel less heavy when you're with them." Lunyai reached out a hand to Songaa, riding beside them. "I know I feel safe now I am with my father."

He turned to them and smiled. "And I will feel safer when we are back with your mother! She would have scared those raiders off, so fierce she…"

Emiren saw the joke die on his lips. He had tried to make light of what he had been through, but it was too soon. Emiren wondered if another fifty years would still be too soon. Songaa sighed.

"Will you sing the Tarakalo with me, Lunyai?" His daughter nodded. "Emiren, Moryn, please listen, and make sure Lunyai teaches you the words when she has time. In both our languages!" He smiled broadly as he said this.

Emiren again put her head to Lunyai's warm back and listened to the father and his daughter sing their song. They sang it in the common tongue first, and Emiren remembered the night she had found Lunyai again. She'd thought her friend was dead, but Lunyai had actually been saved by the Duthka mariner, Moryn. Then they sang in their own language and Emiren began to feel drowsy. The gentle rhythm of the horses and the Tarakan tongue induced a feeling that she was a babe in her mother's arms.

Her thoughts turned to Wulfner, Tacet, and Corann, and she wondered where they were now. Why had Tacet left Argyllan without saying good-bye? Where did he go with the Meridian lord? She suspected her uncle had known more than he let on. And had Wulfner and Corann reached Westhealfe safely? Had they spoken to General Torbal, Lady Cyneburg, and Lord Kenric? Emiren hoped Wulfner had returned home after relating all his news. She smiled as she thought of her big friend back in Ceapung with his loyal hound, Trob, and Balther's hearty laughter.

Neii'Ne stopped.

"There is a man staring at us, Emiren," whispered Lunyai.

Emiren peered over the Tarakan's shoulder.

"Emiren, is that you?!" a voice called out.

Kall, a hunter from Fallowden, was standing on the road, bow in hand, eyes wide in disbelief. Emiren was about to dismount again but Kall held up his hand.

"I will run ahead and tell your parents. Do not stop!" And with that, he turned about and sprinted off along the dirt road faster than Emiren had ever seen him move.

Lunyai gripped Emiren's arm that encircled the Tarakan's waist. "Soon," she whispered.

And soon it was. Emiren felt it mere moments after Kall sped away, and then she heard voices and saw her village ahead. There was her mother, Megari, holding up her skirt and hurrying toward them. She slid off Neii'Ne and ran to meet her.

The instant she was in her mother's arms, the world seemed to fold inward and she was falling. But Megari held her, a mother's strength lifting her daughter. She was safe, yet she felt as if a whirlwind was howling around them. All that had happened came rushing back, like a shriek from a banshee of legend.

Dancing at the Bealtaine fire with Anton, seeing Sylvanus plunge the blade into her friend. Fleeing through Argol, death snatching at her heels. Hiding, sending Tarak away, reaching Argyllan. Leaping across rooftops in the moonlight, only to be seen by Rencarro. His spear, Lunyai's rescue. Wulfner's cart, Trob, Azal. Ceapung, Balther, Lunyai's song. Tacet's actions endangering them all. Being alone, believing Lunyai was dead and not knowing if Wulfner was alive or not. The Duthka village and Corann, reuniting with Lunyai, Wulfner, and Tacet. Lady Cyneburg and the horror that had befallen her soldiers in Morak. Westhealfe and meeting the King's Shield himself. The Sacred Mount, the glow-worms, Nerian's death and the realisation that this Seolta intended to turn the rest of Morak into beasts. Her legs buckled again, and she leaned into her mother. Megari held her up and squeezed tightly.

"Emiren, thank the Spirits!"

"Mum, I thought I'd never see you again," she croaked, tears spilling forth.

Megari pulled her even closer and Emiren felt her fears being quashed by a love that she had been away from for too long.

"Emi…" Her father's voice.

Emiren withdrew from her mother and fell into her father's arms. He stroked her hair as tears fell from his eyes.

"Spirits, it's good to have you back," he sobbed.

Megari joined the embrace and Emiren let their warmth seep into all parts of her being. The dark memories began to recede, and she let her mind wander through the years that had come before all this. She could even think of Anton without it being a sharp stab of agony. She could have stayed like that for a day and a night, but her father pulled back.

"Who are your friends, Emi?" he asked gently.

Emiren let her mother's arms slide off her shoulders and wiped her eyes. She turned to see her three companions dismounted, holding the reins and waiting patiently.

"Mum, Da, this is Lunyai and her father Songaa of the Tarakan people. And Moryn, a sailor who has braved the Western Sea many times. There is so much to tell but all I need say now is that I live because of Lunyai, Lunyai lives because of Moryn, and Argyllan still stands thanks to Songaa and his people."

There was a look of awe on her parents' faces. Then Emiren noticed maybe twenty or so other villagers had passed the gates and were watching this reunion with wide eyes and listening with eager ears. Master Lukas was there, as were Kall and two other hunters. Clara the tallow chandler, Ben a carpenter, even Old Beo had come to see. Then she saw Master Aine standing at a slight distance, his face a mask of worry.

Megari broke the silence that had fallen upon the little crowd.

"Come on, Emiren, let's get you home." Emiren's mother turned to everyone else. "Please let me feed my daughter and her friends. There will be time for talk later."

Quint chipped in, with a gentle smile. "Later? Maybe tomorrow." He then gestured to Songaa, Lunyai and Moryn. "Please come and share our food. I'll find some grain for the horses."

Kall raised a hand. "Leave that to me, Quint. I'll also bring a keg of my liquid grain, if you know what I mean." He grinned, and his hand made a drinking motion.

"Appreciate it, Kall." Quint put an arm around Emiren's shoulder. "Come on, you. Home!"

Emiren looked over her shoulder to see Megari taking Lunyai's hand and leading them into the village. She smiled, but this faded as they passed through the gates. Banseth was not there and Loranna would never again be there. And Anton would never race her to the gate again. She clenched her jaw and wondered if the grief would ever end.

Her faint hope was dashed as she surveyed the scene within Fallowden. The shattered thought then reformed into something harder. Not grief, but a cold despair.

Fallowden had changed. The Throskaur attack on Argyllan and the Helligan assault on Meridia were of course known here, and it looked like the villagers believed the trouble was not over and could reach them next. The wooden palisade had grown a couple of feet and Emiren saw work being carried out on walkways. She saw villagers she knew sharpening wooden stakes and fletching arrows. The young lady gasped as she spotted a rack of simple spears.

Spirits, will the killing come this far?

But of course, terrible violence had already come to the port of Argyllan. What was to stop it crawling and slithering farther inland, or even crashing in from the east?

Her father must have noticed her sudden tension, her head turning side to side as they moved through the village.

"We can't let others risk their lives defending us. We mustn't. Fallowden will try to help Argyllan rebuild, and we will be sure to secure our own home." Quint sighed. "We're not fighters, but we won't be cowards."

Emiren felt a cold fear rise within her as she remembered the Unvasik warrior in the Sacred Mount. Twenty of those giants would be enough to slaughter the entire village. She shuddered and Quint pulled her closer. She was glad her father didn't know the full terror of what was out there in the realm.

"Someone else has come to greet you!" blurted Quint suddenly.

Emiren gave a yelp of delight as Tarak bounded up. She crouched as the wolf leaped at her, and both tumbled to the ground, Emiren laughing as he tried to lick her face.

"Tarak, I've missed you so much."

She picked herself up and kissed his head, breathing in the scent of Argol Forest mixed with his wolfen fur.

"Tarak, say hello to my friends."

Songaa held out a hand and Tarak trotted over to sniff it. "Tarak? An interesting name for a *Tarakan* wolf." Songaa's voice carried a note of humour. Emiren laughed.

"I know. Not very imaginative. I was much younger when I named him. Seemed very sensible then. It told people his name and where he was from."

Songaa chuckled. "It is a good name." Lunyai's father studied the wolf with wide eyes. "By Yaai, he is quite a big one! Perhaps the water here is good?"

"The water is fresh, that's for sure. But I may have indulged Tarak over the years with some choice meat," commented Quint with a wry smile.

Tarak sat on his haunches and turned to Quint in a manner that was so close to human indignation that everyone laughed. Lunyai bent down to hug the wolf.

"You must be happy now Emiren is back, Tarak. Moryn, come and say hello," she said to the Duthka sailor.

"Erm, I will keep my distance. Sea sirens I can handle when I'm sailing, but I was uneasy even with the wolves we Duthka lived with," he explained, his hands up in an almost defensive gesture.

There was a sudden silence and Emiren realised a truth had just been revealed. Her parents were staring at Moryn.

"Duthka?" whispered Quint. "But I thought..."

Emiren put her hand on his arm. "There is much to tell. I have learnt so much these past few weeks, maybe as much as I would have had I actually attended classes with the masters," she joked, hoping to ease her father's worry and stop him thinking too much before he knew the entire tale.

Megari walked over to Moryn and took his arm. "Come, young sailor, you are welcome in our home. My husband likes to cook but I think it would be safer if I did today."

"Oi, oi!" Quint grinned, then turned to Lunyai's father, shaking his head in mock anger. "Do you see what I have to suffer here?!"

Emiren laughed and hugged her father. She was back, with new friends, and with her beloved family.

For now, the darkness had been chased away by the light of those around her.

"Thank you, Megari. That was delicious!" said Songaa, dipping his head. "I would like you to teach one of my tribe's cooks how you made that stew."

Lunyai cocked her head. "Kukala?" she enquired as her father pulled his hair free from a leather band and shook it loose.

Songaa nodded and they both laughed. Emiren felt a surge of joy to be with Lunyai, her father, and her own family, all squeezed around the table in her small home. She cast a glance at Moryn. He seemed distant. Emiren wondered if he felt far from his people, being in the south of Ragnekai.

Megari held up a hand and shook her head as she responded to Songaa's compliment. "It is a small thing compared to what you have all done for us. Much as I want to hear your stories, part of me says this is not the time. I would simply enjoy being with you all."

She gasped and raised a hand to her mouth. "Quint, we forgot to say any Words before eating."

Quint nodded earnestly. "We did forget. Emiren, your mother and I have been waiting to hear you speak the Words again..." He coughed on emotion.

Emiren reached out and took his hand, the familiar calluses, scars from the furnace where he blew glass into wondrous shapes, and hairy patches a warm comfort to a daughter who had missed her father so much. "I'm home now, Da." Quint wiped his eyes and took a deep breath.

Emiren began speaking the Words.

"Aowa mon aoket mon aowa. Kyakyalo te wasen."

Her parents dipped their heads and closed their eyes. Lunyai and Songaa followed suit. Emiren smiled but when she turned to Moryn, her voice stumbled. The Duthka man was staring at her with a strange look. She quickly finished her prayer to the Spirits and frowned at Moryn.

"What is it?"

"Forgive me, Emiren. Many of those words you spoke seem familiar, but I cannot understand them. You taught me a few in Manbung but I yearn to learn more and discover what secrets the past is hiding." He looked around the room. "Could we perhaps show the book to your parents? I believe they would be interested."

Quint clapped his hands. "A book? History maybe? I've a bit of a fascination with the past, truth be told. Let me get a beer for Songaa and I here, and let's have a look at it, Emiren."

Emiren hesitated. She wasn't sure she wanted to open up this tome of yesteryear right now, but she couldn't deny her mother in particular could probably read more of it than her. She reluctantly got up and retrieved the book from her sack. Megari cleared the table with Songaa's help, and Emiren set Cherin's book down. Quint returned with two mugs of ale and passed one to Lunyai's father. Emiren snorted a laugh as she saw her friend regard the mug with interest.

"Da, can you pour one for Lunyai, please?"

"Emiren!" the Tarakan blurted.

Songaa frowned. "You drank ale on your journey?"

"We had a few..." said Emiren quietly.

"*We*?!" cried Quint.

Megari laughed. "Ales all around it seems, dear husband. Kall did bring over a whole keg after all. And don't forget mine!"

Quint shook his head and went off to get some more mugs, muttering under his breath as he went.

Soon they were all sipping on Kall's home-brew, which was fairly potent, and staring at the precious pages before them.

"Where did this come from, Emiren?" her father asked.

"Cherin, Lord Torbal's nephew, had it. He is quite the scholar."

"Lord Torbal? *The* Lord Torbal, the King's Shield?!" spluttered Quint.

Emiren ran her hands through her hair and shook her head. "Yes, Da. I'll tell you about it all soon but, as Mum said, maybe now isn't the time."

Quint nodded and took a quaff of ale, eyes wide over the rim of the mug.

Emiren found the page that had led them to the Sacred Mount. She traced her fingers along the Words and Megari read them aloud. Moryn leaned forward, his eyes keen.

"We didn't find the cure to the madness though," said Emiren sadly.

"Madness?" queried Quint.

Emiren sighed. "I'm sorry Da, but that is definitely best left for another time."

"Cure?" questioned Megari.

"Please Mum, I'd rather just lea—"

"No, I mean I think you've read it wrong, Emi."

Emiren sat up straight. Moryn raised a hand and spoke. "*Cure* is not the correct word?" he asked, his voice betraying a hint of nervousness.

Megari shrugged. "*Chamoket* is closer to *solution* I would say. I used to help with Master Lukas' classes when you were younger," Emiren's mother said and raised an eyebrow. "An age when you actually went to lessons."

Emiren's cheeks heated with embarrassment.

"Anyway, Lukas would use *chamoket* often when teaching numbers. Don't you remember, Emi? Cure would be simpler, I believe it's *chamo*."

Vague memories of chalk on slate flitted through her mind.

"*Ketqan, kyushasem, chamoket!*" she cried, the process coming back to her suddenly. "Yes, solution is more accurate."

"So, it reads *a solution to the madness*?" pressed Moryn.

Megari nodded.

Emiren's brow furrowed. The *madness* was surely men becoming beasts, which was why she had read *chamoket* as *cure*, as it had seemed like a sickness of the mind. *Solution* seemed an odd term to use.

"And we didn't find a cure or solution to the madness," said Lunyai quietly.

Emiren thought about this. The blue worms had sealed Olwyn's wound, but it had been clear the strange creatures had stopped the bleeding and prevented infection, nothing more. Was it possible they could do something else? Could they have been wrong about the limits of the worms' abilities? She looked up at Moryn.

"What do you think, Moryn?"

The Duthka mariner looked troubled. "I am lost here, to tell the truth. The worms did help Olwyn when she was injured, so they could be seen as a *cure*, but it would be strange to call them a *solution*. The other Duthka took the fungus and seemingly ignored the worms, so presumably know nothing about this solution. Unless the fungus is the solution…" His voice trailed off.

Megari had continued to look through the book and was commenting on the many sketches of herbs and plants.

"This is fascinating, Emi. Sister Jessa could use some of this herb-lore. Look, I'm sure this is a drawing of Lorth Weed, and I can read these few words here. *Weed takes away pain.* You know this already," she said, seeing Emiren's expression. "But then look here. Is that not Naga Root?"

Emiren peered at the drawing. It certainly looked like that rather infamous root that seemed to hide itself away in the darkest corners of forests. Rumour was that it had miraculous properties, but Sister Jessa had always told Emiren it was not something worth experimenting with. Megari continued.

"I might be wrong, but it seems you can wrap Naga Root with Lorth Weed, then…*burn it?* That can't be right."

"Smoke it, Mum." Emiren laughed.

Quint shook his head. "And I'd like to know how you seem familiar with that method of enjoying Lorth Weed? Is that what you and Anton were doing…"

The words died as he spoke them.

Quint took one of Emiren's hands. "Sorry. I just forget sometimes."

Emiren nodded, feeling the loss of her friend sharply. "I will visit them later," she said.

The group went silent for a time, Emiren remembering Anton's silly jokes about her hair and eyes. She looked at the others and realised Moryn and Songaa did not know who Anton was or what had happened to him. That was one more story she was not ready to tell this night. She took a breath and offered a smile to her mother, then gestured to the book.

"What else can you find, Mum?"

Megari read on. Emiren felt her father's hand upon hers, the warmth of his touch pushing back the darkness she felt.

Spirits, it's good to be home with Mum and Da.

"So much to learn here," said Megari. "Look, this concoction gives you *clear thought*."

Moryn raised a hand again, making Emiren smile at his politeness. "What do you mean? It helps a person focus their thoughts?"

Megari frowned. "*Bona* means animal or beast so…" she muttered, her eyes staring hard at the page.

At the mention of *beasts*, Emiren stiffened. Moryn leaned forward and Lunyai looked at Emiren with frightened eyes.

Megari continued. "There! *Chamo*. That's definitely *cure*. This Word here. *The cure to*…Spirits, this is difficult to read. *Bona se kyu-shasemko nia chamo*. The cure to the burden of beasts."

Emiren inhaled sharply, then exchanged looks with Lunyai and Moryn. Her mother kept reading.

"It then says *The cure became a…spell*? A cure that was like a spell? Does that make sense to you, Emi?"

Emiren's mind stumbled over what her mother was telling her. What did the book mean by burden? If it talked about curing it, and if burden was the correct translation, then it must indicate that whatever her mother was looking at there, helped animals in some ways. Could it help those that had been turned?

It became a spell? Sorcery?

It didn't make sense but Emiren felt a glimmer of hope that this book held the key to curing the men that had become little more than beasts. *Spell* was perhaps misleading. What might have seemed like sorcery to people a hundred years ago was maybe something that could be explained by herb-lore or poisons now.

"Emi?" pressed her mother.

The Fallowden girl shook her head. "I'm not sure but I think the book contains knowledge that can help those poor souls. Do you agree, Moryn?"

He nodded in reply, his gaze intense.

Lunyai blew out a breath. Songaa spoke in Tarakan to his daughter. She replied in the common tongue.

"Father, Argyllan has not been the only battle in the realm," she said sadly.

"We know. Meridia fell to the Helligan nation," put in Quint.

"And there was fighting to the north, Da, at the Black Stone Ford."

Emiren's father frowned. "But that is in the heart of the Rihtgellen kingdom! Who was fighting who? Is the north in a state of civil war?" he asked incredulously.

"Soldiers from Westhealfe were fighting men who had been driven mad, turned into beasts. Men from *Morak*," explained Moryn, his voice bitter.

The room went quiet again and Emiren felt that reading the book was bringing as much darkness as it was understanding. She gently slid the book away from her mother and closed it, giving all of them a look she hoped they understood.

"So, what have you been eating while you've been roaming Ragnekai?" asked Quint cheerfully. Emiren wanted to hug him. He had understood perfectly.

"Leave it till tomorrow, Emi," said Megari, her expression begging her daughter to delay the hardship till the morning.

"I can't, Mum. I must visit them this day."

Lunyai placed a hand on Emiren's shoulder. "Let me come with you."

Emiren shook her head. "Thank you, but it's probably for the best if it's just me," she said, taking a deep breath.

Lunyai leaned in and hugged her, whispering in her ear as she did. "I will hold you later."

Emiren felt the warmth that only Lunyai could give her surge within. She was ready now to face the sorrow at the inn. She gave her parents a hug, ruffled Tarak's fur, then stepped out into the night with her wolfen companion. The door shut behind her and she suddenly felt horribly afraid. She looked down at Tarak. He nudged her leg, as if to gently push her in the direction of Nicolas' inn. Part of her was ready to go back in and melt into Lunyai's arms now, accept the warmth. Emiren stood for a moment, trying to keep down the emotion.

"There'll be tears anyway," she muttered. "Come on, Tarak."

The girl and her wolf set off toward the inn, the gathering dusk bringing villagers out to light lanterns. Emiren felt the relief of being home again being swallowed by the anguish that came with memories of Anton. Her mind went back to that day and she found herself wondering where Anton had been going, trekking off into Argol by himself. Had he been going to visit a girl?

I'll ask Cale. He'll know if Anton had a lover.

CHAPTER 6

MORYN

22nd Day of Maia, Three Days After Gimmweg Was Attacked

Moryn's eyes gradually became accustomed to the dark as he lay there on the straw mattress in Emiren's home. The single black mass before him had broken into varying shades of the night, the outline of the table and chairs where they had eaten becoming discernible. He breathed in deeply, trying to calm himself. Sleep had taken him soon after her parents had bid him goodnight, but something had woken him up. Maybe that wolf had howled, being shut out in the father's work-shop. He felt that falling back into a slumber would now be impossible.

Athaiq, help me...

Moryn flinched as his mind replayed images from Argyllan. The smouldering piles of bones, the mounds of earth where the citizens of the port-town had been buried, and the anguished outbursts of emotion he had heard again and again whilst they were in Argyllan.

So much death...

Moryn had seen little violence in his life. Indeed, the first killing he had witnessed had been when Corann cut down a fellow Duthka within the Sacred Mount. Idelisa's father's swordsmanship had been terrifying to behold, the Duthka lord seemingly unstoppable. And yet the sight of his daughter had frozen Corann.

"Even the mightiest have their weakness."

Moryn heard the words inside his head, heard that voice, and whimpered. He wanted to run away from all of this. Escape from his past and his future. Be far away from the consequences of his actions.

Why am I even here...in this damn village?

He sighed, the exhale breaking into a sob. He was here in Fallowden because he yearned to know more about this book. They had the book because they had gone to Westhealfe. And they had travelled to that city as a result of a chain of events that began when he had saved Lunyai from the sea.

Moryn clenched his jaw. *I should have let her drown.*

On the return from his final meeting with the Throskaur, Moryn had seen a figure flailing in the rolling waves. The sea had been rough that day but nothing that a seasoned sailor such as Moryn couldn't handle. He had hastily altered the course of his vessel to rescue this dark-haired, half-drowned female. Moryn had hooked her in and expelled the water from her lungs, then headed back to shore with the bedraggled, half-conscious girl. The act had made him feel somehow cleaner after his dealings with the thuggish raiders. A saviour rather than a scoundrel.

Moryn recalled his journeys to the Barren Isles, each one a trial of perseverance. The Throskaur were uncouth and unkempt, ignorant and illiterate, violent and vicious. Before he had sailed there, Seolta had told him not to judge them.

"They are the product of their environment, Moryn. If you or I lived upon those harsh islands, at the mercy of those storms, I doubt we would survive."

Moryn had tried to heed Seolta's words, but the pirates were filthy in their habits, vile in their traditions, and barbarous to even their own. He had been safe there, though, Seolta's gift to them something they valued highly, an artefact of old. To Moryn, it was merely a rusted trident, but to the Throskaur it was a sacred object, something from their god.

So, the Duthka mariner had been an honoured guest in their lands. The Throskaur lords had exhibited a blind fervour and treated Moryn like some kind of prophet. They had probably set this belief into stone when the Western Sea had calmed, just as Moryn had predicted.

They ignore their own history and do not see the truth in their legends. It *is out there…*

Moryn felt most of the tales and myths that they did remember, though, were born out of drunken flights of fancy. Dragons were indeed mythical beasts, ghost ships more likely the result of too much alcohol consumed, and even if mer-folk did exist, which they didn't, Moryn was fairly certain they wouldn't be trying to seduce the loutish Throskaur. Drunken brutes speaking in a woefully broken form of the common tongue, their rancid breath in his face, had not been a particularly pleasant experience.

They could never have been a part of the reborn Marrh.

Yet they had come to Argyllan, as Seolta had said they would. Only to end up being slaughtered by Tarakan arrows and Westhealfe cavalry, something Seolta had not foreseen.

They had killed so many before they were stopped.

So much death…

Conflict surged within Moryn, his stomach tying in agonising knots. Seolta's words and promises had started to become reality and Moryn had now seen the colour of that reality in Argyllan. A horrible, dirty brown upon the grass. And he had smelt it. A lingering stench of burning, acrid smoke that told a hideous story. And he had heard it. Children crying, words of loss overheard, and then the silence of despair.

I did that…

His head began to ache as he connected his actions with the devastation in Argyllan. He knew it was a necessary part of Seolta's design, but that didn't make it any easier to ignore the harsh reality of violence and his part in bringing forth that doom.

Moryn chastised himself for having been so naïve. Seolta's vision of a realm reborn, a Marrh ruled by the Duthka, was impossible to achieve without spilling blood. But now Moryn had seen it with his own eyes: Corann cutting down Duthka, the Unvasik giant killing Nerian, the hundreds of fresh graves beyond the walls of Argyllan; now he understood the true cost of what Seolta was striving for.

"Be strong, Moryn."

Again, Seolta's voice was in his head, this time the gentle tone his master would adopt when encouraging Moryn. Whereas Corann had always been distant and never tried to be any kind of father figure to Moryn, Seolta had filled that void in his life. Far away physically but Moryn shared a strong bond with the man. Seolta trusted him and offered him new paths of learning, each secret meeting with him a time of wonder for the young Duthka. Corann on the other hand seemed to want to bury knowledge, turn his back on new possibilities and hide from hard truths.

Seolta should have become the leader of us all…

Moryn hoped this would happen one day. When Marrh was reborn under Duthka rule, Moryn hoped Corann's people, the Duthka he had himself lived with for almost a decade, they would recognise what Seolta had achieved and come forth from the Abhaile. Maybe some of the other settlements, those deeper in the forest, would also venture south.

But so much death…

Moryn squeezed his eyes shut against hot tears and clenched his fists. The future Seolta promised was a beautiful and pure image in his mind, something that could not be reconciled with the brutality that had killed so many. A war between the north and the south was something Moryn could have turned a blind eye to, but he could not hide from Argyllan. He was responsible for that, he alone.

In his mind the image of a peaceful Marrh crumbled into ash. The Duthka mariner felt an urge to run away from Fallowden this very night. Flee from the savage reality behind Seolta's plans. He cast his gaze around the living area where he lay, his eyes again picking out the dull charcoal outlines of furniture and cloaks hanging. He sat up and wiped his eyes.

Emiren took the book into her room…

So much had been revealed that evening, so much more than Moryn could ever have anticipated. The book that Cherin had passed to them seemed like a companion to the one Seolta had acquired. Two books. One contained healing knowledge, the other knowledge of power. Moryn wondered who had written them. Was the legend of the brother and sister Corann spoke of, true?

There is a solution to the madness…

But if that solution was referring to the fungus within the Sacred Mount, Moryn couldn't make sense of it. Surely the fungus could not be a *solution*. The fungus turned normal men into crazed animals, robbing them of their humanity. The young Duthka could not see how that could be termed a solution. It seemed at odds with the rest of the book, which listed the healing properties of many plants and roots. Moryn could not understand how someone who sought to heal would consider the fungus as solving anything.

Was it an extreme solution? To an extreme problem in a past age? And what did the book mean by the *burden* of beasts? There were too many questions. Too much was unknown. And too much had happened.

So much death…

Moryn wept silently. He was a fool for being so blind to the cost of Marrh becoming Duthka lands again. Seolta had warned him it would take years and many would suffer. But Seolta had always ended any conversation with glorious words of their bright future that would follow. These words had dispelled the dark images. But words spoken now would not wash the blood from Moryn's hands.

Moryn wished he were out in his boat, feeling the wind and the salty spray from the churning waters. Perhaps because he sailed alone, maybe because he was so close to the sublime power of nature, but Moryn could think clearly out on the waves. Here, in this closed space, four walls around him and a roof above, he felt constricted and his thoughts haunted him.

Athaiq, help me…

Moryn again felt the urge to flee. If he was in a boat, he could leave this nightmare, go to a far-off land where no-one knew him or what he had done. His thoughts began to turn. He would be turning his back on Seolta and Idelisa, but he had done what had been asked of him. His part in Seolta's designs was finished.

I am free…

Those three words abruptly came to him and he felt a heavy weight, a terrible anxiety, lift from his shoulders. He realised his head was no longer aching and his stomach was not twisted. He took a breath. Then nodded to himself. It was indeed time to go.

The book!

He had to have the book. He wanted it for himself and knew it could help those that would fight Seolta's vision. It would be better for everyone if he took the book with him. He realised he was smiling.

Yes, all will be well.

Moryn took a deep breath and slowly rose from the floor, trying to make less noise than a gentle whisper. He made no swift motions, knowing a loss of balance and tumbling into something would ruin his new-born plan before it began. He stood straight and then moved to his boots, quietly slipping them on. Next the Duthka sailor retrieved his long-coat from near the door and carefully put it on, focusing on each button as he fastened the warm vestment. He looked at the door to Emiren's room.

No wolf, thankfully. Only Emiren.

He moved towards the door, each step a measured action, gently pressing down on the floor to find a squeaky board before its wail shattered the night. Moryn was then at the door. He curled his fingers round the handle and pushed down. Then gently nudged the door.

The door didn't budge.

Moryn increased the pressure but the door didn't move.

Locked?!

Why would she lock the door? The front door was secured so there was no need to bar this one. The Duthka sailor frowned. He leaned in, peering at the door in the darkness. He could see a tiny sliver of a gap between the door and its frame, and as he ran his eyes down, he noticed a small block of blackness chest-high. A latch.

After a slow, deep breath, Moryn withdrew his knife from the inside pocket of his coat. He took off the leather sheath and saw the blade was a dull grey in the darkness. The blade was only four inches but he had kept it sharp over the years, needing it to cut rope out on the waves. He carefully slid it between door and post, then edged it upwards until he felt the resistance of the latch. Holding his breath, he raised the knife, pushing the latch. He carefully pressed against the door and it drifted inwards, silent as a leaf falling in the heart of that forest.

The book was right there, on a small table to the left, its bulky form crying out silently to Moryn. Emiren's bed was against the far wall, her sleeping form an inky black shape. Moryn saw the curtains behind the bed billow slightly and felt a night breeze. Knife still in hand, Moryn made a furtive step to the table. He lifted the book and then held it fast between his left arm and body.

I have it!

A sighing sound of movement made him tense and cease all motion. He looked at the bed.

"Moryn?" came a sleepy voice.

Moryn lurched through the streets of Fallowden. He had to run, get far away. Someone must have heard the cry. He looked down at his hands. Blood. He wiped them on his coat, gasping as he did.

Athaiq, help me…

He was at the gates and heaved with exertion as he removed the wooden bar locking the entrance, pain lancing in his lower back. It was heavier than he imagined and too much for him to hold. As it came free, he lost his grip on the beam and it fell to the ground with a thud. Moryn whirled around, expecting the entire village to burst forth from their homes. There had been so much noise. But the night stayed quiet, save for the nocturnal scuffling of animals, barely audible over the other side of the wooden palisade. Moryn eased open the gate and passed through, his breathing ragged.

Athaiq, give me strength!

Low voices suddenly came to his ears. He froze, trying to judge where they were coming from. Inside the village. At least two people. He peered through the narrowing gap as he pushed the gate closed. The glow of a torch appeared from the main street in the village, the voices became louder, but they were not shouting. A night patrol engaged in conversation. Tears rolled down his cheeks and Moryn prayed they wouldn't see the gate was unbarred. If his exit was noticed now, he would lose the head-start he so desperately needed.

Only a thin line of vision was available to him now. He saw two men ambling slowly toward the gate. They had a torch. Surely they would see the bar upon the ground. Moryn pulled the gate fully shut and then put his back against the wooden barrier. He listened, his mind telling him to run but his body begging him to stop.

The voices came closer and Moryn heard what was being said.

"It was probably Ivalin and Adele romping, a howl of passion! I caught them sneaking out into Argol night before last. Bloody rabbits, those two!"

A laugh.

"Ha! Wish my Ymma was that feisty."

"Gate's shut so I'm guessing they're behind the storehouse again."

A pause.

"I will miss her at the gates."

"All of Fallowden will."

That woman who was killed by Throskaur...

"Him most of all. The man is broken."

"He didn't speak much before."

"Aye, and now he speaks even less. Were they lovers do you think?"

"Who can say? I never saw anything to suggest that but..."

The voices moved away and Moryn breathed a sigh of relief, wincing. He waited a few more moments, then began moving quietly away from Fallowden. He clutched the book under his left arm still, its presence the only thing preventing him from breaking down and sobbing. His thoughts were otherwise confused, his mind feeling lost at the edge of the open sea. Where should he go? What should he do?

His stomach churned and he abruptly vomited, Megari's stew splattering onto a large rock. He cuffed his mouth with his sleeve, spat a few times, then took a deep breath.

Moryn began walking unsteadily, his mind numb and his hands shaking.

Forgive me...

PART THREE

Chapter 1

Kapvik

23rd Day of Maia, Four Days After Gimmweg Was Attacked

"There they are," whispered Siorraidh.

Kapvik peered into the night and saw two tall shadows. They lurked at the edge of the glow of one of the street lanterns, flickering oil lamps that hung on poles here and there along the main thoroughfare. The village, whose name Kapvik couldn't remember, was mostly sleeping but he could hear the odd laugh drifting along the night air, and a horse snickering, perhaps dreaming of being free. From the two figures, though, there was no sound. They were looking up and down the road that led to the market square and then to the far side of the settlement. Kapvik reckoned they were waiting for someone, but he hadn't seen a single soul for what seemed like an age as he waited unseen with Siorraidh.

"Who are they?" he asked her, his voice kept as low as he could, though he knew he was not adept at whispering. His frustration with Siorraidh and the Duthka in general was growing. If she did not charm him as she did, he felt certain he would have cursed in rage and left these night-walkers to their nocturnal deeds, heading back to his lord

Vorga and the promise of a more worthy quest.

"Helligan agents," she replied, her eyes focused on the two men. "I did not expect to see them in Barleywick again…" Her voice trailed off.

"You have been to this settlement before?" he asked, his brow furrowing.

Siorraidh grinned, her teeth a milky white contrast to the colour she had applied to her face, a deep red in daylight but a dark shadow now.

"I have been many places, my gentle giant." She leaned up and grabbed his face in her hands. "And I would go to many more with you at my side!" she said, then kissed him. Her lips were sweet with something Kapvik couldn't recognise.

The notion of travelling with her to new lands was exciting to the Unvasik warrior, but he also feared he might go mad if he kept following this mystifying lady. What he had witnessed at the summit of the Sacred Mount had shaken him to the core, and he had prayed to Tatkret many times since, seeking a sign that he should bid Siorraidh farewell and return to Vorga.

But where would I go? And why is it so hard for me to even think about leaving her?

He had no idea where his lord was now. Possibly still in Morak, possibly somewhere else entirely. And Kapvik could not travel openly in these lands. Their Duthka allies disguised themselves well but their skin was pale like the lowlanders, and they were of a similar stature. He was a giant compared to most here and his father had told him stories of how the lowlanders stared at the Unvasik with their darker skin. There was no way he could just steal a horse and ride under the sun's glare. He would be lost here were he not with Siorraidh. Kapvik felt suddenly alone and vulnerable.

Vorga, have I been a fool?

"Wait here," whispered Siorraidh and abruptly stepped out of their concealment, the storehouse to a drinking shop.

He made to grab her, but she was already walking toward the two men with no hint of fear, her head wrapped in that colourful cloth and her grey leathers replaced with flowing purple silks. Kapvik knew it was some disguise but was at a loss to explain it. He had given up asking questions as the answers were always too cryptic. He watched her approach them, then heard her voice hail them. She was putting on a strange voice, pretending to be someone else.

Does she know them well? A strange jealousy arose within.

Indeed, they seemed to know her in this guise as they greeted Siorraidh and then all three began speaking in hushed voices. Kapvik was too far away to hear, so he slumped back against the wall and tried to calm himself. He struggled to justify what he was doing here with this woman. Vorga had commanded him to stay with her, but his lord would be furious if he knew how this order had led to a physical relationship, a new world of possibility and perhaps disloyalty. He cast his eyes to the night sky and saw Tatkret's many white eyes, gazing over the realm. He huffed.

I must speak to Vorga again.

Much as he was enthralled with this Duthka lady, she was a wild storm at sea, taking him to unknown places. Vorga was an anchor that could stay this constant tumultuous movement and make him face reality. Kapvik decided he would give Siorraidh a few more days with her strange ways, then demand they return to Vorga or they would part ways. He looked up to see what the three were doing now.

Tatkret!

They were nowhere to be seen.

Kapvik broke from his cover and strode out into the street, no longer concerned if a villager saw an Unvasik tribesman in the heart of their home.

Where have they gone? Is she mad?

Siorraidh and the two men weren't anywhere in the thoroughfare, so they must have headed farther down the side alley where the two had been waiting.

She risks herself. They could b—

A flash lit up the darkness behind a house yards away, followed instantly by a crack as if the sky had been ripped apart.

No!

Kapvik ran to the house, then around it to see Siorraidh standing facing one of the men, her arm outstretched and pale blue sparks hzz-ing near her hand. Kapvik's chest tightened—she had used that thing again. She had called forth the awesome power of the realm and sent it forth. The man facing her looked terrified, his arms held up in a gesture of submission. He slowly turned his head. Kapvik followed his gaze and the two gasped as one.

Lying maybe ten yards past them was a dark shape, smoke rising from it and tiny flames flickering upon it. Siorraidh had killed one of them, using the weapon from a past age. Kapvik felt nauseous but it wasn't the smell of burning flesh that induced this; it was an inner dis-gust that Siorraidh would strike down someone in this way.

"Go back to your lord, Helligan," she said in the common tongue, her voice cold and harsh. "Tell him the north belongs to Torbal."

The man stared at Siorraidh, then at his dead companion, then re-turned to face the Duthka lady. She brandished the rod and he flinched. Then both became aware of Kapvik. There was a tense moment of ut-ter silence, as if all were unsure who was who and what was happening.

"Go now!" She snarled to the man, brandishing the rod.

The man did not hesitate this time but turned on his heel and broke into a run, plunging into the darkness. Kapvik heard him stumble some yards on, but then hurrying footsteps began again and faded into the night.

"What have you done?" he asked her, his voice trembling with anger. "You use this new power to cut down defenceless men?"

Her reaction startled Kapvik. Her throat made an unnatural growl-ing noise and she strode up to him. He was relieved to see the pole slipping into her flowing robes.

"Kapvik, daku ellami-nngit wa-si kaneq-tok!" she hissed, her voice rasping upon his language. "Open your eyes! Do you really believe we will take back Marrh through strength of arms alone? Stop judging each action and think of the destination. I promise you there will be much more you find less than glorious before we are done. This is not a chain of single battles but a war! And wars are ugly."

The Unvasik warrior was taken aback. Not just with what she

said, but how she said it. To speak so deeply in his tongue once again showed Kapvik Siorraidh was a wonder of her people. Yet she was clearly a terror of nightmares to those who opposed her.

He knew she was right, though. The Unvasik could not hope to take back Marrh by force, and he was beginning to realise that Vorga had known this all along.

"Not all wars are won by warriors."

His lord's words came back to him and he felt the tension leave his body, a feeling of ineptitude seeping into him. Was it just he alone who lacked insight? Was he delusional, misguided even? He had marched that night into the Beacuan, the home of the Duthka, with wild ideas of facing foes in battle after battle. But Vorga had told him this would not be how they reclaimed the realm. Kapvik had heard his lord's words but hadn't truly listened.

Siorraidh moved into him and hugged him tightly.

"Forgive me," she said, her voice losing its edge and the woman he was enthralled with returning. "I do not mean to turn my anger on you, Kapvik. I am scared of the future, frightened of failure. I do not like what I have to do at times, but I know I must not dwell on each day, only on where we are heading. And I must not question how we get there."

She pulled his head down and kissed him. Despite all he had seen with his own eyes and what he now knew she was prepared to do, he could not resist her. He hugged her tightly.

"I cannot see the future either, Siorraidh. I thought I knew what would come but I am lost now," he muttered, cursing himself inwardly for how he had become so weak and laden with doubt.

"I am lost too, Kapvik." She kissed his lips again, her hands stroking his beard. "But together we can find our future. Not Seolta's dangerous vision of what the next age will be but our *own* future, far from here. With you beside me, I fear nothing, my gentle giant."

Kapvik's chest surged as her words seeped into his body, crushing all doubt with their bewitching ways. He lifted her from the ground. She let out a tiny yelp, then laughed as he twirled around, her legs flying out with the momentum.

"I will never leave you, goddess of the storm!" he cried.

Voices broke the night, somewhere deeper in the village. Sior-raidh's brief *storm* had woken those that dwelt here.

"Hush!" she chided him. "Our work here is done. Let us find some-where away from this village where you can gaze up at the stars as I look down upon you."

Tatkret, how can I resist this daughter of the moon?

CHAPTER 2

SYLVANUS

23rd Day of Maia, Four Days After Gimmweg Was Attacked

Sylvanus nodded in greeting to the villagers he passed. Rumbleton was a large, bustling settlement, situated as it was on the road from the Gjallag Bridge to Bregustol. But there was a tense hush in the streets this morning. Rumours of the Helligan advance to the south had reached the folk here and Sylvanus had seen more than one wagon stacked with belongings heading north, presumably to leave the village and seek refuge behind the capital's high walls.

Those walls will not save you.

Not all were fleeing though. Maybe they had heard that Meridia had not been sacked, so they believed they would be ignored if they kept their heads down. These used to be Helligan lands, so it was possible the more pragmatic villagers here were of the mind that although the person on the throne changed from time to time, life in a village would always go on as usual.

Not this time though. News of Gimmweg and the Royal Mines should have reached the capital by now.

A cart laden with milk urns trundled by, a gaggle of children rushed past him shouting out something about a stinky bog, and a lady was furiously beating a rug with a stick, dust fleeing away into the morning breeze. The woman looked up, saw Sylvanus, and gave him a smile. The Duthka refugee dipped his head and imagined how different the scene must be to the northeast.

People of the Rihtgellen kingdom fleeing from Unvasik warriors…

He strode down the main street, keeping his pace even but moving with haste. The inn where the meeting would take place was unlikely to be open at this hour, but he wanted to be sure he wasn't being followed so decided a bit of a detour would be wise.

The smell of meat cooking wafted by in the air and his stomach grumbled. A man was roasting what looked like small birds on spits. Sylvanus decided to give in to his cravings.

"Morning to you," he hailed as he walked over.

The man smiled at his approaching customer.

"Morning, sir. Clear skies again today."

"Glorious indeed. One can almost forget the rumours of war," commented Sylvanus, hoping for some gossip in response.

The man frowned and shook his head. "Ever-Father knows what is going on these days! The High King dies and all the lords start strutting here and there." The seller put his hands on his hips. "It's us small folk who end up suffering when the high and mighty play their games."

"Indeed," replied Sylvanus. "I'll take one of these…quails, if I may."

"Quails they are, sir. Juicy and freshly roasted," he said, as he busied himself sprinkling a few herbs on one that was ready to be sold.

"The people of Rumbleton are not worried about the Helligan soldiers crossing the Mimir?" enquired Sylvanus as he handed over two coppers in response to the man's two raised fingers and received the roasted bird.

The seller shrugged. "Roads aren't as safe as they were a month ago, so I reckon the journey to Bregustol carries its own risk. And if the Helligans are coming this way, Bregustol is exactly where they'll be heading! We'll just wave them through," he said with a laugh.

Sylvanus took a bite of the bird and hot juices dribbled down his chin. It was delicious, especially after having eaten cold sausage that morning. He wiped his chin and nodded.

"I shall join the good people here with that wave," he said. Then grinned. "But a few obscene gestures to their backs as they pass through is warranted, wouldn't you say?"

The seller guffawed. Sylvanus bid him farewell and carried on with his stroll. Lord Rencarro's former Second narrowed his eyes as he surveyed daily life in this village, a village built upon land that was stolen. People merrily living their lives upon soil into which had seeped the blood of Duthka and Unvasik many years before. Sylvanus felt no pity as he continued down the main thoroughfare.

They have no idea what the coming days will bring.

"Malesh," hailed Sylvanus, seeing Seolta enter the inn. The Duthka lord was wearing a faded robe and had a swirl of cloth around his head.

"Brother!" responded Seolta.

"In all but blood!" whispered Sylvanus as they embraced. The once Meridian general pulled back and grinned at his mentor and friend. "I feel there is a fresh breeze blowing through the realm," he commented wryly.

Seolta nodded. "And you have created it, my friend! Truly you have achieved so much alone," said the Duthka lord, gripping Sylvanus by the shoulders.

He felt a surge of pride, being praised so highly by this great man who had searched the realm for Duthka thrown afar by violence and tyranny. A man who had gathered those who had lost loved ones to Rihtgellen oppression. And a man who had taught him so much. "I was never alone, Seolta. I had your teachings with me every step on this path."

Seolta's smile faded. "If only my other pupils were as diligent as you," he muttered.

Sylvanus frowned and waited for more. Seolta motioned for them to sit at a table in the corner.

"No word from Idelisa?"

Seolta shook his head and Sylvanus began to feel uneasy. No word from her was potentially grave news.

"I know something of her whereabouts but am concerned as to exactly where she is now and why," he said, tapping one finger on the table.

Sylvanus was about to reply when a barmaid approached. She asked what they would be having and Seolta ordered a couple of flagons of their home-brew and today's pie. When she moved away, Sylvanus leaned in. Seolta sighed and related his news.

"My ally within the Abhaile is with Corann, as expected. But Corann is not where we thought he'd be."

Sylvanus frowned. "He has come to the Beacuan?"

Seolta shook his head. "Corann came south. And seems to know more than he should," he finished, his jaw clenching.

Sylvanus' eyes widened. "South? Westhealfe?"

"I believe he was probably there. But he was definitely within the Sacred Mount with some rag-tag group." Seolta's eyes hardened. "And my ally."

Treachery?

Sylvanus studied his mentor's face and was sure this is exactly what Seolta was thinking. He waited. The man huffed.

"It is no matter. He completed the task I gave him. The Throskaur came."

Sylvanus blinked. He sat back in his chair, thoughts swirling. Rencarro had sent his Velox Riders out with orders to spread rumours of long-boats seen off the coast but here Seolta was telling him they actually came.

Seolta noticed his confusion and smiled.

"Forgive me, my friend. As you know, it is necessary to tell any one of you only what is required. You understand the risk?"

Sylvanus nodded slowly. He had always been aware of this, but he felt uneasy now. He waited.

"My ally sailed to the Barren Isles and secured their, hmm, assistance shall we say, in our endeavour. Argyllan was perhaps surprised to see their ugly faces so close."

Sylvanus reeled. He felt in equal measure awe at the scale of Seolta's designs, but also uncertainty as to what it would mean to have pirates joining them in their new world.

Seolta cocked his head.

"Oh, have no fear. The Throskaur were slaughtered."

Sylvanus stared at the Duthka lord. He couldn't take it all in. Seolta continued, grinning.

"In a bizarre way, we have your former lord to thank for that. I had envisioned the Helligan nation coming west and putting an end to their presence here in Marrh, but I received word that Rencarro led the defence of the city."

"He lives?" blurted Sylvanus, before he could check himself.

Seolta held his eyes. It was perhaps a moment of silence, but it felt like an eternity.

"He lives."

Sylvanus kept his face a mask of nothing. Seolta looked about to begin a lecture, his hand raising and a finger crooked. At that moment, the barmaid came over with two mugs of ale, which she set down upon the table. The tension fell away as they thanked her.

"What about Idelisa?" asked Sylvanus, hoping to turn the conversation away from Rencarro. He felt remorse for betraying his former lord and friend, but had thought Rencarro would grow old in Argyllan as the realm crumbled around him. The thought of him dying under the merciless swings of a Throskaur axe had opened a door into Sylvanus' more recent past. He mentally pushed that portal shut and cast his mind back to his mother.

I will return soon to where you brought me into the world.

Seolta took a long draft of the ale, then set the mug down, his eyes intense.

"Idelisa was supposed to be with me now."

That sounded ominous.

"The group who were with her returned with the fungus we need, but she climbed the mountain with an Unvasik warrior."

"Unvasik? They are that far south?"

Seolta raised one eye-brow.

"Just Vorga's body-guard. I needed him to be far from his lord so I planted a few ideas in Vorga's mind. Why Idelisa would go up that damn mountain with him though, I have no idea. It is troubling…" His voice trailed off as he looked around the inn, as if searching for the Moon Sister here and now.

Sylvanus realised there was so much that Seolta was not telling him. He felt somewhat bitter, considering all he had sacrificed and now accomplished for their cause. He deserved more trust from the Duthka lord. He probed.

"So Vorga is still with us?" he asked, placing a slight emphasis on the last word.

Seolta seemed not to notice. The cloud concerning Idelisa that hung over him seemed to blow away to be replaced by a look of amusement , his eyes were almost twinkling.

"He will do what is necessary, of that I am sure."

Sylvanus shrugged inwardly. Seolta's designs seemed to be bearing fruit. Idelisa would return to her master, of that Sylvanus was sure. She had always been alight with passion when speaking about reshaping the world, and had told Sylvanus many stories about the forests to the north. At this moment, Sylvanus felt tired and wished he could just ride to the Beacuan and rest within the trees and their silent watch.

A snort of a laugh from Seolta startled Sylvanus. His mentor seemed to have truly pushed away any suspicions about Idelisa.

"I believe we have much to tell each other but let me share one aspect of all this I found somewhat entertaining."

Sylvanus smiled, glad Seolta's mood had brightened. He had feared few men in his life but the Duthka lord was dangerous, of that Sylvanus was fully aware. Dangerous to those who opposed him, and perhaps dangerous to those he felt were not obeying him.

"You know that Idelisa was able to locate the High King's little secret and retrieve it, yes?"

Sylvanus nodded. He'd had more than one nocturnal meeting with Duthka agents.

"Exactly where it was hidden though you do not know, correct?"

Again, Sylvanus nodded.

"I have to dip my head to Sedmund for his cunning. And sense of humour perhaps. He hid the book in the Holy Sepulchre!" Seolta sniggered with delight.

Sylvanus couldn't supress a laugh himself and slapped the table. "Divine tragedy one could say."

The bargirl came over again, this time with their pie and the aroma was even better than the roasted quail Sylvanus had enjoyed not long before. The girl smiled at them.

"You gentlemen seem in high spirits today," she commented. "Some of our regulars are worried about Helligan soldiers coming this way." The young girl bit her lip, looking afraid.

"We have heard rumour that the troubles in the south of Ragnekai will soon pass and we can all go back to our lives," responded Sylvanus with a forced grin. "Trust me when I say that all will be well soon."

"Well, I am glad to hear that. People are telling such frightening stories."

She left them again and the two men took a quaff of ale, both smiling over the rim of their mugs. Seolta then continued.

"I do not think Sedmund was able to translate any of the text, which is maybe not surprising when you consider how he kept it hidden from all eyes. I do not understand why he was so secretive, but it doesn't matter now."

Sylvanus pushed for more information regarding the book.

"Were you right in what the book contains?" he enquired. "I could not stay to watch the effects of the fungus on Orben but judging by the bells ringing, I am certain he is dead."

Seolta sat back and smiled broadly.

"The legends have more than a grain of truth, my friend. More like an avalanche of truth," he said, patting his sack that he had upon his lap.

Sylvanus felt a strange giddiness. The book was real and inches from him.

"I cannot read all that is in here yet, but I understand enough. It does contain powerful knowledge." Seolta lowered his voice even further. "If you had stayed to watch Orben turn, I believe you would have been more alarmed than amused," he said, with a crooked smile.

Sylvanus tried to conjure up images of Orben raging like a madman. His mentor continued.

"We turned many men from Morak and had them attack Torbal at the Black Stone Ford. I am told those turned were like a pack of rabid dogs, viciously striking whoever was near. As soldiers, they were worthless. But as oil poured onto a flame, they blazed! Fear and hate will spread like a wildfire."

His master paused, his brow furrowing as if considering something. "They still feel pain though..."

Sylvanus waited for his mentor's thought to continue.

"The fungus seems to shut off their power of reason, turns them into mindless beasts, but they still howl in agony when pierced with a blade. If we could also turn off their feeling of pain, they would fight till they literally dropped."

"An army of the dead," whispered Sylvanus.

"Indeed."

Sylvanus felt his misgivings fall away. He was in the dark as to much of Seolta's plan, but gradually tidings were coming to his ears and it did appear that at long last, the Duthka vengeance had arrived. The realm was sundering, and a new age was dawning. He looked at his lord and saw there was more; Seolta's eyes were now wide with a glee Sylvanus had never seen before.

"This tale has another twist?" he enquired, then knocked back a gulp of the ale, the beer holding a satisfying combination of something sweet and the tartness of gooseberries, unless he was mistaken.

Seolta took a sip of his own ale before carrying on with his story. "As planned, with the help of the Unvasik, we took Morak. And," he couldn't suppress a laugh, "we had guests from Westhealfe."

Sylvanus' eyes widened. "Torbal?"

"No, his sister and her rabble of girls," he replied, his eyes alight with glee.

"I trust Cyneburg is dead then," said Sylvanus, spooning pie onto Seolta's plate, then his own.

"At the bottom of the Icefinger River, I do believe."

"You threw her in?" He gasped.

"No, she jumped!"

Sylvanus raised his eyebrows. *The north and south are suffering.* He took a mouthful of pie, wondering if the quail's egg that popped between his teeth was from the bird he had eaten earlier.

Seolta washed down his own pie with a swig of ale. "After we have eaten, we should leave, make our way to the Ruby Road as soon as possible. I want to make sure the Unvasik are coming as planned, and not sacking the countryside like the bone-headed barbarians they have been for so long. Timing is crucial."

Sylvanus nodded. He was relieved to hear they wouldn't linger in Rumbleton. The former Meridian officer was fairly certain he hadn't been followed but he also felt a growing sense of unease. He had ridden his luck for far too long, with clandestine meetings and lies an integral part of his life, and never once had he been suspected. Now the truth was out, and his betrayal to both Meridia and the Helligan nation surely known, he knew there were many out there who wanted him dead. Sylvanus didn't want to spend any longer in the wider realm than was necessary.

Seolta raised his mug, offering a toast. Sylvanus obliged.

"With your efforts, the entire south is weak, divided, and its leaders dead or absent. Nobody can stop the coming storm."

Sylvanus inhaled, his eagerness to finally return to Duthka lands surging within him.

If only you were there to welcome me home, Mother.

CHAPTER 3

TORBAL

23rd Day of Maia, Four Days After Gimmweg Was Attacked

Torbal clenched his reins tighter and ground his teeth, his jaw suffering the bitterness he felt within. The night before, Wulfner, Beornoth's old soldier, had related to him Nerian's final stand. As always with such tales, the man had perhaps embellished some details, made it more heroic, but Torbal believed it was close to the truth. Nerian had been an excellent battle-sergeant and a noble man. Torbal had seen him defeat a huge Unvasik warrior at the Black Stone Ford when those beast-men had attacked, so the King's Shield felt certain that Nerian had been slain by a truly mighty opponent. Indeed, three of them had been unable to bring him down.

The farmlands of Morak were in view now and Torbal wondered what they would find ahead. The skies had clouded over and Torbal couldn't help but feel this was an ill omen. The last days of spring seemed to be hiding, hastily retreating even, scared of what the summer would bring.

Torbal had pushed the legions hard coming north from the Black Stone Ford, their camp last night a hurried affair and the departure this morning made as soon as the sun had begun to peek over the eastern horizon, the soldiers eating heels of bread and passing round water-skins as they marched.

Torbal had with him sufficient numbers to conquer the walls of Morak, drive the Duthka and Unvasik out from the city, and send them into bloody retreat. Or slay them all. Torbal knew Cyneburg would prefer the latter. His sister had ridden up and down the ranks of the Bradlastax, speaking with as many as she could, steeling courage and carefully nurturing their desire to reap vengeance upon those who had slaughtered their sisters.

They were closing in on the fields now and not a soul could be seen. Torbal began to fear the enemy had emerged from the city walls to spill the blood of common folk too.

"What has happened to the realm?" muttered Wulfner, who rode quietly beside him. Torbal had regretted his harsh tone with the man concerning his friend, Corann. Wulfner was a good man and had done far more than anyone could have reasonably expected of him. The same could be said for the Duthka man, who was now far away, having left the camp to return to his people. His part in this tale was over.

"Too much has happened," Torball replied to Wulfner's question, "and too much is still unknown to us."

The general's mind then turned to a matter he had been pondering before Wulfner and the tall Duthka had arrived at their camp. The general had been considering the future of Ragnekai. He felt certain they could push back the northern threat and also that Ulla could persuade Orben to be content with only Meridia. And if he and Ulla married, Orben would be forced to accept Torbal and his sister as rulers of the realm. That just left the details.

"Wulfner, how well do you know this Rencarro?" he asked, deeming the big northerner to be a good representation of what a commoner not in his direct service would think.

"Not very well, my lord. He is a capable leader and seems to be a skilled fighter, going by what your niece reported. But I have never met him in person."

Torbal nodded. He had figured as much.

"I have met him. More than once. There was an annual council in Bregustol before Sedmund passed away. I did little in terms of diplomacy so did not speak with him at length, but he struck me as determined. And ambitious," he added, hoping to encourage Wulfner to be frank.

The northerner pulled on his beard, a habit the general had noticed in himself of late. "As you know, my lord, I travelled with Tacet, a Meridian, for a number of days. Whilst we didn't talk much about Lord Rencarro, from what little was said, I believe you are right in your estimation of the man." Wulfner coughed. "Forgive my curiosity, my lord, but why do you ask?"

Torbal shrugged. "My niece Lucetta and her company are now in Argyllan, or patrolling that area. I do not think there will be another raid, if one could call it that."

"Invasion?"

Torbal nodded grimly. "I doubt those pirates have the numbers to mount a full-scale invasion of the realm, especially now with so many of the curs dead. They are not the Xerinthian empire, that much is certain. But if they were part of a wider design..."

The big copper-haired man inhaled sharply. "I have had similar thoughts, my lord. So much seems to have happened at just the right time for this Seolta fellow."

Torbal nodded and looked ahead. There was still no sign of anyone working the fields. He didn't like the quiet.

Wulfner cleared his throat in what Torbal could only describe as a polite nudge. "General Torbal, you were speaking about Lord Rencarro..."

"Yes, Rencarro," said Torbal, his eyes fixed upon Morak, which grew in size the closer they came. "My niece showed herself to be a capable leader and quite the warrior, judging by the reports and tales that have come back. So, she has proven herself in battle. Leading a company of soldiers is one matter however, governing a city is quite another. I would offer Rencarro the rule of Argyllan."

Torbal quickly turned his head to see Wulfner's reaction. The man did not look surprised; he was gently nodding.

"Meridia was prosperous under his rule, from what I know."

"It was indeed," the general concurred.

"But I would think he wants to retake his own city from the Helligan nation above all else," said Wulfner.

"If I were him, I would. Most certainly. But he must see that is something that will not be achieved without a great deal of bloodshed, and he has already lost many men to the Throskaur. He is no fool and I believe he realises that marching on Meridia now would be suicide."

Wulfner shifted in his saddle. Torbal could see the man was less than comfortable upon a horse. Being upon one so much of late had actually numbed Torbal to the discomfort. He had fallen back into the rhythm of life on the road, setting up camp each night and rising with the sun. He wasn't particularly enjoying it, and frequently wished he was in a warm bed with Ulla, but he had ceased being bothered by it. The soldier in him had risen again.

"I believe the people would not be averse to Lord Rencarro governing the city," said Wulfner after a pause.

"Exactly. He led the defence of Argyllan until the Tarakans came, and then Lucetta's company. He must be a hero in their eyes."

Wulfner pulled at his beard again and frowned.

"You have some doubts, Wulfner? Please speak them. You have the ear of the King's Shield himself!" Torbal said with half a smile. "Now is your chance to help shape the realm."

Wulfner's eyebrows shot up and he blew out a breath.

"Well," he began slowly, "I was just thinking back to when this all started, after High King Sedmund's death. The Meridians marching west to Argyllan to…" He left the sentence unfinished.

Torbal laughed out loud, startling the other soldiers around him. "Wulfner, I may not be as perceptive and astute as my dear friend Sedmund was, but I am not without insight. It took me a while, I'll admit, but it is clear what he did. Rencarro effectively annexed Argyllan under the guise of protecting the region from raiders."

The surprise registered on Wulfner's face. The former soldier had clearly thought this was still an unconfirmed rumour that he would be out of place to voice.

Torbal continued, "But Rencarro misjudged Orben's cunning and patience. And he was blind to his officer's treachery. Then he was dealt a particularly cruel and ironic blow when the Throskaur actually came." Torbal shrugged. "Some may see that as poetic justice, but I must be practical if I am to be... steward of the throne till the realm returns to calm waters. I need a strong ruler in that port city. The Throskaur may be spent now as a fighting force but we cannot be sure."

Torbal put this down as a decision made in his mind. Rencarro should accept the proposal. Even if he didn't want to stay there forever, it would keep him active and an ally to the northwest. Torbal would promise Rencarro to begin negotiations with the Helligan leadership, but he truthfully didn't expect Orben to ever give up the city without a fight. The general turned back to Wulfner.

"You are a perceptive man yourself, Wulfner, to see what Rencarro was up to. Why weren't more people suspicious of his intentions, I wonder."

Wulfner answered immediately. "They were scared, my lord. Rumours were rampant. When the common folk, like myself, are in a state of fear, they are easily misled. You know the story of The Rotten Baron, my lord?"

Torbal nodded, remembering the tale was a favourite of one of his tutors when he was a lad. Wulfner kept speaking.

"The citizens of Silverland believed the baron's lies about who was to blame for their crumbling kingdom. The baron spread rumours of foreign agents and bandits everywhere, and the people were so eager to avoid responsibility for their own failings, they happily accepted all his falsehoods. They cast their king aside and welcomed the baron into their city. Only when the baron disappeared one night with all the wealth did they realise he had deceived them. Why did they believe the baron? Because he had sparked fear within them. He preyed upon the ignorance of the common people, and it must be said, also their prejudices, and presented himself as the one who could save them all." Wulfner sighed. "The folk in Argyllan saw Rencarro as a strong lord who could deliver them from an unseen peril. They saw what he wanted them to see."

"Smoke, my lord," came a voice from behind the general.

Torbal scanned the scene and saw indeed there were spires of smoke. But it was soon clear that it was not the smoke of burning homesteads but columns rising from chimneys.

"Somebody is home," said Torbal quietly. "Wyman, bring the Bladesung to arms," he ordered the legion Forwost.

Torbal halted his mount and Wyman began reeling off a string of orders. The Bladesung moved into action, dozens of soldiers splitting from the main body; four separate units of forty spearmen, twenty archers, twelve hobilars, and a command group of five, also on horseback. When each flank of the entire company was covered by two of these units, Torbal ordered a slow advance.

"Tell them to be alert, Wyman, but wait for orders."

The Forwost acknowledged the command and sent two of his captains to shadow the units.

Cyneburg approached Torbal and Wulfner on her mount, a majestic grey courser.

"My lady," said Wulfner, dipping his head in respect.

"Wulfner," she acknowledged. "Good of you to stay with us. I know you're not a soldier anymore and going home must have been the more attractive option."

The former soldier offered something of a smile. "I feel like I'm wound up in all this in more ways than one. I'd like to see it over and the realm back to normal. Too much blood has been spilt."

Torbal's sister nodded and clenched her fist. Cyneburg had taken Wulfner's comment as a bitter curse upon the Duthka and Unvasik, but Torbal knew there was more to that last statement. The big man, a former soldier, then a trader, then a guardian to two young ladies caught up in this storm, had been hinting at restraint. Wulfner had expressed concerns the day before, that bringing the full strength of the legions with them against the Duthka and Unvasik in Morak, bringing death to them all, would keep the cycle of vengeance turning. Torbal could see his point but he felt Wulfner had been too long away from military life. He hadn't gone soft, as some might say, but he had become tired of violence.

We all tire of conflict. But this is one battle that must be fought.

This had been an invasion of Ragnekai, on several fronts. There had been a massacre, the Bradlastax. Citizens of Morak had been turned into animals and thus condemned to death. This madman Seolta and his Unvasik allies were a threat to the entire realm. There could be no negotiations now, no calls for peace. The only outcomes possible here would be all of them in flight or feeding the worms.

"Look there, my lord!" cried Wyman.

Torbal followed the Forwost's pointing finger and saw a figure emerging from a farmhouse. He was still a distance away but a cloth covering his face was visible.

"Wyman, take ten riders and see what you can find out from that man. Keep your distance though. He possibly carries disease," said the general, these last few words bringing back the memory of thinking the beast-men at the ford were sick with their strange movement.

They were sick. Very sick.

Torbal sat back in his saddle and waited. He could see Wyman conversing with the man, the fellow gesturing wildly with his arms. The general then noticed others coming out from their homes, all wearing some kind of cover over their nose and mouth.

"Is it a plague, my lord?" enquired Wulfner beside him.

"We shall soon know," he replied grimly.

Wyman returned and gave his report.

"The farmer was surprised to see us, General, saying that a plague has erupted within the walls of Morak and it has become a city of the dead. They heard moaning and movement some nights ago, which may have been the mob we encountered at the ford. The villagers and farmers that live 'round here have mostly stayed within their homes, only going out when absolutely necessary and going nowhere near the city itself." Wyman paused. "They say Morak is cursed."

"May Thunor take this Seolta's head!" exclaimed Torbal, clenching his teeth. "He has sown lies and spread fear. I doubt there is any plague here. The rumour of it, though, has been enough to keep these families away from the city. Which may have been a good thing," he added with an exhalation. "Wyman, send pairs of soldiers to every homestead and farm in the area. Have them assure the people that there is no sickness and the region will soon be safe. But it's best they stay inside until we have rid Morak of these craven dogs. We move!" he cried to his captains.

As they advanced upon the city, its turrets now scraping the horizon, more common folk emerged from their homes and waved to the troops and shouted words of gratitude. The red and blue flags of Westhealfe were obviously a welcome sight. Word spread quickly. Torbal was pleased to see this. Nothing gave a soldier more courage than seeing grateful citizens cheering them on. It gave each man and woman carrying a spear or bow a sense of righteousness, a sense they were about to release these people from the grip of terror.

Wulfner clearly sensed it, too. "A good boost to the morale, my lord."

"Indeed, Wulfner. The words they shout will strengthen our resolve."

Torbal was impressed with Wulfner's general perceptiveness. He began to consider trying to persuade the man to re-join the legions, perhaps in a tutoring role. The younger men could learn a lot from him. Beornoth had spoken highly of Wulfner and it was clear he was of noble character. His thoughts faded as Morak rose ever higher before them.

Ugly city…

It had been built at a time when the northeast had been in a state of small-scale conflict, the soldiers under Sedmund's grandfather's rule involved in constant skirmishes with not only Duthka raiding parties and the odd Unvasik war-band, but also a particularly stubborn bandit-lord who had taken up residence just south of the Deadwood. It had been constructed as a fortress-city in some senses, the walls defensible and the approach to the main gate up a raised road. But under Eorthe's rule, the atmosphere had become something more suitable to making a life. Hundreds of citizens from Bregustol had left the over-crowded capital and come to settle in Morak. The farming had become bountiful and prosperous, and folk would say that the sun had finally shone through the murk that had hidden this region.

But the Winds had not blown kindly of late for the city. Torbal studied the walls before them. Tall, strong, and undamaged despite all that had happened here.

How did they get in?

The general called a halt and the huge force began to spread out, keeping a good distance from the wall. Cyneburg's nightmare in the city had taught them to be cautious. They would not just stroll in through the front gates.

Torbal frowned. *That's odd…*

Having come closer, he could now see the left side of the gates was half open. Cyneburg rode up to him, her Bradlastax in formation on the left flank. He pointed to the gates and she cast her eyes that way.

"Another trap," she growled.

"Maybe," responded Torbal. "But I see no movement whatsoever. Wyman, pass me your telescope."

The Forwost withdrew the looking device from his saddle bag and passed it over. Torbal raised it to his right eye and slowly tracked across the battlements. The only movement was that of crows. He handed the telescope to Cyneburg.

After a few moments of studying the walls that towered before them, she grunted in dissatisfaction.

"What do you make of it, Torb?"

"It would seem to be a trap but if they are watching, they must be able to see the size of the force we lead. Leaving the front gates open seems slightly foolish."

Wulfner coughed beside him. "My lord, my lady, if they have turned the rest of the city into those mindless beasts, it could be that a horde is just waiting to rush out as we approach," he cautioned.

Torbal considered this, recalling that terrible day at the ford. They had been caught unawares, though then, the beast-men rushing their ranks before anyone knew what was happening. He turned to his sister, eyebrows raised in question. She replied with little hesitation.

"We spring the trap. Carefully."

Torbal nodded. He beckoned Wyman over as Cyneburg ushered two of her captains to join her. The King's Shield gave his commands.

"Tight shield wall, slow approach and ready to open a channel so if those things do come hurtling out, they will run down an avenue into a killing zone. That zone will be the halberd troops, here at the bottom of this slope. Archers covering, eyes on the walls. And have the cavalry hang back to watch for any sortie from the walls farther around. Remember the piercing sound that not all can hear. If that comes, then we can be sure the beast-men will follow. To arms!"

Wyman saluted and hurried off. Torbal studied the city before him and still saw no motion except crows descending upon the summit of the walls. And he heard nothing. If those beasts were in there, the Duthka were keeping them quiet.

Wulfner coughed again.

"Wulfner, just say it, damn it! Enough with the polite coughing," he grumbled.

Wulfner nodded quickly. "Sorry, my lord. I'm just concerned that if there are beasts in there, and they charge, we will be killing citizens and soldiers of Morak."

Torbal knew he was right, but he had decided that very morning that those who had become beasts were no longer human and could not be saved.

"They are dead already," he said sadly.

The soldiers marched surely but slowly toward the gates. Torbal stared at the entrance, expecting it to burst wide open any moment.

Come and face us, you damned Duthka! He gritted his teeth in anticipation. *We are ready this time.*

Closer the soldiers marched, their captains shouting out commands to keep steady, hold the shields up, and be ready for anything.

Show yourselves!

The legions were now only twenty yards from the gates and still there was not the slightest hint of motion from within. Torbal glanced at Cyneburg and saw her anger was rising, but also saw the puzzlement he felt himself.

A score of soldiers from each legion broke off from the main group and cautiously approached the gates. Still nothing. Torbal gripped his reins with one hand and found his other hand was lightly encircling his sword grip, ready to withdraw it from its scabbard.

They wait till we are in the jaws, beneath the fangs.

The group of soldiers reached the gates and proceeded to slowly push them wide open. Torbal saw the courtyard through the portal, the one which had become a killing ground for Cyneburg and her Bradlastax. The gates were swung back fully now and still all was quiet. He looked at his sister.

"Are you ready?"

She nodded once, her eyes staring ahead, her jaw clenched.

"Wyman, send in the first unit, but have the gates held open and a clear path if they need to retreat."

The Forwost shouted out the orders and the troops were in motion again. The first unit entered the city cautiously, forming up in a circular defensive shape, archers in the middle of a ring of shields, bows trained upward.

"Send the next two," called out Torbal.

Slowly but surely, the Bladesung and Bradlastax entered Morak. As Torbal rode in, he glanced warily in all directions. The walls were unmanned, the stairways devoid of anyone, and the foremost buildings of the city emitting nothing but an almost insidious hush. The farmers outside the city had called it a city of the dead. Torbal couldn't argue with that sentiment.

Soon rank upon rank of soldier stood in the entrance courtyard of Morak, and still many were stationed outside and holding the gate. No ambush came. A nervous muttering swept through the men and women, they too no doubt feeling the eeriness of what should have been a bustling market town.

Torbal addressed them all in his commanding voice. "Stay alert! There are no ghosts here, but there may be beasts of a tragic nature. If capture of those poor souls is possible, then do so. But if you are in danger, defend yourselves. Do not hesitate. And if Unvasik or Duthka still walk within these walls, slay them without mercy."

Spears were clashed upon shields a single time in acknowledgement.

Where are you, Seolta? And where are the beasts you have created?

Torbal noticed Wulfner had dismounted and was surveying the upper walls, as if he expected there to be foes above them. The general followed his gaze and was suddenly reminded of Eorthe's fate: pushed from a walkway to fall until the rope around her neck brought her to a fatal stop. Cyneburg had wept tears of sorrow and uttered oaths of rage when she had recounted the horrific tale to him. He turned to find her. His sister was sitting upon her horse, absolutely still. Her Bradlastax warriors were all around her, battle-axes in hand, feet planted ready to fight.

Torbal signalled to Wyman.

"Begin spreading out. Slowly advance through the streets. Knock on doors but do not enter any building. We have stepped into the main trap and nothing has happened. Either there is no one here or this city is filled with a thousand smaller areas of ambush."

Wyman acknowledged the order and began to relay it to the troops. Torbal caught Cyneburg's eye and gave her a nod. She returned the gesture and kicked her mount into motion, leading her sisters down the main thoroughfare. Torbal called to Wulfner, telling him to follow them. The man nodded but did not remount his horse, instead trotting up to Torbal's side on foot.

Happy to be back on his own two feet, no doubt.

The city's Great Hall came into view before long and still all was quiet. If this was indeed a trap, then the Duthka were waiting very patiently. Waiting for as many of Torbal's force as possible to be within the city walls perhaps. Waiting to unleash the beast-men.

Wyman rode beside Torbal, his head leaning forward, listening. He raised a hand. Torbal raised his own hand high and the soldiers came to a shuffling halt.

"Do you hear it, my lord?"

"The whistle?" asked Torbal, his body tensing in anticipation of a surge of beast-men from all around them.

Wyman shook his head, closing his eyes and straining his ears. "Movement, a scuffling or scratching."

Torbal clenched the pommel of his sword in the cup of his hand. He looked ahead and saw the doors to the Great Hall were firmly shut, unlike the city gates.

This is it.
Torbal pointed ahead to the hall and Wyman nodded.
"Slow advance. Keep their backs covered."
Come and taste our iron, you evil demons.

CHAPTER 4

SVARD

24th Day of Maia, Five Days After Gimmweg Was Attacked

Seeing the Holy Sepulchre, the largest holy house in Bregustol, once more in the light of day brought the memories crashing back. Svard had watched from across the square as Erland and Stigr were murdered by the religious zealots. He had ordered Cuyler to stop Erland's suffering with an arrow, and that act of mercy had bred a whole new, decidedly unholy mix of problems. The First Ranger would have preferred to stay away from this eyesore, but he was effectively working with Worsteth now, to try to salvage something from this mess, so personal feelings were a luxury he simply couldn't afford.

He quietly cursed under his breath as he saw the crowds approaching the True Sons' *glorious* building. There were as many as there had been that day Svard had lost his two captains, but today they were not just milling around and waiting; today they were filing into the huge church.

A mustering? That Magen fellow does seem to be calling for a holy war. Against whom though?

Svard shook his head. He felt lately that even the Dark Raven had tired of him, and he was now being tormented by the Meridian Widow. Whereas the Helligan Raven was the bringer of death, Svard had heard that the crone deity delighted in cruel games. Ever since that last night drinking with Lorken, it seemed as though some malicious power was taking a perverse pleasure in throwing all manner of misfortune his way, and generally kicking up a shit-storm in Ragnekai.

He had failed to protect Lorken, his lord had been false with him, two of his captains were dead, and now he was making deals with the Royal Chamberlain of the Rihtgellen kingdom, who was himself at the apparent mercy of forces beyond his control. Svard remembered Cuyler muttering *Some game* when they were both with Worsteth.

Some game indeed…

Svard moved forward and joined the orderly press, nodding grimly to pilgrims, workers, and even young boys.

The Ever-Father calling the young to arms? The realm really has entered dark waters.

He didn't need to be a fortune-teller to know this would all end badly, worse than the black pit they were all in now. Sending untrained men and boys into battle was as good as throwing half of them into a god's giant meat grinder. Even the city guard in Meridia, who should have had a few ounces of skill under their belt, had been swept aside by the Sentinels without much trouble. Worshippers with clubs and knives going up against Unvasik with battle-axes was a slaughter waiting to happen.

The Helligan First Ranger sighed quietly. He hoped he would come out of this alive. If he did, when this was all over and he was back in Gamle Hovestad, Svard decided he would entice Kailen to some dinner and ale, and hope that they might find that spark again. If so, he would ask her to join him on a trip south to the port of Hurtig, maybe take a boat to the Belfri Isles. There was a part of him that was contemplating leaving Gamle Hovestad and the Rangers for good. He felt very little loyalty to Orben anymore.

"Brothers, rejoice as you enter the Holy Sepulchre!"

A senior monk, by the look of the silver chain around his neck, was greeting the throng of eager men. He was waving them in, patting some on the shoulder, tussling the hair of boys who were no more than fifteen years and looking very pleased with himself in general.

Unrest is certainly bringing new folk into the congregation...

Svard was three back from this man, waiting behind a couple of dishevelled fellows, their odour tickling Svard's nasal passages. He probably hadn't smelt so wonderful himself when he met Worsteth two days ago, having not had a bath since that ice-cold one in the river crossing. The chamberlain had given him a generous amount of coin though, and he had some to spare after buying more rope. So now he was clean, shaven, fed, and rested. But very much alone.

"Ever-Father be praised, just look at all these fine men answering the call!"

The man was looking directly at Svard now and he tensed. There was no way anyone would recognise his face, and if he was more careful with what he said, he should be just one more *Brother* seeking to please his god.

Ever-Father, Ever-Father, Ever-Father, not bloody All-Father, you fool!

"Praise the Ever-Father!" Svard blurted.

The welcoming Brother beamed with delight at this apparent outburst of worship. He ushered the two in front through and clapped Svard on the shoulder.

"Ah, a strong man I see. May the Ever-Father bless you with the strength and courage to defeat the Unvasik hordes!"

Not what I had in mind. Sounds like they're intent on digging their own graves though...

Svard wondered if many of these men here had any knowledge of the Unvasik. He doubted it. If only half of the people here had been told even a few stories about Unvasik raids, they wouldn't be flocking into a huge church, pledging to meet the giants in battle.

"There is wine and bread within," called the holy man.

Svard smiled.

Ahhh, that's why these lads are eager to get through the door. Nothing like free grog to bring in all the waifs and strays.

The First Ranger figured the majority here would drift away after having had their fill and the True Sons would be left less than encouraged by their mustering efforts. There would no doubt be a few desperate men with a desire to improve their chances in the afterlife, who would follow these holy men to their deaths. Svard was fairly sure he'd be quaffing ale with Lorken when his time came. He swallowed a lump in his throat as he recalled many nights laughing with his friend.

"The Ever-Father touches us all," said the priest gently, a hand patting Svard's shoulder.

First Warrior, save me from these fools!

Svard finally got into the Holy Sepulchre and took in his surroundings. His eyes nearly burst out of his head when he saw figures in grey passing out wine. He casually sidled up closer to one and saw it was indeed one of those Grey Sisters or whatever they were called. That struck Svard as odd, to say the least. Witnessing the murder of a True Son in cold blood hadn't exactly given Svard the impression that the two holy orders were on friendly terms.

What are they doing here?

The True Sons seemed to find nothing untoward about their presence but were treating them with something bordering on disdain.

"Sisters, hurry up and quench our thirsts, Ever-Father above! And be sure to hold still your wagging tongues when Magen speaks!" scolded one True Son.

Svard rolled his eyes. The Grey Sisters he had encountered weren't exactly loud, apart from those two who had been enjoying each other, so it seemed a bit unnecessary to berate them so.

Svard noted that this Magen was going to make a speech. Would he be sending forth the True Sons on a crusade to the Unvasiktok region? To the Royal Mines? Or was this all a ruse and he was about to wrestle control of the city away from Worsteth in the name of the Ever-Father? Svard would listen to the religious lunatic, ask a few questions of True Sons who had drunk a decent amount of grog, and try to find out who had murdered Eswic. And also try and figure out why in the name of the First Warrior these nuns in grey were serving wine here.

Everything is so damn complicated in this city...

Svard jumped as he became aware of a figure at his side. It was a Grey Sister, with a tray upon which were three goblets of wine.

Creepy!

She raised the tray slightly, offering one. Svard took a goblet and smiled a thanks. The woman's face was in shadow so he couldn't be sure she returned the gesture. He wondered if she had a shaven head like those other two. And what were the markings on their heads? Some sign of their adulation for...

Who do they worship anyway?

Svard realised he had no idea what god or gods the Grey Sisterhood worshipped. Maybe his darkest suspicions were correct, and they were witches from some secret coven. He shook his head and tried to clear his thoughts. Letting his imagination run wild about black arts and sultry women was a distraction he didn't need.

Svard lifted the goblet to his lips, figuring a bit of grog might settle him.

A gong crashed, startling him. He lowered the wine untouched and looked to where the sound had come from. Figures were climbing stairs to a raised platform. A hush was settling upon the gathered men, a good few hundred here by Svard's reckoning and no women he could see, save the Sisters giving out wine.

"Brothers!" came a cry.

Bastard!

It was definitely the same man who had condemned his captains. This was the Magen scumbag Worsteth had told him about. This was someone Svard would like to send to the Dark Raven given half a chance.

"We are gathered here today to answer the call of the Ever-Father!" he shouted, his hands shooting up and his head falling back as if in divine ecstasy.

Raven's arse, this slug is full of it...

"The realm is in peril!"

The congregation muttered around Svard, many nodding vigorously. Svard raise the goblet again, thinking he was in for some mild purgatory here, listening to the fool's rant.

"Worsteth…"

Svard raised an eyebrow, lowered his cup again, and waited for what was to follow.

On to Worsteth already, huh? No time for how glorious the All-Father is?

Svard rolled his eyes at his own ineptitude.

Ever-Father! Damn, I'm not cut out for clandestine work.

"Worsteth is a coward!" Magen cried. Booing and hissing followed. Svard shook his head. *Mummer's farce!*

"But no concern of ours," continued the holy leader.

Interesting…

"The peril lies beyond these walls!"

Assenting cries burst forth, accompanied by a fair amount of coughing and what sounded like someone bringing up their wine. Svard saw a couple of men doubling over.

That's what happens when you just hand out the drink!

It seemed like Worsteth wasn't in any immediate danger then, but the ranger kept listening. Magen was leading up to something here. Svard raised his cup to finally take a sip.

"Oi, careful!"

Someone had lurched into him and knocked the goblet from his hands.

Drunken oaf!

The man grabbed Svard's arms to steady himself. His head came up and he stared at the First Ranger.

Oh shit…

PART FOUR

CHAPTER 1

LUNYAI

23rd Day of Maia, Four Days After Gimmweg Was Attacked

Lunyai found her father brushing down Ahoni, singing quietly while he did so. It felt strange to be with him in a village so far from the Tarakan Plains. Her stomach tightened as she realised she would soon have to say goodbye to Emiren and return to their home. She would see her mother and her people again, but her heart ached to think of being so far away from the fiery-haired girl with whom she had been through so much. And with the realm seemingly at war, she knew the future of Kayah was far from certain.

"Good morning, Father," she said, hugging him from behind.

"And a good morning it is, my daughter. Yaai blesses the lands with her warmth this day, and the Grey Ones are off somewhere," he replied, turning and holding her tightly to him. "I thank the All-Mother and Her children that you are back with me, Lunyai. Your journey has been fraught with dangers few Tarakans have known, and yet it has brought new…" Songaa paused and looked uncomfortable. Lunyai stiffened in his embrace. "…friendships that I suspect Tlenaii knows more about than Yaai," He gave her a smile, but she saw something else in his eyes.

Lunyai pulled back from Songaa and turned away, her cheeks burning. Her father knew she had snuck out from Kall's home last night and seemed to have guessed where she went.

Lunyai had gone to comfort Emiren after her visit to the inn, climbing in through the Fallowden girl's window. Her fiery-haired friend had seemed hollow and lost. The Tarakan tried to get her to talk but all Emiren said was that it was all her fault. Lunyai knew this couldn't be true but understood people blamed themselves for trage-dies. She had turned Emiren's face to hers as they lay there and kissed her softly. Then again, their lips lingering and their hands tightening. The world had then seemed to miss one breath and the two of them let their feelings flood forth, exploring each other with an intensity Lunyai had never known, the Tarakan lady experiencing an ecstasy she didn't know existed. She had left Emiren sleeping peacefully and crept back out of the window. Lunyai hoped their Duthka friend, Moryn, had not heard them in their passion from where he slept in the next room. She took a deep breath and returned to face her father.

"We are more than friends, Father," she whispered, looking him in the eyes.

Songaa's body tensed and Lunyai felt her world teeter on the brink.

Please do not be angry, Father.

Then Songaa relaxed and whispered, "I know, Lunyai. Your fa-ther may be getting older and his eyes not as sharp as once they were, but I am not blind yet." He smiled gently. "The All-Mother knows it is not what your mother and I saw in your future, but I can see you shine with Yaai *and* Tlenaii's light when you are with Emiren. That is something to be cherished."

His smile faded then, and he cupped her face in his hands. Lu-nyai felt the warmth in his calloused palms and was suddenly a little girl again, back from running around their tribe's settlement, out of breath.

Songaa spoke again. "We must return to the Plains and Emiren must stay here. You know this." Lunyai opened her mouth to speak but Songaa held up a finger. "I am not saying say you will never see her again, but you will have to say goodbye for a time. The realm is in conflict, my daughter, so pray to Tlenaii to give you the strength to weather any storms that come."

Tears touched Lunyai's eyes. She sniffed and nodded. "Not even the All-Mother knows the future."

"No, She does not," agreed Songaa. "But She and Her children do give us the heart and mind to dream of a future and seek it." He hugged her fiercely. "You must do this, Lunyai. Dream of the future you want, ride after it, but be aware the shortest road may not be open to you. It may be a long journey."

Her thoughts swirled and she began imagining many different futures, some upon the Plains, some here in Fallowden, and one where she stood at the summit of the Sacred Mount, looking out upon a burning realm, the Thunder Rider's hooves a deafening noise all around. She inhaled deeply and let her father's love calm her.

Where is Emiren this morning?

Lunyai hadn't seen her yet and began to let her mind roll. She suddenly felt anxious that Emiren would feel differently now that Yaai had risen and was looking down upon them. She looked around at the village of Fallowden, seeing people moving here and there. Smiles were given generously but they faded as the villagers returned to their tasks, the dark cloud of recent events hanging over them all.

Emiren, are you still sleeping?

Lunyai shrugged and turned to help her father with Ahoni and the mount she was riding, Neii'Ne. Choondei had insisted Lunyai take her, assuring the young lady that his mare could ride like a gale from the Western Sea if the need arose. The horse was beautiful and Lunyai began singing to her.

"Lunyai, there you are!" came Emiren's voice. Lunyai whirled around to see her friend hurrying toward them.

"Good morning, Songaa."

"And good morning to you, Emiren. You look troubled..."

"Have you seen Moryn this morning?"

Lunyai frowned. "I thought he stayed at your home."

Emiren nodded. "He did. We said goodnight to him, but he wasn't there this morning. The book is also gone so I thought he would be out somewhere studying it."

"Emiren!" came a shout. They all turned and Lunyai saw a man striding towards them. He was of a similar height to her father, shoulder-length hair tied back loosely, and a leather vest with dark stains here and there. He bore an expression that frightened Lunyai in its intensity.

"This is Banseth," whispered her father in the Tarakan tongue.

Lunyai held back a gasp. She knew who Banseth was, but this was the first time she had seen him. The Battle of Argyllan had claimed many lives and Banseth's close friend Loranna had been one of them. From what Emiren's mentor from the hospice had said on the road to Fallowden, the man was suffering greatly.

"You are here," said Banseth, one hand carrying a long staff. "The front gates were unbarred this morning and I thought you had headed into Argol early. With the realm at war, that would have been unwise. But…you are safe."

Emiren hugged Banseth.

"Thank you. We are safe. The gates were open?" she asked.

Banseth frowned. "Not open but the bar was off, and…" The Fallowden sentry suddenly looked around. "Where is the other one who came back with you, Emiren? The Duthka man."

Emiren exchanged a look with Lunyai. "I can't find him, Ban. He stayed at our home last night but was gone when I awoke. We don't know where he is…"

Banseth stiffened. "We can assume your friend is the one who left the gate unlocked. Tell him when he returns that he cannot just come and go as he pleases, not with…not with death everywhere." He turned before they could respond and stalked off.

Emiren sighed. "My uncle told me he blames himself for Loranna's death, reasoning he didn't see she was badly wounded until it was too late. I think he has taken the safety of every citizen of Fallowden as his responsibility now."

Lunyai looked around and could almost sense the fear now permeating this village. A young man had been murdered in the forest nearby, Emiren had been pursued by those who would have killed her, and a lady who had vowed to protect the community had lost her life defending those in a city farther north. Lunyai silently thanked Yaai that her father and the other Tarakans had survived the attack.

"So where is Moryn?" asked Songaa, hands on his hips.

"And why did he take the book?" added Emiren.

Lunyai was beginning to worry about the Duthka sailor.

"We should find him," her father said.

"Where is he?" Emiren asked, waving her hands around in all directions. "I dreamt about him last night." She paused. "At least I think it was a dream."

"You dream about sailors a lot?" teased Lunyai.

Emiren shoved her playfully. "Only the rough ones."

Lunyai laughed and they continued ambling along one of the many paths within the leafy haven of Argol forest. Banseth and her father were searching the main paths together, whilst Kall and another hunter were looking for signs of Moryn in the areas where they set traps for game. Emiren had said she would take Lunyai and walk the areas off the visible trails, reasoning Moryn might have got lost if he had wandered without thought. And Tarak was roaming by himself somewhere, possibly just chasing rabbits, Lunyai thought with a grin.

Emiren blew out a breath. "Do you think he just left, without saying goodbye?"

"I worry that he may have heard us last night," Lunyai whispered, feeling her cheeks blush. She looked at Emiren and saw she too was feeling more conscious in the light of day.

They walked on in silence for a few yards.

"We weren't that loud," her friend finally mumbled. "And even if he did, why would he run off?" she asked, clearly not picking up on what Lunyai was implying.

"I think he may have become…sad," Lunyai offered, unsure how to put it. "Sad that it was not him with you."

Emiren stared at her. "Are you saying Moryn wanted to bed me?!" she blurted, her face a wide-eyed grin. "Lunyai! Moryn is a gentleman!"

Lunyai stopped walking and put her hands on her hips in mock indignation. "So, I am not a gentleman?!"

Emiren put her arms round Lunyai's neck and pulled her in. "You are most certainly not a gentleman. You are a siren from the sea, or whatever that song was about," she said, then kissed Lunyai on the lips. A tingle ran through the Tarakan's body, as it always did when they kissed. She brushed Emiren's hair away from her eyes and sighed.

"My father knows."

Emiren's face changed instantly. Shock, maybe fear.

"He heard me come back last night and seems to have guessed the rest," Lunyai continued.

Emiren tensed, her hand gripping Lunyai's. "Was he angry?"

Lunyai smiled. "No. It is maybe difficult for him to ask me about it, but I did not feel any anger."

Emiren's shoulders slowly relaxed. They began moving once more up the trail, the rustle beneath their feet a truly peaceful sound compared to the horror of the battle within the Sacred Mount and all the other days of danger they had faced.

Emiren spoke, her voice laced with anxiety. "I do not think my parents are ready to hear it yet. Fallowden and this whole area has strict views on…this kind of thing," she said, her hand squeezing and releasing Lunyai's in a steady rhythm. "There were two carpenters in Fallowden some years back, who everyone suspected were more than friends. One was supposed to marry Master Aine's daughter and carry on the family business, his father being a carpenter too." Emiren sighed. "They left, though. Nobody told them to go but I think they knew they couldn't have the future they wanted in Fallowden. Mum told me they headed east to Meridia, where I believe it is not uncommon for men to love men, and women to love…"

Lunyai stopped walking and turned to Emiren, whose words had faltered. The Tarakan's heart was pounding. They had lain together in passion but what Emiren seemed to be implying was shaking her. Nobody had ever said they loved Lunyai except her parents, and likewise she had never said it to anyone.

"Emiren…"

The redhead put a hand to Lunyai's face and pulled her close, kissing her gently.

"I do, I lo—"

Emiren stopped. Lunyai tensed.

"Did you hear that?" whispered Emiren urgently. "Listen!"

Lunyai strained her ears but all she really wanted was to move back three moments in time and for Emiren to finish what she began saying.

I want to hear those words…

Voices.

Lunyai stared at Emiren, eyes widening. Emiren's face broke into a curious smile.

"Moryn? Talking to himself?"

Lunyai listened again. She cocked her head. *No, there is more than one voice.*

"Not Moryn, I think," she said. Emiren nodded, her smile replaced with a furrowed brow. She gestured with her head in the direction of the voices. Lunyai shrugged and motioned for Emiren to lead the way. Emiren took a step, then stopped. She raised a finger to her lips and made a shushing sound. Lunyai rolled her eyes and pushed her friend forward. It was either Moryn speaking to one of the hunters, or her father and Banseth.

She followed in Emiren's wake, her eyes gazing at the fiery hair of the Fallowden girl. It was such a beautiful colour, burning like the most glorious evenings when Yaai sunk slowly beneath the horizon and cast Her fire upon The Grey Ones. And yet it also seemed to glow gently like the embers of a Tarakan fire after Naaki and Imala's stories. Lunyai reached out a hand to run her fingers through it but caught herself as the voices drifted to them once more.

That is not the common tongue, nor the Tarakan language!

Emiren had halted too. She turned to her friend and her frown deepened.

"What language is that?" Emiren's voice was so soft, Lunyai barely heard her. She shook her head. Emiren pointed to the left, not ahead where the voices were drifting from. Lunyai nodded and the two of them picked their way through a cluster of what Lunyai thought were cedar trees, the aroma pleasantly massaging her nostrils.

The voices were closer now. There was a harshness to the language. Emiren stopped and crouched down, pulling Lunyai with her.

Both listened and a strange feeling began to rise within Lunyai that this language did not belong here in the forest.

"Jurr vid jun yijah?"

"Hvernig wej yijah!"

"Verdum vid finna yordak Dujka. Moryn."

"Moryn wej petturi! Magwajah!"

Lunyai gasped and grabbed Emiren's arm.

"Did I just hear *Moryn*?" she whispered.

The look on Emiren's face told her she had not imagined it. Who could be talking about Moryn in a strange tongue?

Emiren pointed ahead and made a creeping motion with her hands. Lunyai inhaled sharply and gave her friend one clear nod. Then the two moved slower than a Grey One on a windless day, inching closer to the voices. Emiren's hand again pulled Lunyai down, whilst her other gently pushed aside the leafy mass of a bush. Lunyai peered through the gap. Her body stiffened.

Tlenaii! Who are they?

A group of men were sitting or standing in a small grove, talking in low voices and looking around nervously. Lunyai saw one of them was lying on the forest floor, moaning. The Tarakan's body tensed as she saw the man had been injured badly, a ruddy brown stain covering his bare chest. She winced as she spotted what had to be bone protruding from his left side.

She wanted to tear her eyes away from this gathering, but she was like a Tarakan hare who suddenly found itself staring at a drawn bow, frozen in terror. The men were all hurt in some way, cuts on arms and backs, and hands clutching stomachs. They looked tired and haggard, but all gripped weapons of some sort; axes, long knives or short spears. But it was their faces that shot sparks of fear into Lunyai's being.

Black markings round the eyes and beards of all colours and lengths. One was red and forked, another blue and long, passing through silver rings, and one with numerous strands, some black and some yellow.

Her father had spoken little of the Battle for Argyllan, but he had mentioned their enemy had looked like *Yenali* demons.

"Throskaur," she croaked.

Emiren whipped her head round and her mouth opened to speak. But the badly injured man let out a load groan and one standing began to snarl angrily at him, his arms gesturing in all directions.

"Haltu kafti, mavad'chah! Qoh munu finna vidu!"

The man was clearly in agony and his moaning did not stop. The man who had berated him suddenly knelt down, slapped a hand over his mouth, then slit his throat.

Lunyai and Emiren both yelped. All the living Throskaur whirled, their eyes darting to the general area where the two young ladies were crouched.

"All-Mother..." breathed Lunyai.

"Spirits..."

Lunyai grabbed Emiren's hand and pulled her up, dragging her away and breaking into a run as they cleared the cluster of cedars. She heard no cries of anger from behind but something much worse: pursuit. The Throskaur were chasing them.

Yaai, help us now!

"This way!" shouted Emiren, and Lunyai felt her arm being jerked away from the direction she had been heading. She let Emiren lead them, having faith her friend knew the forest well and could take them to safety.

Hand in hand, Emiren in front, they leapt through the woodland, swerving past larger trees, dodging smaller ones and skipping over great roots that groaned out from the ground. Lunyai prayed her father and the others were close.

Or should I pray they are far away from these men?

"Up that tree!" cried Emiren, pointing to a sturdy oak ahead.

Emiren was up it like a Tarakan vole scuttling up a *sodizin* pole. She reached down a hand and Lunyai grabbed it, her friend's strength allowing her to haul herself upwards.

Lunyai heard their pursuit crash through undergrowth, less than one verse of the Tarakalo behind. She turned her head in panic and her grip slipped. Lunyai's breath left her as she dropped, her hand scraping against the bark, then her legs crumpling beneath her as her feet hit the spreading roots of the tree. She sprawled backwards, her slung bow digging painfully into her lower back. The world seemed to cartwheel above her and then finally her body gasped for air.

She looked up and saw Emiren in the tree.

Lunyai struggled to her feet. Voices and the sound of heavy movement entered the sphere of the great oak. Lunyai glanced up at Emiren, glanced at the Throskaur, and made a decision.

She ran.

She plunged into the forest and ran like she had never run before. Leaves tight on their branches brushed her face as her arms flailed wildly in front of her, pushing Argol's many fingers away from her.

Lunyai heard the sounds of pursuit and sobbed with a bizarre sense of relief.

They are coming after me. Emiren will be safe.

The Tarakan girl was soon lost though. She had no idea even which direction she was heading but kept running, her lungs begging her to stop and rest. But to rest would be to give herself over to an uncertain fate. From what little she knew of Argyllan's battle, the Throskaur had no mercy. And as she and Emiren had just witnessed, even towards their own kin. Now she was a danger to them. If she made it back to Fallowden, the villagers would come out in numbers.

Her mind rolled as she ran, and she had the sinking feeling she had somehow double-backed on herself. Lunyai gritted her teeth and kept going. What else could she do? A thought came to her and she did what she should have done as soon as they fled from the raiders in the first place. She screamed.

In the Tarakan language. In the common tongue. She cried out, the strain slowing her as her body struggled to cope with the combined exertion.

"Father!"

She slid between two trees that leaned away from each other.

"Father, help me!"

She pushed through brush that had grown almost as tall as herself.

"Father!"

Lunyai bounded into a clearing and stumbled to a halt. She could hear no sound and that was strangely frightening, as if the forest was also afraid of these men. Lunyai gulped in the air her body had been desperate for these last moments. She took in her surroundings.

Lunyai's eyes swept left to right, searching between the green leaves, the pale grey trunks and the darker patches of amber seeping from the silent sentinels. So much beauty was there. The green of emeralds, the rich brown of the earth, and the silver lines that slid down here and there.

Blue.

Lunyai saw blue just beyond a tall, slender tree that possessed no low-lying branches.

A blue that was not of nature.

A blue beard.

The Throskaur saw her too and stared.

Lunyai couldn't help but moan.

"Father..." she whimpered, her voice fading on the one word she spoke.

The Throskaur said something. Lunyai couldn't understand but she felt the menace in his tone. But there was a trembling there also.

He is scared too.

She gasped as he raised his axe and pointed it at her. The weapon wobbled in his unsteady hand. Lunyai felt her legs weakening. Her bow was slung over her back, but she dared not even reach for it.

He's crying...

The man wiped at his eyes angrily. Words began to tumble from the Throskaur. Words that seemed full of hate yet croaking with fear.

"Dujka sailor, where? Moryn where?!" The common tongue. He lowered the axe and hung his head, reverting to his own language.

Lunyai felt a strange sense of pity for the man and let her hands fall to her sides. She cocked her head. Then spoke. "Can you understand me?" she asked softly in the common tongue.

His eyes widened and a wailing moan erupted from his throat. He launched himself at her.

Lunyai turned to run but fell backwards, her feet catching upon each other. She crashed to the forest floor. Her eyes clamped shut as she waited for the blow to come.

There was a thumping sound. And a grunt.

Lunyai rolled over and saw the Throskaur lying in a heap to the right. And a wolf poised over him, a growl emanating from deep within the beast.

Tarak?

Tarak!

Emiren's wolf was between her and the fallen Throskaur. The animal had bowled the man over and now looked ready to rip him to pieces. Lunyai struggled to stand.

"Tarak," she breathed.

Then came the sound of people approaching.

Father?

Four more Throskaur pushed through the trees, weapons in hand. Lunyai felt the world darken, as if the Grey Ones were covering Yaai with a ferocity unknown till now. The raiders looked at their comrade on the floor, took in the wolf now baring its teeth to them and began to warily spread out. Tarak's head whipped left to right, jaws gnashing but not moving from where he stood.

He guards me.

Lunyai moved to bring her bow round, praying to the All-Mother that the men were focused on Tarak and would not see.

"*Gajtu ka!*"

An order. Two moved to attack Tarak, one advanced towards Lunyai, the other stooped to help the man Tarak had knocked down. Lunyai scrambled with her bow. Too slow. Too late. The Throskaur raised his axe.

A whoosh of sound, a dull thud, and the Throskaur fell back, his axe falling from his hand and an arrow in his chest.

Lunyai looked around, wildly trying to understand what had happened. She saw her father advancing through the trees to their right, nocking an arrow to his bow.

He released and another Throskaur was felled, one of the two stalking Tarak.

The wolf leaped at his second assailant, jaws clamping around the man's throat.

The one who had given the order pushed his comrade away and brandished a spear. He began howling in his own language, and it was answered by similar cries from farther ahead. Then came the sounds of people crashing through the undergrowth and trees.

"Lunyai." Her father's voice was hard. "Take your bow and shoot. Do not hesitate." His words were a command, uttered in a tone she had never heard before. A tone that said she must obey. Her father withdrew another arrow as he came to stand beside them.

There was a shriek from ahead and Lunyai looked up to see the two Throskaur that were still standing, turn to face someone charging from their right.

Banseth.

The Fallowden sentry was a blur of motion as he charged into them, his long staff striking the head of the leader, then Tarak's first victim. Both Throskaur collapsed to the forest floor. Banseth slammed his staff twice into each man's face, creating a bloody mess.

More Throskaur emerged from the trees, each carrying a vicious looking blade. One immediately fell with an arrow in his throat. Songaa's voice came calmly but sternly to Lunyai.

"You must do it, my daughter."

Feeling like she was in a trance, Lunyai gripped her bow and pulled out an arrow. She raised both to her eye-line and took aim. Her hand was steady. She focused on a man with a green beard, within which were woven bones. She inhaled, then released. The arrow flew.

The Throskaur clutched at the arrow in his chest, sank to his knees, and wheezed something at Lunyai, his eyes full of hatred. It turned to fear and Lunyai could see he knew he would die. She had sent him to his death, just as she had done with that Duthka in the Sacred Mount.

"Forgive me," she said.

"Again, Lunyai. Do not stop," commanded her father.

Banseth was snarling at the new Throskaur, at least five in number.

"Come on, Throskaur scum! You took Loranna from us and I will take your lives!" He launched himself into their midst, his staff twirling. He was being reckless and also preventing them from releasing their arrows. The risk of hitting Banseth was too great.

Three more emerged from the shadows of the forest and advanced toward Lunyai and Songaa.

"Tlenaii save us!"

One snarled and raised a long knife. A thunk sounded as a small axe appeared in the side of his head, silencing him. His eyes rolled back into his skull and he toppled over sideways.

A roar of anger and two figures burst forth from behind them, one brandishing a spear, the other an axe. Kall and the other hunter who had been helping them search for Moryn. Lunyai froze, unable to register what was happening. Beside her, her father raised his bow and let loose an arrow. Another Throskaur fell.

Tarak took down another, rolling out of sight with the man. Lunyai heard a yelp from where they had tumbled.

No, no, please no...

The hunters rushed past Lunyai and engaged the remaining Throskaur. She turned to see Banseth smashing another's head to a bloody pulp. Her stomach churned. She swallowed the bile and raised her bow again with a new arrow.

"Forgive me, All-Mother," she whispered as she released. Her arrow flew and struck a Throskaur who was moving to engage Banseth. It pierced his midriff. He looked down at it, his body shuddered, and he fell to the forest floor, now awash with blood and human bodies.

Songaa's bow twanged again and another fell.

Lunyai looked around and saw the hunters and Banseth had killed the last three. She numbly started counting the dead bodies. Then stopped. *One death of a loved one is a world dying for those that are left behind. And all of us, the Throskaur too, are loved by someone.*

Lunyai gasped as Tarak limped out from the trees. His maw was a sticky mess, his teeth a dark crimson. He was hurt. Lunyai moved to him. She tripped on the leg of a dead Throskaur, sprawled out in the heart of this forest.

The Tarakan lady found herself on her hands and knees facing the wolf. He padded over to her, a whine in his throat. She grabbed him and hugged the animal tightly.

Emiren!

Lunyai wobbled to her feet, her eyes darting this way and that.

She jumped as Banseth let out a howl. It was filled with rage and agony.

"Bastards! May the Barren Isles burn and sink into the sea!"

Lunyai turned this way and that. Emiren wasn't here. She had hidden. Was she safe?

Banseth began sobbing, the rush of battle falling away to the misery of this reality. Lunyai felt numb. Her hands trembled.

In the corner of her eye, she saw Kall approach her father.

"Your bows save our people again," he gasped. Lunyai turned to look at the hunter. He was staring at the blood on his axe. His body tensed and then he vomited onto the forest floor. The other hunter had his eyes clenched shut.

Songaa placed a hand on Lunyai's shoulder and looked around. "Are there more, do you think?" he asked, almost to himself.

Emiren.

She turned to her father and felt as if the forest was dying around her, leaves withering and bark peeling. Her stomach churned.

"Father..." she said, her voice a hoarse whisper. "Emiren..."

Banseth's voice was loud.

"There could be more," he said, a tremor in his words. "We should get back to Fallowden, gather more people, then set out to patrol the forest. I thought they had all been slaughtered..."

Songaa held Lunyai. "Emiren? Where is she?"

"She hid... I ran. I left her," said Lunyai, her words falling and her body beginning to shake.

A twig snapped. Songaa pushed Lunyai away and whipped an arrow to his bow, raising the weapon to the sound.

Emiren pushed past a tree and entered the clearing. A clearing where death had come and the blood of the fallen now seeped into the soil and roots.

Lunyai cried out and ran out to her. She grabbed Emiren and babbled apologies for leaving her. The Tarakan pulled away after a moment and she saw the disbelief and lack of comprehension on Emiren's face.

A whine from Tarak brought the Fallowden girl back to the moment. She cried out and fell to her knees, hugging the wolf.

Songaa crouched by her and began to examine the wound.

"He was cut but not seriously, I think. Yaai be praised, your friend here saved Lunyai. Saved us all."

Silence fell upon the group. What could be said? Lunyai and her father, Emiren and Tarak, Banseth and the two hunters were alive. Around them were the dead. Many dead. Two of the dead Throskaur had been felled by her own arrows. She had taken life once more. Lunyai knew if she hadn't, her father or one of the others might be lying there instead. But she had taken everything from them, each in the space it took to take one breath.

A sound came to her ears and she was confused, not recognising it. Her eyes caught movement and she saw more than one of the fallen Throskaur moving. They were still alive and moaning quietly, their wounds an agony.

Banseth stepped forward.

"Songaa, take Emiren and Lunyai away. We will finish this," he said over his shoulder, his voice bearing no sign of mercy.

Songaa pulled his daughter with him and motioned for Emiren to come. They moved onto a path. Lunyai tried to shut her ears to the sounds of the Throskaur lives being ended but couldn't.

All-Mother, what have we become?

The company made their way back to the village, threading their way carefully through the trees on a trail Emiren knew would take them to Fallowden more quickly than the main path. Not one word was spoken. Lunyai's eyes darted back and forth, scanning the trees for movement or a flash of colour from their ghastly beards.

They were soon back. Banseth rushed ahead into the village, his voice shouting out to the people of Fallowden.

"To arms! There are still raiders in the forest. Everyone, take up a weapon!"

Lunyai passed through the gates and felt a wave of relief. They might not be completely safe from danger but at least here they would see it coming. Argol Forest could hide an enemy in its sighing depths.

Soon villagers were gathering, all carrying some kind of weapon, be it club, spear, or knife. A hand fell on Lunyai's shoulder.

"You will stay here, Lunyai," said her father. "I will go with Banseth and the others and make sure there are no more."

"No, Father," she breathed, shaking her head.

"Do not worry for me. You saw Banseth. He is equal to ten of those demons. And look," he said, pointing to a group that was now standing in a crescent around the Fallowden sentry, "we have numbers this time."

Lunyai hugged her father, then watched as the group left through the gates, heading back into Argol. Their faces were grim and Lunyai saw something dark in Banseth's eyes. She knew he had killed with un-bridled hate. She turned to where Emiren was tending to Tarak, helped by her mother who had rushed from their home with Emiren's father to see what the commotion had been.

Quint approached Lunyai.

"Will this storm ever end?" he asked, his voice devoid of hope.

Lunyai stared at the ground, chaotic swirls of foot-prints visible in the dust. "I don't know," she whispered.

She looked up to see Quint shaking his head. His kindly face was wracked with sorrow. Lunyai inhaled deeply, reached out and took one of his hands.

"The storms on the Western Sea rage like it is the end of the world itself." She offered a smile. "But they do not last. Calm waters return."

Quint slowly nodded. "So, we must be strong and wait out this storm."

Lunyai felt hope was kindled within Emiren's father but struggled to birth a flame in her own heart.

"Tlenaii and Yaai will protect us, and your Spirits will watch over us," she said, giving Quint's hand a squeeze. Then turned her head away, tears threatening to reveal themselves.

For the first time in her life, Lunyai did not feel certain the All-Mother and Her children were with her. She clenched her jaw, fighting to hold down a sob.

"Yes," murmured Quint, pressing Lunyai's hand with his. "We will survive…"

Chapter 2

Kailen

23rd Day of Maia, Four Days After Gimmweg Was Attacked

Raven's damned, rancid, stinking breath!

Kailen slumped upon her mount, an aching fatigue running through her body. She had not slept in over a day and she had been moving almost constantly, riding in the daylight and leading the horse forward at night, wise enough to know a pot-hole in the dark would hobble her new friend. She stroked its mane and cast her eyes forward.

First Warrior, give the beast strength!

She had not seen her pursuit since the sun rose. She had spotted torches far behind her last night, but in the light of day there'd been no sign of any pursuit. Farmers and traders, yes. Children in the fields of homesteads also. But no Helligan soldiers.

Have they given up?

Kailen doubted that but she felt secure in the knowledge she was at least heading in the right direction, the Sacred Mount towering in the distance, a gargantuan signpost to the north.

Eligius had released her from her bondage and in doing so had given her more questions than answers. She suspected he had come back to her with the intention of releasing her, as a person did not normally carry lock-picks around with them. And the sudden cries of *"Fire!"* were either the luckiest of chances or a carefully planned diversion. The waiting horse suggested the latter.

Why Eligius had helped her escape, though, was a mystery. She hadn't hung around to ask him and had been moving ever since.

Her thighs ached and her shoulders were stiff. Her head throbbed and she wished she were in the bathhouse near her sister's home, one that infused the waters with intoxicating mixes of herbs and plants. She desperately needed one of their chamomile baths, with a hint of coconut imported from Xerinthian lands. Despite Eligius seeming so sure of the situation across the Swift Sea, and the fire undoubtedly being of Meridian making, Kailen still wondered if Sylvanus was indeed a Xerinthian agent and soon their empire would sail north once more, intent on conquering the much smaller realm of Ragnekai.

First Warrior, what is happening?

A wave of helplessness washed over her, and she let her head rest upon the steed's neck. The animal stopped and began chewing at the meadow they were in. Kailen felt her body begging her to dismount and flop down upon the lush grass. She gritted her teeth, sat up straight and gave the horse a gentle prod with her heels.

Sorry, Ser Longface, we need to keep moving. I have nowhere to go but north.

She was a fugitive from her own people for the murder of their lord, and the horrible irony was that she had killed Lord Orben. Orben's widow, Lady Hulda, apparently believed she was a murderer and that Kailen had acted upon the orders of Lady Ulla, which meant Orben's sister would now be behind bars. And Kailen would be too, if she set foot inside the walls of Gamle Hovestad.

The Helligan Battle-Sergeant Rorthal had arrested her, then sent men to capture her after her escape, so was obviously not someone she could turn to. The Helligan First Sentinel, Brax, had not been in Meridia, and this had concerned Kailen greatly. Either the Sentinels had gone north, which would make sense given that Orben's ultimate goal had been to control the entire east of Ragnekai. Or—and this was potentially worse—they had headed west to annex the smaller villages and town near Argol Forest.

Svard.

The Helligan First Ranger was the only one she could hope to reason with. Perhaps because they had slept together, or maybe because Svard was distant now and away from Sylvanus' schemes, but Kailen felt she could trust him. This could turn out to be a huge mistake though.

If I can't trust Svard, who else is there?

Her thoughts were bleak, and she felt hamstrung by a sense of utter defeat. How could she hope to even find him? He was in Bregustol, a city of thousands. She rolled her eyes as she realised the best place to look for him might be the city jails as, if he had assassinated Eswic, he may well have been captured after the deed. If he were in a cell, then Kailen would have to beg the First Warrior to break down walls for her.

Her horse suddenly lifted its head. Kailen heard it too. Shouts. Kailen cast her eyes back in the direction she had come.

For the love of the First Warrior...

The distinct red and white colours of Helligan soldiers were emerging from an area of woodland to the south. Mounted and many in number. Her eyes darted left and right, looking for cover, but she was in an open field. Very flat with only ankle-high grass and devoid of any kind of cover.

Damn...

Fear coursed through her body and motivated her muscles. Kailen snapped the reins, squeezed her thighs and let the horse break into a gallop. She chanced a look over her shoulder and saw they were gaining on her. She snarled at the injustice of this nightmare.

Not today, Raven, not today...

She was closer than she realised to the Warrior's Ring, the joining of Ragnekai's four rivers that circled the Sacred Mount. Swimming across was her best option now—the horse hopefully powerful enough to beat the current.

Kailen called forth everything she knew about riding a steed and urged the beast to keep going.

"We're going to take the plunge, Longface!" she shouted to the beast, her breath ragged. "You and me. And you are going to help me not drown!"

Longface snorted in response. Kailen hoped it was an expression of agreement and not the animal's way of telling her she was mad.

She could hear the soldiers in pursuit screaming at her to halt or risk death. The Helligan lady felt she was a step away from greeting the Dark Raven anyway so ignored them.

The river was yards away. She steeled herself for the leap into what looked like an unforgiving flow of the realm's waters. She cracked the reins and cried out to the beast.

"Yaaah!"

The horse surged to the riverbank. Kailen felt the First Warrior was truly guiding the magnificent creature.

Then it skidded to an abrupt halt. Kailen lurched forward, her feet left the stirrups and she tumbled past the animal's head, crashing to the ground.

"Raven's piss!" she groaned, glaring at the horse and spitting out grass. Ser Longface snickered and turned, ignoring the curses that were erupting from her mouth.

Kailen winced as she picked herself up. She saw the Helligan soldiers closing in, still calling out for her to halt. Her body was wracked with pain, but she was damned if she was going to just stand there and wait for them to arrive.

She glanced around and saw a boat coming up the river. A spark lit within her. Looking back, she saw her pursuit was less than two hundred yards away, the riders slowing their mounts, foolishly believing she had nowhere to run now.

Not today...

Kailen began to wave frantically with both arms at the incoming boat. Three men were at the paddles, working furiously to move against the current.

"Rivermen! Please let me on board! I have coin," she cried.

They didn't look like fishermen. Nor traders. That didn't matter now. She paced back a few yards, then took a running leap toward the boat.

"Help me!" she cried as she sailed through the air.

Kailen hit the water and instantly went under. Panic took her as she felt darkness begin to crush her. She flailed with her hands and her palms hit hard wood. Panic surged. She had gone underneath the boat. Her lungs began to swell as the river current tried to drag her down into the blackness below. She kicked her legs and tried to walk her hands along the belly of the boat. She prayed she was moving starboard to port, and not the longer journey of bow to stern. Kailen opened her eyes and saw light.

First Warrior, please…

Kailen's head broke the surface. She gasped for air. Her collar jerked, and she felt pressure under her arms as her tunic was hoisted upward.

"Grab the oar and stay down!" hissed a male voice.

Kailen grasped the oar that was hanging in the water, the current pulling at her legs. She stifled her coughing. Shouts could be heard. She was on the far side of the boat, hidden from the Helligan eyes. Kailen shut her eyes and prayed the proffered oar was a sign these men were indeed rescuing her.

She tensed as one her saviours called out in a strong accent. "Who was that, captain? She dived in the river like she were possessed by a Shade!"

Shade?

Kailen heard a shouted reply. Something about it not being any of their business. She squeezed her eyes shut, hoping.

A laugh from the boat.

"Well, she's nobody's business now! Damn fool woman must have drowned!"

Kailen held tightly to the oar and waited, her body beginning to shiver in the cold river. No more was said. She opened her eyes and looked up at the boat. A man was standing, while another was bracing against her oar. The extra weight had to be no small effort but he was smiling away.

The river dragged at her lower body, begging her to join it in its eternal flow.

"They're heading back. Looks like you're safe for now, my lady," said the one standing, his eyes still directed south.

Moments passed and Kailen's feet and legs began to numb.

"Alright, bring her in," said a commanding voice.

Two of the men hauled her into the vessel. She flopped down on the bottom boards, slightly surprised that she was actually still alive.

"Stay down a while longer, my lady. Until they're out of sight."

Kailen focused on regaining her breath.

Thank you, First Warrior.

One of them started humming.

"Mm-hmm-ahh-mmm… and they're gone."

Kailen sighed with relief.

"Are you mad, woman?" came a harsh voice.

Kailen pushed herself up, warily peeking over the gunwale. Her pursuers were indeed heading into the distance, giving up the chase, and hopefully believing the lie. She hoped word of her *demise* would not get back to Gamle Hovestad and her mother and sister. Ser Longface was nowhere to be seen. She slumped down and abruptly started coughing.

"Yes," she spluttered. "Quite mad."

Kailen was safe for now but had no idea who she was with. In a boat upon a river, exhausted, soaked to the skin, and no longer in control of where she was going. These men had saved her from drowning, and did not seem ready to hand her over, so she felt there was a glimmer of hope.

Kailen took a deep breath and crawled onto one of the benches. She avoided eye-contact for the moment, instead focusing on the boat itself. It was longer than the rafts that ferried people up and down the rivers and looked to be made of sturdier wood. Crude glyphs were burned along the sides in a language she didn't recognise. She stared at the jagged letters.

"Just borrowing it from some Throskaur raiders," came a voice from behind her.

She raised her eyes and looked around at her saviours.

One man was slightly older than the other two, maybe forty years of age, grey hair almost silver in the sunshine. The other two were younger, rather handsome if Kailen was being honest, and none of them had the appearance of traders, fishermen, or ferrymen.

"Throskaur?" she croaked, thinking she had misheard.

One of the younger ones responded. "Well, I say borrowing, but the Throskaur are dead so I suppose we have taken possession of this craft."

Kailen was more than confused. The Throskaur were pirates who dwelt on the Barren Isles. Why would one of their boats be in the middle of Ragnekai? Had this truly been a rescue, or had she just landed herself in the midst of three outlaws who had plans to use and abuse her? Her body tensed.

"Why would Helligan soldiers be chasing such a beautiful maiden?" enquired the second young one.

Kailen couldn't tell if he was mocking her, teasing her cruelly by hinting at carnal ideas, or genuinely wanting to know why she had just jumped into a river and almost died.

Maybe all three…

She cleared her throat and replied. "Those soldiers were not exactly of good breeding. They wanted sport, I believe."

Her eyes darted between the three of them, looking for a smirk that might indicate they had less than noble intentions. She detected only disapproval and disgust though.

"Bloody Helligans," muttered one of the younger ones, his tone laced with a certain coldness.

Kailen stiffened. *Meridians?*

"And where were you running from today?" enquired the older man.

Kailen hesitated. Was the truth the wisest path here?

"I was going to Meridia, but the city is occupied by the Helligans. I would now try my luck in Bregustol."

She noticed the three exchange glances when she mentioned Meridia.

"One good turn deserves another," the older man continued. "In return for rescuing you, how about you share any information you have about the situation in the south?"

Kailen nodded. "Of course. I do not know much but will tell you what I have seen in my travels."

One of the younger men passed Kailen a blanket. She took it grate-fully and wrapped it around her shoulders.

"My thanks. And twice so, seeing as I would have died either on land or in the water without your help," she said, speaking slowly and watching their faces to gauge their reaction to all her words.

"The realm is in a bad way," said one of the younger men. He was maybe nearing thirty years old. His shoulder-length black hair framed a charming face and he was not without lean muscle himself.

He'd give Svard some competition in the inns of Gamle Hovestad.

"Whilst I appreciate you are tired, helping us at the oars would hasten our journey," said the older man, handing Kailen a paddle.

She would have preferred to slouch down in the boat and let them do the work, but she couldn't really refuse, being a guest in debt. She took the oar and joined them in their efforts.

"You have strength in you, my lady," commented the other young-er man.

The compliment and polite address pleased Kailen in a small mea-sure. With all her misfortune of late, she was grateful for any kindness that came her way.

She kept rowing, keeping rhythm with the three men. The exer-tion felt strangely good after bumping around on a horse for so long. But her legs were not in such good humour. Kailen gritted her teeth and put her back into the effort. The men were not slacking and the boat made good progress. She chanced a quick look back and was re-lieved to see the place where she had boarded get smaller and smaller, with no sign her pursuers had commandeered a boat of their own.

"Let us cover a few more miles on the water," said the older man, "then pull in for a rest near the mouth of the Unn, and the fair lady here can tell us about Meridia."

Charming but focused. Who are these men?

As she turned back to the bow, her eyes caught the glint of steel. A fine spear was lying along the burden boards. Kailen got back to pad-dling but knew for sure these three men were soldiers or mercenaries.

"Rowan," said the older man, "sing a song that will keep us pad-dling. Something heroic!"

Kailen expected whichever one was Rowan to break into some kind of ridiculously outrageous tale of brave men rescuing a dim-witted maiden from the clutches of an evil warlock, so she was pleasantly surprised when he began singing *The Journey To Everstorm.*

"The River Unn runs fast that way, yah!
But we head not to the Swift Sea, yah!
Against the current we go this day, yah!
The Unn pulls at my oar with glee, yahhh!

Deep we now must thrust our paddle, yah!
Into clear waters just below, yah!
Would that I were in the saddle, yah!
Of a spirited horse not so slow, yahhh!"

Kailen was impressed with the singer's voice and she quickly joined in with the *Yah* calls, which united their movements, bringing them to paddle in a perfect harmony. The Helligan lady smiled to herself, grateful her luck had taken a turn for the better and that she would reach the northeast before long. Getting to Bregustol would be the next task and finding Svard would be near impossible, but what else could she do?

First Warrior, the Raven is behind me. I can only go forward. Guide my path, I beg you.

They paddled long into the morning and Kailen felt her strength disappearing fast. The Sacred Mount was always on their port side, its rocky face basking in the warm sun. She glanced more than once to it, trying to see the summit.

Did you die up there, Father? Why did you climb a second time?

The older man finally called for them to take a rest as the Unn came into view, so they pulled into the left bank. Kailen expected them to get out of the boat but it quickly became clear this break from paddling would be taken on board. Kailen stretched her limbs as one of the younger men tied up their mooring rope to one of the many wooden posts that dotted both banks of the river.

Raven's wings, this is all a bit different from running around delivering messages...

Kailen was exhausted after her night-time journey, sore now from the rowing, and drowsy due to the sunshine gracing their little vessel. She slumped on the gunwale and closed her eyes, needing a few moments to gather her thoughts.

She woke to a herby smell of smoke. The three men were talking in low voices, so she decided to listen in for a bit before they realised she was no longer sleeping.

How long was I out? And what in the name of the First Warrior are they smoking?!

"Do you think we have any chance of finding him, my lord?"

My lord?

"The Widow is cruel to all of us, so I have hope that Sylvanus will suffer her perverse humour soon."

Sylvanus!

Kailen sat bolt upright and stared at them before she could stop herself. They returned her gaze, the older man's eyes narrowing.

"Who are you? The truth this time."

Kailen stayed silent, trying to figure out who they were and how to respond. Men who knew Sylvanus and were from Meridia themselves by the sounds of it.

Caution be damned!

"My name is Kailen Jacobson, personal aide to Lord Orben of the Helligan nation."

A painting of their surprised faces would have made a fortune. Kailen tensed her body, debating on whether or not to scramble from the boat.

"Helligan. You probably have *quite a lot* of information I would find interesting then," commented the older man.

"I've told you my name. It would be polite to return the gesture."

The older man's jaw tightened and Kailen took a deep breath, ready to make good her escape.

"I am Lord Rencarro."

Now it was Kailen's turn to be surprised. The breath she had been holding puffed out.

"What? Lord Rencarro of Meridia?" she spluttered.

Was this man sitting before her now truly the father of Eligius, he who had released her from captivity?

"I seem to be without my city, thanks to Helligan ambitions. And the treachery of my former Second, Sylvanus." He paused, inhaled sharply, then placed a hand on the spear. "With whom you seem to be acquainted."

Kailen heard the implicit threat in his voice. And then noticed that Rowan and the other one had moved while their lord had been speaking. They were ready to grab her if she bolted from the boat. She closed her eyes and wished the First Warrior would bless her right now and make her life that little bit less complicated.

Three on one seems a bit unfair…

Kailen rocked forward as if she were fainting, letting her body fall toward the one called Rowan. As she folded her body, her hand withdrew the knife in her boot. Exactly as hoped, Rowan made to catch her to stop her fully collapsing. She lunged upward, grabbing his tunic and placing the blade by his throat, her motion causing the boat to lurch violently to one side.

Kailen steadied herself and called out. "Please do not move. I am rather desperate at present and will do what I have to."

Keeping her eyes on the other two and the blade at Rowan's neck, she carefully stepped around him to bring herself at his back, the boat now gently swaying, and soon had all three in front of her. She was surprised to hear Rowan chuckling.

She pushed the blade ever so slightly into the flesh.

"You have a strange sense of humour, Rowan," she said.

Rowan let out a sigh. "Forgive me, but the irony of this situation struck me as somewhat amusing."

Kailen tensed. Was this Rowan some kind of lethal assassin who could easily disarm her without a drop of blood being spilt?

"Explain!" she hissed, sliding her knife and breaking the skin.

"Ow, ow, Widow's teeth! Now this really has become farcical… from my point of view."

"What are you talking about, fool?"

Kailen saw the other two smiling as if this Rowan was an idiot who always got himself in trouble.

"Not that long ago I was in a boat, holding a blade to the throat of a Tarakan girl. I believed she was the accomplice of a village girl who I thought was a Helligan assassin. I was wrong on both counts. Ended up swimming in the Western Sea."

Kailen's anger rose. "Are you trying to force my hand here with your stupid stories?" she snarled.

Lord Rencarro coughed lightly. "Kailen Jacobson, please calm yourself. And please do not kill Rowan. I need his help with some hunting," he said flatly.

Hunting?

Kailen felt sure she knew the object of their hunt. Kailen eased the pressure on her knife slightly and gestured with her chin to Rencarro.

"Will you give me your word that you will not harm me?"

Rencarro frowned. "We have no intention of harming you, but any more blood drawn from Rowan here will force our hand, so to speak."

Shit on the Dark Raven!

Kailen slowly took the knife away and pushed Rowan gently but firmly away from her. He made no sudden movement but took a seat next to the third man, who pointed at his neck.

"You'll have to think up something wild to put in a song for that cut," he said with a grin.

Rowan rolled his eyes and wiped the blood away with a handkerchief from his pocket.

Lord Rencarro spoke again. "That's better. Now, be so kind as to tell us the real reason you were being chased by your own people."

"I would see Sylvanus dead also," she offered.

The three exchanged looks.

Damn it, Sylvanus played this game well…

"Sylvanus betrayed Meridia to Orben, you are Orben's messenger, and yet you seek his death?" queried Rencarro. "I feel I am missing something here."

Kailen once again threw caution to the wind and decided to tell them the truth. She didn't have time for guessing games and hints.

"Lord Orben is dead, murdered by Sylvanus."

Kailen would have liked a second painting of their faces, as this time their jaws were truly slack.

"That doesn't make sense..." murmured Rowan, staring at her.

Kailen lowered her blade. "Sylvanus used some kind of poison to turn my lord into a crazed beast. I belie—"

"A beast? Orben was turned too?!" exclaimed Rowan.

Now it was Kailen's turn to let her jaw hang low. "You have seen others turned?"

"Not seen, but heard about them," replied Rowan.

"Hundreds of citizens from the city of Morak were turned into raging animals. There was a battle at the Black Stone Ford," explained Lord Rencarro. He slammed his hand on the gunwale. "Damn the Widow! There have been no coincidences, only carefully planned deeds carried out."

Kailen was confused but understood at least that Sylvanus had deceived more than just the Meridians and Helligan people. She decided to divulge the truth about her situation, more or less in its entirety.

"I lied about the nature of my pursuit. Those were Helligan soldiers chasing me because I am wanted for the murder of Lord Orben."

"But you just said Sylvanus turned him," said Rowan, eyes narrowing.

"And he did. Lord Orben, or the beast he had become, died in a struggle and Sylvanus saw to it that I am considered the one responsible. I was arrested by my own people in Meridia."

Rowan shook his head. "I am getting lost here. Why were you in Meridia?"

Kailen sighed, the convoluted schemes of Sylvanus muddying the waters. "Lady Ulla and myself believed Sylvanus to be a Xerinthian agent. She didn't know who she could trust, so she sent me to bring back the Helligan forces now in Meridia. Lady Ulla wanted to prepare Gamle Hovestad for a possible invasion."

Lord Rencarro exchanged looks with his men, then gazed up into the sky. Kailen turned her eyes skyward too and wished she were a bird, able to fly far and wide, and see everything from on high.

The third one spoke. "My lord, is this in truth a Xerinthian plot?"

Kailen answered before Rencarro could respond. "Your son, Eligius, doesn't seem to think so."

Rencarro's attention shot to her and his eyes were wide with something Kailen could not read.

Shame?

"You spoke to my son before you were arrested?"

"After. As it happens, your son set me free."

Rencarro's reaction shocked her. He laughed. Loudly. "Eligius continues to surprise me," he said. But then his humour faded and was replaced with something bordering on shame again. Kailen determined the relationship between this father and son was complicated.

Rowan spoke up. "If Lord Eligius believes it is not a Xerinthian invasion, I would place coin on that bet. Your son is by far the most knowledgeable man I have ever met. That Seolta being the one behind all this becomes ever more likely."

Rencarro nodded slowly, seemingly deep in thought.

"Who is Seolta?" asked Kailen.

"Rowan here has been in the northwest, talked with Duthka..." started Rencarro.

Duthka?!

"...and spoken to General Torbal. From what he has learnt, we believe a Duthka by the name of Seolta is the one pulling the strings. And from what you say, I would say Sylvanus is in league with him. Why, I have no idea."

Rowan nodded. "So, Sylvanus never intended to take the rule of Meridia. He just needed to start conflict in the south."

"Weaken the southern factions," said the third man. "Lucian, by the way, Kailen Jacobson. Pleased to meet you," he said, extending a

hand. "And grateful you chose Rowan here to threaten with death."
He grinned and Kailen couldn't help but smile.

"Erm...sorry about that, Rowan. It's been a rough few days. Being arrested by Helligan soldiers was like the Dark Raven and your Widow spitting upon me together."

Lord Rencarro shook his head. "This tale gets more bizarre by the day," he muttered.

Kailen suddenly remembered they intended to kill Sylvanus, which meant they were searching for him. "I take it you were heading to Helligan lands in your pursuit of Sylvanus?"

Rowan nodded. "We were," he said, frowning. He turned to his lord. "I'd wager the Widow spawn is no longer in the southeast, my lord."

Rencarro looked at Kailen and held her eyes. She had the feeling he was seeking a sign that she was lying.

"I'm telling the truth," she said, exasperated.

He gave her a crooked smile and spoke, ignoring her statement.

"Sylvanus would not have come back west, seeing as there are hundreds in Meridia and even some in Argyllan who would recognise him and want to see him pay for his treachery. So, he must have crossed into the north." The lord sighed. "This is still a fool's quest, but I will find him. The Keeper may guide us in some way."

He looked at her. "If you want to get out here, skirt the base of the mountain and head west, we will not stop you."

Kailen knew west held nothing for her.

"My business is in Bregustol." She shrugged. "A last hope, you might say. A fool's quest."

She smiled and he returned the gesture.

"Then I suggest we get moving. The sun is high, but the river currents are not to be scoffed at. We will pass the Unn, then find somewhere to dock along the Mimir, a good distance from the Gjallag Bridge but not too far off the main road heading to the capital. Sylvanus will have taken that road, I assume, so I would look for his passing there. Once into the Mimir we can rest at the oars."

Lucian and Rowan were on their feet and the boat was soon battling the flow of the Warrior's Ring again. They rowed and rowed, the river never relenting in its desire to send them back. After they passed the Unn, Kailen felt her lack of sleep more keenly than before. She considered herself a hardy sort, but she was not used to this kind of relentless exertion. At least she could breathe a little more easily now that she was with Meridians and not Helligans.

Ironic...

"Hard to port!" cried Rowan suddenly.

Kailen momentarily thought her comprehension of basic seamanship was off as she thought port was to the left and they were supposed to be veering right to enter the Mimir. Then she saw the boats farther down the river that sliced between Helligan lands and the Rihtgellen kingdom.

Red and white flags flew on several rafts with many figures visible on the northern bank. Kailen saw black beneath red and white, and gasped.

Sentinels!

She needed no more telling to paddle furiously away from the mouth of the Mimir.

"Give it all you have!" called Rencarro. "Our quest will be short indeed if we crash our single vessel into all of that!"

Kailen felt the Mimir drawing them in, its myriad watery fingers pulling at the oar, an irresistible force of nature that only relented when it drained into the Blind Sea in the east.

First Warrior, give us all strength!

Kailen felt it would be particularly unfair to have escaped Rorthal's men to then end up with Brax's, especially since Meridians were helping her. She gritted her teeth and dipped her paddle again, probing deeply.

But the Mimir was not to be conquered. Their craft was slipping to starboard, its bow turning to point straight down the river.

"Widow be damned!" shouted Lucian. "We're being sucked in!"

Their small vessel gradually but surely entered the Mimir. Kailen looked up and prayed the Sentinels were still too far away to see. But even if they were, that wouldn't be the case for much longer.

"My lord?" called Rowan. "We're getting closer!"

Kailen knew he wasn't merely stating the obvious. Rowan was asking his lord to make a decision.

"Damn the Widow and her ways! We'll have to bank!"

Kailen looked to the north bank and saw nowhere that offered safe port for at least another hundred yards. Small trees and bushes lined a near vertical wall of earth and rock.

"Hard to port!" cried Rencarro. "Ram the damn boat into the trees."

It was not the safest idea but the only viable one. Kailen worked with the three of them, first angling the bow toward the bank, then pushing forward to prevent their craft simply spinning down the Mimir.

"Brace!" shouted Rowan as they drove head-long into the bank.

The collision almost destroyed the boat, the frame suffering more than one shattered board as tree branches pierced the craft. Water began chugging in. It would have been worse had Rencarro not jammed his spear into the bank, absorbing some of the impact.

"Abandon ship!" ordered Rencarro, who was already clambering out, using his weapon as an anchor. He reached out a hand to Rowan, who grasped it.

Lucian pushed Kailen forward.

"Quick, dammit! The boat is being pulled back into the current!"

Kailen lunged forward and grabbed Rowan's outstretched hand. She turned back to see Lucian stumble as the boat tore free from its unorthodox moorings. He fell against the bottom boards and Rowan hollered a name that was not Lucian.

The Meridian scrambled to his feet, but the boat was now back in the current. Kailen glanced upriver and saw the Helligan soldiers were facing this way.

They've seen us!

"Jump!" cried Rencarro.

Lucian did not hesitate, leaping from the wrecked longboat. But his launch was from a moving platform and the jump was poor. He splashed down into the river.

Kailen saw a low-hanging branch ahead and made what was quite possibly the most foolish decision ever in her life.

She let go of Rowan's hand and pushed herself off the bank.

"Lucian! Grab my hand!" she cried as she hit the water. Her left hand shot up to grab the branch as she reached for Lucian with her right. The river pulled at her legs and fear gripped her.

First Warrior…

Lucian shot out a hand and they connected, gripping each other within the cold flow of the Mimir.

A spear slid down in front of Kailen's eyes. Rencarro was bracing behind a tree, Rowan behind him gripping his lord's belt.

"Reach!"

Kailen screamed with exertion and pulled Lucian toward her.

It was enough. He got a hand on Rencarro's spear and pulled. The pressure on her right arm instantly lessened and Kailen focused on her left, which was losing its grip.

Lucian found his own tree just as Kailen's left hand slipped from the branch, the bark tearing the skin of her palm. The Mimir pulled mercilessly at her legs and she found herself facing death by drowning once again.

But Lucian did not let go of her right hand. Her body twisted painfully but she did not go under.

Her left hand flailed for purchase of something, anything.

It found, or rather was found, by a strong grip.

"I've got you!" cried Rowan.

The four of them managed to scramble up the bank and onto flat ground, where they all collapsed. Kailen didn't want to move for a year and a day.

Thank you, First Warrior. Seems today is not the day I die.

"Get up!"

Rencarro's voice was a harsh command.

Kailen took a breath and rolled onto her front, pushing herself up to stand. She surveyed the scene. Their craft was floundering, but still heading down the river to the Helligan soldiers.

And those soldiers were now coming this way.

"Run!" shouted Rowan.

And once again, Kailen was in flight. Her body was wracked with fatigue and bruised in a hundred places, but the thought of being captured again conquered her physical agony.

Valkyna, give us wings, I beg you!

CHAPTER 3

MORYN

23rd Day of Maia, Four Days After Gimmweg Was Attacked

Forgive me…
  Forgive me, Athaiq. Forgive me the violence I brought to Argyllan…
  Forgive me the death…
  Moving farther away from Argyllan had done nothing to lessen Moryn's agonising guilt over what his deeds had wrought. Mentally he was a mess. Physically he wasn't much better. He winced as the pain reignited in his thigh.
  Emiren had stirred in her sleep, Moryn had panicked and fled from the home. He had clumsily collided with one of the wooden posts that held the porch roof and jabbed himself with his blade, still in his hand. He had cried out, the book had dropped and he had believed all was lost. But he had recovered, picked up the book and ran as fast as he could, his leg burning in agony and his hand slick with his own blood.
  Moryn had taken the Forest Road south, away from Emiren and Lunyai, away from Argyllan and away from Seolta. The Duthka sailor limped the remaining few yards to the settlement's entrance.

"Welcome to Lowenden," said the sentry, although there was little enthusiasm in his words.

Moryn took a deep breath, trying to push down the pain and bring the concentration he needed.

"How fares your town in these dark times?" he asked as gravely as he could.

The sentry straightened. "We are well here, looking out for each other," he said, almost as if his pride had been hurt. Then he sagged slightly. "We are safe thanks to the Meridians."

Moryn tensed. "Meridians?"

"Yes, some stayed on despite the trouble to the north." The sentry studied Moryn. "Where have you come from?"

"I have travelled from Argyllan."

The man's eyes widened, and a hint of fear touched his face. "You were there when…" He left it hanging, as if to mention the word *Throskaur* would be to tempt them this way.

"Fortunately, I arrived after the attack. There are many dead," said Moryn, almost choking on the last words.

The Duthka mariner wondered if the sentry was a perceptive man, but a moment's look told him this was not the case. Moryn judged he had never had to deal with anything more than a drunken trader asking after his wagon that had mysteriously vanished during the night.

"Dead… We heard what had happened and many of us…" He puffed up his chest. "Many of us were ready to march north and help our neighbours."

Moryn forced a smile.

"I am sure they all knew help was on its way," he said, trying hard to keep the cynicism from his voice. "I heard many folk there speak of Lowenden and its kind people. And wise masters."

This seemed to satisfy the man's feeling of impotence. He nodded and gestured to the town behind him.

"Well, we certainly welcome anybody here and the masters are wise, to be sure. Teaching my eldest now. Reckon he'll be smarter than his old man any day now." He chuckled.

Moryn smiled again, his stomach folding in on itself with nervousness.

Athaiq, give me strength now.

"And where might I find these masters?" His voice croaked. He coughed and tried to gather his thoughts. "I am a scholar from Westhealfe, truth be told, travelling the roads, trying to avoid the troubles. I would like to ask them to impart some of their wisdom to me, as my own master has sent me to gather knowledge of the southwest."

"Well, we don't have anything so grand as a university here, like they do in Bregustol, so I've heard. But the school is in the southwest quarter," he said, gesturing in that general direction. "If you can't find any of the masters there, I know Master Francis can usually be found in The Old Scroll." He winked.

"The Old Scroll?"

"Yes, an inn at the end of Market Street. Small place but the sign was freshly painted last week. You won't miss it."

Moryn thanked the man and decided to head to the inn first. He wanted to be discreet and felt it better to approach one man having a drink than announce himself at a school in front of children.

He walked into the town, his feet feeling like heavy logs dragging at his legs, the right one not too badly injured but he would have preferred to sit down and rest. Moryn took a deep breath and tried to push away the more crippling sense of guilt, doubled now by a sense he was betraying Seolta.

Forgive me, my teacher, I am not strong like you and Idelisa.

It wasn't long before he found The Old Scroll inn. Exactly as the guard had said, the sign had clearly been freshly painted. The white background was as clean as fresh snow, the black letters sharp, and the scroll itself a truly beautiful image to Moryn's mind. Books and writing were second only to sailing on the waves to the Duthka mariner, with reading being his main activity when he was back in Corann's village. Moryn pushed open the door and a bell tinkled above his head.

The taproom was bright thanks to large front windows and a number of skylights in the roof over the bar. Lanterns were lit farther back, chasing away any gloominess. What gave Moryn something of a thrill were the bookshelves leaning against almost every section of wall not being used for coat hooks or lanterns. Back in the Abhaile he had a small collection of books, gifts from Seolta over the years, so this was like a great library to the Duthka man.

The inn was not so crowded, with maybe a dozen customers sipping at ale or slowly eating pie whilst reading from a book. It seemed you could borrow a lantern from the bar to give you more light to read. With the smell of good food, a whiff of pipe weed, the books and the hush that enveloped the place, Moryn could not help but smile. He felt more at home in this inn than he had ever done living with Corann and his people.

Moryn stepped up to the bar and greeted the innkeeper, a jovial fellow of maybe fifty years, grey hair gracing the sides of his head and a shiny pate on top.

"What'll it be, sir?" he asked, giving the counter a wipe as he did.

"A small beer, if you will."

"Anything for your hunger?"

Moryn tensed, wondering how the man could have known he was hungry.

"Got some good pies freshly baked if you are."

Fool.

Moryn realised it was just a typical question for an innkeeper. The man didn't know him or how he had come here.

"Just the beer, thanks."

The innkeeper nodded and drew a beer for him into a small wooden mug. "There you are. When you're ready for the next, I'll pour it and then it'll be one copper," the innkeeper said with a cheerful smile.

Moryn thanked him, took a sip, then raised a hand. The innkeeper raised his eyebrows questioningly.

"You wouldn't happen to know a Master Francis, would you? I heard he frequents here."

The innkeeper grinned but shook his head. "I am sure Master Francis is right now teaching classes at the school."

Damn...

Another voice carried over. "Why would you want to speak to that old fool anyway?"

Moryn turned to see an old man to his right, leaning on the bar and sipping at a full pint of ale.

"Well, I was told by... Is he not a *wise* master?"

The innkeeper chipped in. "Master? Yes. Wise? Opinion is divided on the matter, young sir." He chuckled.

Moryn sensed there was some private joke going on here and his frustration rose. Were they teasing him?

"Wiser than an innkeeper who needed help spelling Scroll!" cried the old man.

Him?!

Moryn realised the old man was Master Francis and smiled. It wasn't that he found their silly banter amusing, more that he had found the man without too much trouble.

"Master Francis, I presume," he offered.

"Ah. Seems like you are wiser than the pair of us old badgers," the man replied, moving away from the bar and doing a theatrical bow. "Master Francis at your service!"

"Thank...erm, thank the winds that I have found you."

The Master raised his eyebrows, which were bushy and prominent under a head of white, unruly hair. The man was plump but not obese, smaller than Moryn but perhaps still of an average height.

"You have piqued my interest, good sir. Why would a stranger to this inn be seeking me with such enthusiasm?" He paused. "Do I owe you money?"

Moryn forced a laugh. "Nothing of the sort, Master. I have something I need help translating. If you have some time, I would appreciate your wisdom."

The Master smiled warmly. "How could I refuse such an offer? Shall we look at it here?"

Moryn frowned. "Some place more private would be preferable. The text is rather old and perhaps of a personal nature to myself," he explained, trying to look embarrassed.

"Understood. We shall examine your text at my home." He raised a finger. "But first, let us share some ale and chat."

Moryn reluctantly agreed.

It was an insufferably long time later that Moryn stood in Master Francis' home, peering over the man's shoulder as he devoured the writing before him.

"Absolutely fascinating!" he said for the hundredth time.

Moryn hoped for more insight than this. His patience was wearing thin, but he repeated Seolta's words in his head.

"Never rush something you desire greatly. That is how mistakes are made and plans are undone."

Moryn inhaled slowly and deeply, and waited for more.

"The Words are indeed those that we hold sacred in these parts, but the structure of the sentences is more like the Tarakan language. Hardly surprising when you consider the Tarakan used to inhabit these lands before we came..." His voice drifted off as he read more. Moryn tried to process this nugget of information.

The book was written by a Tarakan or perhaps of a race of people that were around before the horse-people. Was Seolta's book written by the same person? Moryn didn't think so.

"I'm no expert," muttered the master, "but the handwriting would suggest a woman wrote this."

Corann's words echoed again in Moryn's mind. When they had been in Westhealfe, speaking with the general and the lord, Corann had spoken of a legend concerning a brother and sister. Moryn had been surprised as he had never heard of it, despite having listened to many fireside stories when he lived with Corann's people. Could this book be the sister's and Seolta possessed the brother's? *What happened to the siblings?*

Moryn gently directed the master to the page Emiren's mother had been reading from, concerning a cure to *the burden of beasts*. The gift, it had been called.

"The gift became a curse."

Curse?!

Emiren's mother, Megari, had translated that as *it became a spell.*

The master looked up at Moryn and raised his eyebrows. "Intriguing! Sounds quite sinister if you ask me. Hmm, they cured the burden of beasts, whatever that may be, but in doing so, they unleashed a curse!? Spirits, where did you get this book, my lad?!" he asked, his tone one of awe. "This is a treasure, a wonder even."

Moryn forced a smile. "My mother passed it on. I think her grandfather gave it to her, so it has been in the family a while."

The master looked sceptical and Moryn cursed himself for not having created a better story on the road to Lowenden.

"Well, it is old certainly. I wonder where it came from before it entered your family's possessions."

Moryn felt strangely annoyed by this thought. He had no idea who his parents had been, but this man was suggesting the book was too grand a thing to have been with his ancestors by right. Something hard entered Moryn's mind, a coldness.

Don't judge me, old man. You have no idea what I have seen, what I have done.

"We should get this to the capital. The king will…well, Sedmund is dead, but I am sure scholars in Bregustol will want to see this. It could provide a much greater understanding of the realm's history, perhaps help in settling territorial disputes."

Moryn was shaking his head but the master carried on regardless.

"And the herb-lore in here. I am no physician but I feel certain there is knowledge here that would save many lives. We must…"

He stared at Moryn as his voice trailed off.

"What is the matter? Surely you agree this book must be shared."

Moryn's jaw clenched. "No."

"No?! My lad, I know this might be precious to you but—"

"No," he repeated, wishing the man would shut up so he could leave.

"But…"

"No, no, no!" Moryn knew his voice was rising.

The master's hands fell to the book and Moryn sensed he was trying to take it from him.

"No, no, no!" he cried. Moryn became unaware of his own actions.

The master struggled, his hands flapping at the Duthka sailor.

"No!" Moryn shouted, rage coursing through him and tears blinding his eyes. He squeezed with all his strength.

The master continued to beat his fists against Moryn, but he was a weak, old man, too feeble to defend himself.

"No, no, no, no!"

Moryn's eyes were shut now but he didn't stop. He felt detached from everything except a numbing fear that the book was being taken away.

"No!" he whispered.

The master was not struggling. Moryn could still feel his weight though.

In his hands.

"No..."

Moryn opened his eyes and his body froze. His hands were tight around the master's throat. The man's eyes were open but vacantly staring somewhere beyond Moryn. His face was a strange colour, a dull grey-blue.

Breath came to the Duthka sailor and he gasped, releasing his grip. The master slumped to the desk, his forehead striking the wood with a thud. A heavy silence descended upon the room.

"No..." whispered Moryn. "No...get up." He shoved the master but there was no response.

"Get up, get up, please get up...no, no, why did you do that?"

His eyes frantically looked around the room. He felt the walls were watching him and the candles in the lanterns were flickering angrily. The flames had seen what he had done.

Moryn patted the master on the back. "I'm sorry...I didn't mean to...it wasn't me."

Moryn's legs gave way and he stumbled, falling into the wall behind the desk. He slumped his head against it, then slowly turned to look upon what he had done.

The man was dead.

His stomach churned horribly and he gagged. Bile came up and he spat it out.

Athaiq, what have I become?

"You find Master Francis then?" called the gate sentry as Moryn hurried through.

He turned but didn't stop, keeping his feet moving sideways like a crab. "I...erm, no, sadly I could not find him."

The sentry frowned. "Well, there are other Masters who would be happy to help... Where are you going? Meridia? Surely not the Tarakan Plains. No more towns to the south, only homesteads. Hey!"

Moryn ignored him and began to hurry, his leg protesting and the book in his sack, bumping against his body, a horrible reminder of what he had done within the walls of Lowenden. The Duthka sailor kept going and did not look back once. He heard nothing more, so he reasoned the guard had given up.

He'll know it was me. They'll all know it was me...

When they eventually found the body of Master Francis, word would spread, the innkeeper would remember the stranger who went to the Master's home and the guard would be sure to remember Moryn leaving in haste.

I can't go back that way.

Moryn kept walking and soon came upon one of the homesteads the guard had mentioned. There were a few men and women working in the fields, and some children playing with sticks near the home. Some stopped what they were doing and waved at him. Moryn returned the gesture and quickened his pace, despite his leg still being sore.

I must get away from all these people...

The road wound onward and, in another mile, Moryn was nearing another homestead. A man was leaning against a gate post, smoking a pipe.

"Good day to you, sir!" he hailed.

Moryn raised a hand in greeting and smiled but said nothing. He hoped the man would not wrangle him into a conversation. He kept his eyes on the road ahead, which veered right. Moryn could make out the dark shape of some kind of rock formation in the distance. He heard nothing more but from the corner of his eye saw the man watching him.

Just let me pass by...

"If you're heading to Meridia, then you might want to reconsider. City is occupied by Helligans."

Moryn stopped, turned, and forced some cheer into his troubled self. "Perhaps I am a bit lost. I wanted to head south, not east."

"South? Well," he said, raising his arm and pointing in one direction, "keep going that way and you'll reach the Tarakan Plains."

Lunyai...

"You don't look Tarakan to me though, so I'm not sure where you are heading," he finished with a frown.

"No, I do not want to meet Tarakans. What else is south? Is there a port somewhere near?"

The man chuckled. "Spirits, you are a bit lost, friend. No port for miles. Meridia that way," he explained, thumbing at the rocks, "and the Plains this way."

"And this way?" asked Moryn, pointing in a direction halfway between those two points.

The man's expression darkened and he made some strange gesture with his left hand.

"Just the Izachu Wildlands..."

Moryn hadn't heard of this place before. *Wildlands* didn't sound like a very safe place, but he was beginning to think that hiding from Emiren and Lunyai, Corann and Olwyn, Meridians and Helligans, and even Seolta, was his best course right now.

"Does anybody live in these wild lands?"

The man shook his head vigorously. "Spirits, no! You'd be all alone if you went there."

Perfect.

Moryn smiled and dipped his head. "My thanks. I feel some time by myself is what I need."

The man stared at him as if he were mad, then made that odd gesture with his hand again.

Moryn turned on his heel and began walking, turning off the road onto a trail that ran in his chosen direction. He chanced a look back and saw the man still standing there, watching him.

Superstitious folk. How wild can these lands really be if there is no one there? Overgrown with wild weeds?

The Duthka man tightened the straps on his rucksack and pushed on, a growing sense within him that he was shaking off his shackles.

I will walk a new path.

CHAPTER 4

PAEGA

24th Day of Maia, Five Days After Gimmweg Was Attacked

Paega felt physically and mentally a world better than the day before. His wound had been treated by the True Sons and was healing, and he had been well cared for. Then this morning he had received a handwritten note from his eternally silent master at the forge that his position was waiting for him when he was fully recovered. It turned out that Hrodgar was a fervent follower of the Ever-Father and had felt immense pride in the fact his apprentice had risked himself to take down an enemy of the church.

Strange days…

So Paega had decided not to decline Magen's request he come to the Holy Sepulchre and join the worship as they readied themselves for the Ever-Father's work. Or whatever the holy leader had said. The young man looked around the huge cathedral and felt a mixture of awe and anxiety. Awe at the imposing architecture, and anxiety at the gathering of so many men eager to prove themselves worthy of divine praise.

Paega began drifting to the back of the great hall, away from the

True Sons. Magen was busy talking to various brothers of importance and didn't seem to notice. The mood in the hall was one of a festival, with men laughing and clapping, almost all of them drinking wine that was being handed around by those strange grey nuns. To be honest, it really didn't seem like a call to arms for the True Sons. Paega wasn't complaining though. Even if the Unvasik had attacked the village of Gimmweg, he thought it unlikely they would march on Bregustol. If Paega himself had all those rubies, he'd sit there and count them. Bregustol was bound to send soldiers up the Ruby Road anyway, likely calling for aid from Westhealfe. The battle would be far from here.

"Wine, my lord?" asked a female voice.

Paega almost jumped out of his skin. One of the nuns was standing right beside him with a tray, upon which were two goblets of wine. Paega took one, thanked her, and continued his casual retreat from the fore of the church. He took a sip of the wine. It tasted different to that sweet, fruity one he had been given in the hospice but wasn't too bad.

Difference between red and white wine maybe, he thought as he swirled the claret drink. All the other men gathered here were drinking the wine freely, so it certainly wasn't bilge-water being passed off as good stock. He took another sip and found himself easing into the more bitter taste. Paega had a gulp and shrugged. His shoulder still ached but being called *my lord* and being given wine certainly improved his mood. So did being farther away from Magen. The holy leader was too intense for Paega's liking.

Give me my hammer and the heat of the forge, and I'll be happy.

Paega figured they would all get drunk, Magen would give a rousing speech, more wine would be knocked back, and then everyone would go home to sleep it off. Paega would then head back to the forge, thank his master for his patience, and assure him he would return to his work soon.

Ever-Father, you have smiled upon me this day.

He began his prayer but suddenly felt something inside, a swirl in his stomach.

I'm drinking wine in this holy place! Is that allowed?

Paega looked up to the high ceiling sheepishly. He wondered if the Ever-Father could see him now. He was supposed to be able to see all His children wherever they were, so He must be able to look over them in the Holy Sepulchre of all places.

Forgive the wine, Ever-Father. It helps to dull the pain.

Paega cleared his throat, despite the fact he wasn't speaking aloud.

Ever-Father, please help me to return swiftly to the forge and my life there. I am a woefully poor servant of Your will without my hammer.

He had never been any good at thinking up fancy words for his prayers, but he thought that last bit sounded quite decent and hoped He was listening.

Paega felt an itch on his chest and scratched it. It was getting warmer in here, with all the hundreds of bodies, many of whom hadn't washed in days, Paega reckoned. He gulped down his wine and saw another grey nun. He moved over to her as casually as he could, not wanting to seem eager for another drink. The woman's face was hidden in her cowl so he couldn't tell if she was giving him an admonishing look.

"My thanks," he said, taking a full cup and placing his empty one on her tray.

Where do they get the money to pay for all this wine?

It really was getting warmer in here, hot almost. Paega felt the need to get out and breathe in the fresh air, or as fresh as air was in the capital. He noticed a couple of True Sons looking as hot and bothered as he felt, scratching their necks and puffing their cheeks.

Time to get some air…

He was about to head out when a gong sounded, loud and clear over the general hum of conversation. The hall went quiet immediately and everyone looked to the far side. Paega saw Magen climbing onto a stage and groaned inwardly.

Here we go again. Please don't call me up there to show these men what a truly heroic servant of the Ever-Father looks like!

Paega hoped there was some other poor bastard who had impressed Magen recently, another faithful servant of the Ever-Father whose courage would rouse the masses here. His stomach churned again; the wine was disagreeing with him. He'd had two cups. Or it might have been three.

"Brothers!"

Magen's voice rang out in the Holy Sepulchre. Paega carefully inched his way farther back within the crowd. His feet felt oddly heavy.

Damn this! Am I drunk?

"We are gathered here today to answer the call of the Ever-Father!"

Paega cast his eyes toward Magen but couldn't make out the True Son patriarch. He squeezed his eyes shut and shook his head. He didn't feel well. He bumped into a man and was about to apologise when he saw the fellow was feverishly scratching his own chest and muttering. Paega tried to ask the man if he was alright.

"Are you schick...shishu..."

What's happening to me?!

Paega couldn't speak. His mouth was moving but he couldn't control it. He heard Magen's voice somewhere but couldn't make out the words. People were speaking around him, but they sounded like a swarm of bees approaching.

Ever-Father, help me...

Shouts erupted around him and he raised his eyes to see people shaking their fists. He felt too hot now, like a fever was wracking his entire body.

He stumbled and bumped into someone else, knocking the fellow's cup of wine from his hand. Paega grabbed hold of him to steady himself, raised his eyes, and blinked.

He knew this man.

Something stirred within him.

Danger. Paega sensed danger. His body tensed and he felt fear.

PART FIVE

CHAPTER 1

WULFNER

23rd Day of Maia, Morak

"Slow advance. Keep their backs covered," ordered the general, his voice strong in the eerie hush that had swallowed the northern city of Morak. It was silent except for the rustling and scraping coupled with whimpering noises that were escaping from the Great Hall. A hall now being approached by soldiers of Westhealfe.

Wulfner moved forward with the men and women. His mind swirled frantically with images of what was about to happen – beast-men charging, spear-wielding soldiers standing firm, poor souls being impaled on iron tips. If he could stop the carnage, he knew he should. But with sharp points here and mindless men undoubtedly within, what could he hope to achieve?

The doors stayed shut but the sounds from within grew. Someone was in there. Or something.

"Open the doors," came Torbal's voice, loud and clear.

Damn, damn the Winds, shields would be enough here. Lower the spears!

Wulfner struggled to get Torbal's attention, but there were too many bodies between himself and the general now. He turned back and watched two soldiers grab the rings set into the doors. Wulfner tensed as they pulled.

Screams erupted. From within. The two soldiers yanked the doors open wide and fell back. Something shot out, something small. It darted through legs, and then Wulfner heard a disgusting squelch, a horrific squeal, and a soldier cursing.

"It's a bloody pig!"

What?

As the soldiers lowered their eyes to the ill-fated swine, Wulfner shoved past them to stand less than five yards from the threshold. He peered into the gloom. The glow of a torch appeared and beside it a woman's face, her expression one of sheer terror.

"Spears advance!"

Wulfner spun to see the soldiers hunched behind shields step forward, lethal points jutting out from the mass, advancing upon him and the open doors. Instinct told him to get out the way, but he had seen a woman in there. Frightened, not crazed.

"Halt!" he bellowed, squeezing his eyes shut and spreading his arms wide, creating a woeful barrier.

A strange hush fell.

Wulfner opened one eye and saw soldiers staring at him as if he had gone totally mad.

"Get out the bloody way, you old fool!" cried someone.

Wulfner found his voice again.

"There are people in there. Not beasts. People!" he shouted. "Stay your weapons!"

A general murmur grew within the ranks as soldiers tried to see into the darkness of the hall.

"Mercy…" came a ragged voice.

Torbal's commanding voice then rang out. "Bladesung, stand down! All ranks, pull back!"

Wulfner breathed a sigh of relief.

Bless the Winds. They blow kindly this once…

"What happened here?" Wulfner asked the mother. The situation had settled now, and the big northerner had found himself comforting the lady whose petrified face he had seen in the hall.

She looked at him and her eyes were vacant with dark shadows hanging below. "Happened…"

"Did those who attacked leave? The Unvasik. Where did they go?"

The mother squeezed her child's hand, her grip tightening, crushing the small hand within hers. The child began to cry with the pain. Wulfner gently took her wrist and pulled it slowly toward him, his other hand pushing the child back. At first, the mother would not let go of her son but Wulfner persisted with his soft but firm coaxing, and she relented. She fell into him and began sobbing. Her son grabbed Wulfner's leg and wouldn't let go.

What horrors did they see?

Wulfner stroked her hair and patted the boy's head, all the while trying to keep his balance, the lad pulling his leg this way and that. He couldn't stop the memories of Rowena and Sunniva surfacing, but he also saw Emiren and Lunyai in his mind's eye, and knowing they were alive and far from all the torment gave him strength.

The mother said something, but it was just a mumble to his ears. He leaned back and dropped his hand to her shoulder, applying a slight pressure to open up some space between them. The woman looked down and saw her son gripping Wulfner's leg. Her face crumpled into a mix of anguish and disbelief.

"They took him."

Wulfner frowned. "Your husband?"

She nodded. "They changed him."

Wulfner sighed, wondering how much more of this nightmare the realm would go through before it eventually woke up. This wasn't a dream though. The realm was awake.

"You saw him?" he asked, his voice low, afraid he was plunging the lady into terrible trauma.

"I saw him…" She sobbed. "But it wasn't him. His eyes were mad and he was moving like an animal." Eyes clouded with tears rose to Wulfner's own. "Where are they? Where did they go?" she cried, pleading with Wulfner for answers.

Damn Seolta! Damn his soul…

Wulfner couldn't give her the truth. He couldn't tell her that her husband, the boy's father, had probably drowned somewhere past the Black Stone Ford, and had now been swept out into the Western Sea, slain by his own people. Or was maybe lying on the riverbed, feeding the various creatures that scavenged there. A chill rushed through the northerner as he saw the perverse genius in Seolta's designs. Kin would kill kin, and then their kin would nurture hatred in their hearts and seek revenge on those who had killed their loved ones. Seolta could just step back and watch as the realm disintegrated into fratricide.

"What did they tell you? Why were you in the hall?" he asked, trying to shift her attention away from her husband's fate.

The woman coughed, wiped her eyes, and caressed her son's head. "At first we were told to stay in our homes by the Lady Eorthe. Word went around that the city had been taken by enemies and we should stay inside. Except for the men…"

Wulfner shook his head. Seolta had taken the men away and turned them into beasts, leaving their wives and children to an uncertain future.

"Our home is on the main thoroughfare. We heard them coming. I looked out…" Her voice cracked with a sob. Wulfner gently squeezed her shoulder, not knowing what else he could do to offer comfort.

"I looked out and saw the men moving like they had been raised from the dead. Then I saw him…"

May the Winds blow Seolta far beyond the Jagged Heights!

She looked up at Wulfner. "They moved us from our homes after that. They told us a plague was spreading and we had to abandon the southern city. They lied…"

The realm has been flooded with lies. Who knows what is true anymore?

She kept speaking, her voice strangely hollow. "We heard the sounds of battle some days ago. We thought aid had come. We thought we would be saved from those witches and evil giants. But the noise stopped after a while and all was quiet again. The next thing we heard was their voices again, shouting from beyond the door, telling us to stay inside as the plague had got worse. They told us there were dead bodies on the streets."

The Bradlastax...

Shouts rang out and Wulfner looked up to see what was happening. Soldiers were running here and there, and cries of anger became louder. He strained his ears to pick out what was being said.

"Here too!"

"Bastards! They will pay for this!"

"Captain, Hod found at least twenty of the Bradlastax in a bakery on main street. The smell..."

"Sir, the barracks..."

"May Oblivion take their souls!"

Wulfner felt for these soldiers who were making grisly discoveries. Morak truly had become a city of the dead. And the bringers of death had moved on, maybe returning to their own lands.

Wulfner gently pulled free from the mother and her son and retraced his steps back to the entrance courtyard. Morak had become a grotesque aberration that cruelly twisted the pain of loss within him. Rowena and Sunniva had been murdered outside the walls of Morak, their herb-gathering group set upon by Duthka. Two out of over twenty had survived, fleeing back to the city and raising the alarm. By the time soldiers came to the scene of the attack, the Duthka were nowhere to be seen and the innocent victims of a hatred begun years before, were strewn around on the grass, eyes staring up at a deep blue sky.

Forgive me, my precious ones. I should never have brought us here.

Wulfner remembered how the city had seemed so very ugly when they had arrived here, his company bolstering the existing troop compliment. The walls had always been more black than grey, something to do with the stone in these parts, it was said. Over the two years his family were here, though, the Lady Eorthe brought new life and plenty of colour. Little things like hanging baskets of flowers were put up throughout the city, houses and shops were given splashes of bright paint upon their rafters, and banners were hung here and there to break up the monotony of streets.

The big northerner cast his eyes around and saw flowers wilting in baskets, not having been watered in a week or more, he guessed. Colour still adorned the buildings but now it seemed somehow perverse considering the slaughter that had occurred here. And no banners danced in the wind.

It was then he noticed the smell. The stench of old rubbish that had been left in the streets, the odour of rotting meat and the stale stink of despair. Wulfner tried to recall the scents Rowena had always commented on. The faint whiff of pine from the Deadwood, the sweet smell of lilacs in the baskets, and the delicious aroma of freshly baked bread. He tried to bring these sensations back, but his memories were silent images only, pale and harsh.

Wulfner jumped as a company of Bladesung marched past. He heard shouts and orders being given, then hurrying boots.

And so Morak becomes a fortress once more, soldiers perhaps outnumbering the inhabitants… No, outnumbering the survivors.

Wulfner clenched his jaw. When he had stepped foot within the walls of Westhealfe again, just over a week ago, he had felt a beauty tinged with sorrow there. Morak was different, awash with pain and suffering. There was no beauty here.

How many ghosts now walk these streets?

"Wulfner."

He looked up to see the Bladesung Forwost, Wyman, approaching him. Wulfner made to stand but the officer motioned for him to stay seated.

"I thought you had gone mad in that moment, but it seems you have more courage than half my lads put together," he commented, shaking his head.

Wulfner shrugged. "Maybe I'm getting old. When you have fewer years left, I guess it pushes you to move before thinking."

Wyman frowned. "I thought that was how it is when we are young. Leap before you have a good look at where you'll land, something like that," he said, eyebrows raised.

Wulfner nodded and pulled at his beard. "The young have courage born from inexperience. The old are not brave so much as we have finally realised how fleeting life can be."

Wyman seemed to ponder Wulfner's words. His face contorted for an instant; he coughed and turned away. Wulfner knew the horror of the here and now had struck him, and his defences had buckled.

Happens to even the hardiest of soldiers.

"What does General Torbal plan to do now?" enquired the northerner.

Wyman inhaled, then let it out in a huff. Wulfner sensed the Forwost's mettle was being tested far more than his own. The two of them saw the same hideous reality but Wyman was responsible for the lives of so many. Wulfner was just a lone piece in this twisted game, a man-at-arms on the Garak board, a game popular in Westhealfe. Wyman was an Overseer or a Sergeant in that game, a far more important piece that one had to employ skilfully.

Maybe I should heed Corann's words and head back to Ceapung…

"I believe the general will give the order to track down the murderers. My gut tells me we'll be heading into the Deadwood."

Wulfner hung his head. The killing would go on and on unless he could do something.

Trob, Azal, ask Balther to look after you for a while longer.

CHAPTER 2

SVARD

24th Day of Maia, The Day After Morak Was Retaken

Oh shit…

Svard was standing in the gargantuan Holy Sepulchre, in Bregus-tol, the capital of the Rihtgellen kingdom, far from his home in Helli-gan lands, with a man now grabbing his arm. And Svard knew this man. It was the smith who had tackled him days before, there could be no doubt. The iron grip, the scarred arms packed with muscle, and the bandage around the shoulder where Cuyler's arrow had struck. Svard panicked and struggled to free himself, the fear of being wrestled to the ground again surging through his mind. It was definitely the same man but there was something crazed about him. His eyes were wild, and a pitiful moaning sound seeped from his lips.

Raven's beak, what is this?

Svard became aware that other men around them were behaving like animals, growling and scratching their bodies feverishly. The smith gripping him now was not alone in his madness. Svard aimed at the man's shoulder with his free arm and shoved him as hard as he could. The smith fell away, a bizarre coughing erupting from his throat. Svard was free. He stared at the smith. The man's right arm hung in a slack fashion, but he made no attempt to examine his bandaging or the injury beneath. The fellow looked at Svard and the crazed expression fell away to be replaced with vacant eyes and a slack jaw. It was as if he had no sense of where he was.

Has he lost his mind? What is happening?!

Svard hung his head, instinct telling him he needed to avoid any more attention. The smith had reacted like a submissive animal, his humanity disintegrating like the last log that lingered in the ashes of a fire long lit. Svard shivered involuntarily. He flicked his eyes left and right, looking at the men all around, all who seemed to have gone mad. They were ignoring him, just shuffling about within the Holy Sepulchre. He heard raised voices. Words were being spoken. He glanced up and saw several of the grey nuns moving in between the seemingly mindless men and talking to each other, then shouting at the True Sons and those who had come to the mustering.

"Crunnich samliad! Rask lath!"

To Svard's astonishment, the women started cuffing the men around the head. Those hit just cowered and moved onward, as if they were being herded. The voices of the grey sisterhood grew in volume, but they weren't speaking in their language any longer; it sounded like they were imitating animals themselves, hissing and growling in their throats. To Svard's horror, the men were responding to the women, and shambling over to one side of the hall. They were commanding the pitiful wretches!

Witches!

The Helligan First Ranger suddenly felt very vulnerable. He remembered the strange markings on the shaven heads of the two lovers he had spied upon, and a chill ran down his spine. Were these women part of some ancient coven of witches that practiced dark arts? Whoever they were, these women in grey did indeed have some vendetta or rivalry with the True Sons, and Svard could only think they had used some kind of sorcery on these poor bastards, stripping them of their minds.

So why am I not affected?

Svard kept shambling along with the other men, following a group who were being directed to an area near the main doors. Some were being herded to the inner depths of the Holy Sepulchre, but Svard wanted to be as close to an exit as possible. His foot kicked something. He looked down. A cup skidded across the floor, a patch of spilt wine where it had been.

I didn't drink…

The True Sons and the eager flock who had answered their call to holy war, had been knocking back the claret as if there would be no to-morrow, and the grey nuns had been encouraging great consumption. *Poison? Maybe there isn't a tomorrow for this lot…*

He was sure that if he revealed he had not drunk the wine and thus was unaffected, he would be killed outright. He had witnessed the fact that the Grey Sisters were not averse to ending life without hesitation.

The hissed sounds, which Svard took to be commands, continued. Some were like a guttural growl, some were like sharp intakes of breath, and Svard even heard a few low whistles. Yet he reckoned there were words within the grunts and grumbles. An ancient tongue may-be, forbidden words unearthed from a dark past that controlled those who had consumed whatever was in the wine. A figure bumped into his side, making him flinch. The man moaned like a wounded cow, but then simply changed his direction slightly.

First Warrior, what have they done to these people?

Svard kept moving along, keeping his shoulders slouched like the others, head hung, and scratching his body every so often. He prayed none of the poisoners would notice he was not as mindless as those around him. Svard shook his head from side to side, hoping he looked like a frisky hound or something, snatching glances at what was going on.

A group of the Grey Sisters was up on the platform where the True Son leader had been giving a speech, and they were surveying their handiwork, nodding and pointing as if discussing something mundane like where to put some furniture in the king's chambers. They seemed completely unperturbed by the fact that maybe a thousand men were packed into the Holy Sepulchre and were now ambling around like cattle ready for slaughter.

Oh no, Dark Raven, no...

Svard wished he hadn't conjured up that image. Were they about to go around and casually slit the throats of everyone here? Was this holy house about to become a slaughterhouse, its stone floor to be awash with the blood of a thousand? If so, Svard would have to make a break for it. He had his weapons on him so fighting his way out was possible. But if they could control these men, he could quickly find himself at the centre of a horde of frenzied beasts.

Not the way I want to go.

After more shuffling though, it became clear that mass murder was not on the cards. The men had been divided into groups, it seemed, corralled into corners or the sides of the huge church. Svard's stomach knotted as he saw they were being prepared for something—and it wasn't death. At least not death by execution.

They're going to send us out into the streets...

Svard's mind whirled as he tried to imagine what they hoped to achieve and arrived at an ominous conclusion. This was all connected. The High King's death, Orben's move to expand the Helligan nation, the murder of the holy man, Orben's mysterious accomplice Kailen had spoken of, Worsteth's suspicions that General Torbal was going to wrest the rule of the capital from the chamberlain, and the revelation that Svard's own Lady Ulla was in bed with the King's Shield.

Am I going mad like these poor wretches or is this all part of some grand design? Is Ulla a witch too?!

The group of men he was with were now at one side, and another hissed command seemed to be the order to halt. Svard did so and felt like he was in the midst of a horde of revenants. His bowels churned. He was painfully aware that he was in as much danger now as when the smith had grabbed him after the execution of his captains days ago.

Svard tensed. One of these strange animal-men was pawing at him, like a dog would to get attention. The First Ranger growled at him, doing his best impression of an angry hound. Svard was as much hor-rified as relieved to see the man cower, then shy away.

They have become little more than simple beasts…

Svard slumped against a wall, wanting to have nobody at his back, and kept up with his scratching motions and random guttural noises. He had a reasonable view of the women in grey robes so he could keep track of what they were doing at least. They were hissing their harsh words at a handful of the turned men. It sounded like they were spitting out short, sharp gusts of wind from their mouths. There were words within this unholy cauldron of noise but nothing Svard could make out. It was if the strange nuns were sucking in the will of each man, then flinging it back out in a curse, a black blast of air that howled around whatever dark language they spoke.

"Hasss, dek de dek, shoowaaa-hasss, tahsen gah!"

Svard was frightened. Witches and dark sorcery were beyond his skills and wits. *First Warrior, I can fight a man with a sword but I need your help with this.* Svard squeezed his eyes shut and pleaded with his God. He needed a higher power to guard him now, surrounded as he was by malevolent mages and men descending into madness.

Svard peered over again at the nuns and saw that one of the men being hounded was the holy leader, Magen. As much as Svard wanted to see the man hang for ordering the execution of Stigr and Erland, he was hit by a wave of sympathy. His gut told him what was about to happen would be something he would wish upon no one.

A group of four sisters crowded around Magen and four other mindless men, the poor bastards just slouching and making strange sniffing noises. One of the women made a harsh sound and cuffed one standing next to the holy brother.

Raven's…

Svard almost lost his composure as the man leaped at Magen and began to pound his fists upon the holy leader's head. Magen tried to defend himself but his reactions were sluggish. The three others were quickly smacked and given commands, putting Magen at the mercy of four. In moments he was unable to ward off the blows due to being unconscious. But even then, it didn't stop.

Svard lowered his eyes but he could not close his ears. The sound of fists pounding Magen was like a cook madly tenderising some beef. Then there came wet smacking noises. The Helligan First Ranger felt nauseous. He slowly breathed in and tried to calm his nerves.

Magen was now very much dead. The grey robed ones looked to be studying the results of an experiment, chattering away in their language and pointing. One then pulled back her hood and Svard saw ink markings similar to the ones he'd seen on the two lovers.

Who are you people?

Svard had hunted bandits in Bresden Forest, infiltrated the High Chief's camp on the Belfri Isles, taken down the kingpin of the Hurtig criminal underworld and had captured Rencarro's son in Meridia. He had faced danger and death many times and survived. But this was beyond him. He had never faced dark sorcery before.

The First Ranger's thoughts turned to Lorken and the grand notions he had conjured up for the future of his friend's family before they marched to Meridia. Svard had envisioned a greater Helligan nation, no longer bowing to High King Sedmund. He had imagined a glorious future of safety and prosperity for Darl, Torg, and Eira. Svard then recalled his foolish oaths of vengeance to Jenna. Even those were dust in the wind now.

Lorken, this would be a grand tale to tell you over a few ales.

Svard shut his eyes but the snuffling and whining of these things penetrated his skull remorselessly.

But you're not back in Gamle Hovestad…

The First Ranger felt failure more keenly in that moment than ever before. He clenched his fists, inhaled deeply, then let his shoulders drop.

Maybe I'll see you soon in the First Warrior's Hall, old friend.

CHAPTER 3

RENCARRO

24th Day of Maia, The Day After Morak Was Retaken

"First time I've been here," commented Tacet. "What did you say was the name of this village, Kailen?"

"Rumbleton," she replied, turning to Rencarro as she did. "Do you think he will be here?"

Rencarro shrugged, his legs tired after a gruelling march north, away from the Helligan Sentinels. Those soldiers obviously had more pressing business than pursuing a few wayward boatmen and had not pursued them.

On their journey north, Rencarro and his companions had seen no sure sign of the traitor Sylvanus and had passed few travellers on the road. The main reason for that was that folk were heading north, away from the rumours of a Helligan advance. They had only passed a group of monks or some holy order, hooded in drab, grey robes and muttering away to themselves in prayer.

"We can only hope," he said softly.

Rencarro watched as two men tried to pull and shove a stubborn ox off the main street than ran through this settlement. The beast seemed reluctant to leave the even paving for the more rugged side-street where the Meridian spotted a waiting cart. He was about to order villagers nearby to help but then stopped himself.

This is not my village. I am no longer lord of anywhere…

All his life Rencarro had borne far more weight upon his shoulders than the average man. Being an only child, he had grown up knowing he would inherit the rule of Meridia after his father, and thus had been prepared and tutored for the station since he was an infant. His mother had taught him the financial intricacies of governing a city, something Eligius had taken a keen interest in also. And his father had taught him amongst other things to keep your head down, let others be noticed, and then rise when the opportunity presented itself. When Sedmund died, Rencarro had thought the moment had come to set out on a path that would see his city, with himself at the helm, become a far more powerful faction in the realm.

It had all seemed possible…

Yet here he was in a village north of the Mimir River with two of his men and a Helligan fugitive, his city lost, his eldest dead and his younger son, Eligius, having demonstrated far more wit and grit than Rencarro had ever given him credit for.

When Sylvanus is dead, I will come to you, my son.

As they moved up the main street, they heard much talk about the Helligan capture of the Gjallag Bridge but there was a general lack of concern surprisingly. A carter rolled by, his wares piled high. Two women were laughing loudly with each other, perhaps sharing some gossip or a saucy tale. There was a street-seller roasting something that smelt very appetising. And a priest, by the look of his garment, was calling out blessings, telling any who would listen that the Ever-Father was watching over them all and would bring good fortune to their village if they prayed.

Not sure prayer works so well these days…

Eligius had never had much faith in the power of prayer, and Rencarro now felt the lad had the right of it. Rencarro knew he wouldn't return to Meridia to stay, but he wanted to speak with his son again before he left the realm, perhaps make amends for his failings as a father.

Sailing to the Radiant Isles had become more than a fanciful idea; he had decided he would definitely go there after he had brought justice to Sylvanus. He smiled inwardly as he remembered his last meeting with Camran before leaving Argyllan. Rencarro had blamed him for introducing the Meridian lord to rum, in good humour of course.

Damn that Camran!

Tacet cleared his throat and spoke in a low voice. "Shall we split up, my lord? Ask around and then rendezvous at the midday bell, presuming it is rung here?"

Rencarro nodded and Salterio agreed this was as good a plan as any. He turned to the Helligan woman.

"What will you do, Ms. Jacobson?"

She looked at a loss for a moment, pulling at her left ear. "If you have no objections, I will do the same. I have a few theories that may be easily discounted with a bit of local news."

Rencarro nodded. "Please meet us here at midday then."

The Helligan agreed to this and headed off to the west of the town.

"Will she come back, do you think?" questioned Salterio.

"I have no idea," replied Rencarro. "If she finds out something and shares it, good. If she moves on, then good luck to her. She too has reason to see Sylvanus dead, but I sense she has other obligations as well."

Rencarro then rubbed his hands and raised his eyebrows questioningly. "So, you are Rowan and you are Lucian. Who am I?" he asked with a grin.

Tacet responded. "Maybe just keep it simple. Ren."

Rencarro mulled it over. It was as good as any name and it was unlikely anybody here would even know who the Lord of Meridia had been anyway.

"Ren it is. And I am a former merchant, now looking to buy some land up here."

Salterio puffed out a breath and chuckled. "Wish it were under different circumstances, but I have to say I could get used to this. Roaming the realm with my lord and Rowan here, staying nowhere too long and seeing where we are led by the Keeper and the Widow."

Rencarro understood the sentiment. These two men were experts at this kind of thing and no doubt enjoyed the open road and being somewhere nobody knew them. For himself, this was a new experience, but not an entirely unpleasant one. As Salterio had suggested, on another day, this would be quite the adventure.

"Keep your enquiries subtle. Sylvanus is obviously far more cunning than any of us could have ever imagined. If he is around and sees us or learns men are asking for somebody who looks like him, he will flee." Rencarro frowned. "To be honest with the two of you, I am the one at a loss here. You need to tell me how to gather information without asking too many questions."

Tacet smiled. "Strange days indeed. Alright, Salterio can head off now, starting at the north end of the village, and we can stroll around the south, casually chatting over a few methods and techniques."

"Excellent!" responded Rencarro.

And so, they did as Tacet had proposed. Salterio hurried off and was soon lost to their sight. Tacet and Rencarro took a leisurely pace, with the Velox rider explaining various tricks of the trade. The Meridian lord had to laugh at more than one of them.

Rencarro's humour faded as he saw a man slumped against a storefront, a bottle of something dribbling its contents into the dust, its owner barely conscious. Drunk before noon. Rencarro thought about his friend Camran again, the Argyllan quartermaster so many miles away. The man had been drinking far too much since the battle. Rencarro didn't judge him. Both had seen a great deal of blood spilt that day and both had nearly died. Rencarro had the fortitude to lock it away and let the pain out in small doses, but his quartermaster friend had no such strength. Trying to persuade Camran to come to the Radiant Isles with him was perhaps not the best idea. His friend would be better off heading south to the Tarakan Plains for a time, living close to nature and away from the memories. Or with his brother in Fallowden.

A strange tale it has been, he mused as his thoughts turned to Camran's niece, whom he had almost killed. Rencarro thanked the Keeper that mistake had been averted, though it had not been without a healthy amount of pain for him. Tacet had related to Rencarro his journey with the two girls and a northerner, and the Meridian lord marvelled at it all, recognising how important perhaps Camran's niece and her village were now. They kept alive a centuries old language and some old book of herb-lore, that had been hiding in a library in Westhealfe, was written in that tongue. Who knew what diseases they might be able to cure with this newfound knowledge?

Could they have saved Shansu from the Shadow Within?

"Nothing," replied Salterio, his face a picture of defeat as they sat together in an inn a while later.

Rencarro slapped his shoulder.

"Do not despair, Lucian," he said encouragingly. "Ours is a fool's quest with little hope of success. But if we do find him, then we will have set right at least one matter in this whole sorry state of affairs." Rencarro rapped lightly on the table. "Let us eat and forget the cur for a time. I feel like you two have many stories worth listening to. If I had known my Velox riders were enjoying themselves so much on their missions, I would have cut the expenses allowance in half!"

All three laughed, and Rencarro again felt an urge to forget about Sylvanus and make a life on the road with these two rogues.

The Helligan woman returned from the outhouse at that moment. She came over and took a stool. "I must apologise in advance and tell you I have very little in the way of coin," she said, her eyes darting between them. "Very little as in none at all."

Rencarro shook his head. "My life gets stranger. I have enough for all of us, but I cannot ignore the farcical nature of all this. I will *knowingly* buy an ale for the personal messenger of the man who annexed my city," he said with a look of bemusement.

Tacet laughed. "When this is all over, I will write a song in honour of the bizarre tale we find ourselves in."

Kailen offered a smile. "That will be quite a ballad, Rowan."

A bargirl came over to them. She had a cheery air about her and Rencarro reckoned she was popular with the customers.

"What'll it be then, sirs?" Her eyes fell on Kailen and she blinked, noticing she was not a *sir* but a woman. "And ma'am! Sorry, milady, too used to fellows in this inn."

Kailen waved away her apology.

"Four mugs of the house ale and whatever is cooking," the former lord of Meridia said.

"Will have them here in no time," she replied with a flutter of her eyelashes.

As she left their table, the three men exchanged a look. Rencarro caught Kailen rolling her eyes. He let out a belly-laugh. He couldn't help it. The absurdity of what they were doing, where they now sat, the Lord of Meridia no longer in command of his home city but a hero in Argyllan, and the realisation that his Velox riders were a couple of handsome young men who played as much as they worked. And now they were drinking with their enemy. He slapped the table. Then became aware he was attracting attention. Other customers were staring at him.

"Miserable lot," muttered Salterio.

Tacet puffed out a breath. "Don't blame them. They're not fleeing the Helligan advance, but I'm not sure they have that much to laugh about right now."

Rencarro calmed himself. "Quite."

The barmaid returned with four frothy mugs of ale and set them down. "Pies will be along soon, milady, gentlemen."

Rencarro thanked her. "And forgive my outburst of merriment moments ago. Old memories can do that to me at times."

The barmaid gave them another gorgeous smile. "Oh, don't you worry, sir. It probably seems a bit glum in here to travellers such as yourselves. We're just a bit anxious about all those soldiers coming this way. Better than Unvasik giants though!" she said with a shudder.

Rencarro glanced at Tacet, then cocked his head. "Unvasik?"

"Haven't you heard? Unvasik raiders sacked the Royal Mines and the village of Gimmweg about a week ago. Word is that refugees from villages along the Ruby Road have been pouring into the capital."

Salterio choked on his ale. "Widow be damned…" he muttered.

Kailen cursed something under her breath.

Rencarro tried to put this piece of information within the larger context. Unvasik in Morak *and* Gimmweg? Were the tribes staging an invasion? The timing was frighteningly suspicious.

"Well, I am sure Bregustol will send a legion of good men to send them packing," said Rencarro, although in reality he really had no idea what the situation was in Bregustol and who would be making such decisions. He began to think about it but Tacet's question to the barmaid distracted him.

"Have there been many travellers coming through your village?"

"A few. But they don't stay, not with all this trouble. My cousin told me something happened up in Morak too, but nobody seems to know much about that."

All of them were well aware of the horror that had occurred there, but Rencarro felt it better to spare this lady the grim details. He looked at his Velox rider and saw Tacet was thinking something. He waited to see where he would go next with his enquiries.

"Sorry to keep you from your work, good lady, but I have a strange question," he said with eyes that practically oozed physical attraction. It was all Rencarro could do not to snort with laughter again. This was how Rowan the Rhymer gained the trust of young women.

Too damn charming!

"Not too busy, my dear, so ask away," she replied, looking more than a tad excited.

Rencarro noticed Kailen turn away to hide her smirk.

"Have you seen anybody coming through with ink markings upon their head?" asked Tacet.

Rencarro was surprised but could see he was investigating if the Duthka had been seen in these parts. The Meridian lord had been totally unaware their people still inhabited the forests to the north, but it seemed the Duthka had not faded into the depths of history.

"Funny you should say that…"

The whole table tensed.

"There were a couple of gentlemen in here yesterday. I remember them firstly because they were in high spirits, a bit like yourselves. One said something about a good wind blowing through the realm." She put her hands on her hips and shook her head. "By the Ever-Father, I have no idea how they could think that!"

Rencarro looked at her, listening intently.

"Anyway," she continued. "One of them was wearing a wrap of cloth around his head. Bit unusual as most men in these parts wear hats or nothing at all on their bonce. But I saw him tightening it up after they'd been here a while. I glimpsed something under the cloth and hurried over to collect their empties..."

She paused and her cheeks flushed.

"Oh, you must think I'm terribly nosey. Typical bar-girl!"

Tacet reached out a hand and took hers, gently stroking the back with his thumb.

"Anyone would be curious. If that had been me, I would have rushed over and pulled the damn thing off," he said, turning to Rencarro and Salterio and laughing, all the while holding the girl's hand and caressing it.

He is good.

The girl relaxed, although Rencarro saw her eyes darting down to Tacet's hand every now and then.

"Well, I went over, picked up their glasses and saw one of them had some kind of markings under the cloth. A jagged swirl or something."

The northerner whom Tacet had travelled with had told the Velox rider a fair bit about the Duthka and their markings. The man had fought against them, it seemed, in a campaign that Sedmund had kept secret from the realm at large, and so was fairly knowledgeable about them.

Salterio perked up with a question. As he asked it, he took the girl's other hand.

Keeper, save me from these two! thought Rencarro.

"And the other fellow," Salterio said, gently massaging her hand with his thumb and forefinger, "did he also have his head covered?"

Kailen coughed into her hand. Rencarro thought he had heard something said within the cough.

"Oh no." The barmaid giggled. "He was going bald."

Rencarro stared at her. Tacet and Salterio both stopped their tactile teasing of the young lady. All three men went rigid. Kailen's attention was also on the barmaid.

"What?" the young lady spluttered.

"This other man," said Rencarro slowly. "Was he a bit older than me, maybe nearing fifty years of age? About a head taller than yourself. What hair he did have, a dark grey? His features weathered, one might say." Rencarro continued to describe Sylvanus in as much detail as possible.

The girl raised both hands to her mouth, pulling them away from Rowan the Rhymer and Lucian of the Lyre.

"Ever-Father, it's as if you're seeing into my memories! Is he your brother?" she asked, her eyes wide and a smile blooming.

Rencarro's gut tightened. Sylvanus had been here. Only a day ago. Truly it seemed like the Widow was playing games with him now.

"Not his brother but a good friend to us all," said Tacet, recovering more quickly than his lord. "Do you have any idea where he went? Has he come back to this inn?"

She shook her head. "I waved goodbye to them from the front door there. They had spent a fair bit of coin here, so I felt they deserved a proper farewell. They headed north up the street, but I couldn't tell you where they went." She turned sad eyes at them. "What a shame you missed your friend! He would have been happy to see you, I would think."

Rencarro forced a smile. "I'm sure he would have been delighted to see us."

The girl flashed another smile, then headed back to her work.

Silence hung in the air at the table, each of the four staring at their drinks, lost in their own thoughts. Kailen was the first to break the hush. "Can someone please explain the significance of the ink markings?"

Tacet looked at Rencarro, who gave him a quick nod. The Velox rider then proceeded to tell the Helligan all about his journey into the Frozen Forest and his altercations with the Duthka.

When he had finished, Rencarro leaned forward. "Ms. Jacobson, is there anything you know that might relate to the Duthka? Did Orben speak of allies in the north? Do you think he had forged an alliance with the Unvasik?"

Kailen shook her head, looking mystified. "I don't know. Lady Ulla was always party to all Lord Orben's planning, but this time it was different. He shut her out, and of course, myself also." She bit her lip and squinted. "So, if Sylvanus was here yesterday, who was the other? A Duthka agent."

Rencarro drummed his fingers on the table. "Possibly this Seolta himself. If they headed to the north of the village, can we assume they left and moved on? If so, their obvious destination would be Bregustol."

"Sylvanus and Seolta plan to spread chaos in the capital, do you think?" queried Salterio.

"If their goal is indeed to divide the realm and ignite civil war, then yes, I would say Bregustol is their next target."

It was all becoming clear to Rencarro. Sylvanus was part of whatever grand plan had been erupting like sores across the realm. He was allied with the Duthka, allied with a people Rencarro thought lost to the brutality of history. Meridia falling to the Helligans, Marcus' death, both were single threads in this hideous web that Sylvanus and the Duthka lord had spun with the Unvasik.

The Throskaur raid too...

Rencarro was sure now that the pirates were part of it. How they were summoned or persuaded to join, Rencarro couldn't fathom, but it couldn't be a coincidence that they had struck so soon after Sedmund had died.

Did he die? Or was he murdered?

So many dead. And with Helligan forces to the south and Unvasik attacking in the northeast, the blood would continue to flow. Suddenly vengeance upon Sylvanus seemed small and insignificant. What difference would it make if Rencarro killed his former Second? Marcus would not return, his city was lost to him, and the conflict in the realm was now careening down a hill like a runaway wagon.

Nothing will change if he dies.

Tacet was lightly pounding his fist on the table. "Damn the air he breathes!" he snarled. "And let the Abyss take Seolta!"

Kailen stood up. "Please excuse me again. The ale has gone right through me."

They nodded and she headed to the outhouse again.

Rencarro noticed Tacet frowning. "What is it?"

"She said the ale had gone right through her, but she's only had a mouthful," he observed, pointing at her mug.

The three exchanged looks. Then there came a shout from outside.

"Thief! Somebody stop her! That's my horse, dammit!"

CHAPTER 4

SONGAA

24th Day of Maia, The Day After Morak Was Retaken

Songaa watched the hive of activity around him, his heart heavy. Fallowden had changed even in the short time he had been here. The appearance of Throskaur within Argol Forest yesterday had understandably terrified the folk here, but also rallied them. Every villager capable of using a tool was feverishly working away, building up the palisade even higher and strengthening walkways. Down in the village proper, more defences were being constructed. The raiders they had killed yesterday were probably the last but the villagers were right to do all they could to protect their homes. Who knew what else lurked in the forest of Kayah's future?

"Promise me, Emi, promise me you'll be back before the next Moonday," croaked Megari as she gripped her daughter's shoulders.

Songaa truly felt for Megari and Quint. Emiren would be back in Fallowden within a week but to say goodbye to their daughter now after all that had happened was a hardship he would not wish upon anybody.

"Mum, I promise," Emiren assured her, kissing her mother's cheek and stroking her hair. "I'm sure Moryn went to Manbung to join Ol-wyn and Turi. We'll catch up to him and make sure he gets there safely."

Quint huffed. "Why did he head off by himself anyway, before dawn without a word? Not the kind of friend I'd go running after," he grumbled.

Songaa couldn't disagree with Emiren's father. Moryn had been foolish and selfish to wander off without telling anyone. It was nothing short of reckless. Songaa could only think the young man had a good reason for his actions. Whatever it was, the Tarakan elder still meant to admonish the Duthka sailor when they found him. He stroked Ahoni's mane and cast a glance at several people of Fallowden who were sharpening wooden stakes. Songaa said a short prayer to Yaai and Tlenaii to watch over these folk day and night.

"I know," Emiren agreed with her father. "I am furious with him too. But he has the book, which as we discovered last night is full of valuable knowledge. If Moryn were to be robbed on the road, or worse, if the book got back to this Seolta, it would be a disaster. Any hope of curing those turned mad, would be lost." She sighed. "And it seemed like those Throskaur yesterday knew him. If that is so, they may hunt him."

Songaa couldn't make sense of the Throskaur knowing Moryn's name but took a step forward to speak. "Megari, Quint, I can well understand your feelings here. Not knowing where Lunyai was for a time was a waking nightmare." He tried to smile reassuringly. "But you know where Emiren is going and I will be with her all the way."

Quint shook his head. "I certainly feel better knowing you will be with her, Songaa. And Lunyai here. But to be honest, I feel bad about that too! You, heading away from your home again. The folk here already owe you and your people a debt of gratitude we can't repay."

I hope you never have to try, thought Songaa gravely.

Emiren hugged her mother again, then her father. "I'll be back before you know it. And then we'll face the troubles together. When I'm in Manbung, I'll also make sure to pass on word that the Argol region needs help. General Torbal might remember me, and if he hears that there is danger here too, he may send soldiers."

Megari sighed. "I don't know what to hope for…"

Songaa again could not argue with this sentiment. To wish for no soldiers to come was a risk, yet to wish for spears and shields to march the Forest and Coastal Roads, this was also a dark thought.

"Let us hope there are no more Throskaur, no beast-men and peace will return to Ragnekai," Emiren said, her face full of an optimism and determination Songaa envied.

Quint put a hand on Emiren's shoulder. "I think you've grown ten years in the last few weeks. You talk about raiders and battle as if they are an everyday occurrence," he said in a tone laced with sadness.

Songaa studied him and saw Emiren's father did not carry the expression of a proud father in that moment, but of a man struggling to control his own fear. Songaa knew the fear he carried was that he might never see his daughter again.

The Tarakan reached out and placed his own hand on Quint's shoulder. "We will be on horseback and I promise you, we will flee at the first sign of trouble. The company of riders who came to our aid in Argyllan is still patrolling the lands. Also, we have a rather mighty ally with us," he said, pointing to Tarak, who was waiting patiently. The wolf would come with them, mainly because Emiren wasn't sure the animal would suffer her leaving him again.

Quint nodded but his eyes were tearful.

"Da…" whispered Emiren and leaned in to hug him. "I'll be back soon. And this time I won't be running off again."

Megari pulled her husband's arm. Songaa could see she was putting a brave face on this parting now.

"Come on, dear husband. We're making a scene here," she said with a chuckle. "Let's get back and finish off Kall's home-brew."

The farewells were over. Megari and Quint were walking back to their home, with no backward glances, no final waves. Songaa knew this was for the best. Pretending their daughter was off to the next village was undoubtedly easier than thinking about the reality.

Lunyai helped Emiren up onto the horse and the three of them left the village with Tarak trotting along beside the two horses, Ahoni and

Neii'Ne. Banseth gave Songaa a grim nod as they passed through the gates.

We have killed together, on two different days. No words are necessary now.

They quickly fell into a good pace and were soon heading north along the Forest Road, all three keeping one eye on the road and one on the forest to their left, its beautiful greens hopefully hiding no more of the Throskaur. With Banseth and others, Songaa had spent the rest of the day yesterday patrolling the forest paths. Nobody heard anything nor saw signs of passing. Songaa prayed those who were killed were the last of the raiders.

All-Mother, please spare us from more death. And I pray that Lunyai never has to kill again…

He had spoken with his daughter about her actions. It had been a very difficult conversation, with neither of them having the necessary words to express themselves. Songaa had found he could not justify the killing, could not say with conviction that the Throskaur deserved to die. But equally, he knew that if they had hesitated, Banseth or Emiren or any of them might be dead now.

His mind turned to the dream that had entered his sleep the previous night. It had been similar to the one that had come to him the night he learned Lunyai was missing, only this time his daughter stood with him on the island. Tlenaii was again massive on the horizon, seemingly touching the All-Mother, a son returned to a place of love. The sea was glass again. The *tatanka* had been there again but it had moaned as if in pain, then keeled over. The glass sea had not shattered as before, instead becoming a black ooze into which the *tatanka* was enveloped, the darkness covering all traces of the beast, as if it had never been there. Tlenaii had then faded in the space of two breaths to a grey shadow.

Songaa shook his head to dispel the images. He had never known dreams to come true, but he couldn't shake the feeling that Tlenaii was giving him a warning. A warning of what, he wasn't sure.

Their mounts seemed to be enjoying getting out onto the open road again, a friskiness in their step and a feisty snicker every few yards. He hoped they would simply come across Moryn, sitting under a tree, reading the book.

And then Lunyai and I can return home.

Songaa saw the Plains in his mind's eye and wondered if going home and life going as before on was at all possible. Could his people live on the Plains, hoping all would be well in the wide realm? It seemed more a dream than a realistic hope. With all he had heard from his daughter and others, and what he had been through in Argyllan, the Tarakan was sadly certain that the realm would not heal in the foreseeable future, and when it finally did, it would bear terrible scars and deep wounds. Wounds that would heal and be forgotten for a time, but which would begin to itch one day, bringing back bitter memories, and it would begin again.

Wounds fester if you do not take steps to heal them properly.

Songaa pondered on whether the Tarakan people should gather into one large tribe. Greater numbers meant they were safer, but it would change their entire way of life. Life on the Plains was good and in harmony with the All-Mother. One tribe stayed in a region for two years, caring for the All-Mother and seeking guidance from Her children. Then the tribe would hand over those lands to the next, as they in turn moved on to another home. It had been this way for generations and there was peace and happiness. Bringing the tribes together would lead to a great concentration of people in one region and would strain the All-Mother, perhaps make the land barren.

His thoughts continued to swirl as they nudged the horses into a decent clip, Songaa's mare Ahoni snorting in the morning air tinted with Argol's scent. Tarak seemed happy bounding along beside them.

As they rode on, Songaa noticed Emiren and Lunyai were being very quiet and wondered if it was because he was so close to them. With this in mind, he reined in Ahoni a tiny fraction and allowed a few yards to open up between them. Before long, conversation began to flow between the two young ladies, and he felt he had made the right choice to hang back. Tarak seemed to sense his intentions and kept pace with him. Songaa smiled.

This one is a clever wolf.

After another half a mile of riding, he began to hear laughter from his daughter and Emiren. It was a wonderful sound after the darkness of recent times. He wished he could laugh more but knew it would take his wife Chenoa and her subtle teasing to bring back his belly laughs. Songaa watched the two young ladies together on the horse.

The vitality of youth and the promise of the future.

Songaa wondered at that future. If all the trouble faded and life returned to what it had been, what did the coming years hold for Lunyai and her friend? Songaa could see the bond between them, the warmth that seemed to swell when they were together and the unmistakable look they shared when they held each other's eyes. As he had said to Lunyai, it was not a future Chenoa and he had envisioned, but how could he yearn for something different now he had seen the love that was growing between them?

Part of him wanted to tell them to ride to the Plains together and leave him to find Moryn by himself. A fear lurked in his mind that danger would find them if they stayed in these lands. His troubling dreams were not helping him to dispel these concerns.

But at least he could sleep.

Songaa wondered if the innkeeper, father to Emiren's murdered friend, could find any rest under Tlenaii's watch.

To lose a child...

Songaa almost broke down there and then with the thought of Lunyai actually being dead, not just missing. Even though he hadn't known where she was, he had held a belief that he would see her smile again, hold her in his arms and hug her tightly. But the very idea that he would never see the curiosity shining in her eyes, never hear her sing the Tarakalo again, and never know what future she would have had—all this tore away at his heart.

All-Mother, please give the innkeeper and the brother the strength to keep living. And let the memory of the son never lose its gleam.

Songaa looked up and saw Lunyai had halted her mount. He tensed. Songaa pulled Ahoni up to them and saw they were staring ahead.

"What is it?" he whispered.

"Listen," breathed Lunyai.

Songaa closed his eyes and focused on the sounds around him. He heard the wind in the trees. He heard a bird singing a short tune over and over. And he heard his own heart beating.

What does she…

There!

It was the unmistakeable sound of hooves clip-clopping along the road, somewhere ahead of them. Songaa's right hand slipped to his bow, his left falling to the fletching upon an arrow, and his thighs tensed, ready to bring Ahoni round.

He stared ahead.

Then Lunyai laughed and Songaa nearly fell off Ahoni.

"Quiet! What are you…"

Then Songaa laughed too. He could hear the Tarakalo being sung by more than one voice.

The three of them waited and before the next verse was over, two horses came into view with grey-haired Tarakan ladies atop the animals. Naaki and Imala. They saw Songaa and the girls and their faces broke into huge smiles. All the riders nudged their mounts forward and soon greetings were being exchanged.

"Why are you here?" asked Songaa, not trying to hide the fact he was overjoyed to see them. "I thought you would be on the road home now."

Imala smiled gently. "We sent the others ahead along the Coastal Road, but I told my sister that we couldn't leave you and Lunyai to ride back alone."

Naaki spoke up. "So, we have come to accompany you." She raised an eyebrow. "Though we were expecting to meet you at the village. You have left already it seems."

The expression on Songaa's face must have said it all.

"You are not going back to the Plains," stated Imala.

"Not yet," replied Songaa sadly.

CHAPTER 5

KAPVIK

25th Day of Maia, Two Days After Morak Was Retaken

The light mist of rain that fell upon the lands around Bregustol gave the night an ethereal feel, the damp darkness a welcome to wraiths. Kapvik remembered when he was younger and had to take his turn manning the watchtowers during the dark nights up in Unvasiktok. Some of his people believed Tatkret's black-hearted brother, Sila, sent the mists to obscure their view of the Ropa-Obita, but Kapvik believed The Watcher would not allow such a thing to happen. A time would come when Tatkret would cast His brother from this world and the wraiths would fade, the mists would clear and the icy touch of Sila's breath would be no more. Or so it was said.

Where will I be when that happens?

Kapvik turned to his mysterious Duthka lover Siorraidh, who walked beside him through fields of shadowy thickets and whispering grass. She looked up at him. In the daylight, she was beautiful; at night, she was bewitching.

"All is well, my gentle giant. I have word that Seolta and Vorga are both now moving forward with the plan, but on different paths," she told him.

Kapvik frowned, not entirely sure if this was good news. Were the Unvasik being sent forth into battle again while the Duthka watched? Was Seolta manipulating his lord?

"Where is Vorga?" he asked.

"You worry too much, Kapvik," said Siorraidh. She must have noticed the tension in his voice. "Our lords have their parts to play and I have no doubt they will succeed. Your lord is a mighty warrior, mine a careful planner. They may not be trusting partners, but they are on the same side. As are we," she finished, with a questioning smile.

Kapvik reluctantly nodded. Maybe he was thinking too much, but everything had become so complicated. When he had marched down from the Unvasiktok tribelands, he had expected the following days to be one battle after another, with the Unvasik showing the lowlanders why they should be feared. He had known their soldiers were well-trained, but he had believed then that his prowess was far superior. Kapvik felt like a fool now for having been so naïve.

"Life was simpler back in my lands," he grumbled, although he did spare a grin.

Siorraidh chuckled. "Simpler? Yes. But would you leave this new path behind? Would you leave me?"

They stopped and she reached up. Her hand was on his beard, stroking his jaw, and her eyes were a show of playful innocence. "I would not change anything in this moment," she whispered and Kapvik once again felt his resistance shatter like thin ice under a heavy boot. He slowly inhaled, then leaned down and kissed her lips.

"No, I would not change this moment." He straightened to his full height. "But I cannot escape my doubts."

We all have doubts, Kapvik. Only a fool sees clear skies every day.

"Can you really not see my thoughts?" he questioned. "It is very strange to have you within my head."

"It makes you uncomfortable?" she asked, a pained expression on her face.

"No. If anything, it soothes me. But when I think about it, it is... strange." He laughed.

"Think of it as hearing my voice not with your ears, but with your heart, Kapvik."

He sighed. "You have a witch's tongue, that much is certain."

She laughed and squeezed his arm. "Come, we must hurry and be gone before the sun rises and the folk around here wake."

"And where are we going this time? I thought you said we were heading to the capital." He looked ahead in the pale light of the coming dawn and saw the dark shapes of high walls. They were still at least a few miles away from Bregustol. "Unless you can also make us fly, I don't see how we can get there before the sun is up and people around here start screaming that the Unvasik have come."

Trust me! came her voice in his head.

Kapvik ran a hand down to her shapely backside and imagined her naked form.

"Trust me..." he muttered, shaking his head. Kapvik reckoned they would soon meet more Duthka and they would have some ingenious way of getting them all into the city. He hoped it didn't involve him hiding in a hay cart. Maybe they had a hooded cloak big enough for him. *I will still be noticed though. These lowlanders are so small...*

They walked on another few hundred yards, Siorraidh quickening her pace as the sun broke the horizon to the east, a golden glow gently seeping into the land that by right belonged to the Unvasik and Duthka. His lover suddenly stopped.

"Kapvik, please remember not to mention what we found at the summit," she said, almost pleadingly. "Seolta must not know. If he learns what I carry, he will take it. By force if necessary."

Kapvik growled in his throat. "Let him try! I would break his skull."

She leaned in to hug him, whispering, "I know, my gentle giant. But you could not deny Vorga as well."

He begrudgingly conceded she was right. He let out a huff. "I will say nothing. Now let us stop talking and move!"

"We are here already."

He rolled his eyes. "I suggest we keep walking and stop the games."

"No games," she replied, her eyes alive and teasing. She then pointed to a barrow or some such mound just ahead to their left. "Hurry!"

Kapvik followed her, frowning as he went. So, they would hide in some musty tomb until night fell again? This was becoming tedious.

It was a barrow, but it looked as if it had not been visited in many years. The steps leading down to the stone arched entrance were overgrown with all manner of weeds and grass. Moss blanketed the stone in patches and Kapvik could already detect a musty odour from within.

Siorraidh did not hesitate and entered the darkness. Kapvik sighed and followed her in, almost bending double to get through the arch. It was pitch-black within and the Unvasik warrior felt his patience wearing thin.

"Stand still for a moment, Kapvik," she whispered. "I don't want you falling over the crypt here."

He heard her shuffle farther away and guessed she was retrieving a flint and tinder or something. His breath caught in his chest as a portion of the darkness before him slid away to reveal a tunnel lit with flaming torches. A figure was visible beyond, now ushering Siorraidh in. He heard some words exchanged.

"Eirik Duthka, eirik Idelisa!"

"Eirik Duthka."

"Quick!" she called back to him.

He moved to the light and saw that some kind of heavy curtain had concealed the passageway.

"You Duthka seem to have thought of everything," he whispered, quite impressed by how Siorraidh seemed to carry no doubt.

After the first few yards down the tunnel, Kapvik was able to proceed without stooping. They passed several Duthka, all carrying bundles, travelling in both directions. Siorraidh would give a stern word to each one, and they would respond with a quick reply and a dip of the head. It appeared she was second only to Seolta. This thought made Kapvik admire her all the more; she was a truly impressive lady, as enchanting as the first snow, as mysterious as the sights he had seen within the Sacred Mount, and wiser than any he had ever known.

A stab of doubt hit him. *Why would such a magnificent creature be interested in a mountain tribesman like me?*

He cursed himself for once again letting weakness slip into his mind unbidden. He was Vorga's Fist, not some green youth who had never faced the Ropa-Obita. Doubts should not come anywhere near him. And yet they did.

She will be the death of me…

He grinned to himself as he thought this, wondering whether it would be the ancient weapon she now possessed or her witch's tongue that would send him to the Hall of Bones.

After walking for another five hundred yards at least, Siorraidh led him down a left-fork in a passage, then a right-fork at another junction. More passages opened up before them and Kapvik could see there was a whole network of subterranean tunnels. Being underground wasn't the most enjoyable experience he had ever had, and he wondered how the Ropa-Obita lived like this, shunning sunlight and running from Sila's Breath.

"The Duthka built these tunnels?" he asked his lover.

She replied over her shoulder, her pace not faltering in the slightest. "No. They have been here for hundreds of years. Seolta has a theory as to why they were made, but he will not tell me. He likes to keep his secrets," she said with a laugh.

"And now you have yours."

She stopped abruptly and turned to him. No words came from her mouth. Her voice was in his head, forceful and pleading.

I beg you, Kapvik, say no more about that. Seolta will not hesitate to kill me to possess the rod.

Kapvik clenched his teeth, picturing himself taking Seolta's head from his shoulders with a well-aimed swing of his mighty axe. He pushed the image aside and nodded.

"How much farther is it?" he asked, despite not knowing where exactly they were going.

"Still some distance so let us make haste," she replied, turning back and setting off again at a quicker pace. Down the tunnels they moved, darkness stretching out before them, broken by small islands of flickering flames.

They finally entered a large chamber and Kapvik had a feeling they had passed under the outer walls of Bregustol and were now within the city itself. He realised these tunnels were how the Duthka came and went without arousing suspicion. They could enter and leave the city without anyone knowing.

Siorraidh moved over to a ladder, beckoning Kapvik to follow her. Without hesitation she climbed up. Kapvik let out a sigh and followed her, testing the lower rungs first to see if they would bear his weight. The ladder was clearly a new addition to this underground network, judging by its sturdiness and the absence of rot.

The Unvasik warrior climbed up after her, wondering where they would emerge. His stomach suddenly tightened as he realised they might be about to meet Seolta and Vorga.

How will I explain myself if he has heard I have lain with a Duthka woman?

Siorraidh disappeared above him, through another curtain of dark material. He followed her and, pushing through the cover, found himself looking up at a stone ceiling with wooden rafters. An old building but one of strength, he reckoned.

Siorraidh offered him a hand, as his head and shoulders rose above the floor. He took it, dipping his head in thanks. The Duthka lady grinned and he felt a surge in his chest.

Damn her charms…

"What is this place?" he asked.

"One of our many safe houses within Bregustol."

Kapvik saw two figures in long, grey robes walk through the room, exiting at the far side without a word to Siorraidh. A third followed behind but this one stopped and spoke to her in a low voice, this person also obviously female. He couldn't understand a word but sensed important news was being related. He waited patiently, surprised these people in grey seemed unperturbed by an Unvasik warrior entering their secret hideout.

He heard a door open to their left and peered over. Another grey-robed figure came through and before the door was shut again, Kapvik caught a glimpse of what was beyond—a row of beds with people lying upon them.

A rest place? A house of healing?

Siorraidh finished talking to the other and turned to him.

"All is ready."

"Ready for what?" he asked, feeling more than a little uneasy with the Duthka and their ways.

"Ready for the coming storm, my gentle giant," she replied, squeezing his hand.

Kapvik looked into her eyes and saw her beauty, but beyond that he saw something else.

Who will control the storm?

Siorraidh might be carrying a weapon of godly power, but Kapvik feared not even she could control a storm once it had been unleashed.

Winds, rain, fire…lightning! They cannot be tamed.

CHAPTER 6

LUNYAI

25th Day of Maia, Two Days After Morak Was Retaken

As they trotted into the town of Manbung, the Sacred Mount towering behind them, Lunyai felt Emiren's head heavy against her back. She worried that the girl from Fallowden, so used to navigating a forest on foot but a new-born in terms of horsemanship, was feeling the strain of sitting so long in the saddle. She turned her head to see her father was looking their way with an expression that said he felt the same.

"She sleeps," he said in the Tarakan language.

"She was not born on the Plains," observed Lunyai with a sad smile.

Emiren's head lifted from her back and she sighed with grogginess. "I'm sorry, Lunyai. I must be the worst person to ride with," Emiren said, trying to stifle a yawn.

Songaa laughed. "You keep Lunyai's back warm, I think."

Lunyai had had to make extra effort to control her mount, Emiren being close to a dead weight at times, but she wouldn't have wanted anything else. Having her so close had kept her warm on the out-side and within, her chest swelling every now and then as she thought about a future with Emiren.

"Where is this inn?" asked Imala from behind them.

"Not far," replied Lunyai.

"I think we are bringing attention," commented Naaki.

Lunyai looked around and noticed more than one of the townsfolk stopping for a moment to watch the riders clip-clopping into their town. There could be no mistaking the fact that they weren't from this region, with their buck-skin clothing, long black, or grey, hair tied with bones and decorated with feathers, and their darker skin tone. Lunyai hoped that some of them would remember her from before, but knew it would likely be only Iden and Darelle of the Merry Mount Inn who would recognise Emiren and herself. She wondered if Turi and Olwyn had returned to the Abhaile already. She was pleased with herself for having remembered the forest's true name and not the un-kind title the people of Westhealfe had given it.

Frozen Forest indeed! I found so much warmth there, just as I did in Fallowden.

"Do you think Moryn came this way?" asked Emiren behind her.

Lunyai felt this was their last hope, to find Moryn here in Man-bung. They had not seen him or heard any word of his passing from travellers on the road. The Tarakan lady felt betrayed by his sudden departure. Since he had saved her life, she had felt there was a bond between them, one that warranted at least a word of farewell.

"Maybe," was all she said in reply.

They were soon at the Merry Mount Inn and saw a man standing outside the front door, head back and breathing in the morning air. A tall man in black hosen and a leather vest, ashen fair hair above eyes that were closed.

"Corann?" Lunyai couldn't believe her own eyes.

Emiren gave out a yelp.

"Corann!" she cried.

Is Wulfner here?

Corann opened his eyes and saw them. His first reaction was a warm smile, followed swiftly by confusion. Emiren was sliding off their horse as the other Tarakans pulled in.

The redhead from Fallowden rushed to the Duthka man and leapt up, hugging him and almost making him stumble. Lunyai could tell he was not used to such displays of affection.

"Corann, I can't believe you're here. Where is Wulfner?" asked Emiren, her words tumbling out in an excited stream.

The man's expression fell and Lunyai's heart lurched.

No...please, Tlenaii, no...

Corann gently pushed Emiren back and offered a smile.

"Wulfner is with General Torbal, I believe, although I hope he had had a change of heart and is now on his way back to Ceapung. We parted company after meeting Torbal at the Black Stone Ford." Corann looked at the small company. "Fellow Tarakans?" Then he frowned. "Where is Moryn?"

Lunyai dismounted and joined Emiren. She gestured to her father and the others. "Corann, this is my father, Songaa, and also Imala-shi and Naaki-shi of the Tarakan Plains. They came with us in our search for Moryn."

Corann's eyes flashed. "What? Moryn went missing?"

Emiren explained. "He left Fallowden before dawn two days ago, without a word to anyone. He has the book with him. We thought he had come here to find Olwyn and Turi, but we have seen no sign of him."

As if summoned by the mention of her name, Olwyn stepped out of the Merry Mount Inn. Her look of surprise and joy at seeing Emiren and Lunyai again was genuine. Her subsequent mask of worry when she heard about Moryn was vastly different.

Further talk was cut short as Darelle came out.

"What's all the clamour out... Lunyai! Emiren!" The innkeeper's wife stared at the Tarakans, then burst out laughing. "You've brought your people with you! I knew our pies were good but not this good!"

In the space of what was only two songs, the company were sitting at a large table in the Merry Mount, their horses stabled for them by a lad who was clearly in awe at the Tarakan steeds and their beauty. A delicious aroma was wafting through from the kitchen, along with Darelle's voice, singing a song about long-lost friends. Turi had given them all crushing embraces, tears spilling from his eyes, but saying nothing. Olwyn seemed much healed after her injury. Lunyai looked around at the odd group and couldn't help but grin.

She turned to Emiren and saw a flush in her cheeks. Emiren's eyes lifted upward and Lunyai felt a tingle run through her. This was where they had first slept together, a night of nervous passion. Lunyai cast a glance at her father, but he was busy gazing around the inn.

Yaai, Tlenaii, You guide me down the strangest of paths. All-Mother, let this moment endure in my memory forever.

The group, made up of people from all over the realm, ate well and made light conversation. Lunyai knew they would have to discuss serious matters soon but for now she was content to hear about Olwyn's recovery and their stay here.

"We have no coin, of course, money not being used in our village, so at first we felt ashamed. Darelle and Iden have been taking care of us as if we were family though."

Lunyai smiled, thinking that there were good people in the realm, more kind people like Darelle and Iden than malicious folk like Seolta.

"Turi has been helping out, and Iden swears he has done a month's work in the few days we have been here."

Corann said something in his own tongue and patted Turi's massive bicep. The big Duthka waved away the comment bashfully. Lunyai felt he really was a gentle bear.

The talk turned to darker happenings and Imala told them more about the Throskaur attack on Argyllan and Songaa's timely arrival. Corann in turn gave them his story, riding with Wulfner, then saying goodbye at the Blackstone Ford. Lunyai wished her father could have met their big northern friend.

Emiren then related their encounter with the Throskaur in Argol Forest. Lunyai clenched her fists under the table, the burden of having killed again weighing heavily upon her. Emiren was still speaking but Lunyai felt her hand upon hers, out of sight of the others. Some of the tension within her eased.

Lunyai shook her head as she added that the Throskaur had spoken Moryn's name.

"I just can't understand how they knew him though. It doesn't make sense. Unless he met them in the forest after he left Fallowden." She huffed out a breath.

The table fell into silence, everyone lost in their own thoughts, trying to find explanations for the unexpected turn of events and reasons for Moryn's odd behaviour. Lunyai found her gaze settle on Corann's face and she saw something there. Something grim. His jaw tightened and his eyes were practically burning their icy-blue.

Tlenaii...

The Duthka leader's fist suddenly came down hard on the table. His face was as dark as a thunder-cloud. They all looked at him, startled.

"He had met them but not in your forest," he whispered, his eyes closing and a breath escaping.

Lunyai turned to Emiren but it was clear she too didn't understand. The young lady from Fallowden held up her hands in confusion.

"When? He was with us when they attacked Argyllan, far away."

Olwyn said something in the Duthka tongue to Corann, her face a mask of puzzlement. The Duthka leader let out something close to a sob. Then he inhaled sharply and spoke.

"The Barren Isles are somewhere off the north-west coast, across the Western Sea."

Lunyai knew that already. She looked at Olwyn and saw tears forming in her eyes.

"Olwyn?"

The Duthka lady spoke, her voice cracking as realisation dawned. "They knew Moryn because...he had been to the Barren Isles."

Lunyai gasped, Emiren breathed a word of denial, and Turi suddenly let out a wail, then buried his head in his hands and began to shake with grief. Corann placed a hand on his friend's back. The truth had reared its ugly head and it was a loathsome beast indeed. Lunyai found herself choking on tears. Songaa was speaking rapidly to Naaki and Imala.

Tlenaii, no. Moryn saved me... He could not have done anything so hateful.

307

Emiren was the first to speak. "Moryn told the Throskaur to come? That can't be true. Why?"

Corann's voice was like cold iron. Lunyai instinctively leaned back, the rage within the Duthka palpable.

"He was always a loner, living on the edge of the village, always out to sea by himself. We never questioned it. He brought back fish and stories of the Western Sea and its temperament. He was gone days on end. Nobody saw anything strange…"

Corann's eyes widened.

"Now I see why he hid so far back within the Sacred Mount. He didn't want to fight his allies."

The Duthka lord choked back tears and hung his head. Lunyai could barely hear his whisper.

"He knew. All this time he knew my daughter was alive. He knew Idelisa was…"

Olwyn sighed with sorrow, her face a picture of emotional agony. Lunyai could see the pain etched deep in her eyes. Their friend and fellow had been false for maybe many years. The Tarakan struggled to comprehend the sense of betrayal they were feeling. Turi was muttering quietly. Emiren placed her hand on his back, and the company sat that way as moments passed. Lunyai sang the Tarakalo within her head.

Emiren finally broke the silence. "So where is he now?" she asked hesitantly.

Corann shared a look with Olwyn, then replied to her. "If he has indeed betrayed us and the realm, and he is a thrall of Seolta, then I would think he is returning to his master."

Lunyai turned it over in her mind. "But he could have left us long ago. Why did he come with us to Argyllan?"

Olwyn spoke, her voice heavy. "Maybe he wanted to see if the Throskaur had done their work."

Emiren gasped. "No, he wanted more of the book translated. He was eager for my mother to read it."

Corann stared at her. "What else was in the book?"

"We think it may have knowledge that could help those turned, give them back their humanity."

Corann pounded the table with his fist again. "So, he has stolen the book, will take it to Seolta, and then the beast-men will be forever cursed. Seolta has no reason to help those he has intentionally doomed."

"He has to cross the Icefinger," said Olwyn, her face hard and her eyes alight with a fury that unsettled Lunyai.

Corann nodded. "The ford is the obvious place to go. As one simple traveller, he may pass the soldiers there without any trouble."

Lunyai tensed as Corann began speaking angrily in his own language. Olwyn joined in and the two seemed to be cursing Moryn, though the Tarakan couldn't be sure. She looked at Turi and saw utter devastation in his face.

Is it really true? All-Mother, please give me a sign that Moryn is true and not serving Seolta.

It seemed barely the space of a few songs and they were gathered once more outside the Merry Mount Inn. Their horses were ready and Tarak seemed impatient to be moving again. Corann had strapped his two swords to his back, the blades a paradox of reassurance and danger to Lunyai's eyes.

"I am so sorry, Darelle. We have enjoyed your hospitality but have no coin to repay you," said Olwyn, her eyes lowering in shame.

Lunyai found it interesting that neither the Duthka nor the Tarakans used money. Her people did trade with the few merchants who ventured onto the Plains but there was never any coin passed, just the exchange of goods. Tarakan medicines and bows for iron tools and strong rope. The Duthka, it seemed, also made what they needed and shared it equally.

Both our peoples keep to themselves. Maybe coin is necessary to become part of the wider realm...

"Nonsense!" cried Darelle in response to Olwyn. "You have earned your keep ten times over."

Beside her, Iden nodded. He then slapped Turi's thick arm. "Turi here has been a blessing, lifting barrels and fixing up the stables." He shot the two of them a questioning glance. "You sure you won't stay a while longer? The summer festivals in Manbung are quite something to behold."

Lunyai looked at Corann and could see sorrow in his eyes.

He knows this summer may hold little joy.

Olwyn wiped her eyes and shook her head. "Thank you, Iden. You and Darelle have shown us the beauty in Marrh. I hope one day we will be back. I hope one day that…"

She didn't finish and Lunyai could understand the lack of hope within all who had heard of the horrors of beast-men, seen Unvasik axes, or listened to Throskaur screams. Hope was a faint glow behind a thick fog.

The small company either embraced Iden and Darelle, shook hands, or dipped their heads. Lunyai mounted her horse and held out a hand to Emiren. The warmth of the Fallowden girl on her back was comforting.

If I am with Emiren, then there is hope.

CHAPTER 7

TORBAL

25th Day of Maia, Two Days After Morak Was Retaken

Deadwood. A fitting name…

Torbal could hear the weary sounds of his soldiers traipsing through the forest but little more. The crunch of their boots on the undergrowth was clumsy and loud compared to the silence of the trees around them. Torbal's forces had divided, about two-thirds entering the woodland on foot and the rest staying at the border, guarding the horses and wagons. The first mile within the forest had been tense and slow. The soldiers had kept a tight formation and practically inched their way forward, ready to raise their shields and defend themselves at any moment. But nothing had happened.

Just like Morak.

The folk who had been hiding in their homes in Morak had said the Unvasik and Duthka had left one night and nobody knew where they had gone. Torbal's men had found tracks outside the city that showed a sizable number at least had headed back to the Deadwood.

But why?

To take Morak with apparent ease, win a victory against Cyneburg's legion, and then just leave seemed odd and a strategical blunder. Torbal was certain though that Seolta, and Vorga who had to be with him, were not stupid. So much had happened that had so obviously been carefully planned; this retreat from Morak had to be intentional. Torbal could only think they knew he would come with a large force and whilst Morak was defensible, they didn't have the numbers nor experience to hold its walls. But if that were the case, why take the city in the first place?

We are always one step behind them, he thought with a heavy sigh.

They weren't in total darkness within these trees, but the sunlight had a difficult time piercing the dense canopy above them. Torbal imagined night in here would be pitch black. If they found nothing within the next mile, turning back would have to be considered, as making camp in such limited space would leave them horribly exposed.

"Still nothing, General," said the Bladesung Forwost Wyman to his side. "I don't like it."

"Neither do I. They definitely came into the forest and possibly have returned to their own lands. But I do not believe this Seolta has retreated. And Vorga, the mighty Unvasik High-Chief himself, turning tail and running? Unlikely."

Wyman nodded in agreement but offered no explanation.

Torbal huffed with exasperation. "Where in Thunor's name did they go then?"

Wyman shrugged. "The capital?" he joked, with a crooked smile and a shrug.

Bregustol…

Torbal stopped walking. Wyman paused, then raised his hand to signal an all-stop when Torbal did not resume their march.

"Bregustol…" he muttered. Thoughts began to swirl.

"General?"

"Wulfner told us they took a huge quantity of the fungus from the Sacred Mount. We assumed it was for Morak. But there were no more beast-men there," he said urgently.

Wyman's jaw dropped. "They took it to the capital…"

"And we are heading deeper into this damn forest, farther and farther away from Bregustol."

Torbal saw it now. Seolta meant to turn the people of Bregustol into beasts and had lured the Westhealfe soldiers away from the threat, after having already dealt two blows to them, one serious to the Bradlastax, and one less so at the Black Stone Ford.

"We've been played, Wyman."

Wyman nodded grimly. "Looks that way, sir. Shall we turn the company and leave this cursed place?"

Cyneburg approached. "Why the halt, brother?"

Torbal explained his thinking as quickly as he could. Cyneburg listened and her face darkened.

"Cunning bastard! Bregustol will be a bloodbath if he turns even a quarter of them. It will be chaos on the streets."

Torbal couldn't disagree. He felt like a fool for having been deceived so boldly. The fungus had not been brought this way. The Unvasik and Duthka were now undoubtedly nearing the capital, possibly in force, more likely in stealth.

"Give the order, Wyman. Get the company turned around and let's get out of this bloody place."

"As you say, General," replied Wyman with a salute. He turned and opened his mouth to shout, but suddenly grasped his head with both hands.

Several other officers and soldiers near Torbal did the same. The King's Shield knew what had caused this reaction.

"No…"

The trees to either side of the company burst into life as large forms erupted from the murk and hurtled into both flanks. A hissing sound filled the air and several soldiers fell, clutching shafts in their necks and chests.

"To arms!" cried Torbal.

The order was unnecessary, as the Bladesung soldiers and Bradlastax shield-maidens were already defending themselves.

Torbal looked in horror at the large figures that had crashed into their flanks—Unvasik. Each was well over six foot tall, some undoubtedly more than seven, and all broad with it. They were attacking with a mad frenzy, swinging their fists and grabbing soldiers.

Wyman shouted for Torbal's bodyguard to form a circle of defence. One stumbled as he rushed in, falling to the ground with a short spear in his back.

"Pull back!" roared Torbal. "Form ranks, shields up!"

But chaos was everywhere. They were not in open fields now and there was no river to use to their advantage. The trees and the tight confines made any attempt at forming up impossible.

Torbal saw three Bradlastax cutting down an Unvasik warrior, their axes digging deep; the man's bellow was only silenced when one of the Westhealfe sisters took his head with two chops. The three paused to catch their breath and it was the death of one, an arrow taking her in the throat.

Cyneburg screamed in rage. "Bastards!" she cried and broke from their defensive ring, her axe held high.

Torbal watched her for the space of two heartbeats, then roared his own battle-cry. "Westhealfe! Westhealfe! Kill the animals!"

Wyman took up the call and within moments it was each soldier for himself. There could be no tactics here, no shield-wall and no thundering cavalry charge. This was kill or die.

Together Torbal and Wyman swiftly advanced on one Unvasik who was leaning over a Bladesung spearman, clobbering him with clenched fists. The man was already dead but the Unvasik pounded away, a terrible growl emitting from his mouth.

He has no weapon…

Torbal did not hesitate and slashed his blade across the back of the hulking warrior. The Unvasik arched, his head went back, and he roared. He turned and swung a fist at the general. It didn't connect; instead it fell to the forest floor. The Unvasik stared at the stump where his hand had been in confusion. Wyman's bloodied sword then entered his stomach. The Bladesung Forwost twisted and withdrew, bringing forth a dark mess of innards. The Unvasik slumped to the ground, his eyes crossing grotesquely.

"The Duthka have turned the Unvasik!" Torbal shouted to Wyman.

Wyman stared at him for a moment, then realisation dawned in his eyes.

The whistles had blown and the Unvasik had poured forth but without weapons. They were attacking mindlessly, exactly like those poor souls at the Black Stone Ford. Fighting against beast-men from Morak was a terrible thing; being attacked by beast-men from the Unvasik tribelands was a new nightmare.

To Torbal's right, a group of Bladesung plunged into the trees to engage enemies who had been hidden.

The Duthka masters to these animals.

Torbal quickly looked around and saw no immediate danger to himself and Wyman. He surveyed the battle beyond them. It seemed to be less chaotic than it had been, with the Bladesung and Bradlastax gaining the upper hand. The howling of wolves could be heard deeper within the trees, along with shouting in an unknown language.

"Wyman, with me. We'll slay them one by—"

A roar that seemed to have come from Oblivion himself exploded just ahead. Torbal looked and for an instant thought the Ever-father's Fallen Son truly had come to slaughter them all. A giant was grabbing soldiers and flinging their bodies into the trees, or smashing his huge fists into their heads, knocking them to the ground. His beard was woven with silver and he was perhaps over eight feet in height—the biggest human Torbal had ever seen. Unvasik, but like a monster of legend.

Torbal could only watch as the terrible titan grabbed two Bradlastax warriors by their necks and smashed their heads together with a sickening crunch, their helmets offering little protection against the brute strength. He flung their lifeless bodies away and snarled, saliva spitting from his jaws.

"Bastard!"

No...

Torbal's sister confronted the beast with her mighty battle-axe, her feet planted and her swing one of pure rage.

The giant raised a hand to ward off the blow. There was a strange metallic clang as the axe connected with the brute's wrist, and Cyneburg's weapon dropped from her hands.

The Unvasik seemed confused for a moment, then lurched forward and grabbed Torbal's sister with both hands. With an unholy roar, he lifted her high above his head and then threw her. Cyneburg flew through the air and crashed into a great oak, bouncing off it and plummeting the few yards to the forest floor.

Torbal wasn't fully aware of what happened next. There was a surge near him and a swarm of Westhealfe soldiers, Bradlastax and Bladesung, attacked the giant with insane ferocity. The brute's roars of rage became gurgled chokes as he was assailed from all directions. He fell and they continued to hack away, axes rising and falling, blood flicking onto leaves and bark.

The general hurried over to where his sister lay, a cold certainty within him that her body was broken. He dropped to his knees and gently held her face.

"Cy. Cyneburg, it's me. Can you hear me?"

His sister slowly opened one eye. The other was closed, caked with blood from a head wound.

"Torb?"

The sounds of battle died away around him, but he took little notice. The cries of triumph and oaths of rage, even the wolf howls—they meant nothing in this moment.

"Easy now, sister. Easy..."

What could he say? Cyneburg was beyond aid. Her lower half was twisted unnaturally and her legs were becoming darker as blood spread.

"Damn it..." she croaked.

"Don't speak, Cy. Just..."

She coughed and flecks of blood spattered her chin. Torbal stroked her hair and was flooded with memories of their youth together, his big sister toughening him up with her rough play.

"Family..." Her voice was weakening.

"I will care for them, Cy. I will care for your family."

"Names..."

Torbal didn't understand.

"Say their names..."

Torbal choked on tears. "Kenric, Lucetta, Cherin."

Cyneburg's mouth formed a faint smile. "Again…"

"Kenric, Lucetta, Cherin," repeated Torbal, his voice cracking as he uttered the names of her beloved husband and children.

Cyneburg made a sound. Torbal stroked her hair and said their names once more.

"Kenric, Lucetta, Cherin."

He clenched his jaw.

"Kenric, Lucetta, Cherin."

Her body went limp and her head lolled to one side in his hands. Torbal shut his eyes.

"Kenric, Lucetta, Cherin," he whispered.

The Bradlastax and Bladesung trudged wearily ahead, slowly emerging from the forest. Most of the soldiers carried stretchers crafted from cloaks and spears between them, upon which were wounded comrades or fallen friends. Four shield-maidens carried Cyneburg's body. Torbal could hardly bear to look upon her.

Kenric, forgive me…

The general turned and beckoned to Wyman. The Forwost began to walk over to him, his face mirroring the despair Torbal felt. They had lost over thirty Bradlastax and twice that number of Bladesung. Torbal hadn't waited around to count the number of Unvasik and Duthka corpses; he had ordered a withdrawal as soon as it was clear the immediate threat was over.

The general inhaled sharply as the Forwost approached. "Wyman. Have the wounded taken back to Morak and be sure the city is alert, and defences are set. And send riders south to the Black Stone Ford. Order two-thirds of those stationed there to march on Bregustol." Torbal felt numb as he gave out the commands. Wyman's acknowledgement was similarly devoid of emotion.

Torbal was beginning to feel a certain hopelessness to it all.

Seolta is truly an evil man.

Wyman had agreed that the giant who killed Cyneburg was probably Vorga, judging by his size and the amount of silver he wore. Seolta had betrayed his Unvasik allies, of that there could be no doubt. But why? Again, it seemed foolish from a strategic point of view. Why destroy your allies? But Torbal couldn't help feeling Seolta was well aware of what he was doing and that everything was proceeding along a path he had been crafting for years.

Is Bregustol the goal?

Torbal saw Wulfner helping out a wounded Bladesung soldier. He bitterly recalled Wulfner's advice not to hunt them into the Deadwood. The man had been right and Cyneburg was now dead due to their burning desire to reap vengeance. Torbal wished with all his heart he had been more patient.

Patience...

That was one trait this Seolta seemed to have in abundance. The man had clearly been planning for years, carefully positioning his people all over the realm, and sowing seeds that were now rising through the soil and spreading themselves to trip the reckless. The Duthka lord had committed an act he knew would outrage his enemies and bring them forth without due care, vengeance blinding them.

Just as glory blinded Rencarro, rage blinded my sister and me.

Cyneburg...forgive me, sister.

CHAPTER 8

KAILEN

25th Day of Maia, Two Days After Morak Was Retaken

Kailen smiled sweetly at one of the guards manning the sturdy gates of Bregustol.

"Gates are closed for the day. Come back tomorrow!" he growled.

Kailen sauntered a little closer and affected her best Meridian accent.

"Business has dried up down south, handsome sir. Was hoping to earn a few coppers on the streets here," she said, placing a hand upon his chest and trying her best to flutter her eyelashes, which were quite short unfortunately.

First Warrior, forgive me for this lie!

The guard looked at her, glanced at her stolen horse and then focused his gaze back on her with the most cynical eyes Kailen had ever seen. He shuffled back a few inches, enough to send the message he didn't want her hand anywhere near him. She tried to sigh erotically. He looked at her as though she were drunk.

Raven's arse, I wasn't born to be charming…

The guard let out a huff and stood aside to let her pass.

"There is a brothel in the southwest quarter that takes in all manner of… working ladies. Quite cheap so you won't earn much coin. But safer than the streets." He frowned. "And probably more chance of getting a customer."

Kailen smiled again, as demurely as possible, but all she wanted in that moment was to break this fool's jaw, then ram his spear up his backside.

"My thanks, noble sir," she replied, and he waved her through.

"You'll get more for the horse at the Saddle Street stables," he called out after her.

If I find Svard, he owes me a few ales for this.

Kailen entered the throng of people moving up and down the main thoroughfare. The street was wide, with a central lane big enough for carts in both directions, avenues for pedestrians on either side of it and even space for street vendors, crammed against the walls of houses and shops. It lacked the more elegant nature of the streets of Gamle Hovestad but Kailen was sure Bregustol had far more coin changing hands.

She decided to take the guard's advice and began asking the way to Saddle Street. It wasn't on the other side of the city thankfully, being only five hundred yards from where she was now. She headed there and managed to sell her ride with no trouble. She accepted a very low price but seeing as the horse hadn't been hers to begin with, she'd made a profit.

I can now add horse-rustler to my list of misdemeanours.

She felt ungrateful for having left Rencarro and his men, especially considering they had saved her life. Twice, in fact. But they were moving far too slowly for her. Kailen needed to find Svard and she knew he was in Bregustol, so the capital was the only place to be.

The Helligan lady left Saddle Street and let herself be taken along with the press of people, not really knowing where in this sprawling chaos she would find the First Ranger. She knew the jails were a likely contender for his current whereabouts, but she wanted to at least try other possibilities first. The thought of Svard behind bars was depressing.

Damn it, Svard, where are you? The dark raven has shit on me and I need your help.

Kailen was in a truly sorry state. A fugitive from the Helligan nation, far from Lady Ulla and close to harbouring no hope as to her current objective. Nonetheless, she pressed on and began stopping at vendors to chat and try to learn something of value. She didn't buy anything, much to their annoyance, but did gain some insight as to what had been happening in the capital, or more accurately, what the capital was feeling about events in the wider realm.

Bregustol seemed to have shrugged at Meridia being annexed, frowned at rumours of Unvasik raiding the city of Morak, and grumbled about northern tribes stealing rubies from the Royal Mines. The people here were almost looking forward to Helligan forces coming this way so the north could show the south their grit.

Damn fools, the lot of them.

Kailen had learned much from her brief time with Lord Rencarro and his two men. She was still trying to accept the reality of a Westhealfe legion being massacred by Unvasik and a forgotten forest tribe, common men turned into raging beasts by some fungus, and Throskaur pirates attacking the port city of Argyllan at a suspiciously vulnerable time for the realm. Eligius had seemed so certain it wasn't a Xerinthian invasion. Kailen still hadn't discounted that, but she could see now that there was a clear threat to the realm from the north and from within its various cities, towns, and settlements.

First Warrior, is the future a dark one?

Kailen reckoned the answer to that was a solid *Yes*. She shivered as she imagined the Dark Raven flying overhead, its wings blocking out the sun and its cry misery to the ears of all below.

I need a drink...

"The Helligans have crossed the Mimir. I fear dark times are ahead," murmured the barkeep to two fellows to Kailen's left.

"I knew it! I bloody knew it," the nearest man blurted out, slapping the counter as if this was a good thing. "Told you so, didn't I? Hey? Hey?!"

The other fellow just took a pull from his flagon and was silent.

Kailen cursed her luck for ending up at a counter with a braggart and his inebriated friend. She took a quaff of her own ale. It wasn't too bad, but she reckoned the beer in Gamle Hovestad was superior. She caught the loudmouth watching her from the corner of her eye. Without turning, she spoke.

"Nothing to see here."

The man whistled, then chuckled. "Forgive my infusion to your thoughts…" he began.

What?

"I was just constipating recent happenings in Ragnekai with my friend here," he stated with an air of wise authority that didn't quite succeed due to his apparent desire to use *big* words.

"Is that so?" said Kailen flatly. She turned her head and smiled. "Anything coming out yet?"

The man grinned, glad to have secured her attention. "My noble friend here believed that a Xerinthian invasion was impotent."

Raven's arse, someone fix this man's brain!

Figuring she could shut down this discussion quickly, she agreed with the mangler of the common tongue. "I have come from the south and assure you there are no signs of an *imminent* Xerinthian invasion. Your friend is *mistooken*."

The man narrowed his eyes for a moment. Then grinned inanely.

First Warrior, is this my punishment?

The braggart turned back to his friend. "Told you they was Helligan spies!"

Kailen tensed. She coughed politely and the man turned back to her. She wanted to smack his stupid face but needed any information she could get.

"There were Helligan spies in Bregustol?"

He barked a laugh. "There were. There *were!*" He winked. "Do you get it?"

First Warrior, no!

It felt like molten iron was being poured into Kailen's stomach.

"…I told my not-so-clever friend here that it wasn't a Xerinthian invasion. He's in love with the idea that the Xerinthian Empire will be back soon. His dad fought or something."

"Might still be!" his friend piped up, seeming slightly aggrieved. "And it was my uncle who fought. And died, I'll have you know."

Kailen's mind raced. Did this idiot's joke mean that Helligans had been killed here? She picked up her mug, put it to her mouth to hide her shaking lips, and listened.

"You're just sour that fellow punched you," his friend added.

The first one threw up his hands. "Fellow? He was a bloody Helligan spy too!"

Svard?!

The man carried on, puffing out his chest. "I took a blow for the Rihtgellen kingdom that day," he said, proudly thumbing at his nose, which was clearly bent out of shape.

Both of them laughed and took a swig of their ale. The Xerinthian invasion-believer started shaking his head and held up a finger.

"He wasn't a spy. He just got fed up with your grousing, my friend."

"You know nothing! Why did the other one send an arrow into the man they hanged then? Huh? Answer me that!"

An arrow?

Cuyler?

"Arrow shmarrow. Nobody else saw it."

"The others were all too busy running away like mice and you were as drunk as a tanner on Frensday night!" he cried. The argument was tedious, but Kailen was forming images in her mind.

Someone had been executed and Kailen felt it horribly likely that this person had been a Helligan Ranger. Two others had been witness, and one was possibly Cuyler, judging by the arrow.

"Alright, alright, say there was this master archer from Helligan lands. Why did he kill his own man then, hanging as he was by his neck? Huh? Answer me that!" he finished, mimicking his friend.

Mercy. It was an arrow of mercy.

The bent-nose man frowned. "Maybe he knew something grand and they didn't want him squealing to the True Sons," he proposed, clearly unsure of himself.

"You are so full of horse-shit," his friend cackled. "If he had some secret knowledge, it was moments away from disappearing at the end of a rope!"

Kailen felt sick listening to them speculate on the death of a Helligan Ranger. She realised it had gone quiet and found the two men looking at her.

"What's up with you now, lady? A little inundated?"

Kailen struggled to restrain herself.

"It's been an exhausting day," she said through slightly clenched teeth, then downed her beer in one. "Another," she said to the barkeep, figuring she would knock this one back too, then leave these two fools to their posturing.

The more inebriated fellow lost interest in Kailen but the bent-nose one was casting very unsubtle sideways glances at her. She turned to him and forced a smile.

"So, what happened to the archer and the man who smashed your face in then?" she asked sweetly.

He missed the mockery in her tone and put on a serious, self-important tone of voice. "Well, word on the street is that they escaped."

Thank you, First Warrior...

He paused, then looked around dramatically as if he was worried someone might be eavesdropping. "I could find out more, you know. I am, as they say, well connected."

His friend snorted a laugh and received a jab for his troubles.

Bent-Nose smiled conspiratorially at Kailen.

First Warrior, save me from fools!

He carried on, oblivious to her growing anger. "Maybe you and I could take a walk, and I'll show you the Holy Sepulchre where it all happened," he said, his hand moving toward hers on the counter.

Kailen had had enough. She gasped and pointed to the other end of the bar. "An angel of the Ever-Father!" she cried.

As expected, the two men, the barkeep and others within earshot instantly whipped their heads to look.

Kailen stepped off her stool, grabbed Bent-Nose's hair with her right hand and the back of his head with her left, then slammed his face on the counter. The instant his head connected, the noise brought the attention of the room back. She let go and threw her arms up in a display of shock.

"Ever-Father help him! He slipped and struck himself."

Bent-Nose slid to the floor, out cold, his nose a bloody mess. His friend burst out laughing and pointed at the stupid wretch. The barkeep looked around, confused.

"What just happened?"

Kailen put two coppers on the bar and walked out. Giving that man a new angle to his nose had refreshed her spirit to a degree, and she felt a new determination to find Svard. She knew she was clinging to a hope that it was him and Cuyler that the two drunks had encountered. She also knew that that hope came with the death of another Ranger.

Damn the Dark Raven!

CHAPTER 9

EMIREN

26th Day of Maia, Three Days After Morak Was Retaken

Emiren was glad to be riding with her beloved wolf Tarak, Corann, and the Tarakans. For the child in her, it was something she could tell her parents when she finally returned, assuaging their anger by letting them know she was well protected. And not the only one embarking upon a journey that perhaps lacked conventional wisdom. For the person she was becoming, for whom necessity conquered fear, it gave her more hope they could help stop the hate flowing through the realm. If they could track down Moryn, retrieve the book, and then cure those who had been turned, it would be a small victory. And also a mercy.

Emiren still found it hard to believe she was now heading, once again, to an area of Ragnekai she had never been before. She had spent all her life in Fallowden, Argol, and the occasional visit to Argyllan or Lowenden. But since the day Anton had been murdered, she had travelled far and wide, to Ceapung and into the Abhaile, where Olwyn and Turi would be heading now. Also to Manbung, had entered the Sacred Mount, and now she was journeying to the Black Stone Ford.

At least this time I am not running from something but running to it.

The two Tarakan sisters who rode in their company were named Naaki and Imala. Lunyai had spoken with them a great deal as they rode and Emiren had listened quietly, and learned a thing or two when Lunyai had brought the conversation into the common tongue. At first, Emiren had been embarrassed she was so ignorant of so much of the realm beyond Fallowden and Argol Forest, but the sisters' fascination with what Emiren knew of herb-lore and all that Lunyai and she had been through had chased away some of the shame. Their presence in this small company raised Emiren's hopes that she would return to Fallowden. Later than promised, but home safely.

Forgive me, Mum. I didn't want to leave again.

It wasn't absolutely certain that Moryn had betrayed his own people and was in league with Seolta, but his disappearance was suspicious. And if he had indeed been in contact with the Throskaur, he was truly damned. Emiren had thought his reaction to the devastation in the port city was due to the same revulsion and anguish she felt at seeing so much death. But what if it had been guilt, a realisation as to what his deeds had wrought?

Emiren held out a glimmer of hope that they were wrong though. She knew that it was easy to go back through the past, recent or distant, and ascribe reasons to actions that fit the tale you had chosen was the truth.

He deserves a chance to explain why he took the book and ran away.

But if Moryn was indeed a traitor, and had taken the book to Seolta, who knew what evil the Duthka lord could bring to the realm with both tomes in his possession? The power to turn and the burial of a cure that would save those poor souls. If Seolta could translate more, then possibly more ancient learning would be in his hands. Emiren was beginning to realise that knowledge in itself was neither good nor evil; it was simply there to be learnt, and then used in whatever way the one who acquired it saw fit. Learning how a sickness spread could help stop the disease afflicting many, or one could learn how to disperse the disease far and wide.

As she sat in the saddle behind Lunyai, Emiren felt a new determination within her and squeezed the Tarakan's waist. They *would* find

Moryn and retrieve the book, General Torbal and his soldiers *would* capture Seolta and gain the second book, and Emiren *would* be part of a movement within the realm to safeguard the knowledge and be sure it was used to help people and not to fulfil the goals of hate and revenge. She imagined Lunyai by her side in all this, the two of them riding together, delivering healing to those in need. The image cheered her.

Spirits, guide me to this future. And watch over Lunyai.

So many...

Emiren had seen soldiers marching in Westhealfe and remembered the Argyllan city guard, but never had she seen hundreds upon hundreds of men and women in light armour, carrying weapons, helmets upon their heads. The camp at the Black Stone Ford seemed immense, larger than Fallowden itself.

"The warriors of the realm are busy of late," said Imala to Emiren. The young lady from the small village could only smile sadly. She remembered her father telling her a story about a hero of legend, Beosarg, and the words this man said numerous times in the story: "A bored warrior is likely to lose his next battle, but his boredom means the lands are at peace. A busy warrior will probably defeat his next opponent, but the fact he is busy means war is upon us." The young Emiren had insisted Beosarg was wrong and the warrior was bored because he was a boring oaf. Her father had laughed.

Da, I'll be a better listener when I get home. I promise!

Emiren and Lunyai waited with Imala, Naaki and Tarak at the edge of the camp, all the riders dismounted. Songaa and Corann had asked permission to enter and speak to the captain or lord or whoever gave the orders.

"Do you think Moryn did come this way?" asked Lunyai, leaning back into Emiren and letting her head fall onto Emiren's shoulder behind her so that their cheeks touched.

"I don't know what to hope for anymore," whispered Emiren,

wrapping her arms round Lunyai's waist, just as she had done all their long journey upon Neii'Ne.

"Here they are," said Naaki, pointing to their two companions emerging from between two neat rows of red and blue tents. Songaa and Corann waited till they were all in a tight circle before they related their news.

"There has been no sign of him, or any other lone traveller," reported Corann, his expression one of defeat.

"The roads are quiet, according to the stable-master of this legion. The trouble in the realm is discouraging people from making long journeys," said Songaa, resting a hand on Naaki's shoulder.

Emiren sighed, one hand dropping to ruffle Tarak's fur.

Where are you, Moryn?

Corann huffed. His face was a mask of pain. Emiren could not imagine the sense of betrayal and loss within him. His daughter, who he had thought far away from the troubles in the realm, was with Seolta, and very much involved in the violence. And it seemed Moryn had also deceived him, someone he had believed a friend and member of their community.

"I'm afraid I have more news that bodes ill for those we care about," said Corann.

Emiren tensed.

"Wulfner joined the legion that went north to Morak. I told him to go back to Ceapung and wait out the storm, but I fear he is someone who cannot turn his back when others are in need," he said sadly.

Lunyai turned and hugged Emiren, the love they shared for Wulfner as strong as that which was growing between them. Wulfner was with soldiers so he was better off than a single nomad wandering the fields and forests; yet being with soldiers meant you were more likely to be heading to storms and violence. *I wish all warriors were bored now, with nothing to do.*

"Spirits, watch over Wulfner," she murmured.

"We will see him again, Emiren, of that I'm sure," whispered Lunyai beside her.

Emiren found her words comforting, but part of her knew they were just words. People made promises all the time and broke them despite the best of intentions. Anyone could believe in a bright future, but nobody really knew what tomorrow would bring.

Songaa made a low whistling sound. "By Yaai's light, what should we do? I do not know which road to take now. If Moryn hasn't gone north to Seolta, he could be anywhere. If he is false, then I can see it will bring more misery to Kayah. If he is true to all of you, then I am sure he is on a safer road than this," he commented, gesturing past the lines of tents and weapon racks.

Naaki sighed. "Once more we have a difficult choice to make, Songaa. The boy does not seem to have come this way, so I believe finding him is beyond us, even if we were to roam far and wide for a hundred cycles of Tlenaii's watch."

Emiren couldn't disagree. Finding Moryn seemed nothing short of hopeless.

"Corann, what do you intend to do?" asked Songaa.

The Duthka man frowned, then slowly shook his head. "Olwyn and Turi will tell my people to move farther into the Abhaile and pray the malice fades." He looked at Emiren and she knew he was not going back to join his people. "I would speak with Idelisa." He paused. "I must hear her voice once more."

Corann would cross the ford, seeking his daughter. Wulfner was north, maybe in Morak. Emiren had no idea where Tacet had gone but she suddenly had a cold feeling he too was moving into danger.

Songaa nodded and gripped Corann gently by the shoulder. "A father sometimes has no choice."

"Tarakans!"

The shout came from a robust looking soldier heading their way.

"This is the legion's captain," Corann told them in a low voice. "I wonder what he wants."

The man cast his eyes around their little group. His eyes fell on Emiren and stopped.

"Ah, you must be the one!" he said.

Emiren's heart leapt. *Me!?*

"I heard from your friend Wulfner that you can speak to animals."

Emiren frowned. "That would be Lunyai here."

Lunyai started, then turned wide-eyed to Emiren. "I can't speak to animals."

Emiren put her hands on her hips. "As good as. You can calm any horse. You even got Lord Rencarro's horse to knock him down!"

Lunyai shook her head. "A lucky chance. You're the one whose best friend is a wolf!" she said, grinning.

"You spend half your waking ti—"

"Ladies, please!" interrupted the legion captain. "If *both* of you could come with me, it might be quicker."

Emiren and Lunyai shared a look.

"Alright," they said in perfect unison. Tarak let out a whine.

The entire group followed the captain. He didn't seem to mind but was clearly in a hurry. They soon arrived at what looked like a holding pen. Emiren looked past the fence and gasped.

People were inside. Men. They were moving this way and that, and their movements were very much inhuman, and more like animals.

"These are turned ones?" she blurted, sadness mixing with fear.

The captain turned and he looked very uncomfortable. "This sounds like madness but whoever is the animal-talker, can you try to communicate with these things? Not all of them are eating what we throw in and I'd prefer them not to starve to death before Lord Cherin gets here to examine them."

The man was clearly embarrassed to be asking this and that added to Emiren's rising anger at the way he called them *things*.

"We will try," she said before Lunyai could say anything. "To help these *people*."

The captain clapped his hands. "Good!"

Then he walked off.

"That one could do with emptying his head of all the dung within," commented Imala.

"I agree, sister," said Naaki.

The pen seemed to have been made by sectioning off an area of the enclosure meant for the horses. Songaa moved to where the horses were, followed by the two sisters. Corann stood back, staring at the ground.

Emiren nudged Lunyai. "Go on then. Try to talk to them," she said. Emiren wanted to make light of this bizarre situation, but there was tragedy underlying it all.

Lunyai held up her hands and her voice was laced with exasperation. "That captain does not understand Tarakan ways," she complained.

Emiren leaned in and gave her a quick kiss on the cheek, certain that Songaa and the others were not looking. "Neither do I, but I want to learn."

Lunyai tried to hold back her smile. "I will teach you everything I know."

One of the turned men had his hand through the dividing fence and was trying to touch a horse. The mare snickered and trotted away.

The horses were clearly unsettled by the turned-men, and Emiren didn't blame them. It was like something from a bad dream, beings that looked human but acted like animals. She wondered if they would be released from this torment upon death.

Lunyai moved to the horses and started comforting them. Emiren smiled watching her friend's gift for calming animals, nodding to herself that Lunyai did indeed communicate with them. She took a step closer to listen to what Lunyai was saying and was surprised that Lunyai was making sounds more than actually speaking. A purring hum was followed by what was probably her tongue clicking. The horses quickly settled down, and Emiren was about to pay the Tarakan a huge compliment, but she suddenly felt a stillness to her right and heard Tarak emitting a low growl. She looked around at the turned-men.

Spirits!

They were staring at Lunyai, heads cocked and making their own sounds, but quite softly. All had stopped pacing around in the enclosure and were now calmly standing by the near side, arms hanging by their sides, with what Emiren could only think were expressions of curiosity.

"Lunyai," she whispered.

Lunyai turned and gasped to find herself suddenly the focus of their attention.

"What are they doing?" she whispered back.

Emiren studied them and then began to smile. "I believe they were listening to you!" She pulled Lunyai closer to her and gestured to the poor fellows. "Look at how they are losing interest now that you've stopped whatever sounds you were making."

The turned-men were starting to move again, looking away from Lunyai. Emiren decided to test her theory.

"Lunyai, repeat the sounds you were just making to the horses."

The Tarakan frowned. "Sounds? You mean the Tarakalii?" she asked.

Emiren shrugged. "If that is what you were just doing, then yes," she said, gesturing for Lunyai to hurry.

Lunyai huffed out a breath and took a hesitant step forward, then began to make the same sounds as a few moments ago.

The effect was almost frightening. The turned-men instantly flinched as if startled and came shuffling back to the fence, their eyes wide. Some seemed almost happy. Lunyai turned around to Emiren and gave her a quizzical look.

"Do they understand me, do you think?" she asked in a faint voice.

This certainly seemed to be the case.

"The Tarakalo, what is it?"

"Tarakalii," Lunyai corrected. "The Tarakalo is our song that binds our sense of time. The Tarakalii is what binds us to the All-Mother."

Emiren felt slightly embarrassed to ask but she had to test her theory. "Is it a means of communication?"

Lunyai shook her head. "Not really. It is something our parents teach us from the moment we are born, much like the Tarakalo. We can't talk with the horses about the weather and such, if that is what you mean," she said with a grin.

Emiren let out a small laugh. She hadn't imagined the Tarakans could chat away with animals as humans did with each other, but she felt she was on the verge of discovering something.

"No, I wasn't thinking that. But do you use it to tell your horses to do something?"

Lunyai's face clouded slightly. "It is not a way to command nature," she said sternly.

Emiren held back her frustration. "I know, Lunyai, I know. Please help me to understand it." Emiren pointed at the turned-men. "Look, they have lost interest again."

Lunyai seemed uncomfortable.

"Please make the sounds again," urged Emiren.

Lunyai seemed less than happy about this but obliged. Once again, they ambled over to the fence, a childlike wonder in their faces. Emiren listened to what Lunyai was doing and tried to imitate her.

Her friend laughed. "It sounds like you are gurgling sour milk!" Lunyai placed a finger on Emiren's throat. "Bring the sound forth from farther down. Your village had cats, I saw them. Like a cat purrs."

Emiren tried again and this time sounded less like a dying frog and more like a sick cat.

"Better!"

A laugh from behind startled them. It was Imala, her kind eyes wrinkled with humour.

"It takes more than one singing of the Tarakalo to learn the Tarakalii, or so we say on the Plains," she said gently. "You must calm yourself first before you seek to calm others. Breathe deeply. Then reach out to these poor men, Emiren. Not with your hands but with your heart."

The young lady from Fallowden listened to the Tarakan Elder and was taking in all she said. She was encouraged that Imala seemed to understand what she was trying to do, but she wanted to try out something different. She kept trying to make the same sounds as Lunyai. Emiren felt she was getting closer as she had the attention of some of the turned men now. She stared at the man closest and uttered one of the sacred Words her village held so dear, and that had been found in Cherin's book.

All the turned-men abruptly began scratching themselves.

"What did you do?" asked Lunyai, alarmed.

Emiren ignored the question and tried again. This time the Word was clearer, at least to her ears.

"Shyula, shyula."

The turned-men began to lower themselves to the ground. They did it with haste but there was no violence to their movements, no pushing of others to make space as they lay down in the dirt. Then, one by one, they shut their eyes.

Emiren felt a hand on her arm. Imala.

"Child, how did you do that? What did you say?"

"I told them to sleep," replied Emiren, not quite believing what had happened herself. She looked down and saw Tarak had also responded and his head now lay heavy on her foot.

Emiren then noticed a soldier approaching, carrying a bucket. He stopped abruptly and stared into the pen.

"I don't believe it..." he murmured. He held up the bucket and asked, "Can you make them eat this fruit?"

Emiren looked at Lunyai. Her friend shrugged.

"You asked them to sleep. Now ask them to eat."

Emiren did so, feeling slightly guilty for rousing them again. The results were unnerving. The turned men began to munch away at fruit the soldier had thrown through the fence. Emiren felt a conflicted mix of emotion within her. The men looked content to be eating but the very fact that they were humans behaving like animals was harrowing.

If only we still had the book...

Emiren's thoughts drifted back to what could happen if Moryn was indeed a traitor and had taken the book to Seolta. She prayed to the Spirits that the Duthka lord didn't have the ability to translate all the text.

Hopefully he is not as wise as the Masters in Lowenden.

Lowenden!

Emiren froze and grabbed Lunyai's arm as it hit her.

The Tarakan yelped. "Ow! What is it?"

"Moryn. He didn't come this way," Emiren said with a gasp. "He took the book to Lowenden. He wanted to translate it, but my mother couldn't read all of it. He asked about the masters there..."

Lunyai stared at Emiren. "So, he is still in the south?"

"Maybe," she replied. Emiren felt a small glimmer of hope within her. Was it possible they had misunderstood everything? What if he had simply become so excited he took the book to Lowenden by himself, not thinking about the worry he would cause?

Spirits, please let that be true!

"Should we ride back?" asked Lunyai.

Emiren thought about it and could see no reason to keep travelling this way if Moryn was indeed in Lowenden. She couldn't be sure but there had been no sign of him riding north. He had been on foot so if he had come this way, they should have caught up with him. It was possible they'd missed him somewhere along the roads, but Emiren felt surer by the moment that Moryn had headed south to Lowenden.

She held Lunyai's eyes and smiled, suddenly feeling that they were closer to going back to their homes, and maybe she and Lunyai could be together.

"Yes," she breathed, taking Lunyai's hands. "Where did Corann go? We must tell him."

Emiren felt a surge of excitement as she began to imagine a future with Lunyai, far away from the troubles of the greater powers in the realm.

Galloping hooves and shouts broke her reverie. She turned and saw riders entering the camp, all wearing the colours of Westhealfe. The men dismounted and hurried to the legion's captain, who was already striding toward them.

Emiren shared a look with Lunyai, and they both joined the flow of soldiers gathering close to the newcomers. The atmosphere was tense and Emiren's visions of days spent with Lunyai in Fallowden and out on the Tarakan Plains began to fade once again.

"Our forces were ambushed in the Deadwood. We lost many." The soldier let out a howl of emotion. "Forwost, Lady Cyneburg was killed!" he wailed.

Emiren and Lunyai gasped as curses and cries of anguish erupted from the gathered soldiers. The towering, fierce leader of the shield-maidens, General Torbal's sister, was dead.

Spirits, when will this end? Have they not suffered enough?

Lady Cyneburg had seen her sisters massacred in Morak and now she had fallen in the Deadwood. Emiren presumed it had been at the hand of the Duthka and began to worry that some here would know

Corann was one of the forest-dwellers.

He should have gone back with Olwyn and Turi.

But Emiren knew he was seeking his daughter, hoping to bring her back to him. She feared his heart would be broken beyond all repair if he did find her.

"The Duthka turned the Unvasik into beasts, Forwost!" blurted one of the soldiers who had returned with these ill tidings.

"What? Why? The Unvasik were their allies when they took Morak."

Lunyai squeezed Emiren's hand. "Can you imagine a giant like the one who killed Nerian, turned into a howling beast?" she whispered.

It was a horrifying image. Emiren thought back to her village and her parents. Raging warriors with no mind bursting through the gates of Fallowden was a terrifying thought. Her people had simple spears and only a few like Banseth could fight.

The soldiers were still speaking.

"General Torbal commands the Heoroth legion to march to Bregustol immediately," he reported, passing over a scroll. "It is believed that the Duthka will turn the entire city to mindless creatures. The general thinks the enemy does not want to capture our cities, but to destroy them from within."

The legion's captain did not hesitate nor even open the written word. He began shouting orders, telling his men and women to break camp and be ready to march.

Lunyai's hand touched Emiren's arm. "Wulfner was with the general…" she moaned.

Emiren's heart ached. Their big friend might be alive but the tidings that been brought to the camp meant there was a mounting chance he had fallen.

"What do we do?" asked Lunyai.

Emiren noticed Songaa was standing behind them, and Naaki and Imala were also approaching. The three Tarakans looked sad and Emiren knew why. She looked down at Tarak. His head was raised, his eyes looking up at her, and his throat was releasing a mournful whine.

CHAPTER 10

SVARD

26th Day of Maia, Three Days After Morak Was Retaken

Svard felt exhausted, delirious, and his nerves were truly frayed. He had been in the Holy Sepulchre for two nights now. At least he thought it had been that long. His mind had started playing tricks on him last night, as what he presumed was the setting sun gave its last light to the stained-glass windows. He had thought he had seen the First Warrior in one, a mix of colours merging together to form the Helligan deity. Svard had croaked out something, his mouth and throat parched, buckets of water here and there the only source for quenching his thirst. He had seen the First Warrior turn away to be replaced by a shadow he feared was the Dark Raven.

But it had been one of the nuns in grey, standing before him, a scarf covering her nose. Terror had woken his mind to the reality, and he had acted like a drowsy hound. The figure had moved off and Svard had almost cried with relief.

The Helligan First Ranger tried to focus, but his thoughts were ragged and broken. The stench of urine and feces was almost unbearable, his own waste staining the floor a yard away. The constant growling and snuffling and whining had driven him close to madness. Facing an enemy on a battlefield he could handle. Staying still and silent, perched up a tree, he had done many times. Shivering on a cold, wet night, waiting for nasty bastards had been an annual occurrence for the Rangers. But every time there had been a way out, a path he could take to escape from a situation turned rotten. Here, in this gargantuan ugly monster of a church, he was trapped. Filthy dirty, hungry, throat parched and most definitely trapped. And alone.

First Warrior, if this is to be my end, give me the strength to make a stand. Don't let me die in a puddle of my own piss…

The notion of starving to death amongst all these turned men was chilling. Svard wanted his death to be quick, not something he could feel coming for days.

Dark Raven, I will look you in the—

There was an eruption of sound to his left. His mind was addled and he had trouble at first ascertaining what was making the noise. He listened, his head pounding due to lack of water, and could make out voices. It sounded like the Grey Sisters were issuing more commands.

"Hasss, hassa hassu, dek de dek, tahsen gah! Tahsen gorsha!"

The beast-men around him rose to their feet, their movements jerky and unnatural for an animal, let alone a human. He tried to mimic them, his dry throat scratching out the best bestial sounds he could. Then came the sounds of doors creaking open, and Svard felt a glimmer of hope within him. Stiff and tired as his limbs were, he drew forth on all that was left and made ready to break if they left the church.

The horde began to move out through the doors. Svard steadied his breathing and shuffled into the bizarre procession. There was a faint light coming through the arched doorway, so Svard figured dawn was approaching.

Where are they taking them?

He corrected himself.

Where are they taking us?

The First Ranger presumed this gathering of beast-men, an insult to the natural order, would soon be commanded to attack innocent civilians and cause chaos. But to achieve a greater shock, sending them out in broad daylight would have served better. At this hour, there were few in the streets so Svard deduced the grey nuns were now positioning their unholy troops, perhaps awaiting some sign to strike.

Svard drifted to the edge of the horde and then let his pace slacken a touch. Someone bumped into him and he instinctively looked to his side.

He stifled a gasp as he saw the smith again. The man was just ambling forward and paid Svard no attention whatsoever.

Poor bastard...

Svard would have liked to punch the man on another day but all he felt now was pity. The fellow probably had family or a love somewhere, and now he was as mindless as a sheep.

The First Ranger slowed even farther back, scratching his chest. A grey sister walked past him but didn't seem to notice he was deliberately falling behind.

He saw his chance. Ten yards ahead there was a very narrow alleyway running off from the street they were shuffling down. He shook his head, made a few growls, and took a look over his shoulder. He saw no figures in grey, only more beast-men. He was five yards away now. Lowering his shoulders, he tried to make himself as small as possible. The alleyway opened up as he came near.

He half-fell, half lunged into the darkness of the side-street and slumped down against a wall, hiding his head and praying he hadn't been noticed. He listened intently and heard the sound of leather scuffing on cobblestones but no raised voices. He waited.

Please, First Warrior, blind their eyes!

The horde passed. He stayed with his head down, listening as the shuffling footsteps faded farther down the street. He inhaled slowly and then released the breath, allowing his body to calm itself and the tension inside to dissipate.

Thank you, First Wa—

He heard something close. Careful footsteps. Soft footfalls. One of them had noticed.

Svard gritted his teeth and made ready to draw his blades. He didn't like the idea of killing a woman, but he was ready to slay a witch. He gripped the handle of one of his knives and tensed.

"First?"

Svard looked up.

Cuyler!

Svard struggled to his feet and almost fell into Cuyler's arms. The terror of the past two days flooded out of him and he gripped his captain, Cuyler a strong hand that stayed his descent into madness.

"First Warrior bless you!" he gasped.

"Come, quickly! We need to move away from that nightmare."

Svard lay on a bed in a small room. Cuyler had guided them back to the inn he had been staying at—having stayed in Bregustol when he should have headed to Barleywick, rendezvoused with Gudbrand and Stian, and then returned to Gamle Hovestad.

Thank the First Warrior Cuyler is not the best at following orders.

"You shouldn't be here," Svard croaked, turning his head to his captain, who was sitting cross-legged on the floor, tending to his arrows.

"Rangers never leave one of our own behind. You know that, First." Cuyler blew out a breath. "Not sure any of us should have come here in the first place," he replied sadly.

Svard couldn't argue with that. "How did you know I was there?"

Cuyler snorted a mirthless laugh. "I didn't know for sure. Been looking for you since that mess the other day. Left a few scratched messages near the meeting point. No sign of you or from you, so decided to find out what was what for myself. Paid a nocturnal visit to our friend in the ministry. He works late so I was able to have a chat. He told me you were doing some investigating for him, looking into what this mad holy man was up to. So, I figured that ugly bastard of a church was the best place to start. A lot of people were lining up to get in a couple of days ago, and then nobody came out."

Svard nodded, remembering the mustering.

How wrong all those hopeful men were...

"Something seemed up," continued Cuyler, "so I've been watching the place. I've had a couple of cold nights but by the looks of you, First, reckon I had the easier job."

"Damn nightmare..." he muttered. "Ragnekai is dining with the Dark Raven, the Widow, and Oblivion it seems. All the dark gods are adding their poison to the mix."

Cuyler said nothing in response.

"Let's get some sleep until midday, then we'll go and see our friend again," wheezed the First Ranger.

Cuyler nodded.

Svard let his head sink into the pillow. It was lumpy and smelled musty, but Svard quickly fell into disturbing dreams of beast-men everywhere, some now commanding pitiful humans.

Cuyler stroked the ugly visage of one of the gargoyles that perched in silent watch atop the Royal Ministry. Climbing the roof-tops in the middle of the day hadn't seemed the smartest idea but gathering clouds did bring some gloom. Cuyler stopped touching the silent beast and stared at it. "What possesses those with a mountain of coin to pay for these things?" the captain wondered aloud.

Svard shrugged. "To look handsome by comparison?"

Cuyler seemed to chew on that. "Reckon I'll get one for my woman then. She's always saying I lose something each time I'm away," he moaned as he secured some of the rope to the stone monstrosity.

Svard clapped him on the shoulder. He felt a world better for having slept some and eaten a hearty meal.

"Best not, friend. She might fall in love."

Cuyler sighed. "Probably already has left me for some charming minstrel. Been a long one this, eh First?"

"You're not wrong," said Svard, then stopped and pounded the stone lightly. "And a bad one for the Rangers."

Cuyler was silent.

Damn Orben, damn Magen, and damn this whole sorry shit-heap we're in.

Svard gripped the rope and prepared to descend to Worsteth's balcony.

There was a crash below, the sound of a door being kicked in or something being smashed.

Cuyler looked to Svard. "That didn't sound good," said the captain.

"Raven's arse! So much for the sneaky entry. Come on!"

With that, Svard jerked the rope to make sure it was secure, then jumped from the roof above the window. He swung back in and planted his feet dead centre. His boots connected. The door caved under the impact and Svard found himself tumbling into Worsteth's chamber and bowling over someone in the process.

He struggled to stand but the figure he had collided with was armed. He swung a blade Svard's way.

There was a whoosh of air, a thunk, and the blade stopped, followed by the fellow crumpling to the floor with an arrow in his neck.

I owe Cuyler more than one ale when we get back!

Svard was on his feet then, sword sliding from his scabbard and a knife emerging from his sheath. He quickly surveyed the scene. Worsteth was behind his desk with two figures circling him on either side. Two more were closer to Svard, one rushing to the window at Cuyler, the other snarling something and advancing upon the First Ranger. Svard didn't want Worsteth dying on him just yet, so he would have to finish this quickly before the chamberlain was knifed to death.

He let the man come in with his weapon, one Svard had never before seen the like of. A double-handed thing, a curved blade embedded in a wooden shaft with handholds at the back. The man wielded the weapon as if he were rowing a one-man longboat, swirling the thing in circles.

Raven's beak, not what I expected!

The blade spun up in an arc, then came down with surprising speed. Svard brought his sword up and took the force of the blow, letting his own weapon absorb the impact and bring his assailant closer. Then he rammed his knife into the man's armpit, twisted, and pulled. The dagger came free, slick with blood.

The man's own weapon slipped from his dying grasp and crashed down upon Svard's wrist, knocking the dagger to the floor. Svard let it go and watched as the look of shock on his foe's face fell to one of terror, eyes that saw death close in. Svard shoved him off and moved to the two advancing on Worsteth, horribly aware the chamberlain had just screamed. He had faith Cuyler would best his opponent.

The one nearer Svard turned and raised two short swords, ignoring Worsteth in the face of a much greater threat. Svard lunged forward and brought his blade down with as much force as he could muster. It was blocked by the man's two blades held in an X. Svard kicked at the man's groin, the boot on his long leg connecting. The man let out a grunt and stumbled back. Svard turned his attention to the desk and Worsteth, hoping Cuyler would take care of the one he had just kicked. If he had even won his first fight.

The chamberlain had ducked behind his chair and the assailant had his blade stuck well and truly in the furniture, letting out a stream of what were presumably angry curses. Svard switched his sword to his other hand, withdrew his second knife from his belt, and hurled it, just as the assassin had pried his blade free and was poised to stab Svard's Rihtgellen ally through the top of his skull.

Svard's aim was true, but the man twisted his body in an almost unnatural fashion, and the knife punctured the wooden wall behind.

Damn it!

He launched across the desk and crashed into this man who had displayed exceptional agility, figuring brute force would give him an edge. They tumbled into the chair and both crashed to the floor, the man ending up on top of Svard

Not good…

The First Ranger's sword was still in his grasp, and he moved to cosh his enemy with the pommel. But a knee came down on his wrist, a forearm across his throat, and Svard found himself unable to even squirm with the man lying across him.

The man's forearm pressed down, the weight of his body behind it. Svard's own body instinctively struggled for all he was worth, the fear of death surging through him. His foe was heavy, and Svard was doing all he could just to stop the arm crushing his windpipe.

First Warrior, I need your strength…

There was a strange sound, like a boot being lifted from a bog, and the man grunted, then slumped, his blood spattering onto Svard's face. The Helligan Ranger heaved the body off himself to see Worsteth kneeling with a small knife in his trembling hand, the blade a dark mess.

Svard looked up and gasped. Two short swords were raised above him and the chamberlain.

No…

The man lurched to the side, an arrow in his upper arm. Svard scrambled to his feet, kicked the man in one thigh, pulled his knife free from the wall where it had embedded itself, then rammed it into the poor fool's neck. The would-be assassin spluttered blood, spasmed, and then crumpled onto Worsteth's desk, creating an unholy mess.

Svard offered a hand to Worsteth, who took it as if he were in a trance. The First Ranger turned to find his captain standing there breathing heavily, bow in hand and a nasty display of blood dripping down from his nose.

"First one butted me…" he said, spitting out a glob of blood.

Svard offered a smile. "Looks like you gave him back worse," he observed, seeing Cuyler's foe lying halfway onto the balcony, blood seeping from a head wound.

At that moment, more armed men burst into Worsteth's chambers. Svard crouched defensively until he saw they were wearing the uniform of the ministry guard. The captain, the one Svard had encountered before, gaped at the scene before him, then shouted, "Arrest them!"

Svard and Cuyler took a step back, ready to defend themselves, but Worsteth found his voice and stopped things escalating.

"Stand down, Captain Eahlstan, stand down!" he panted. "These two men just saved my life."

Eahlstan stared at Svard and Cuyler, his suspicions clearly still well in place; Svard reckoned this captain didn't recognise him from before.

"Chamberlain, who are they? And..." He gestured to the five bodies in the room. "Who in the Abyss are they?"

Worsteth put his hands on the desk to steady himself. Then whipped them away as the widening pool of blood touched the tips of his fingers. The chamberlain took a step back, inhaled deeply, and stared at Svard. The First Ranger thought the man was doing quite well considering he had probably accepted he was going to die moments ago. He hadn't pissed himself and that was more than could be said for many had they been in his shoes.

"Chamberlain, Captain Eahlstan, can we all sheath our weapons? I don't like having a conversation facing several points," said Svard, nodding toward the sword brandished by the captain, and the pikes held rather more nervously by his men, four in number.

Worsteth agreed. "Yes, Captain, let us all calm down. The ones who were a danger to me are now dead, thanks to the intervention of my allies here."

Captain Eahlstan wasn't so easily convinced though. "I'd like to know who your allies are first, my lord. And how they just happened to arrive in the nick of time?" He took a step forward, peering over Svard's shoulder out to the balcony. "And how they gained entrance to your chamber."

Worsteth huffed. "Captain, I appreciate your diligence, but we do not have the time for that right now. I want to know who this lot are and..." He stopped speaking, staring down at the dead man slumped on his desk. "Ever-Father, no!"

Svard saw he was looking down at the inkings on the dead man's skull. "You recognise them? The Grey Sisters have them too."

Worsteth looked up at the Helligan ranger, confusion all over his face. "Grey Sisters? No, these are Duthka markings. These men are Duthka."

"Duthka?" Svard frowned. He had heard of the Duthka people but thought they had died out years ago, a result of High King Sedmund's grandfather pushing them north and into forests.

Captain Eahlstan stepped forward. "Chamberlain, we have trouble in the city."

Svard knew what was coming.

"There are reports of numerous fires breaking out all over Bregus-tol."

Not what I was expecting.

"And mobs going mad!"

Ah, there it is.

Svard turned to Worsteth and saw he was having trouble taking it all in. He was about to sit down, but he stumbled on the corpse of the man he had killed and had to grab his desk for balance. His hands came into contact with the sticky dark mess again.

"The Abyss take them all! What is happening?" he cried, wiping his hands upon his robes.

Svard was trying to put it all together himself. "Captain, would I be right in saying the fires are breaking out in hospices, specifically those run by the Grey Sisterhood?"

Eahlstan nodded grimly. "At least three are."

Svard turned to Worsteth. "And you say these markings are Duth-ka?"

Worsteth stared at him. "Yes, yes they are. Why? How did you know where the fires are?"

Svard wasn't sure he was correct in his assumptions yet, but the evidence was mounting.

"I believe those grey nuns are Duthka. They started the fires themselves and they are definitely responsible for the mobs. I barely escaped from the beast-men in the Holy Sepulchre."

"Beast-men?!" exclaimed Eahlstan.

Svard ignored him. "Chamberlain, I believe the Duthka are the unseen enemy we have been talking about. And it seems they have been here in Bregustol all along, hiding beneath grey hoods."

Worsteth gasped. "Sedmund!"

"The High King?"

"They killed him. It was them. Has to be. We thought they were caring for him… Oblivion be damned!"

At that moment, running footsteps echoed in the hallway outside. Eahlstan and the guards tensed but Svard could tell it was a lighter set of feet approaching in a hurry.

"Steady now, everyone," he cautioned.

Moggy, the messenger lad from before, burst into the room. He was about to speak but stopped, aghast at what he saw in the room; several dead bodies and unknown men holding weapons. The poor boy stumbled backwards.

"Moggy, it's alright," cried Worsteth. "The danger has passed. What is it?"

Moggy stared at the scene and Svard felt sorry for the youth. He also felt Worsteth was not exactly giving the lad an accurate summation of the current situation.

Fires and beast-men in the city? The danger has run amok.

Moggy found his voice. "My lord, the Unvasik have been sighted. A horde of two thousand at least, they say, marching up the Ruby Road."

Raven's arse...

"And, my lord, Helligan forces are approaching from the south."

The danger is definitely not past. The storm has come.

Svard shared a look with Cuyler.

And we are stuck in the middle...

Another figure stepped into view. Svard looked past Moggy and thought he was hallucinating.

"Kailen?"

Moggy stepped aside. "And this lady, Chamberlain, she bears Lady Ulla's seal. And a message from Lord Orben."

Svard stared, slack jawed, as Kailen stepped into the room. She surveyed the scene of mild carnage.

"Looks like you have everything under control, First Ranger," she said, eyebrows raised so high it looked painful.

Svard didn't know whether to hug her or slap her.

PART SIX

CHAPTER 1

KAPVIK

26th Day of Maia, The Storm of Ragnekai

They emerged from the tunnel under a grey sky and Kapvik felt a light rain coming down. He looked around and was surprised to see where they were. The city walls were a few hundred yards behind them, open fields ahead of them. To the far north Kapvik could see the Jagged Heights, a great wall behind the trees of the Beacuan. To the east of this was his home, Unvasiktok.

Will I ever return?

His eyes came down from the mountains and he found himself looking upon a large force, marching upon a wide road. He stared out at the huge mass of figures approaching the city.

"Unvasik?" he muttered, disbelief mingling with excitement.

Siorraidh took his arm and tugged. "Yes, the Unvasik march upon Bregustol. And Helligan soldiers come from the south."

Kapvik turned around and saw red and white flags in the distance, held high above a vast number of troops, all amassed before the south wall of the city. A tingle coursed through his body.

Battle! Finally. Tatkret, cast your eyes this way!

Siorraidh pulled his arm again. "Kapvik, we must leave," she said to him, urgency in her voice.

Kapvik frowned. There was a rumble of thunder not far off.

"Leave? The city is about to fall. Victory is near! Why would we leave?" he asked, bewildered that this brave woman would flee from the battle, especially now she carried a weapon of awesome power, one that carried the power of a storm.

Siorraidh let go of his arm and sighed.

"Victory? For who? Look at the Helligan forces. They are many and far more skilled than those you fought in Morak. Bregustol may not have such warriors but they have soldiers, walls, and defences," she said, her finger pointing up at the large bolt-throwing weapons on the battlements. "And if Seolta's designs have gone according to plan, soldiers from the west will come."

Kapvik was confused. He looked at her, the pattering rain beginning to drip from his hair in front of his eyes. What was Siorraidh saying? The city would soon be in chaos with the beast-men let loose, and more would turn. He had seen what would happen beneath the city itself and believed his people would gain entrance to Bregustol. His people were great warriors and could easily conquer these lowlanders.

The Unvasik have come!

Another roll of thunder sounded, and this time he had seen the flash of lightning in the corner of his eye. He looked to the north at his kinsmen marching toward the city, perhaps a thousand of them, maybe more. Kapvik turned his head south to study the Helligan forces. Many, so many. More than his brethren. He gazed up at the walls and saw movement. The Unvasik warrior clenched his teeth as doubts began to form. He turned back to Siorraidh and held her eyes, searching for an answer that was different from the one he feared. His lover had a drop sliding down one cheek that Kapvik knew was not rain from above.

"Kapvik, don't you see? We have never had the numbers to rule this realm. It was never about conquering these people. It was about cleansing the lands, starting a new world by bringing back the old one. But first we have to remove the stain with which they have covered our lands."

Tatkret, no… Give me a sign she is wrong. The time has come for the Unvasik to reclaim their lands!

But as the skies darkened above him, realisation was dawning for Kapvik. He was beginning to understand what she was telling him, and the pieces were sliding together with a brutal clarity. His wild dreams of besting the lowlanders in battle and ruling over them had always been a notion disconnected to reality; he suddenly saw that as clear as the icicles back home. His stomach knotted.

The Duthka, led by Seolta, had begun something that would see the realm crumble. Death would blanket every village and farm, bring down each city and destroy the civilisation here. Seolta wanted to ignite an age of killing and mistrust. The city-states would wage war upon each other and become weak and divided. The beast-men would run rampant, killing with abandon, already as good as dead themselves. The ruling powers of the realm would bleed each other dry, and the land would become a tangled mess of smaller communities. Seolta would then seize the realm. He would come with the Duthka who were now safely far away from the coming violence.

A flash and thunder cracked the sky again, this time closer. Kapvik cursed himself for not having questioned why the Duthka who had left the Beacuan were so few in number. He felt a fool for having believed the grand ambitions of the Duthka were meant for the Unvasik people as well. He looked at Siorraidh and knew she had lied to him at the beginning. Since then, she had hinted at all not being what it seemed, but he had been so enthralled by her that he had not delved more deeply.

"Come with me, Kapvik," she said, her tone almost begging. The skies blinked with more bright white in the distance, and then came the rumble, rolling ever closer.

The Unvasik warrior saw something in her eyes and felt a strong urge to go with her, leave this place and the approaching battle. But where would they go?

"The storm is upon us, Kapvik," she said urgently, as the wind started to pick up strength.

Siorraidh was beginning to look around frantically. Kapvik saw the Helligan soldiers advancing, great machines of war visible in their ranks, towers as high as the city walls—and other strange things Kapvik had never seen before. Shouts could be heard from the walls above. He cast his gaze back to his brethren. His brothers had stopped, and he knew they were waiting for something to happen. The storm had indeed come.

But there is no victory for anyone here. Only death...

Kapvik turned to his lover, anguish eating away inside him. As the rain became heavier, he wondered if Vorga had known all along this was what Seolta planned? Where was Vorga now? Where was Seolta? Kapvik looked past Siorraidh and saw a group on horseback in the distance, maybe half a mile from the city's east wall.

Seolta.

Siorraidh turned to look at the riders, then raised a hand to his face, wiping away the falling rain. Her own face was glistening with the sky's life-blood, tears from above sliding down the face that had charmed him so.

"Come with me," she said, her voice cracking with emotion. "We do not have to travel back to the Beacuan with Seolta. We can find our own path, ride together just the two of us, and seek out new lands. Come with me, Kapvik, and share the power!"

Lightning streaked across the sky, just beyond the city, and the boom of thunder was deafening. Kapvik realised he was crying too. He angrily cuffed his eyes and took a few steps away from Siorraidh. The love he felt for this woman was darkening with the betrayal he now understood. Seolta wanted the Unvasik to die here. Marrh was not to be ruled by Vorga and Seolta. Kapvik's people were not to share in this new world Seolta wanted to create. They would have been rivals, and the Duthka lord would not suffer that.

Kapvik's rage grew even more. "Your new world is for the Duthka only!" He snarled. "Seolta wants us all dead. Where is Vorga now?" he demanded.

The neutral set in her expression told Kapvik all he needed to know. "Vorga is dead?"

Siorraidh held his eyes. "Even if he is not dead, he is a mindless beast," she said, the sadness gone from her voice and a coldness creeping in.

Kapvik gripped his axe tightly, his head boiling with anger as his heart felt all too keenly the pain of Siorraidh's lies. Not even the drumming rain could cool his temper now.

"Duthka witch!" he cried and advanced upon her.

Her hand emerged from her robe holding the rod, and Kapvik felt the air tingle. He hesitated.

"You would strike me down with your lightning?" he asked, his heart being crushed with the weight of sorrow.

"You would cut me down with your axe?" she countered.

Kapvik lowered his weapon and searched her eyes for something.

"You are everything to me…"

The words were out of his mouth before he could stop them. What he felt for her was too strong, like an avalanche from the Jagged Heights that crashed through his defences.

"My gentle giant…" she said softly, her eyes glistening. "Come with me, I beg you. There is so much out there, over the sea. This realm is doomed."

Forks of blinding light blazed for an instant. The crack of thunder made the ground tremble. He felt himself tearing down the middle. The time to flee was almost gone, with the Unvasik close, the southern soldiers pressing forward and the city preparing itself to bring death to these *invaders*. Kapvik shook his head and growled.

"Go, witch! Leave me. If this realm is to die, then I will die with it and the Duthka will have to build upon my very bones! My wraith will return and haunt you all for eternity. Run, Siorraidh, run to your master!"

The Duthka lady turned and hurried away, leaving Kapvik stunned. He had expected her to continue to plead with him and had hoped she would stay. He had wished Siorraidh would somehow change his reality and rush back into his arms.

But she didn't even turn back as he stared after her. Instead, she faded into the grey layers of water that cascaded from above.

Kapvik threw his head back and roared in anger, turning to face the city. As if in answer to his cry, a section of the eastern wall suddenly shifted, a dull rumble followed by a gargantuan grating groan. Then the wall began to collapse, toppling into and out of the city, shattering as it struck more stone beneath. Human bodies fell with it, their screams audible over the crumbling of Bregustol's defences.

A great roar sounded from the Unvasik force and Kapvik's people began to move. There was a flash from above, bright enough to see Tatkret Himself, and a boom loud enough to rattle the Hall of Bones.

He hefted his axe and whispered a prayer to Tatkret the Watcher.

Tatkret, watch over me. The Unvasik have been betrayed. I have been a fool! Battle is the only road open to me now.

The Unvasik tribesmen were now at the broken walls, some already climbing in. Battle had begun and blood would drench the crumbling stones. Kapvik looked south and saw the towers of the red and white soldiers creeping toward the walls.

Tatkret cannot help but look upon this. This battle will be the most glorious ever…

Kapvik knew he was lying to himself though. There was no glory to be had here—only death.

CHAPTER 2

RENCARRO

26th Day of Maia, The Storm of Ragnekai

"By the Keeper, look at them!"

Salterio's voice was one of awe, and Rencarro couldn't disagree as they looked upon the red and white ranks of the Helligan army amassed before the walls of Bregustol. The soldiers were in tight formation, the discipline all too visible. The gloomy sky above seemed to be darkening further, as if to set the scene for the violence to come, and a mist of rain was tangible in the air. Spears and other long-shafted bladed weapons bristled above helmets, and the dark mass of siege engines could be seen nestled in the midst of the Helligan soldiers.

"The Helligan nation has clearly not come to sing and dance," he commented grimly to his companions.

Tacet shook his head and let out a few choice curses. Rencarro scanned the Helligan forces.

"Seolta and Sylvanus were indeed long in their planning. I cannot be sure from this distance, but I would say that the Sentinels are here in full strength, accompanied by at least half the regular forces."

Surveying the scene ahead, Rencarro's thoughts began to swirl.

The Helligan nation was about to assault the walls of the capital, plunging the realm into deeper conflict. Whilst he didn't care anymore about a power struggle in the realm, since he had been effectively removed from that ladder, Rencarro began to envision the future that was taking shape before the walls of Bregustol.

The realm will suffer. Ragnekai will fall…

Rencarro scowled with a deep bitterness. The taking of his city had been but an early deed in this grand design. Orben may not even have known the greater goal. It was clear to the Meridian lord now that Seolta desired for the powers in Ragnekai to bleed each other drop by drop, until all were weak and weary with fatigue, husks of what they once were. Was it possible to stop this bloodshed now? Unlikely. Again, he saw nothing left except vengeance upon Sylvanus. He would end his former's Second's life the way he had ended Marcus'.

Tacet let out a sigh beside him. "The Widow and the Dark Raven will delight in what is to come," he said coldly.

A distant grumbling sounded from high and far above. The rain was gathering pace in its downfall.

"And it looks like the skies are bringing their own wrath," said Salterio.

Rencarro turned to his two Velox riders. "I would say the storm riding in the sky is about to be joined by a more violent storm upon the land, one coloured red. If either of you wish to turn back now and return to Meridia or Argyllan, I will not think any less of you."

Salterio and Tacet shared a look.

"We can halt neither storm," said Tacet, casting his eyes to where there had been a flash in the sky.

Salterio nodded. "Blood will flow here as surely as the skies weep."

"But we can still separate Sylvanus' head from his body," said Tacet, no humour in his eyes.

Rencarro nodded too. "Miss Jacobson did ask that when we have killed him, we kill him a second time."

"And I owe Emiren one for her friend," added Tacet, "so I guess we'll be killing him three times."

"Let us kill him once for every Meridian death his treachery brought," snarled Salterio, withdrawing one of two javelins he had bought in Rumbleton. Not expertly made but sharp enough. Rencarro unstrapped his own spear, the only weapon to have survived their river journey, and this had been made by a master craftsman.

"But where in the Void is he? Surely not inside the city itself."

Salterio looked around helplessly. "Where do we start, my lord? If I were him, and the objective was to destroy Bregustol, I'd want to watch."

Rencarro agreed. "Yes, with so much effort and time put into planning this hideous show, I can't believe he and Seolta would just head off, hoping all went according to plan."

A flash of white sliced through the air maybe a mile from Bregustol and was followed a breath later by an ominous peal of thunder. The pitter-patter of rain was now a steady but gentle shower.

Rencarro withdrew the telescope Camran had gifted him and put it to his eye, scanning the gloomy scene before him. The Helligan forces were here in considerable numbers, two thousand roughly if he were to make a guess. The order and discipline were impressive, and Rencarro could see that his city would have been taken even if he hadn't gone west with his men.

The Helligan nation has not forgotten how to wage war.

The Meridian lord trained the scope on the walls of Bregustol and saw no shortage of defences upon the walls, which must have been well over fifty feet high. Yet he could not see much movement, especially not at the battlements above the front gates.

Tracking east, he suddenly found himself looking at a small group of people emerging from the ground. He blinked to make sure he wasn't imagining this. A dozen or so figures were climbing out of the ground, there could be no doubt. Most began running away from the city but two remained standing, one large and the other a small figure.

Urchins from the sewers?!

Rencarro followed those moving east and saw they were heading for horses, some of whom were already mounted. Were they escaping from the coming battle? Who were they? He strained his eye at the lens and tried to see if they wore any colours, perhaps the blue and red of Westhealfe. Most were hooded and wore dark colours. He couldn't make out further details. The telescope stopped on one rider and Rencarro tensed. He felt something within his gut.

Keeper! Is that…

Rencarro beckoned Tacet to look through the telescope at exactly the same position.

"Is it him?" he demanded urgently. "Is that Sylvanus?"

Tacet was silent for a few moments, before slowly speaking. "My lord, I believe it could be him. I cannot make out his face but there is something in the way he holds himself on that horse. Erect but head titled to one side."

"We must get closer," he hissed.

"And quickly!" cried Tacet. "The Helligan forces are moving. These fields will soon be slick with more than just mud."

"Damn the Widow!" cursed Rencarro. "We can do nothing about that now but if that is Sylvanus…"

"He will die!" Salterio growled.

Lightning forked through the sky, bathing the fields and city with sheer white for an instant, and then the sky roared.

Rencarro set off in the direction of the figures, Tacet and Salterio close behind. The smaller of the two figures, who had remained by whatever hole they had risen from, was now heading toward the horses. The larger one had not moved. Rencarro turned his attention back to the riders and began to feel a hard certainty within him that ahead was indeed his treacherous former ally. His eyes narrowed.

Keeper, thank you. You have guided me to him. I will have my vengeance and the Widow can have his soul.

His thoughts were interrupted by a terrible rumble that was definitely not thunder. It was the sound of stone crumbling, a wall falling.

Keeper…

CHAPTER 3

SYLVANUS

26th Day of Maia, The Storm of Ragnekai

Sylvanus frowned as Idelisa came running over to them. She cut through the cascading rain, her grey cloak giving her the appearance of a ghostly apparition. She had been locked in conversation with the big Unvasik for a relatively long time, when she should have made straight for them as soon as she left the tunnels.

Curious. Has she been making her own plans with the barbarians?

Beside him, Seolta's mood seemed to reflect the worsening weather. He looked decidedly less than happy, and it felt to Sylvanus that there was a more local storm brewing. Did his mentor also suspect deceit?

Did she fall for that brute?

Sylvanus glanced at Seolta again and saw his expression was softening as the lady approached. His lord had always had a weak spot in his heart for Idelisa, a fatherly affection that perhaps clouded his judgment.

He gazed out to the Unvasik horde, massed before the eastern wall. An unruly but terrifying mob. Sylvanus shrugged inwardly. With his true kin, he would soon be gone soon from this place. He would finally go home as the realm disintegrated.

Seolta's designs are sound. They have worked.

Idelisa was now yards from them. She hailed them wordlessly, raising a hand and avoiding eye contact. She moved to mount a horse, but Seolta reached down a hand and grabbed her shoulder, the rain dampening them all.

A huge noise shook the very ground.

Sylvanus jumped in his saddle, the deafening rumble startling him. He looked up and his eyes widened in awe as the eastern wall of Bregustol folded in on itself; debris fell and a handful of soldiers plummeted, screaming, to their deaths. He stared at the devastation, then heard the Unvasik war-band roar in triumph.

The walls of the usurpers fall…

He turned back and saw neither Seolta nor Idelisa had so much as flinched.

"You are well, Idelisa?" Seolta asked pointedly, drops of water dripping off his head, now exposed and displaying the inkings Sylvanus would soon have applied to his own skull.

Finally.

He felt giddy with the chaos unfolding before him, a sign of how Seolta's cunning, and the thought that he would soon be able to embrace his Duthka heritage.

Idelisa paused, seemed to be gathering herself, then looked up, her face difficult to read. "It has been a hard journey, Seolta. I am tired and want to leave this place."

She made to get on the horse but Seolta kept his hand where it was, pressing down, a clear sign he was not finished. Sylvanus felt his anger rise, his breathing quickening.

"I can imagine you would be tired after climbing the Sacred Mount," Seolta said, his voice laced with a hint of menace.

Sylvanus felt uneasy. Here they were, about to see the fruits of their labours, and yet his mentor was questioning his favourite pupil's actions.

We should distance ourselves from the battle to come. This conversation can be held another time!

Idelisa stared up at Seolta and there was something Sylvanus had never seen before in her face. There was an unwavering determination there. Idelisa's right-hand slipped into her robe and Sylvanus tensed, thinking she was about to draw forth a blade.

"We should move farther away," he urged, his eyes on Idelisa's right arm. "The Helligan forces are moving and we will be caught in the middle if they engage the Unvasik."

Neither responded to his pleas. The Duthka refugee watched the pair with anxious eyes. He felt a strange vibration in the air around him, as if the rain was shuddering with fear. One moment became two; two moments became three, the silence an almost unbearable tension. Sylvanus gripped the reins, wanting to slap sense into both of them.

Then the fight seemed to leave Idelisa, her shoulders sagging and her hand emerging from her robe, empty.

"I believed there was something up there." She sighed. "I was wrong."

Seolta's eyes narrowed. "What did you think was there?"

"Seolta, we must put distance between us and the battle," hissed Sylvanus, but the Duthka lord ignored him.

Seolta removed his hand from her shoulder and sat back in his saddle. "One of the primal engines?"

Primal engine? What is he talking about?

Idelisa nodded. "I wanted to find it for you," she said, her voice laced with sadness. "I wanted your praise."

Seolta sat in silence for a few moments. Idelisa still stood by her horse, waiting. Sylvanus fidgeted in his saddle, the sense of betrayal deepening.

They're hiding too much from me...

"You have my praise, young one," said Seolta softly, and his voice was full of the love Sylvanus knew he bore for Idelisa. "You have always had my praise."

Sylvanus relaxed slightly, knowing this storm at least had passed. The storm in the sky however was now bearing down upon all who were in or around Bregustol.

The skies are dark but the future is not.

"Come," said Seolta, motioning for her to mount, "Sylvanus is right. We must make haste and find a suitable place to observe the coming cleansing."

Idelisa was quickly on her horse and they could finally leave. Sylvanus looked back to see if the Unvasik brute had followed Idelisa, but the warrior was lost to the gloom of the falling rain. His gaze ran to the south and he found himself looking at three figures moving towards them, not part of the Helligan force. They were on foot but looked to be running.

Who are you?

Sylvanus strained his eyes and saw one carrying a long spear, its blade silver despite the grey blanket covering the sun.

Athaiq! It can't be! He cursed loudly.

"What is it, Sylvanus?" demanded Seolta.

"Someone looking for vengeance, I do believe."

Seolta's eyes shifted to where Sylvanus was looking, and he huffed. "They are on foot, we have horses. Leave them to their futile pursuit. Come!"

He will not stop hunting me.

Sylvanus jumped as Seolta's hand touched his arm.

"Brother, leave it! We have no time and only a fool would risk his life to satisfy the desire for revenge."

Sylvanus wasn't sure if his mentor was talking about him or Rencarro. The three figures were maybe five hundred yards away now and still sprinting. It was his former lord and comrade, of that Sylvanus was certain. He knew he should listen to Seolta and leave, but his body was already leaning away from the Duthka lord's grip.

"Sylvanus!"

He turned to Seolta and shook his head.

"Forgive me, my friend, but this is something I must do."

He gripped his reins.

"No!"

Idelisa's voice rang clear, startling them both.

Sylvanus was momentarily confused until he cast his eyes back to Rencarro. He saw what had caused Idelisa to cry out.

Seolta pulled at his arm. "They will die. Sylvanus, you have no part to play in this."

Sylvanus felt conflict within but saw the truth in those words. He turned his horse and began to head east. Idelisa was already on the move.

Farewell, Rencarro.

Sylvanus resisted the urge to turn around and watch.

CHAPTER 4

TACET

26th Day of Maia, The Storm of Ragnekai

His lord was sure it was Sylvanus, Salterio agreed, and Tacet reckoned that the Keeper had thrown good fortune their way for once, and it was indeed the traitor. Tacet's breath was short from running. They were now gathering speed, and his lungs and leg muscles quickly felt the strain.

Widow, you tire me!

Yet Tacet's blood churned with an excitement he had not felt since the day he had ridden like the wind to deliver the news to Rencarro that High King Sedmund was dead. Here was Sylvanus and if they could catch him, Rencarro would have his vengeance, and many others would know justice. Even the sight of the eastern wall collapsing had not swayed them in their hunt; all that mattered now was avenging all whom Sylvanus had betrayed.

Eligius would know his brother's murderer was dead. Emiren would hear her friend's killer had paid for his crime. The surviving Meridian cavalry would learn this lying piece of shit would be feeding the worms. And the citizens of Meridia would be told one day that the man who had deceived them all, had felt the steel of Rencarro's spear within him.

Tacet looked ahead and saw Sylvanus, another rider, and a small figure on foot still hadn't moved. They seemed unaware of the approach of Rencarro, Salterio, and Tacet. It truly seemed like the Keeper was holding the Widow at bay and keeping Sylvanus there for them.

We're coming for you, false bastard!

They were closing in, lungs bursting, close now, and this gave them all the strength of will they needed to not falter. Tacet saw Sylvanus turn and notice them.

Look now, you scum! Death approaches. You will die to—

"Keeper!" gasped Tacet as he noticed a figure in his periphery vision, charging toward them.

"Danger to the left!" he cried.

Salterio and Rencarro saw the threat and all three skidded to a halt, dropping into a defensive stance. Tacet stared at their attacker.

No, it can't be!

Tacet had no doubt this was the same Unvasik warrior they had fought inside the Sacred Mount, the one who had felled Nerian and bested Wulfner and himself. Tacet's gut churned. With the traitor of Meridia, Tacet had felt they had the upper hand, all three of them having decent fighting skills, Lord Rencarro in particular. But this hulking giant was a different matter.

Keeper protect us…

The huge battle-axe came swinging in, slicing the air and sending them all tumbling backwards to escape certain death from its blade.

Tacet rolled and quickly sprang to his feet. They needed time so Tacet hurled his small axe at the warrior, his aim good but the spin unlucky. The handle bounced off the Unvasik giant's shoulder and whirled away behind him. The warrior growled and his eyes found Tacet. There was recognition on his part too, his deep voice snarling something in the Unvasik tongue.

Rencarro moved in with his spear, its length giving the Meridian lord some distance and protection from the deadly weapon of the Unvasik. Salterio took a step back and launched one of his two javelins. Their foe got his axe up in time and the short spear made impact with a sharp clank and dropped to the ground.

We must attack him bef—

The Unvasik warrior apparently had the same thought. He rushed in, pushing Rencarro's spear aside with his axe and was barrelling toward Tacet.

Shit…

Tacet got his short sword up and slashed at the brute. The Unvasik tried to twist away but the tip of Tacet's blade caught and a red line appeared across his upper arm. Tacet wasn't sure it was anything more than a scratch on the bicep to this monster though.

Their foe kept moving, his axe whirling above his head, aiming at Rencarro, who was spinning his own weapon. Axe and spear sliced past each other in the air and both men took a step back. The Unvasik growled with fury.

Salterio shouted, "Look at me, you shit-eating hog!"

It had the desired effect, as the Unvasik turned to face Salterio and gave Rencarro the moment he needed to breathe. Salterio hurled his second javelin. It flew through the air.

Tacet thought he was delirious when the next thing he knew the javelin was clutched in the warrior's hand.

He caught it?!

The giant discarded the spear with a look of disgust and charged at Salterio. Tacet's fellow Velox rider fumbled to draw his short sword and tripped backwards. The Unvasik moved in.

"Arrghhh!"

The bellow of pain from the Unvasik was hideous. Rencarro's spear had pierced his side and now the Meridian lord pushed on the shaft with all his weight.

Tacet watched, frozen to the spot. The warrior snarled defiance as the spear sunk deeper.

Rencarro let out his own cry as he shoved harder.

"Die, you monster!"

The Unvasik grabbed the shaft, despite the spear being a foot into his body, and, incredibly, pulled it.

Keeper, who is this beast?!

Tacet saw with horror how close Rencarro was to the warrior. The giant had drawn him in. With an unholy roar, he swung his axe around. It bit deep into Rencarro's chest. The Meridian lord's eyes bulged.

The two of them went silent, blood running down their bodies, colouring their legs, turning the grass beneath their feet a dirty brown.

Rencarro and the Unvasik warrior toppled sideways, crashing to the floor, the spear still running right through the giant, the axe still embedded in the Meridian ruler.

"My lord..."

Tacet stared at the two fallen men before him. His body was paralysed. He was vaguely aware of Salterio rising from the ground and carefully approaching. Tacet's friend plunged his long-knife into the Unvasik warrior's chest, cursing him.

Tacet came to his senses and dropped to the wet ground by his lord, praying beyond all hope that the Keeper would grant them a miracle this day.

But it was clear Rencarro was gone. Tacet's lord stared at the clouds above, the rain a thousand tears upon his face. Tacet gently ran his hand down from his lord's brow, closing his eyes.

"Go to your wife, my lord. Find Marcus and be together once more," he whispered.

Salterio slumped down beside him and laid a hand on Rencarro's chest. "Keeper, watch over our lord. No longer will he suffer the Widow," said Salterio, his voice cracking.

Tacet looked over his shoulder. "We have failed..."

The two Velox riders sat there, Tacet vaguely aware of shouts and cries in the distance, and a rising chill as his clothes became wetter. He looked up to see the mountain tribesmen clambering over the ruined wall of Bregustol. The rain fell harder, its heavy drops sliding down his face. The skies were dark with clouds of the deepest grey, some almost black.

Damn you Widow, damn you…

A streak of lightning appeared directly above the city and the sky boomed with thunder. The storm was upon them. Tacet looked at Rencarro and the Unvasik, their dead bodies joined in a bloody embrace of weapons. He choked on tears.

Widow…damn you.

CHAPTER 5

SVARD

26th Day of Maia, The Storm of Ragnekai

Weeks ago, Svard had set out with Helligan forces to take the city of Meridia, the first step in Orben's strategy that would see them become the superior faction in the realm. Now he was striding along a street in the capital Bregustol, Kailen and his captain Cuyler at his side. Flanking the three of them was Captain Eahlstan of the Bregustol City Guard, and following behind were twenty soldiers in deep blue uniforms.

First Warrior, have I gone mad? Is this just my insane mind?

Kailen nudged him. "What's the best we can hope for here, First Ranger?" she asked, pushing wet hair from her face.

He knew she wasn't mocking him; she was asking the First Ranger to apply all he knew to make a judgment about their current situation, which was rather dire.

"That Brax stand down…" he began.

"That would be nice," she interrupted.

"…and not to get killed," he finished.

Kailen huffed. "Yes, I find I am quite attached to this life of mine. Death would not be ideal." She threw up her hands as they continued walking to the south wall. "And if I do live, it would be preferable not to spend the rest of my days in a Helligan gaol for the crime of murdering our lord."

"The way things are going, I'll probably be joining you," he said with a shrug.

"Oh joy…"

Captain Eahlstan had perhaps tired of their banter, because he spoke up. "Do you think your man will pull back?"

Svard and Kailen turned to each other. Both knew it would take a miracle to even find Brax once the battle had begun, and a second miracle would be required to persuade the First Sentinel to call off the assault. The sky flashed and a peal of thunder followed, sounding like two great galleons scraping along each other's bows.

Eahlstan cleared his throat. "I see."

Svard sighed, then clapped the captain on the back. "Look on the bright side. Things can't get any worse!" he said cheerily.

The stone street beneath their feet trembled.

"Raven's beak!" cried Kailen. "What was that?"

All of them looked this way and that, trying to understand what had happened. A crash was heard to the east, then another. This was followed by low rumblings and faint screams. Eahlstan gasped.

"The walls. They're bringing down the walls!"

That didn't sound right to Svard. If the crashes had been heard to the south, he would have assumed Brax had decided against a heroic assault and started hammering the city with catapults. But he had never heard of Unvasik being familiar at all with siege warfare.

These Duthka taught them?

He realised Eahlstan was looking at him, needing someone to tell him what to do.

Raven's arse! Am I leading the defences of the city that my own people are besieging?

Kailen grabbed his arm. "Come on, First, orders! Now!"

Svard huffed. "Alright, everyone take a breath."

Eahlstan and his men did so in almost comical unison.

"If Captain Eahlstan here is right, the east wall just took a knock. I'd be surprised if it was fully down, but we need to clear the area of citizens and organise new defences in that area regardless." He gripped Eahlstan's shoulder. "Pull men back from the wall or what's left of it. Set up barricades in the streets leading away from where the damage is. If you can muster archers, do so. And quickly!"

Svard knew half of what he was saying was unlikely to be possible, but he could hope, couldn't he?

"If the wall is down, there will be rubble. Unvasik trying to enter the city will have to climb over it. Kill them as they come. Should be as easy as knocking apples at the summer fayre."

Eahlstan nodded and Svard hoped his courage was building.

"Unvasik have no discipline. Barricades, archers, and shield walls with spears should be enough to make them turn back. They're foolish raiders who have got an insane idea Bregustol is an easy target. Show them that isn't the case, Captain!"

He clapped him on the back and the captain saluted, which added another bizarre layer to this mummer's farce, given that Svard was not his superior officer and also happened to be a native of the city-state now at the south wall.

The captain turned to his men.

"Coenred, get to the Fyrdweard barracks and make sure they have mobilised."

The soldier Eahlstan had addressed, ran off with no hesitation, looking like a scared rabbit.

Eahlstan barked out the signal to move.

"To the east wall. Let's show these savages what real soldiers look like!"

And with that they were off, hurrying away in formation.

Svard turned to Cuyler. "I hate to do this to you, friend..."

Cuyler shrugged. "They need someone who can shoot straight."

Svard smiled, trying to put a brave face on it. "Just make sure they hold back and throw everything they have at the Unvasik. And be the first to run if things look grim."

Cuyler imitated the salute Eahlstan had just made and grinned. Svard grabbed his arm.

"And watch your back for these beast-men. First Warrior alone knows how many of them there are. Could be half the city!"

Svard's captain huffed out a breath and nodded. Then spun on his heel and jogged off after the ministry captain and his men.

Kailen looked at Svard and her expression said it all.

"Yeah, I know," he said. "And Cuyler knows it too. If the Unvasik do get into the city, Eahlstan's men are as good as dead."

"Do you think Eahlstan knows that and was just being courageous for his men?" she asked sadly.

"No, unfortunately not. Still, he has some evidence of training. Cuyler will give them something to cheer when he starts dropping the Unvasik."

"Oh, glorious battle…"

Svard ignored her, instead setting off in the direction of the south wall. She soon caught up to him.

"How do you plan to get Brax's attention, First Ranger?"

"I plan on walking out the front gates and…"

"What?"

Svard was looking up. The south wall had come into view beyond the houses and churches, and peeking over the wall were Helligan siege towers.

"Raven's claws!" cursed Kailen. "They're here already."

"Shit…" he muttered. How could they hope to stop a fight once it had begun in earnest?

"Svard, look!" cried Kailen, grabbing his arm again.

Svard followed her pointing finger and saw the nightmare created in the Holy Sepulchre. A horde of men were shuffling out from a side street, coming onto the main thoroughfare and heading to the south gate.

They'll open the gates and the beast-men will attack Brax and his men…

The pit they were standing in seemed to get a yard deeper, and Svard felt they would soon be drowned. Not by the rain that was coming down in sheets now, but by the blood of hundreds of men fighting those who were not their true enemy.

He turned to Kailen and he knew she saw the despair in his eyes. She shoved him roughly.

"First Ranger, you've been in far worse than this. Get a hold of the situation, dammit! We're all under the Raven's wings now so anything is better than standing here doing nothing."

Svard snorted a humourless laugh. "If we do get back to Gamle Hovestad alive, you owe me a few mugs of Warrior's Mirth," he told her, jabbing a finger in her chest.

She rolled her eyes. "I'll be in jail, remember? So, we'll have to knock cups through the bars."

Something stirred within Svard then. Smothering everything that was their nightmare now in this moment came a righteous anger at the injustice Kailen faced. She might have killed Orben, but their lord had already been as good as murdered by this Sylvanus scum. Kailen was a loyal Helligan and had been there for him after Lorken's death. In more ways than one. Svard was damned if he was going to survive this mess only to be back home with Kailen facing jail.

His mind suddenly reeled.

It won't be jail... They'll hang her.

The realisation struck him like one of the streaks of lightning flashing downward from the skies.

The Dark Raven can kiss my arse!

"Come on," he said and started moving, Kailen close behind him. "We have to get as close to the towers as possible without being on the end of Brax's pole-axe!"

Svard ran to what looked like a guardhouse to a stairwell. He ignored the beast-men one street over, knowing he could do little about them. If Brax saw him, he would at least hesitate and Svard would have a chance to yell something at the First Sentinel.

A few words could save a thousand lives...

There was nobody manning the post so Svard entered, Kailen at his heels. He saw the spiralling stairway ahead and hurried to it. He took the steps two at a time, his hands palming against the walls every so often as he lost balance in his haste. He felt strangely reassured by Kailen's presence, her quick foot-falls close behind. If the Dark Raven were about to take him, at least he would have a chance to shout something worthwhile to her.

Thanks?

Svard had never been good with words and had no idea why people read poetry. Kailen would have to make do with a shrug and the memories.

They neared the top of the stairwell, the cool spray from the ceaseless rain gently lashing their faces as it swirled into the turret. Svard heard a clang and knew the closest siege tower had just dropped its boarding ramp. If there were any defenders there, they would be taken down with crossbow bolts. Svard pitied them.

My people are bred for war…

They emerged through an archway onto the ramparts. Ahead were Sentinels pouring out of the sides of the siege tower and scrambling off the boarding planks onto the battlements. There was not a defender in sight, which was probably a good thing. Svard shouted out as loudly as possible in his native tongue. A few turned and began to advance upon him. He could see none of them were Brax.

Damn…

He hailed them again in the Helligan language, but a ripple of thunder drowned out his voice. He began to think a hurried retreat was the best course of action here.

Then the stone beneath his feet lurched.

First Warrior!

The entire wall seemed to heave as if it were a gargantuan leviathan waking from slumber. A Sentinel pitched forward before his eyes, hurtling down into a gathering whirl of dust.

Svard found himself falling backwards as the section of wall where he stood dipped. He landed on his arse and began to slide, the rampart now at an impossible angle.

Kailen screamed his name. He jerked his head and saw her reaching out a hand. But she was over ten yards away.

The stone beneath him crashed into more wall and Svard was thrown off into nothing.

He gasped, arms and feet flailing. Then plummeted.

Chapter 6

Paega

26th Day of Maia, The Storm of Ragnekai

It felt hungry. Hot and restless. It bumped into others. It heard grunts and growls.

Paega...

It jumped. It had heard something. A voice it knew. But it could not remember anything.

Paega, be safe...

It searched around for the voice but all it saw were stone streets, stone buildings and stone walls. Stone. The stone felt wrong. Stone was not its home. Hunger rumbled in its stomach.

It heard shouting from somewhere behind, then cries and screams. Was it in danger? It hunched and shuffled past others, trying to move away from the threat.

Come back one day, son...

The voice again. It swiped the air, trying to stop the voice it couldn't see. It felt strange. It felt something it did not know. The voice was no threat.

Then its ears burned again, the shrill noise stabbing inside its head.

The pain stopped. New sound came.

"*Hasss, dek de dek, tahsen, tahsen, moa, shoowaaa-hasss, moa, tahsen gah!*"

It had to obey. It moved with others. It became part of one.

"*Qilqan, qilqan!*"

It looked. Figures moving ahead. Big ones, small ones. *Qilqan.*

"*Aodeq!*" So loud.

It hurried to the people. It struck the first one, a small one. The small one fell to the ground.

Paega, I will miss you…

It turned around, searching for the voice again, something within it yearning to find that soft sound.

"*Aodeq! Aodeq!*" A harsh sound now.

It turned back. *Qilqan. Aodeq.* It leaped at another one, a bigger one. It pounded its fists into this one's head. The figure screamed, tried to block. Something hot spurted into its eyes. It couldn't see. It growled in its throat.

There'll always be a need for horseshoes but who needs armour now?

Something flashed inside its head. An image of a man. A man. The man had been smiling at…him. He was a man. He was…

"*Aodeq!*"

He shook his head, wiped his eyes, and hammered a small one on the head with his fist. The small one…a child, crumpled and collapsed to the stone below.

Who needs armour when there is no war, Paega?

Paega. Paega. He smacked his own ears, wanting that word to disappear. The word seemed to bite at something within.

He grunted as something crashed into him from behind. He stumbled forward, bumping into a man. The man swiped at him with an arm, clacked his teeth and hissed.

He pushed the hissing man away. That one turned and struck another man. Not a man. A woman. She screamed and fell. A man behind her roared in rage and bashed the hissing one's head with something.

You wield the hammer like a god, my son!

Hammer.

The hissing one's head was the wrong shape, dark red smothering his face. He fell down.

Paega, come back.

He tripped over a body on the floor and found himself clawing over another form, this one moving, struggling and calling out something. The woman looked at him and screamed, her hands hiding her face.

He felt a sudden urge to flee. Danger was all around. His instincts told him to run. He scrambled to his feet and moved away, stepping on bodies and broken wood. He was confused.

He sniffed the air. Burning. Fire. He had to move away from the fire.

He heard a *ting-ting*. He looked around. Where did it come from? He saw men, women, and children running in all directions. He saw men beating each other.

A terrible howl. Men with long poles, sharp at one end. They were sticking their poles into men. Men fell.

Smoke. Burning.

He ran. And fell. He couldn't run as he knew he could. His legs were strange, awkward. He went down onto his hands and moved along on all fours. This too didn't feel right.

Light came, then darkness instantly followed.

"Fa...f-fa, fa, fa..."

The sound was coming from his mouth.

A great rumble sounded somewhere above. He cowered and looked up. What was there? Danger?

Paega, we will miss you.

He gnashed his teeth, swinging his arms around him, trying to dispel the voices that floated in and out of his ears, but were nowhere to be seen.

He crouched and shook his head.

He grunted in agony as his ears were attacked again by the harsh sound. He tried to shut it out, smacking his head, but the noise came again.

"Fa-fa-fa, p-p-p..."

He scrambled along the stone, trying to get away from everything.

But he heard a voice and he couldn't resist it. He turned around and loped back into the crowd of others like him. He slipped and fell, his face connecting with something warm and slick. He pushed himself and looked at it. A man. But this man had been hurt. This man was staring up but not moving. He pawed at the man, pushed his head, but there was nothing.

"*Aodeq!*" came a cry close to him.

He had to kill these people.

Another image swirled inside his head. He saw a lady and recognised her. She was smiling at him. She disappeared.

He felt abandoned. Where was his mother? He should be following her and the others. But she was gone again.

He gasped and swatted at the air again. He had seen the lady's face, huge and right before his eyes. She had spoken, a finger touching his nose.

You are Paega. Can you say that? Pay-gah. Pay-gah. Paega!

He felt his mouth tense.

"P-p-p…pai…"

Light and terrible noise again. Screams and shouting. So many people, so much danger to him and his pack. He had to kill the threat. He had to protect his own.

He felt heat. He looked up. Fire. Fire was danger. Fire could kill.

He turned and tried to get away from the flames.

"*Aodeq!*"

He couldn't resist the word. He turned back and moved into the raging mass of his own and the dangerous ones. He swung his fists wildly.

Paega, we're always here.

He gasped and shook his head. The voices disappeared and were replaced by terrible screams screeching through the air. He moved back into the pack and immediately felt safer with his own kind. When he had moved away from them, he had felt suddenly vulnerable. Now he was back with his kin and felt stronger, and they were moving. Moving as quickly as they could, it seemed. Colliding into each other, but all now hurrying to the wood in the stone.

Paega, have you seen your sister?

He growled in his throat. The endless voices made him feel safe but confused him. They were not his pack; they were not here by his side always. He felt tense but he couldn't stop the soothing voices drifting to him. They were somewhere near him yet also far away.

The wood at the bottom of the stone...a door...began to open. Roars of many voices erupted and Paega felt suddenly terrified. His pack slowed. Ferocious roars came hurtling at him. He saw red and white colours ahead. Paega saw it was danger and yet they were still moving toward it. He didn't understand. He wanted to flee but shouts came from behind.

"*Qilqan sea tah, aodeq ken tah qilqan!*"

The urge to attack the threat surged within him. Paega pushed forward with all his strength. He felt a pain in his shoulder but ignored it. The danger was ahead and he had to kill the danger.

His pack suddenly lurched forward, as if the threat had fled. He ran and found there was open space before him. He ran and saw red and white people on either side. His pack kept moving. Some jumped at the people but Paega kept loping forward.

Paega, I will miss you so much.

He stopped. The woman he saw in his head was so clear, so lovely and kind. He knew her.

Mother?

The thought came to him and he struggled with it. The woman was the one who would protect him. She would shield him from the threat. He looked around, trying desperately to find her. He had to find her. With her, he would be safe.

Something shook behind him. The ground shuddered beneath his feet. Terrible sounds exploded into the air.

He turned around and saw the stone falling. Wooden towers splintered and fell apart as the stone crashed into them. People fell and others screamed.

Sound and sensation smothered him. All he wanted was to find his mother, but he could hardly see who the figures around him were anymore. The red and white colours were difficult to make out with a grey mist descending on them. The mist hurt his throat. He retched and felt something shoot up from within. He spat it out and saw it was dark.

Mother? Help...

Something sliced his leg and he fell, crying out with sound but finding his tongue did not respond. He was on the ground. It was muddy and soft, smelling of something he knew was not clean. His head lolled back, then was kicked. Pain became his world.

Mother, where are you?

He looked up and the sky became white for an instant. A deafening crack shook his body. He knew his death was close. His instinct to survive was strong but his body was numb and would not move.

CHAPTER 7

TORBAL

26th Day of Maia, The Storm of Ragnekai

Bregustol burns!

To the south-east of their position, rising smoke was visible above the grey mass of the capital, darker streaks in the deepening gloom of the storm's shadow. The single columns appeared motionless from this distance, but Torbal knew all were drifting upwards, fires below belching out ash and fumes.

"We're too late, General." Wyman cursed to his side.

"Too late to stop it happening but we will be the ones who finish this," growled Torbal.

At that moment scouts came galloping back. They shot off a quick salute to the King's Shield and their legion Forwost, then relayed grim tidings.

"A horde of Unvasik are assaulting the east of the city, my lord. Hundreds of them, over a thousand maybe. The wall there has fallen but we saw no catapults or trebuchet," the lead scout said between breaths.

Torbal clenched his jaw. How did a wall fall without siege engines? It could only be down to some dark trickery by Seolta and his allies, perhaps sabotage from within the city. If the Unvasık had come down the Ruby Road, maybe the Duthka were already inside Bregustol, sowing chaos, possibly commanding hordes of beast-men in the streets. A whole wall falling though? Torbal could not see how that had been accomplished.

Did that book of Sedmund's truly contain the secrets of fire and Seolta has unleashed its fury?

That was a particularly grim thought and Torbal prayed he was wrong. The realm was already ablaze with hate and vengeance. The falling rain could extinguish neither blaze. Torbal cursed under his breath. What kind of man was this Seolta? He had deceived them all, even betraying his mighty Unvasik allies. If the Unvasik were attacking Bregustol now, why had Seolta robbed his side of warriors, turning them into beasts within the Deadwood?

Is the man completely mad?

It was if Seolta had no intention of conquering even one city in Ragnekai; he simply wanted to watch the realm burn.

Torbal nodded to the scouts and they headed off to relay the news to the infantry who were marching up behind Torbal, Wyman, and the Bladesung cavalry. A company of maybe thirty Bradlastax warriors were also mounted. Torbal turned to their leader, his voice catching as he spoke to someone who was not his sister but now held her command.

"Ealdgyd, take your riders some distance to the east. The Bladesung will drive into them directly from the north, hitting their left flank. Circle round and come in from the rear."

He turned to Wyman.

"Twenty Bladesung to accompany them."

The Forwost nodded. Torbal continued. "We have over a hundred horses in the main charge. Wedge formation, you and I at the head. We—"

"My lord!" interrupted Wyman. "We cannot risk the King's Shield."

Torbal held his eyes. "The High King is dead. Ragnekai bleeds. I will not sit back and watch our lands die."

Wyman inhaled sharply but made no further protest. Torbal turned to a captain.

"Garvin, relay orders to the infantry. Double-march, shortest route to the north wall. Use that wall as their right-flank. Wheel tightly at the north-east corner and advance on the Unvasik. We will charge once, punch through their lines, withdraw, and then come in again, becoming the hammer to your anvil."

Torbal waved him on and turned to Wyman. He looked in the Forwost's face for any doubt. There was none.

"Let Thunor guide our blades and the Winds be at our backs!" said Wyman fiercely.

Torbal nodded and held out a mailed glove. Wyman grasped the general's forearm and they held the grip for a moment. Torbal released and nudged his horse out in front of his riders, trotting first up the line, holding as many eyes as he could, then back down the lines to the other end. He returned to the middle and took a deep breath.

"Ealdgyd and the Bradlastax will sweep in from the north-east, cutting them down as they run!"

A roar of approval answered.

"Wyman and the Bladesung, follow me. Wedge charge straight into the heart of these demons. Push through. Do not let yourselves be caught in a melee. Then we form up again and charge a second time. The infantry will be the wall of spears where they will die!" he cried.

The infantry were already marching past the riders. Torbal saw the copper-haired Wulfner in their ranks, a head taller than those around him, striding forward.

May the Winds blow kindly for you this day...

Torbal realised why he could see the man's hair.

Get a helmet, you fool!

Torbal turned back to the mounted Bladesung and withdrew his sword, thankful it didn't catch but slid from the scabbard in a smooth motion, whispering against the leather. He held it aloft.

"For Ragnekai! For Westhealfe! For Cyneburg!" he roared with all the strength and love he could pull forth from his aging body.

The wave of sound from the mounted soldiers was worthy of

Cyneburg's memory. Their number was far fewer than Torbal needed to engage these mountain giants but their courage could not be
doubted.

They had to break through. Fighting in single combat would lead
to certain defeat. Scattering their foes, picking off as many as possible
one by one, then herding them into the shield wall; this tactic had a
chance.

*Kenric, forgive me. Know that I ride now to avenge your beloved wife,
my sister.*

CHAPTER 8

WULFNER

26th Day of Maia, The Storm of Ragnekai

Wulfner gritted his teeth and kept marching, painfully aware he was probably a good ten years senior to the oldest soldier in the ranks around him. His legs ached but he felt he still had a good well of stamina left in him. If he was honest with himself, it was the mental strain taking its toll more than the physical. The ambush in the Deadwood had shaken him. The fight within that dark forest had been a nightmare Wulfner would never forget. Hulking giants suddenly emerging from the dark depths of the trees, wildly swinging at the Bladesung and Bradlastax, and hurling soldiers through the air. The legions of Westhealfe were not trained for that kind of chaotic combat and had suffered.

The Bradlastax had lost their talismanic leader, Lady Cyneburg. General Torbal had lost his sister, and Lord Kenric would soon learn his wife was dead. Having travelled with Lady Cyneburg and heard the tragic tale of the massacre of her Bradlastax, her death had left Wulfner feeling hollow and bereft of hope. The King's Shield had brought back a measure of morale by telling them to hold their rage within and unleash it when they met their foes once more. Wulfner had nodded solemnly when he heard the general's words, but he'd had to reach deep within himself to reignite a sense of purpose.

I'm too old for this.

The rain was coming down in earnest now and while Wulfner welcomed its cool caress, he would have preferred dry ground for any fight to come. A slither of fear was winding upwards from his gut.

Will we be fighting Unvasik warriors with weapons this time?

He remembered the Sacred Mount, seeing Torbal's battle-sergeant, Nerian, cut down. The huge mountain man had then winded Wulfner with the butt of his axe. And let him live. Wulfner had seen a look in the man's eyes, a look that bordered on pity.

He knew it was an unfair fight. He let me live…

Wulfner let his head fall back and opened his mouth. Not much of the falling rain touched his tongue but he momentarily felt detached from the man-made horror that surely awaited them ahead.

As if to challenge this notion that nature was a calming friend, the sky lit up and the clouds grumbled angrily. The atmosphere was ominous, and the big northerner wished he were back in Ceapung, with the whiff of peat fires, the sizzling sounds of fish on Balther's grill, and the look of awe on his friend's face when he heard Wulfner's tales.

Except it won't be awe. It'll be sorrow I see.

If I make it back…

Wulfner heard the call to halt and shuffled to a stop. His hands found his thighs and he sucked in a few breaths. He caught the soldier next to him watching.

"Twenty years ago, I did this and laughed. Now I can hardly breathe," he joked.

The soldier smiled nervously. "Did you see battle, back then?" he asked and Wulfner realised the majority of these men and women had tasted their first battle yesterday and were undoubtedly shaken.

Wulfner quickly looked the man over and saw his mail was clean and his tunic rich with the colours of Westhealfe. No mud, no blood. This soldier had been one of those who waited on the border of the Deadwood, guarding the horses and wagons. He hadn't been part of the deadly chaos within the trees, so he was yet to be tested in the arena of rampaging, merciless violence.

Wulfner answered his question carefully. "I did. I saw blood spilt then, and I saw it yesterday. It's not nice…"

Damn the Winds! I have no words to help this man.

Wulfner extended a hand. "Wulfner, native of Ceapung."

The soldier brightened. He took Wulfner's hand and shook it vigorously. "Got an aunt who lives there. I'm Bairon, native of Thurham, small village near Manbung."

Wulfner forced a grin. "Well, when this is all over, let's go and drink Thurham dry!" he said, clapping the young man on the shoulder. Bairon returned the good humour, oblivious to the chasm between Wulfner's forced optimism and reality.

Wulfner peered over the ranks before him and saw General Torbal was giving orders. He looked past the general and saw the dark mass of Bregustol. Then he saw the spires of smoke.

Bairon gasped. "Bregustol is under siege? Who is attacking the city? More of the Unvasik?" he asked, his voice quivering.

Wulfner didn't need to answer.

An officer rode up and started shouting orders. The Unvasik were indeed ahead. Wulfner wasn't carrying a shield so he would not be part of any wall, but he had a mace, his big hammer left at the Black Stone Ford.

The infantry began to move, the march double-time much to the displeasure of Wulfner's muscles. He kept pace with Bairon to his left but knew he was feeling the strain more than his young companion. He felt ashamed but suddenly wished he had not spoken with Bairon. He now felt a responsibility to keep the young man from harm. He puffed a laugh.

It'll probably be him saving my old hide.

The infantry was alongside the cavalry and Wulfner saw Torbal whipping up courage. So many years in the legions and he had never come close to anyone of high standing; now in his twilight days he had spoken directly with the First Lord of Westhealfe, reprimanded the King's Shield, and journeyed with Lady Cyneburg. He shook his head at the bizarre nature of this last month.

The infantry passed the riders now and began to pick up the pace, the jangle of mail and the clomping of boots a steady rhythm. The telltale signs of a city under siege reached his senses; the acrid stench of burning, cries that were either taunting in nature or signalling pain—Wulfner couldn't tell which—and the ringing of bells. All the while, the storm above seemed to be drawing strength from the rage below it. Boots began to hit the ground with a wetter sloshing sound, the fields beneath their feet melding with the downpour.

Rowena my beloved wife, forgive me for this foolishness. I'm just trying to do the best I can.

He cast his eyes up at the dark clouds, wishing he could see a clear blue sky and feel a breeze. A blinding jagged line ripped the sky and the thunder was like the world tearing itself in half.

Sunniva, be a good girl for your mother. I might see you sooner than I expected, little one.

Wulfner clenched his jaw and fought back the emotion. Bairon really didn't need an old veteran sobbing as they entered whatever despair lay ahead. He huffed and focused on keeping up with all these younger men and women.

Winds, blow fortune our way, I beg you…

CHAPTER 9

TORBAL

26th Day of Maia, The Storm of Ragnekai

The cavalry began to wheel to their right, now at a point directly north of the Unvasik assaulting the fallen eastern wall. A straight charge should devastate their right flank and bring disarray to the mountain warriors. The scouts had said a thousand; Torbal didn't disagree with that estimate.

By the grace of Eostre, steel our hearts.

Torbal kicked his mount into motion and Wyman moved in beside him. The general saw the Bladesung take up position behind, spreading out to form the wedge. Ealdgyd and her Bradlastax warriors were moving with speed, taking their mounts off into an arc that would bring them round to the rear of the invaders.

Ulla, forgive me if I fall here. So many words I would say to you. Forgive me my doubts. Know that my love for you is stronger than ever.

Torbal picked up the pace, moving the company into a steady canter. Bregustol rose before them. The stench of smoke was heavy in the air as the Unvasik horde came into view. They were a fearsome sight, even from this distance. The war cries they bellowed, the sheer number of them, and all the knowledge Torbal possessed of these mountain giants would have quelled him were he not at the head of such a company. A company of brave men and women. A legion of trained soldiers, protected by chainmail and shields, wielding blades and spears that could pierce Unvasik flesh.

Torbal snapped his reins and emitted a cry. "Yah! Onward!"

The company increased their pace, swiftly moving into a gallop. The ground trembled and the hooves threw up slops of mud, the terrain becoming dangerously swamped with the relentless rain.

The Unvasik became aware of them.

The distance between the two forces was less than half a mile and would disappear in no time at this speed. He was vaguely aware of shouting coming from the wreckage of the north wall and hoped the defenders of Bregustol would rally as they saw allies.

Torbal felt the rush of impending battle course through him and knew there was no more time to think.

No time to fear.

"For Cyneburg!" he roared.

"For Cyneburg!" cried Wyman.

Others took up the call as the gap shrunk to a hundred yards and the Unvasik weapons became visible.

Torbal fixed his stare upon a warrior before him, brought his sword high, then chopped down as he sped past the giant. The impact he felt surge up his arm and the grunt of agony told him his blade had dealt a deep wound.

Torbal heard all manner of stomach-churning sounds around him as he pushed his mount on. Bodies being knocked down by one and a half thousand pounds of charging horse. Not even an Unvasik giant could withstand such an impact. Screams of death, cries of pain, and oaths of rage filled the air. The hideous sound of a horse's wail as it met an axe or broke a leg in a collision.

Torbal didn't look back but rode through the Unvasik, delivering another downward cut to one who was trying to flee. The general's blade opened up a gaping wound in the man's upper back and he fell howling, his hands desperately reaching behind to try to stem the blood.

The Bradlastax had engaged the Unvasik to the rear, their shrieks of fury like avenging spirits of legend, their battle-axes hacking left and right. Unvasik fell to their merciless attack.

Torbal pulled clear of the chaos and spurred his horse on. He chanced a glance over his shoulder and saw Wyman and others emerging behind him.

May all I ride with still live.

Torbal knew that was a false hope though. Despite their advantage on horse, the Unvasik would undoubtedly have taken down some of his men. He had seen their might at the Black Stone Ford.

The general slowed at what he judged was a good distance, then began to wheel his mount, his sword raised high and pointing to his left. Wyman appeared beside him, spattered with blood but seeming uninjured.

"We have them, my lord!" he cried, the thrill of battle wild in his eyes. "They cannot stand against the power of Westhealfe."

Cries caught Torbal's attention, and he turned his head to see riders to the rear of his column grasping at necks and arms. He saw no arrows. What was happening? Then a rider jerked and toppled from his horse, crashing to the ground and disappearing under the mass of hooves.

Thunor, what is this new madness?

A rider passed him, pulling at his cheek. Torbal saw blood but nothing else. The man stiffened in the saddle and slumped forward, saved only by the man next to him grabbing his comrade until the two horses came to a halt.

His men were being struck by something unseen.

We must finish this!

Torbal looked at the scene of devastation and saw to his dismay that fewer Unvasik had fallen than he had thought. Many stood and were advancing upon his company, trying to cut the distance and prevent the horses from gathering speed in another charge. And smaller figures were running in between the Unvasik. The Duthka were here.

Ancestors, guide my sword now…

CHAPTER 10

WULFNER

26th Day of Maia, The Storm of Ragnekai

The ground began to tremble under-foot, and he heard a more constant thunder approaching from behind them. Wulfner shot a glance
over his shoulder and saw Torbal at the head of the cavalry, the horses
now gathering pace. The infantry cheered them on. On any other day
it would've been a majestic sight, but knowing they were charging
into Unvasik tribesmen tempered the heroic sentiment.

Death is about to swallow many of us.

Wulfner realised he was scared. And if he was scared, he was sure
Bairon and many other soldiers here would be frightened beyond belief.

"The invaders will know the wrath of Westhealfe!" an officer cried
out from the front.

"Westhealfe, Westhealfe!" cheered the ranks.

"Westhealfe!" shouted Wulfner.

*What does it matter where we come from? In battle all of us are just
dancing upon a rickety bridge with an abyss below.*

Wulfner heard the terrible clash ahead as Torbal's cavalry drove into the Unvasik. He had never seen such a charge in his life and was glad his view of the carnage was obscured. He suspected some in the front ranks would be hit by crippling fear at the sight.

Emiren, Lunyai, take care of each other. No more troublemaking!

The infantry wheeled as they finally arrived at the northern wall, the right-flank hugging the stone to ensure the force could not be surrounded. Orders were shouted and officers pushed and shoved men into formation, creating a shield-wall. Wulfner let himself drift to the left-flank, where there was less of a tight shape of soldiers. Bairon was no longer with him.

May the Winds blow kindly on you this day, lad…

A horn blew and they advanced upon the Unvasik, the sounds of death and agony coming forth to meet them. Wulfner's stomach tightened. He gripped his mace but felt suddenly wholly inadequate against what he was about to face. He couldn't even best one of these giants with the help of two other hardy men. How could he expect to be victorious in the chaotic melee of battle?

Rowena, I am a fool.

The formation jerked to a halt and blood-curdling screams erupted from the shield-wall. There were no Unvasik out here on the left-flank and Wulfner began searching for an officer. He had no experience in this kind of warfare, but reckoned the left-flank should curl around and come in at the Unvasik right-flank. No officer could be seen, and no orders could be heard.

Damn the Winds!

"To me!" he cried, wondering if he was going mad. "Advance and take them in their flank!"

Wulfner began striding forward. He saw others with him and was thankful for that. They came to the front line and he saw Unvasik crashing into the shield-wall. Wulfner's eyes widened with horror. The wall was buckling, such was the might of these giants.

"Westhealfe!" he cried and charged forward, his mace held high.

Wulfner had his eye on one Unvasik warrior who seemed intent on battering the shield-wall with a hammer. This one would feel a mace in his skull.

Wulfner was upon him.

The mountain tribesman turned and saw the northerner.

Shit...

The Unvasik snarled and his hammer swung around. Wulfner lurched back on his heels and would have fallen had a soldier not kept him upright. He quickly regained his footing and readied his mace.

The Unvasik's face twisted in agony. Wulfner glanced down and saw a spear protruding from the wall, piercing the giant's side.

Wulfner didn't hesitate. He hefted his mace and swiped it at the man's head. It connected with a sickening crunch and the Unvasik crumpled to the ground.

Around him, others were engaging the huge warriors. They had given the shield-wall some respite, which now shunted forward. Wulfner pulled back, searching for anyone in trouble.

One soldier was back-tracking, trying to avoid deadly swings from an Unvasik axe. Wulfner strode over and made ready to swing the mace again. A yard away from his foe, he lunged forward, but his feet slipped in the ever-muddying field beneath their feet. His boots slid forward and fortune favoured him. Wulfner's foot connected with the Unvasik's left leg and the giant warrior stumbled. This was all the opportunity the beleaguered soldier needed, and he thrust his spear into his foe's neck. The gurgling, dying beast of a man collapsed on top of Wulfner and his breath left him.

Get off, you dead sweat-sack!

Wulfner heaved the corpse off him and staggered to his feet. The man he had saved, and who had saved him in turn, was staring at him.

"Well done, lad!" shouted Wulfner.

But then he realised the young man was actually looking past him, eyes wide with terror.

Wulfner turned and almost lost his bladder. A score or more of Unvasik were coming at him.

Why me?

The big northerner looked down and saw the dead Unvasik at his feet had a lot of silver in his beard.

A chief... Damn the Winds!

His lucky slip had become a rallying call to this one's tribesmen. Wulfner stooped to grab his mace and planted his feet.

"Come on then, you freaks! Let an old man show you what real courage is!" he shouted, not believing a word he said.

He heard a whimper to his left; the young soldier who had killed the chief was standing with him.

Brave lad…

CHAPTER 11

KAILEN

26th Day of Maia, The Storm of Ragnekai

Pain woke her. Kailen gasped and twisted her body, but this only re-
sulted in agonising stabs blossoming around her left shoulder.

What happened?

She tried to recall why she was in this dark place, dust floating in
the air and what felt like a hundred sharp stones pressing into her back.

The tower began to collapse...

She remembered the stone beneath her feet shifting and then tumbling back. She retraced her memories, seeking out the reason for her
being at the top of a tower.

We were trying to stop Brax's attack...

Svard!

In her mind's eye she saw the First Ranger sliding down a pitching
slab of the battlements, then being hurled forward as the stone crashed
into a building below. She had tried to grab his hand, but he was too
far.

First Warrior, no!

She struggled to stand but found the rubble around her was less than stable. As she rose to her feet, small rocks began to cascade farther down into darkness. Kailen halted her movement and tried to suppress the panic rising within.

Above her head, white flashed and a boom shook the structure, teasing more debris to loosen, and more dust to swirl in the air. It got into her lungs and she had to cough several times to clear her airways.

Raven's beak!

Her eyes began to focus, picking out shapes and giving her a sense of perspective. She had fallen some way down the spiral staircase but had come to a halt upon this layer of rubble. She couldn't be sure, but it seemed as if part of the wall here had crumbled inward. There was no gaping hole, yet she could feel the wind on her face. She put out a hand and found a hard, solid surface. She winced as she leaned in; her left shoulder was not in the best of shape.

Kailen clenched her teeth and tried again to stop her anguish from surfacing. She had seen Svard fall. She didn't think anyone could have survived that. All he had been trying to do was stop his own people attacking this city, and now he was certainly dead, smashed upon the cobblestone streets of Bregustol. She choked on tears.

First Warrior, guide him to Your Hall…

Kailen lowered herself into a crouch, a numb sensation flowing through her body and mind. What could she do now? It was probably too late to even try to find Brax, and even if she did, it was possible he had received the same orders as Rorthal and would knock her down before he listened to her. How long had she been unconscious anyway? Kailen strained her ears and realised she couldn't hear the sounds of battle nearby. She heard rain falling and the rumbles of thunder above, but no sounds of Sentinels storming the walls.

The wall fell…

Many Sentinels would have died as the wall collapsed. Their siege tower would have been damaged or completely destroyed. The Helligan assault would be in disarray. She remembered seeing the beastmen. The only conclusion she could reach was that they were now fighting the Helligan soldiers out in the fields before Bregustol, and no doubt dying in droves.

Poor bastards. They will share the same fate as Orben.

Kailen felt an overwhelming sense of despair. Svard was dead, Bregustol was in chaos, and she was a fugitive from Helligan justice. Loneliness gripped her and she slumped down again onto the rubble, her shoulder protesting and stones skidding this way and that. She didn't care. All was lost.

Mother, Runa, please know that…

She couldn't finish the thought, at a loss for what she wanted her family to know. Know that she had killed their liege? Know that she was in Bregustol now and would never return to Gamle Hovestad, except in chains? Know that the realm was rupturing along ancient cracks in the land, old wounds that had never healed? Her mother, sister, and herself—none of them knew the truth about her father. Had he died up there on the Sacred Mount? Did he find what he was looking for? Did it matter anymore?

She gritted her teeth against a sob.

Just know that I love you both.

She listened again to the sounds outside the ruined tower. It was much quieter than before, but she still heard distant shouts and what sounded like…singing?

Who in the Raven's gut is singing at a time like this?

Kailen took a cautious breath, then gradually straightened, fearful of the precarious wreckage she stood upon. She paused to gauge where the draft was coming from, then inched slowly in that direction. The darkness began to mingle with a faint glow, something flickering, sending the shadows this way and that.

Fire?

She listened and heard the tell-tale crackling of flames, smelt the smoke. The city was already burning, that much she knew from the lad who had taken her to Worsteth. Maybe all of them would burn to death in the capital, everyone becoming ashes of an insidious design now reaching its culmination.

Kailen carefully moved forward, knowing the flames might mean this was a dangerous path, but at least she'd be able to see. Voices caught her ears as a new light began to seep into the patchy black. Her sense of caution was overwhelmed by a desire to see the sky again and to meet a living soul. Whoever it was.

The voices were speaking in the Helligan language.

"Can you hear me, Jarl?"

Silence.

"He's gone. Damn the Raven!"

"First, what now?"

First?

Brax?

"We are Sentinels! We fight. We win. Got it?"

"Yes, sir!" came a chorus of voices in response.

Kailen called out but her throat rasped with the all the dust. She coughed.

"What's that?" came a shout.

"Brax!" she called out, clearer than before. "Brax!" Stronger now, louder.

"Who's that?"

"Brax, it's me, Kailen."

Kailen heard footsteps on the crumbling stones, crunching and sliding. She held her breath, not sure if the First Sentinel would be pleased to see her, arrest her, or just kill her to remove one problem.

A block suddenly fell out of the wall, and she could make out Brax's face in the dim light. A flash of lightning illuminated his visage further and Kailen saw he was grinning stupidly.

He doesn't know.

"What in the name of the First Warrior are you doing here?" he shouted. "Raven's arse, Kailen, the realm is twisting reality!"

She struggled to reach him as he pulled away another block, giving her room to crawl out of the tower. The former messenger to Lord Orben accepted one of Brax's strong hands and soon found herself facing the Helligan First Sentinel in what looked to be a ruined corridor that had run through the wall, but now had lost anything above waist-height. She fell into him, relief as deep as the Swift Sea flowing through her, relief that Brax was here and relief he wasn't ordering her to be put in chains.

"Kailen, what are you doing here? What is going on?" He looked around. "And where is Svard?"

Kailen choked on her reply.

"He fell, Brax. He fell."

The First Sentinel was silent, as were the dozen or so of his men standing nearby, their uniforms stained with dark patches, sprinkled with grey.

"We'll mourn him later," said Brax, his tone defiant. "Right now, you need to get away from the city. Something happened out front and those mad men are moving off. We have a chance now to march right in, take th—"

"Brax, no! You must stop the attack!"

He looked at her. "Kailen, the Helligan nation is taking back what is rightfully ours. Why would we stop now?"

"It's all a trap, damn it!" she cried. "All of it. Orben was manipulated by a cunning Meridian called Sylvanus. Our lord was turned into one of those beast-men. Brax, Orben is dead!"

That got his attention, well and truly. He stared at her. She hurried on, knowing each moment lost might be another death somewhere.

"Brax, Unvasik are at the east wall, Duthka have lit fires within the city, and those crazed men are everywhere. We have been pieces on the board in someone else's game. All he wants is for us all to die and the realm to collapse."

Brax was listening but frowning with what Kailen feared was doubt or disbelief.

"Don't let them win, Brax. Call off the attack. Bregustol is not our enemy!"

His eyes narrowed and Kailen saw she was losing him.

"Brax, Svard was trying to reach you when he fell. He died trying to stop this madness. Please, Brax, you must pull back!"

A streak of lightning lanced down and the sky grumbled. Kailen heard the sounds of chaos around them but it was the silence of Brax, the Helligan First Sentinel, that held her attention.

First Warrior, I beg you, make him see the truth!

Brax gave his head a slow shake, left to right, and back again.

Raven's bastard black wings!

Kailen opened her mouth to protest further but a shout sounded somewhere beneath them. Both Brax and Kailen turned to peer down into the dust and gloom of the city below.

The voice cried out again, a lone call in the Helligan language, coming from somewhere below.

"Raven's…stinking…shit-filled…arse!"

Kailen's heart leapt.

Chapter 12

Emiren

26th Day of Maia, The Storm of Ragnekai

Emiren felt like she was in a bad dream that would never end. She did not jerk awake to a beautiful sunrise though. This was all too real; her eyes were open and this was a waking nightmare where they galloped ever closer to an unknown horror in the realm's capital, Bregustol. Emiren, Lunyai, Corann, the Tarakans and the riders of the Heoroth legion. And Tarak bounding along beside them all, seemingly thrilled at hurtling across fields and down roads, every square of land a new realm for the wolf.

Rain was coming down now, accompanied by flashes of lightning heralding thunder that rumbled deeper than the Western Sea. Emiren had never known a storm this powerful so early in the year. The fiercest ones normally came at the turn of summer to autumn. The young lady from the small village of Fallowden, so far away now, had thought she had been thrown about in the boat that day on the Western Sea. A horrifying day when Lunyai had seemed drowned in the waves and Emiren had also been injured, cracking her head. But as they rode now, she knew that had been nothing compared to the true power of nature's wrath.

Lunyai kept calling out to Neii'Ne, their majestic mount, almost singing to it in her language. Each time she did so, Emiren could swear they picked up pace or the fatigue fell away from rider and horse alike. The Tarakan people truly were a wonder. And Lunyai was a beautiful moon that glowed with something Emiren desired more than she could express.

There are no words for how I feel about her.

Words. The Words. Emiren still couldn't believe the sacred Words — of Fallowden, Lowenden, and all who lived on the borders of Argol Forest—were truly words of power, just like her mother had told her as a child. Had Emiren not been clutching so tightly to Lunyai and fearing a fall, she would have smiled at the thought of her mother knowing how right she had been.

These Words can command those turned. I can help them, I am sure of it.

Emiren believed she could initially calm them, ease their suffering, and then try to understand more of what had happened to them. If they could retrieve the book Moryn had taken, they might even be able to give the poor souls back their humanity.

Lunyai cried out, one hand briefly leaving the reins to point ahead, then back to gripping the leather as she called out more words in the Tarakan language. Emiren peeked over Lunyai's shoulder, terrified she would lose her grip. And she almost did when she saw what they were riding toward. The capital city of Bregustol was ahead, its western and southern walls rearing up under the ever-darkening clouds.

It's huge!

Emiren had thought the north-eastern city of Westhealfe was a giant's land, with its high walls and buildings rising three or four stories. But the grim walls here were higher still, and the grey shapes of spires and towers pierced the sky. Columns of smoke also rose, the smell tickling her nostrils, mixing in with the fresh smell of the rain bringing life to the soil under the horses' hooves.

The sky lit up again as lightning seared the clouds, the boom of thunder like the bellow of an ogre in a frightening story. But what the storm illuminated was far more terrifying than monsters of the imagination. Emiren saw gaping wounds in the southern walls, piles of stone as high as small mountains leaning into the city. And there were soldiers, hundreds of them, fighting before the destruction.

Shouts exploded all around and Lunyai slowed the horse. Emiren looked around and saw the company of riders were stopping, the legion's captain calling them to halt. Lunyai's father, Naaki, and Imala moved their horses up beside them, their eyes brimming with the same fear Emiren felt. Corann's face was inscrutable. Emiren didn't know if he was scared or ready to ride ahead and search for his daughter, without a thought for his own safety.

"Bregustol burns!" cried the legion's captain. "The Helligan nation has come north!"

Emiren looked back at the soldiers fighting before the city walls.

Helligan soldiers?

She gripped Lunyai's waist tighter and felt her friend's hand upon her arm. They were truly in the heart of the storm now, on the edge of a real battle. Not a fight like the one they had survived inside the Sacred Mont but a chaotic, swirling rage like her uncle Camran had been a part of in Argyllan. Emiren stifled a whimper. She did not want to go any nearer. How could Lunyai, the Tarakans, and herself possibly survive the carnage of such a battle?

Spirits, watch over us, I beg you.

"Captain, what should we do?"

Songaa's eyes rested upon Lunyai even as he asked the question of the soldier. He was a father fearing for his daughter. Emiren was glad her own parents were not with them. It hurt to think how she had broken her promise to them, but she was grateful they were far away and would not see the realm being cruelly twisted and its people falling. She looked down to see Tarak gazing up at her, amber eyes untouched majesty in the deepening discord she felt encroaching upon them. *I'll never send you away again, Tarak.*

"Captain?" pressed Songaa.

The soldier stared ahead. Emiren was relieved there was no rapid reply to Songaa's question. She remembered Anton yelling *Charge!* when they were much younger and playing kings and queens. That was how it happened in the tales. The heroes rode forth upon shining steeds and smote their enemies. The stories never told you how many were killed in the charge, or what was left on the battlefield when the screaming stopped.

"We will wait for the infantry to arrive," he said.

"But it will be many songs before they come!" protested Lunyai. "Can we not stop this fighting?"

Emiren wanted to kiss Lunyai then. The Tarakan was far braver than herself, and still possessed a pure innocence despite all they had been through.

Lunyai had killed three men now and Emiren knew it weighed heavily upon her. She wanted to stop the fighting so there would be no more killing. Emiren wished they were gods that could part the clouds and bring peace to those below.

The captain ordered a couple of riders to scout ahead, then return when they had a clearer picture of the situation. He then responded to Lunyai's plea.

"Sorry, my lady, but right now we don't have the numbers to do anything other than die upon Helligan spears if we charge in. When the infantry arrives, we can form up and slowly advance. With any luck, the Helligans will have to break off the assault at some point and there may be a chance to parley."

Emiren saw then how lords and captains did not have the luxury of viewing the life of one person in the same way she did. They had to look at the risks, estimate how many would die if they acted, how many would be killed if they didn't act, and what path was most likely to lead to victory.

They cannot think of a single life. They must decide which is the least terrible road to take.

The rain continued to cover them with its cool touch. Emiren licked her lips and tasted nature. So pure and so devoid of hate. She wished the falling drops would take away the rage that she saw ahead, but the violence of the thunder and lightning seemed to be at one with the madness on the ground.

The riders returned and Emiren strained to hear their report above the hum and hiss of the weather. Tarak emitted a low growl, his head lifting to the forlorn sky above.

"They are Helligan, Forwost. Looks like they are fighting mad-men, like those the Bladesung fought at the ford days ago. They are men with no armour, shield, nor helmet, just rampaging and leaping at the soldiers. Two sections of the south wall are half collapsed and one Helligan siege tower is no better than kindling. It's like the Abyss has opened up and spewed forth blood and hysteria…"

Emiren felt a wave of sorrow upon hearing that more had indeed been turned. She had hoped General Torbal had been wrong in his belief that Seolta was going to turn the city of Bregustol into mind-less animals. But the Duthka leader had carried out the deed, and so doomed many innocent lives.

We must help them…

"I can save those turned," she blurted out.

The captain turned to her and frowned. "I saw what you did at the ford, my lady, and I don't doubt your ability. But getting any closer to the Helligan forces would be suicide. You'll either be taken down by a battle-blinded soldier or bludgeoned to death by one of those beast-men. Stay here until we have sufficient numbers to persuade the Helligans to stand down."

"But while we wait, those poor souls are being slaughtered!" pro-tested Emiren, knowing in her heart that she had to somehow stop the fighting and pull the turned ones away from the conflict, however dangerous it might be.

Songaa nudged his horse Ahoni forward and spoke. "Captain, we are Tarakan and I am sure the Helligan soldiers would see we are not from your cities. If it is only us approaching, we may be able to con-vince them we are no threat and may even stop the beast-men attack-ing," Songaa explained.

Emiren felt Lunyai tense. Her father was right that the Helligans should recognise Songaa, Lunyai, Imala, and Naaki as Tarakan with their darker skin tone, their decorated hair, and the way they dressed. They might see herself as an enemy, but if she showed them she could control the turned ones, they had a chance.

The Forwost looked less than overjoyed with the plan but he seemed to be considering it.

Imala spoke. "Please, captain, if we can save innocent lives, then we must try. If they see us helping them, we may also be able to persuade them to lower their weapons."

The man slowly nodded and Emiren felt a spark of hope.

"I don't like it, but I have no alternative to offer. We will hold here. If Oblivion, or whatever evil you believe in, comes down though, do not hesitate to flee. And I suggest your friend there stays back some," he finished, pointing at Corann.

Songaa was already kicking Ahoni into motion. Lunyai followed, Emiren seated behind her and Tarak keeping pace. Naaki and Imala fell in beside them. Corann joined them but kept his mount behind. Emiren heard Naaki shout something to Songaa in their language but he didn't respond.

Lunyai called back over her shoulder. "She is angry with what the captain said. The Tarakan people do not believe in evil gods, only in the evil of those who walk the realm."

Emiren clenched her jaw. Her people believed in the Shades of the Evercold, but they did not enter this world for all but one day of the year. She couldn't argue with the Tarakan belief.

Do the Helligans, Meridians, and those in Bregustol believe in an evil deity so they can turn a blind eye to their own malice and failings?

She didn't have time to think further. They were close to the battle. Here, to the rear of the violence, Helligan soldiers were in ranks, ready to be sent in by captains on horses.

Songaa hailed them. "Helligan soldiers, we come to help! Please let us help!"

One mounted officer turned his horse toward them, studied them quickly, and then shouted out an order. Emiren's stomach lurched as they were suddenly confronted by a dozen or so soldiers with long poles, vicious axe-blades at the ends.

Spirits, calm them…

Songaa stopped his horse Ahoni, and held up his hands, palms out. "We can help. Please believe me. This girl can command those beast-men to stop attacking. You must let us try!"

All around was suddenly bathed in a white light and the thunder cracked. Emiren felt Lunyai's body trembling. She squeezed tighter and leaned forward to speak in her ear.

"We are together, Lunyai. We will be alright."

Emiren didn't believe her own words, but she wanted to take away some of Lunyai's fear. She wanted to be more for the Tarakan. She wanted to be everything for her.

"What can you do?" asked the Helligan captain doubtfully, his accent something Emiren had not heard since last year when a group of traders from Gamle Hovestad came all the way to Fallowden.

There was a silence and Emiren realised everyone was looking at her. She cleared her throat.

"They hear the call of this whistle," she said, holding up the bone whistle from around her neck. One of the soldiers at the ford had given it to her, saying it had been found after the battle there. Emiren had been reluctant to take it, seeing the dried blood on it, but had accepted the morbid gift after a moment.

The Helligan's eyes widened. "Those whistles have been sounding over and over. Not all can hear."

Emiren continued, "At the Black Stone Ford, I was able to command some of them to sleep. I think I can do it again." Emiren had little faith it would work as well now, with thunder growling overhead and the terrible sounds of battle drowning out the voices of any and all. But she would try nonetheless.

The captain turned to look at the battle. Emiren followed his eyes and almost fell from the horse. A soldier cleaved a man's arm and blood spurted as the poor soul howled. A turned one brought down a rock, again and again on a prone Helligan's head. And more of these pitiful men were pouring out through the ruined gates ahead. It was a grotesque sight, a portal between two partially devastated walls, out of which were streaming crazed men who ran rampant.

"Do it!" cried the captain. He turned and began shouting orders in his own language.

Emiren gaped as soldiers suddenly formed two blocks, curving toward the battle. An avenue was open and the captain motioned for them to ride forward.

Emiren felt a torrid mix of heat and cold within her belly, followed by a shudder that slithered up her spine. Her breath caught in her chest and she gasped, inhaling in short, sharp bursts.

Mum, Da, I'm so scared…

She squeezed her eyes shut and clenched her teeth, then took a deep breath.

The Spirits are with me.

Songaa led their small group between the soldiers, his pace sure but Emiren knew he must be terrified too. He stopped and Lunyai nudged their mount up beside him.

"Now, Emiren!" he cried, his voice straining to be heard.

Emiren put the bone whistle to her lips and blew as hard as she could. Some soldiers dipped their heads, as did Naaki and Imala. Emiren felt a tingle deep within her ear but no pain. She looked ahead and saw turned ones facing her.

"*Shyula!*" she cried as loudly as she could.

Some cocked their heads and stopped moving.

Emiren screamed in horror as Helligan soldiers darted in and cut them down.

"No!" she cried. "You cannot kill them!"

But she realised then that all she was doing by commanding them to sleep was lining them up for slaughter.

She slid from the saddle and ran forward, Tarak at her heels.

"Emiren, no!" cried Lunyai behind her.

But she did not turn back. She knew she had to save these poor men from Helligan blades.

She was dangerously close to the chaos now. Her heart thudded a frantic beat. She blew the whistle again and this time cried out a different command.

"*Loloqei, loloqei!*" Come, come!

Emiren heard a shout from behind and the Helligan soldiers began to shuffle backwards. The command had been given to cease the attacks.

Spirits, thank you. Please let me save them…

"*Loloqei, loloqei! Lolona!*"

More than one turned man was loping in her direction. Seeing their crazed eyes coming closer, Emiren suddenly feared she was beckoning death toward her. She looked down at Tarak and saw he was ready to pounce. Emiren placed a hand on his ruff and gently applied pressure.

Peace, Tarak, let them come.

More joined the bizarre parade of turned ones now shambling toward Emiren. She stepped backwards and called again. She heard gasps and exclamations from the Helligan soldiers but could not understand what they were saying. She didn't care. All she knew now was that those turned were not attacking the Helligan soldiers and in turn, the men with spears and axes were not cutting down common folk whose only crime was being in Bregustol this day.

Spirits, keep them coming. Let me lead them away from this violence and hate…

She was aware she was passing the horses of her friends but did not look up, even as she heard voices singing in the Tarakan language. Songaa, Lunyai, Naaki and Imala were sending forth the Tarakalii, doing all they could to help Emiren. She focused her attention on the ever-growing mass she was enticing onwards and felt a flicker of flame kindled, a light that led the way out of the darkness. Emiren looked at the poor souls following her as she backed away. Those near the front were mere yards away from her now and she saw a strange calm in their faces—one almost looked like he was smiling. Songaa and the others were flanking the strange procession, and she knew they would ride in if she seemed in danger. Tarak was by her side too. She wanted to hug the devoted wolf.

She wasn't in danger. The farther they walked, the more the men following her seemed more like sleepy kittens than the mindless, raging creatures she had witnessed only moments ago. Emiren felt a surge of relief within, knowing that she had saved at least some lives in this carnage.

But what happens when we stop?

CHAPTER 13

PAEGA

26th Day of Maia, The Storm of Ragnekai

He was not dead. He was in pain. He was on his back, upon the marsh-like ground. He still saw the sky above, grey shadows gliding across it. He felt water pattering upon his skin, then felt a warmth on his face and searched for its source. He found it. A dull glow pushing through the darkness.

The sun…

The warmth on his face increased in strength and light began to push away the dull grey shapes above.

Clouds…sun…I know these words.

He heard a sound and it was a good sound, not like the sound that pierced his eyes and made him do things. This sound was kind, like his…mother.

Paega.

He reached for the face before his eyes, but his arm didn't move. He turned to look, and horror surged through him. His arm was gone. Blood was leaking out from a ruined stump.

Paega moaned.

I am Paega…

Images came to him unbidden. The good sound continued, and he sensed others were moving. Figures lurched past him. He tried to call out, but pain swallowed his voice. He saw the kind lady before his eyes, her face so gentle.

Mother.

His mother was there, and she was smiling. Was she making the good sound? He listened and the pain began to fade.

The world above darkened. A cold like ice began to seep through his body. The good sound became distant and he panicked.

Please don't go…

Paega knew his name. He knew he had a mother. But he did not know where he was or how he had come here. The world grew ever darker.

Come home, Paega, come home.

He closed his eyes and it was if he were no longer there, in agony upon the wet grass. Paega saw his mother, his father, their village.

I am home.

The image dissolved and darkness fell.

Mother?

Chapter 14

Songaa

26th Day of Maia, The Storm Of Ragnekai

Songaa prayed inwardly to the All-Mother and Her children.

Forgive those who have corrupted the natural order, our Mother. Ask Your children to guide us to a better future. One without hate.

With his daughter and Naaki and Imala, Songaa kept sending forth the Tarakalii, adding their voices to Emiren's efforts, soothing the changed ones, cooing and rolling their tongues. It seemed to keep any from straying from the ever-growing line that was following Emiren.

Songaa decided he was no longer needed and turned Ahoni around, seeking out the Helligan captain. He found him with no trouble; the man was stood there watching the corrupted men of Bregustol shuffle after Emiren. He looked up as Songaa trotted toward him.

"The girl has power within her. Is she a witch?" he asked, his eyes full of suspicion.

Songaa held down his anger at the captain's ignorance. "Not a witch. She uses an ancient language and simply wants an end to this senseless killing." Songaa slid off Ahoni and walked to the captain. "Helligan captain, please listen to me. You are fighting someone else's war. A man known as Seolta has set the realm against itself. I know you took the city of Meridia, and then Lord Rencarro saved the port of Argyllan from Throskaur raiders."

The officer's eyes narrowed but he kept listening.

"Unvasik and Duthka attacked the city of Morak. Soldiers of Westhealfe were ambushed by Unvasik in the northern forest. Do you know all this?"

The captain snorted a humourless laugh. "There are Unvasik throwing their lives away at the eastern wall as we speak."

Songaa's heart sunk. Violence was everywhere.

The captain spat on the ground. "We have orders to take the city of Bregustol. I didn't think the Unvasik would be here trying to do the same..." His voice trailed off.

Songaa shook his head. Seolta was sending forth his allies and had somehow brought the Helligan nation north. What did he hope to achieve?

Death...

The answer was simple but so cold. The Duthka lord whom Corann had spoken of was the embodiment of all the evil deities the other people in the realm worshipped. Songaa looked over his shoulder but couldn't see Corann.

Where is he? He could better explain the threat.

Songaa turned back to the captain. "They are your men and you have orders, Helligan captain, but I would advise you to lower your weapons. There is only death for your men here."

The captain said nothing but Songaa saw he was thinking. Lunyai's father did not fully comprehend orders and obeying a lord. Tarakan society had nothing like it, the elders guiding the young ones, who in turn gave their parents and relatives respect and new hope. He knew these officers could not just decide for themselves what to do, but he hoped this one at least would have the courage to consider the reality and then the wisdom to see that nothing would be gained from letting the blood-shed continue.

Songaa searched around again for Corann. He saw Naaki and Imala on their horses, on either side of the strange procession, but no Corann.

And no Lunyai.

Panic hit Songaa. *Where are you?*

He bolted away from the Helligan officer and scrambled back onto Ahoni. His eyes roamed the rain-swept landscape. Emiren and her following of turned men to the south. The Westhealfe soldiers now visible to the west, approaching this madness. The walls of Bregustol were a ruin to the north but at least there was no killing taking place; the Helligans were holding their ground for now. Songaa turned his gaze east and saw a strange sight.

Two figures were emerging from the grey haze of falling rain, heading south away from the city. They were carrying something. An overwhelming fear exploded within Songaa and he kicked Ahoni into motion.

Please no, please no, that cannot be Lunyai. All-Mother, I beg you!

He was soon upon the two figures and saw it was two men carrying a body, and it was not Lunyai. Songaa choked on his relief.

One of the men looked up at him. "Songaa?"

Songaa stared at the bedraggled fellow. He had seen him before somewhere but couldn't remember. He slid off Ahoni once more and approached the two men. He stared at the body they carried.

Is that Lord Rencarro?!

Songaa looked at the one who had spoken and realised it was the Meridian who had travelled with his daughter. His eyes flicked between the Meridian, his companion, and the fallen lord.

"What happened?"

It was all he could ask.

"We tried to bring down Sylvanus but the Unvasik warrior... May the Widow take his soul!"

The Meridian spat on the ground, shared a look with the other, then resumed their journey south, still carrying the body of their fallen lord away from the hideously unnatural storm to the north.

"Corann has lost his mind," he said as they trudged off. Songaa didn't understand. What did this man mean? He looked at the Meridian and saw utter defeat in his face.

"Corann? You have seen Corann?"

"He rode past us. He's going after Seolta. He'll get himself killed." The Meridian paused, frowned, then his eyes suddenly widened, and it was as if he truly saw Songaa for the first time.

"He'll get Lunyai killed..."

Songaa was back on Ahoni in the space of two breaths. He kicked the horse into motion and pushed the steed into a gallop. Songaa's eyes searched the dark fields. To the north he saw battle, presumably the Unvasik warriors the Helligan captain had spoken of. The city itself seemed to be groaning in agony and despair.

Songaa desperately tried to see through the gloom, hoping for a sign of his daughter.

Why did you go? Are you following Corann?

Utter despair coursed through his body. His daughter was probably riding with Corann now, seeking out the man's daughter. But that woman was probably with the most ruthless and dangerous man of whom Songaa had ever heard. He could see no other outcome than the death of his daughter.

Lunyai, what are you thinking? You cannot face such an evil man...

CHAPTER 15

SYLVANUS

26th Day of Maia, The Storm of Ragnekai

Sylvanus felt nothing but satisfaction as he watched the battle unfold from a safe distance. The Westhealfe cavalry had crashed through the Unvasik horde, but the mountain tribesmen were not simple Meridian mustered men, or even Helligan soldiers; they were giant brutes, each one equal to five of their foes. The Unvasik were sure to lose but they would take many with them into the Void, the Abyss, or whatever after-life they believed in.

At the south wall, the Helligan army would kill the beast-men, and in turn be killed by the Bregustol garrison and the northern legions of the Rihtgellen kingdom.

And thus the realm bleeds. And dies a slow death.

Sylvanus clenched his jaw with a grim satisfaction.

Marrh will be reborn.

With the storm now upon them and rain coming down in murky sheets of grey, their view was less than sharp, but Sylvanus had seen Idelisa's Unvasik lover charge into his former lord, Rencarro. He assumed Rencarro was dead but the fact he hadn't actually seen the outcome of that little skirmish gnawed away at him.

He must be dead…

He turned to his true master, rain sliding down both their faces and stated in a clear voice, "Chaos reigns, Seolta."

His mentor nodded, his gaze settling on Idelisa. "We were patient for a generation and now we see the rewards. The two of you have achieved more than I imagined possible. I am proud of you."

Those five words were so simple but reached the core of Sylvanus. He had always thought it an exaggeration when people talked about swelling with pride, but he truly felt himself grow in that instant, as if an energy within was expanding and surging forth. He let out a breath and regained his composure. A glance at Idelisa told him it was more complicated for her.

Did she fall in love? Or does she think she failed somehow?

Sylvanus' mind turned to what his two friends had said when Idelisa joined them.

What is this primal thing they spoke of? Why was I told nothing?

All of his pride and sense of greatness suddenly vanished as he felt a cold fingernail rake inside his mind. He shook his head, trying to dispel images of the Widow. He had never truly believed in the Meridian deities, but years spent with them had coloured his thinking to some degree.

There is no Widow, no Dark Raven, and no damn Ever-Father! Only Athaiq.

He shifted in his saddle, then cast his gaze once more across the fighting at the eastern wall.

The Westhealfe cavalry had regrouped after their second charge and were now picking off the Unvasik on the edges of the melee. It was a smart move as they would no doubt lose horses or even kill their own in the blind turmoil in the heart of the battle. Infantry were pressing from the north and looked to be holding their lines.

Sylvanus looked south. As he did, a sheet of lightning illuminated the fields. The three of them were too far away to pick out the detail from the chaos and Sylvanus could see no sign of the Unvasik warrior or Rencarro.

Are you dead, old friend?

"I think it is time we left this place," said Seolta beside him. "I have seen enough. The Unvasik will lose, many soldiers of the realm will be slaughtered, the beast-men will die, and Bregustol will burn. That much is certain. We will return to the Beacuan and await reports of the devastation."

Seolta placed a hand on Idelisa's shoulder.

"We will take the Ruby Road, then head across fields when we reach the first village."

Idelisa nodded but it was obvious she was troubled. Sylvanus checked Seolta's expression and saw his master's eyes narrow. The trust between the two of them had not been restored, and Sylvanus knew his lord would not be content until it had been.

And I will not be able to rest until I know Rencarro's fate...

He turned to Seolta. "Please go on ahead. I would take a closer look at the Helligan assault." He grinned, hoping to throw Seolta off his true intention. "They are following my plan after all."

Seolta was seemingly deep in thought, distracted by Idelisa. He nodded once. "Be quick about it. Do not risk yourself in any way."

Sylvanus dipped his head, then turned his mount and kicked the horse into motion.

Athaiq, show me his dead body so I can sleep at night.

Not wanting to be spotted by a stray soldier, he kept a very wide berth of the raging human storm that was playing out before the walls of Bregustol. The capital's defences were ruined and he knew it would be carnage within the city itself. The Sisters of the Moon, disguised as healing women in grey, would have started fires all over and the beast-men should be running amok. The citizens would be panicking and that would only be adding to the confusion and havoc.

A rider emerged from the gloom ahead, galloping north. Sylvanus halted his mount and strained his eyes. It was a man, but it didn't look like Rencarro.

He caught more movement out of the corner of his eye and saw a second horse and rider, following the first. He couldn't be sure, but this rider looked like a girl. The two were heading in the general direction of Seolta and Idelisa.

Who are you?

Sylvanus was about to wheel his mount around and pursue the newcomers, but his attention was drawn to movement where the south wall met the east.

No, no, no!

CHAPTER 16

WULFNER

26th Day of Maia, The Storm of Ragnekai

Wulfner wildly swung his mace, desperate to land a blow that would cripple his assailant. The Unvasik snarled at him, rocking back on his heels and easily avoiding the weapon's arc. Wulfner took a step back, his courage melting at he saw the confidence in the warrior's eyes.

He knows he can beat me...

A gurgled scream erupted to his right as an Unvasik axe cleaved an arm from a soldier, the spear still gripped in the hand as the limb dropped to the ground. The poor man crumpled to his knees, blood spurting from the stump.

Wulfner's eyes flashed back to his foe and saw an axe swirling high. Instinct took over and he whirled his mace backwards over his head. As it returned to his front, he released it underarm. The ball of spiked iron hit the mountain man square in the face, sending him crashing backwards onto the water-logged meadow. He didn't get up.

But now Wulfner had no weapon.

His legs shook as his eyes darted left and right, searching for a shield or anything, and watching for new threats. He saw the severed arm and the spear it still clutched. The Unvasik who had taken the arm was either dead or engaged with another. Wulfner grabbed the shaft and prized the dead fingers from it. He brandished the spear at the shadows hurtling around him.

"Over here!" came a shout.

Wulfner turned and saw a knot of soldiers, doing their best to form a schiltrom. He bounded over and inserted himself into the defensive formation.

"Thank you," he blurted, his breath ragged and his nerves shredded.

"They're too strong!" whimpered a soldier behind him.

"Shut your mouth! This big man just downed one. General Torbal will reach us soon. Stand your ground, all of you!"

Wulfner was grateful for the brave officer in that moment. His legs were about to give way and he knew his hands were shaking.

Please, let the cavalry break them!

More howls of rage and grotesque cries of agony filled the air. Shouts in a language that was not the common tongue broke through the endless chatter of the rain. Large shadows emerged from the mist, their shapes becoming distinct as they drew closer.

"Ever-Father save us!"

"We'll die!"

Wulfner stared at the ten or so giant warriors trudging towards them. The leader held his axe aloft and bellowed out something terrible.

The Ceapung native glanced around him and saw his company numbered fewer than twenty.

They would die.

More shouts echoed from further back.

More are coming...

The group of Unvasik advancing upon their brave but pathetic formation stopped in their tracks. More than one turned and started their own chorus of calls.

"What's happening?" squeaked a lad to Wulfner's left, shy of twenty summers he reckoned.

The clash of weapons filled the air again and this time, bellows of pain that could only be Unvasik.

Torbal is here?

Then Wulfner heard shouts in a different language. Not Unvasik, not the common tongue.

Is that Helligan?

Wulfner felt confusion swirl with his fear as he saw tight formations of soldiers emerge from the grey rain and mercilessly cut down the Unvasik.

Pole-axes shot forth from several phalanxes, their long poles reaching past the battle-axes and slicing deep into the mountain men.

"Stay still, lads," called out Wulfner. "Let the Helligans do their work!"

"Helligans?"

Wulfner didn't understand it either but he didn't care.

The Winds...

CHAPTER 17

SYLVANUS

26th Day of Maia, The Storm of Ragnekai

Sylvanus watched the Helligan soldiers march up from the south. He saw them engage the Unvasik and knew Seolta's plans were unravelling.

Why have they broken off their assault of the south gates?

Keeping his distance, he pushed his horse onwards, the cries of battle increasing in volume to the east of the city. After a hundred or so yards, Sylvanus came across a single, large body lying on the muddied ground.

The Unvasik who was with Idelisa...

That did not bode well. The Unvasik lying there dead meant Rencarro and whomever he was with were still alive.

They bested him?!

He knew it was foolish, but he couldn't stop himself now. He had to find out if Rencarro was dead or not. Not knowing would mean the Duthka refugee glancing over his shoulder for the rest of his life.

As he came closer to the south wall, he spied a column of figures moving away from the city. He stared at the line, his eyes narrowing.

The movement was odd, inhuman.

The beast-men?

He kept his horse moving in a path parallel to the column of beast-men. He peered to the front of the line. A glimmer of light shafted down upon the scene before him, the sun desperately trying to chase away this storm. Sylvanus gazed ahead. Someone was leading the beast-men!

Who has the power to control them?!

Except for the Duthka, Seolta had been sure only Sedmund had seen the book, so its secrets should have been kept away from prying eyes. Who could possibly have power over those turned?

His frustration rose and he edged closer to the column, several rays of sun-light now piercing the gloom and illuminating the fields. He strained to see who was leading the beast-men away. He knew he was putting himself in danger now, but the thought that someone was undoing plans so carefully conceived and so long in their making, this was something he could not let pass. He picked up his pace and drew ever closer.

There was a figure at the front. A woman.

Red hair...

Sylvanus stared. He was now thirty yards away.

It can't be...

This was an unbelievably cruel twist of fate. He must be mistaken.

Twenty yards now. He edged closer still, ignoring the fact that he was visible and vulnerable. The woman turned to look at the beast-men she was leading. He gasped.

It is her!

It was the girl whose lover he had killed in Argol. The one he had chased but couldn't find. A girl who should be dead. And now, here she was, guiding the beast-men away from the battle.

Sylvanus' breath shortened as his panic rose. This wasn't supposed to happen. If their designs were known, if the north and south united, all would be undone.

Rage erupted within him. *That damn village girl is ruining everything.*

He let out a bellowing cry that was half fury, half anguish and swiftly withdrew the dagger that had slain the three bandits a few days ago. She had escaped from him before, but not this time.

Sylvanus whipped his reins and his mount lurched forward.

His eyes focused on the girl and he tightened his grip on the blade. *You will die!*

His right-side felt two sudden impacts. Pain erupted like a wildfire within him. He flew from his horse, hitting the ground with a thump, his lungs losing all their air. His mouth desperately tried to suck in more as he tumbled and rolled with the momentum of the fall. Sylvanus howled in agony as two sharp points probed deeper.

Athaiq...

Rain covered his face as he lay on his side, his arms numb and no sensation in his neck.

Athaiq, no, not now.

He tried to lean up, but pain blossomed throughout his torso as if the rain were tiny streaks of fire raking his body.

The fletching from an arrow was poking out from under him. His vision clouded as he tried to comprehend what had happened. He felt the vibration of boots upon the earth, getting closer, approaching where he lay.

No, no, no... I am to return to my mother's land...

The world seemed to spin above him.

I am to...

He should have ridden away with Seolta and Idelisa. He should have heeded his master's words. Vengeance was a fool's quest.

A voice came. "Those old Tarakan ladies did it. He was charging at the girl."

"Who is he?" asked a male voice in the common tongue.

"I know him," said a female voice. His eyes turned and he saw her enter his field of vision. The redhead. Behind her Sylvanus saw a rainbow, the sun shimmering through the rain. It was beautiful.

"He murdered my friend."

Sylvanus' eyes locked with hers and he saw the hate there. A hate mixed with loss. His breath became ragged. His heart began to race. He felt true fear.

Mother…
"Well, here's what we do to murderers," said a gruff voice.
The spear lifted high.
Sylvanus gasped. The redhead cried out.
"No!"
I am Duthka.
The shaft came down.

CHAPTER 18

EMIREN

26th Day of Maia, The Storm Of Ragnekai

Emiren stared down at the corpse of Sylvanus and felt numb. This man had murdered Anton and betrayed his own people, and as such Emiren could find no forgiveness or pity. But seeing his lifeless form before her brought a sense of nihilism, a feeling that life itself was meaningless.

Is death the only thing that binds us?

Emiren heard a commotion behind her and turned wearily. The men whose minds had been poisoned were becoming skittish with no commands coming forth. She saw Naaki and Imala trotting over to her on their Tarakan mares.

"Emiren, please look away from this one now. Return to your connection with these poor men," said Naaki, pushing damp hair back from her face.

"Let them sleep," added her sister, Imala, her voice cracking. "Let them sleep…"

Emiren inhaled deeply, raised her face to the cascading rain and paused for a moment. The sun had broken the clouds and now a Spirit Arc was gracing the sky. She let the beauty of the realm touch her and let her mind roam Argol Forest. She saw rain-drops slide down leaves, racing each other as she and Anton used to do. She heard the twitter of birds and the rustle of tiny forest beasts. She could almost smell the scent of Argol, a purity that had not been defiled by malice. Something nudged her hip and she looked down.

Tarak.

Emiren smiled at the wolf and felt the chaos recede and only this moment to exist. She went back to the turned men and put the whistle to her lips. She blew gently and then began speaking more of the Words, trying to weave in the sounds Lunyai had made.

Purr like a cat...

The young lady from Fallowden conjured an image of a cat and let the vision soak into her vocal efforts. She spoke from the back of her throat, humming the Words. Then rolled her tongue around a few sounds. She closed her eyes and let the Words flow like the Old Stream in Argol, an almost happy gurgle.

Emiren told the turned men to be calm, not to be scared and then she asked them, not commanded them, to sleep. She walked up and down the bizarre line of maybe two hundred souls, bidding them all to rest. The young lady from Fallowden held back a sob as one turned round and round in a circle before settling himself upon the wet and muddy ground.

Just like a dog...

They were beautiful in their serenity, but tragic in that they were normal men robbed of their humanity.

Emiren let a hand fall to Tarak and stroked his damp fur. She looked around for Lunyai to see her reaction to this strangeness. Naaki and Imala were there, still singing the Tarakalii but Emiren couldn't see Lunyai. Her eyes searched the rain-soaked fields around them.

Where is Songaa?

Corann?

Emiren's eyes darted here and there. She took a few steps, her legs suddenly feeling weak.

Where are you?

Emiren turned to the Tarakan sisters but they still sang, seemingly unaware their three companions were gone.

Spirits, where are they?

She hurried now, Tarak beside her. She began to run, belatedly realising that most of the Helligan soldiers had gone. She saw the soldiers from Westhealfe marching along the south wall, the head of the company now turning north as they reached the wall's end.

What happened?

There was no violence here but she could hear battle in the distance. She still couldn't see Lunyai, Songaa or Corann.

Where did you go?

Her head swung left and right, her eyes seeking the girl she loved.

Lunyai…

Emiren's heart began to pound within her. Her stomach knotted. Her legs shook and then gave way. She fell to her knees and grabbed Tarak, pulling him close. She began to sob.

"Tarak, where is Lunyai? What has happened? Spirits, please…"

She looked up at the parting clouds above and cried out.

"Lunyai!"

CHAPTER 19

LUNYAI

26th Day of Maia, The Storm Of Ragnekai

Lunyai was gaining on Corann and in turn he was gaining on his daughter and the man. All four horses galloped at a ferocious pace, hooves clattering upon the paved road, the animals surging through the cascading rain.

Father, forgive me one more time…

Emiren had succeeded in leading the turned men away from battle and at that moment, Corann had wheeled his mount away and sped off. Lunyai had hesitated less than a breath of the Tarakalo, then set off after him. She knew what pulled him, who he hoped to find, but could not let him face his daughter alone. Lunyai feared anger would over-come him. She would not let the love that she knew existed between father and daughter be denied because of blind rage. Corann and his daughter must have the same bond she shared with her own father.

All-Mother, help me now. Help me turn anger to love.

Lunyai prayed as the horses continued to charge up the wide road, the distance between the two pairs of riders decreasing by the moment.

Lunyai got a glimpse of the second rider and fear gripped her.

Is that Seolta?

Lunyai's terror rose, her heartbeat thudding in her throat, threatening to overcome her. She had never met this Seolta, never heard his voice, but in her mind, he was a corrupt energy that poisoned the natural world. He was death in the wind. Lunyai suddenly deeply regretted she hadn't at least shouted a farewell to her father.

What if this ride is my last?

The two riders ahead veered left off the road and began tearing across the water-logged fields, spray and muck snapping in all directions. Hooves pounding beneath them, Lunyai wished she were on the Plains with Emiren behind her, clutching her waist. The storm she was flying through now would soon come to a head and the Tarakan could see now it would be a violent one. Lunyai's chest tightened with pain and sorrow flooded her being. She yearned to hold Emiren one last time, and found herself whispering another prayer to the All-Mother, knowing her own mother would cry endless tears.

All-Mother, protect those I love. Yaai, Tlenaii, watch over them.

The new terrain had slowed the riders ahead and Lunyai saw Corann was almost upon the man. She could see what Corann was about to do. She wanted to scream for him to stop and not throw his life away.

Lunyai dug her heels in and eased the reins slightly, guiding her steed to move wide of those in front. If she were directly behind, she might kill him.

They were so close now. Corann behind the man, Lunyai not far back from Corann, and his daughter pushing ahead at the front.

The man looked over his right shoulder but Corann was no longer there. He twisted the other way. His sudden movement caused a jerk and his mount faltered slightly. In that instant, Corann lunged forward and grabbed the man's robe with one hand. His other hand came forward and made contact. Lunyai gasped as both of them fell back from their steeds and tumbled to the ground.

Lunyai pulled up her horse, relieved she had predicted what would happen, and wheeled the animal around. Corann's daughter did the same. Both were now yards from the two men, who were now scrambling to their feet and drawing their weapons. Seolta a single sword, Corann drawing forth both his blades.

"Stop this! Enough have died!" cried Lunyai.

The two men ignored her, circling each other, Corann twirling his swords, Seolta holding his vertical. She looked to his daughter, praying she would call an end to this madness; her father and her lord facing each other. She would lose, whichever man was victorious. But Corann's daughter stared at them, silent and motionless.

Corann began speaking to Seolta in the Duthka language. Lunyai could understand nothing but the tone was one of disgust. Seolta spat backs word angrily. One hand left its hold on the sword and gestured to the land and sky, then pointed at Lunyai herself.

Tlenaii, what have I done? I only want this to be over...

"Idelisa!"

Corann's voice was beseeching. He was a father begging his daughter to return to him. Lunyai prayed to the All-Mother for the woman to see her father's sorrow, clear as Tlenaii's light upon his face.

His daughter said nothing and hung her head. Seolta raised his weapon, uttering words that dripped with scorn.

Yaai, Tlenaii, how can I stop this?

Lunyai's hand drifted to her bow, but then she let it fall to her side. She couldn't use it. Not now.

Lunyai squeezed her eyes shut and prayed. But her thoughts were instantly shattered by the clang of metal on metal. Corann and Seolta were engaged.

A deadly dance began once more. Lunyai had seen Corann fight in the Sacred Mount and thought then he was a swordsman without equal. But as she watched with horror their blades swirl, Lunyai knew Corann did indeed have an equal. Seolta was darting here and there, his sword parrying one of Corann's, then flicking past to be stopped inches from Corann by the second blade. If anything, Corann looked to be on the back foot, losing ground to his Duthka kin, despite wielding the extra weapon.

Lunyai couldn't breathe. She stared at the other woman.

Why doesn't she try to stop this?

Corann's daughter still sat upon her mount, her eyes watching her father fight, but her face and body showing no sign she would try to intervene.

Lunyai desperately tried to think. Her mind went back to that night in Argyllan, when she had saved Emiren and knocked Rencarro to the ground. She could do the same here. The Tarakan stared at the whirling blades and constantly moving combatants. The only thing she could do was make a straight charge at them, hopefully sending them sprawling. She looked up to the sky and clenched her teeth, steeling herself, gathering courage. It might result in her death but she could not just...

The clanging sound of metal on metal suddenly stopped.

Lunyai dropped her eyes to the two men before her.

They were locked in an embrace. Protruding from Corann's back was the tip of a blade, its metallic shine covered with a dark shade.

"Tlenaii..." moaned Lunyai. "Oh, please no..."

The blade disappeared and Corann slumped to the ground, his two swords clattering against each other as he fell. Lunyai stared at Seolta standing there defiant, breathing heavily. The Duthka man shouted something at his fallen opponent, then sheathed his sword. He continued to look down upon the still form of Corann.

Lunyai raised her gaze to Corann's daughter. Her expression had not changed, though her eyes were blinking.

The Tarakan looked back to Seolta and inhaled sharply. The Duthka lord was looking up at her. He stared into her eyes. Lunyai felt as if she was gazing upon a dark sea and the tide was rising.

Father, forgive me...

Seolta abruptly turned around and walked to where Corann's daughter sat motionlessly upon her steed. Lunyai let her breath release and slumped forward to hug Neii'Ne's neck, her hair mingling with the animal's mane.

It's over...

She heard nothing though, no words spoken and no sound of horses moving away. She peered past her mount's head. Seolta was standing there and Corann's daughter was now holding something, a small curved pole resembling Tlenaii in His crescent form.

What is that?

Seolta spoke. The woman answered. Seolta hung his head and laughed. The woman was not laughing, just holding the pole in her hand, which appeared to be gloved.

What is happening?

Seolta's voice became angry. It sounded like he was admonishing her.

Lunyai felt the air around her tingle.

What is this?

Seolta clearly noticed it too. He backed away a step and held up one hand.

Corann's daughter uttered one word.

"Athaiq."

The air around the pole fizzed and crackled. A brilliant white bolt of light shot forth from it and slammed into Seolta, throwing him into the air. He crashed down yards from where he had been standing, his chest a smouldering ruin. Lunyai yelped. She stared at the scene before her.

Corann lay dead, the back of his robe a darker shade now. Seolta was also dead, the scent of burning flesh drifting in the air. Lunyai's stomach churned and her chest tensed. She raised her eyes and saw Corann's daughter was now pointing the pole at her. Her breath froze in her chest, becoming an icy dagger, the fear like a net that engulfed her, drawing ever tighter.

"Please no..." she begged in the common tongue. "Please..."

The air began to tingle again, and the crackling sound scratched at Lunyai's ears.

"Mother..."

But the woman lowered the pole, looked down upon her dead father for a moment, then returned her attention to Lunyai. She spoke in the common tongue.

"Do not follow me, Tarakan."

She nudged her mount over to the horse that had born Seolta, lifted the flap of a saddle-bag and removed a thick tome. Corann's daughter then turned her mount. She kicked her heels, snapped the reins, and flew off towards the north.

After a few moments, Lunyai choked out the terrified breath she had been holding. She slipped off her mount and knelt down beside Corann. He was truly gone. Tears surged forth and Lunyai knew they were tears for Corann mixed with tears of relief that she still lived.

"Lunyai!"

Her head snapped around, and she saw her father galloping toward her. She couldn't move. Even when Songaa's arms wrapped around her and pulled her close, she still felt paralysed. Lunyai looked at Corann lying there, unmoving, and felt an agony within, the pain of knowing a daughter let her father die. Her muscles found their life again and she hugged her own father fiercely.

"Forgive me, forgive me for leaving you all again," she blurted, tears spilling.

"No, no, my daughter, be still now. Breathe, think of your mother's voice, and breathe."

Lunyai swallowed the air and tried to calm herself. She heard her mother's voice inside her head, telling her to sit still as Imala told a story, whispering that she had grown taller than her, and then telling her to be safe upon the Peregrika, the Tarakan pilgrimage to the Sacred Mount, the beginning of this terrible journey.

The two of them continued to hug each other, for how long Lunyai couldn't tell. Approaching hooves brought them to their feet. They wearily looked to see who the riders were and Lunyai felt a wave of relief as soldiers in red and blue pulled up. Not hooded Duthka nor huge Unvasik tribesmen.

Songaa stood to greet them.

Lunyai felt the chill of the storm lessen and cast her eyes to see Yaai pushing away the Grey Ones and creating a Tarakan Bow for the All-Mother to see. Lunyai took a slow breath, the majesty of the realm visible to all.

Then she lowered her gaze and looked upon the two dead men. One a friend to her and father to a woman now long gone; the other a cunning, merciless mind who had set the realm on fire. Seolta had been killed by some kind of sorcery, the likes of which Lunyai didn't believe existed, even in legend. Lightning had burst forth from that rod and struck him. How was that possible? Thunder, lightning, rain, wind, these were powers of the All-Mother and Her kin, not elements humans could wield. Only the secret of fire had been gifted to people thousands of years ago. Was this the work of their god?

"I think the storm is passing," said Songaa, returning to Lunyai. "For some, at least. These men rode with General Torbal."

Wulfner?!

Her father continued. "They say the Helligan forces stopped attacking the city and marched to face the Unvasik. It is a...slaughter, they say," he finished, his face twisting in sorrow.

So much death...

Lunyai looked up and saw more and more shafts of Yaai's light breaking through the clouds. The rain was lighter. She hadn't noticed. A rumble of thunder, somewhere in the direction Corann's daughter had ridden, told her the storm was moving on.

One storm had soaked the land with a pure water from the skies, the other had drowned the fields in blood. Lunyai hung her head and wept.

PART SEVEN

CHAPTER 1

TORBAL

Two Months After The Storm Of Ragnekai

Ulla had chosen everything perfectly, Torbal noted with admiration as they sat in the Great Hall of Gamle Hovestad. The food was plenty but not displayed in ostentatious fashion; the music was neither triumphant nor was it muted; instead a subtle background sound that hopefully put the guests at ease. And the seating as perfectly arranged as could be. Torbal realised he was smiling, and that sparked a twist of emotion within.

So many lost. So much undone.

The general surveyed the scene before him, taking in as many of the guests as he could.

And yet there is much that is perhaps better now.

"What are you thinking, my love?" Ulla's voice, a hushed murmur to his side. He turned and looked at this beautiful woman. Ulla was a glorious sunrise that he once feared had blinded him. And she was a blazing sunset he had thought he might never see again. Now she was his wife, their marriage sealed the previous week, the ceremony a quiet affair.

Torbal smiled gently and replied.

"I was thinking…" He paused. "That there is much to think upon."

Ulla stroked his hand with her fingers.

"Don't think too much," she said, her eyes holding his. He saw the same raw emotion there that he was holding down. "Nobody can calm every storm whirling within so soon. One step each day," she whispered, then leaned in and kissed him lightly on the cheek. He felt young again and his cheeks flushed with warmth. Ulla breathed a short laugh.

"And how much have you had to drink already?" she chided. "What are you drinking anyway?"

Torbal hesitated a moment. "Maiden's Whisper," he told her.

Ulla's eyes widened. "I thought that was a mild ale for young lads, not a cup for a veteran general."

He had no words, so he just smiled and drank long and deeply.

Torbal felt the time was right to make his speech so he nodded to Ulla, then tapped his knife lightly on the pewter goblet. Those closest heard it and fell to a silence. The hush spread quickly, the musicians came to a swift finish, and soon all the guests were looking this way. Ulla gave Torbal's arm a squeeze as he stood.

Thunor knows I need you now by my side, Ulla.

The general cleared his throat and let his eyes travel around the hall. So many were here, perhaps a hundred at least. Lucetta had come with her brother Cherin and one of her captains, Hugh. Duthka from the fallen Corann's tribe were sitting at a table to Torbal's left, no doubt mourning his death. Ulla's sister-in-law Hulda was with her children at the other high table, still dressed in black, but he had seen her smile more than once. The rather odd mix of Wulfner, Tacet the Meridian, Emiren and Lunyai were sitting together, all looking up at him expectantly. Lunyai's father and a couple of other Tarakans sat slightly farther back. Town mayors, village matriarchs, homestead chiefs, military captains; Ragnekai was well represented in this hall. Torbal spotted the captain of the Helligan Sentinels.

Thank Thunor they sided with us…

Torbal knew the fields of Bregustol would have become a graveyard for everyone had the Helligan forces not broken free from the deceptive designs of Seolta and marched upon the Unvasik horde. The once High King's shield saw it as a moment in history where a coin was flipped, this time thankfully landing in their favour. Tensions remained, though, and the general would have to work hard in the coming months to create an atmosphere where the different peoples and cultures could live together in a new harmony, with differences celebrated, not exploited.

The realm must never be ripped apart again.

"My friends," he began, his general's voice easily carrying through the hall. "I thank you for coming here today, a day that I hope will mark the beginning of a better future. It will not be easy and there will be much to discuss. We will agree and we will disagree, but I implore all present to be vigilant so as to never let the realm slide into such darkness again."

There were nods and murmurs.

"I do not ask any of you to forget history, as those who do risk following the same path to suffering. But let us not judge each other by this history. Let us see in each other a new friend that will help us to rebuild. Let us forge a stronger realm that cannot fall victim to manipulation and treachery. Let us *trust* one another."

He gave his final sentence more weight, then raised his goblet to his eye-level.

The response was good, with many shouting agreement and lifting their cups.

We must learn to trust so that we are not blind to enemies seeking to set us against one another.

Torbal inhaled a deep breath, knowing he needed to deliver his next words without his voice failing.

"Many of us have lost someone dear."

He paused to allow people to remember their loved ones. Heads were lowered and he heard more than one sob. But hands also gripped shoulders and people leaned in, comforting those near them.

There is hope.

"May we keep them forever in our hearts."

He raised his cup above his head, waited for all to follow suit, then lowered it to take a drink. He put his cup on the table as the guests drank, then suddenly found himself wondering what came next.

A light clap came from his side. Ulla. She stood and gently applauded his words, a smile upon her face and a strength in her eyes he felt he could rely upon today and every day till he died.

The guests joined in with the applause and Torbal sat down, relief coursing through him. He nodded to his wife to signal she now had the room. Torbal was certain her speech would be more eloquent than his.

The room fell into silence once more and Ulla cast her eyes around the guests. Torbal gazed at her and felt his breath catch in his chest.

So beautiful.

Ulla was past fifty in years but retained her youth far more than himself. She possessed a shapely figure, the forest green dress she was wearing perfectly accentuating the curves of her body. Her ashen blonde hair was mounted upon the back of her head, a garland of some flower nestled within the twirl. A delicate rosy glow to her cheeks and those eyes that Torbal felt reflected all that was magnificent in the realm. Glorious, yet as gently inviting as a golden autumn grove.

You and the realm are as one in your majesty.

His wife began to speak, her voice warm like a summer evening, her words laced with the beauty of all four seasons.

"What more can I say here, friends? It is true we have lost so much and sit here with heavy hearts, mourning those we loved, trying to hold dearly to the memories of those taken from all of us."

Torbal let his eyes wander and saw emotion overcome more than one guest. He found Lucetta staring ahead, her jaw set but tears sliding down her cheeks. Cherin's head was hung. Torbal knew Kenric was devastated and he would need both his children to get through the coming months. They would help him to govern Westhealfe in a way that would honour Cyneburg, and also maintain its prosperity in this uncertain world into which they were carefully treading.

Ulla's voice reached out again. "And yet I see an opportunity before my eyes in this very room. A chance to build a better realm, a realm that has thousands of hearts, all beating as one. A realm with a mighty chorus of voices that will sing in harmony as we work and toil to repair what has been broken. A realm where no one city is of higher standing than the others."

A wave of murmurs arose. It sounded more like curiosity than resentment though, and for this Torbal was hopeful. He looked up at Ulla and she turned her eyes to him. He nodded and she went on with her speech, the following words their proposal for how to shape a brighter future.

"With this in mind, Torbal and I renounce any claim to a throne."

Surprised gasps echoed around the room.

"We ask of you all that you consent to our becoming guardians of all of Ragnekai. We will build a great hall at the foot of the Sacred Mount, and there we will reside. The hall will be a place of friendship for all the realm. Words shall be spoken there, wounds will be healed and peace cherished. Torbal is not your king and I am not your queen. Ragnekai no longer has a king."

Torbal felt the astonishment roll around the hall. Ulla pressed on with her words; words that were shaping the realm even now as they left her lips.

"We will act as counsellors, if you will. Mediators. We will strive to guide the realm along a road that leads somewhere none of us can foresee. But we will keep looking ahead with open eyes to recognise threats long before they arise. We ask that you give us your blessing and pledge your support in this endeavour. Together we will make this journey and together I am certain we will succeed."

Torbal was taken aback by the sudden clamour that greeted Ulla's words. Roars of approval, hands clapping the table-tops, and heads vigorously nodding.

She certainly is persuasive…

He raised a hand to his mouth to hide his grin as Ulla moved on with her speech.

"Lord Kenric will continue as First Lord of Westhealfe, and may the memory of Lady Cyneburg give him the strength and wisdom to keep peace and prosperity there."

Torbal clenched his jaw at the memory of his sister's voice.

"The realm is beautiful, Torb."

If only you could be here now, sister. I believe you would even say a kind word to Ulla.

"Chamberlain Worsteth will carry on with the rebuilding of Bregustol and all corners of the realm shall help him. Too many innocent citizens died there. The Ruby Road, its villages and the mines were also devastated. The north-east suffered greatly. Let us work together to rebuild the region."

The chamberlain was not in attendance but Torbal did not think it amiss. The man was incredibly busy, the city still in mild turmoil and with much still to do to bring the former capital back to a functioning level of normality.

"Lady Hulda will govern Gamle Hovestad until her eldest child Siggi comes of age. May we honour Orben by strengthening the ties between north and south."

Torbal glanced over at Orben's widow. He had heard of her kindness from Ulla and how the Helligans adored her like they would a mother. She might not have the cunning of her late husband, but she had the love of her people, and that was far more important. If she moved in a direction, they would follow.

"Lord Eligius will govern the city of Meridia. I hear Rorthal and the lord have taught each other much since the storm ended," she said, casting her gaze around the hall.

A mischievous smile lit up her face and Torbal heard a hearty cheer over to the left. He looked and saw a burly soldier, presumably the Helligan Battle-Sergeant, with one arm around the shoulder of Rencarro's son, the other holding aloft a horn of ale. Torbal studied Eligius' face and found there was not much to read there. The lad had lost both his father and brother in the recent turmoil, and his mother years ago, so had little to smile about. He would need steady support and Torbal reckoned a no-nonsense officer guiding him forward was for the best.

May there be many of these unions that help bind the realm.

Ulla went on. "The Argol region will carry on as they always have, helping each other and caring for the region. Argyllan suffered greatly and will need help to fully rebuild and become a stronger port. The world is larger than many of us know."

Torbal heard the underlying message there. Although Seolta was certainly to blame for the storms Ragnekai had survived, he wasn't convinced that there was no threat from the Xerinthian Empire, or that the Throskaur were not out there in greater numbers. He was also far from happy that the two books had not been recovered.

They must be found. There is too much powerful knowledge within their pages that can be put to nefarious use.

"And I hope with all my heart that the Tarakan people and their lands are treated with the respect and honour they so richly deserve. I believe we could learn much from their ways."

Torbal couldn't argue with that. The Tarakans had given up a great deal of their land when Torbal's ancestors had come across the Western Sea, and they had never fought to reclaim it. When he was a young soldier, learning history and seeing only glory in battle, he had viewed them as weak. Now he saw in the Tarakans a strength that was greater than all the armies of Ragnekai. Torbal wondered if he could persuade a few of them to join them in their hall by the Sacred Mount. Their serene wisdom would be invaluable.

"And let us all strive to build friendship with those that were exiled from their own lands."

Torbal knew this was a delicate matter. Seolta was the one responsible for the recent suffering but his hate was born from wounds inflicted upon the Duthka long ago. Torbal knew it was imperative people understood this and did not see the Duthka people as a defeated *enemy*.

Ulla continued. "We cannot change history but we must understand it, learn from it, and so avoid creating such evil again."

Torbal looked around and saw nodding but also a few frowns. Ulla's words had been well-chosen, framing Seolta as a dark force that had been created by their own misdeeds, and so hopefully pushing away the notion that the Duthka were to be punished in any way. But it was clear all was easier said than done.

"We hope that our Duthka friends will join us at the foot of the Sacred Mount and help guide us to bringing the entire realm into an age of peace."

Ulla raised her glass, a signal for Torbal to stand also. He did so and the two of them stood side-by-side, looking out at the many different peoples that would work together to rebuild Ragnekai, and shape it into something worthy of all who had perished.

"And now I ask you all to eat, drink, and talk with each other. Remember those who are not here and honour their memories. But also, I ask you to laugh and joke, and so help us all to imagine a tomorrow that is full of joy and hope."

She raised her glass.

"To the future!"

The hall boomed in response.

"To the future!"

It was not long before the hall settled. Torbal touched Ulla's arm.

"I believe it is time for us to mingle, to ensure your words have met the approval of all, and perhaps get a sense of what we will need to do in the coming months."

Ulla knocked back her wine, touched her lips with a handkerchief and leaned over to place a kiss on his cheek.

"You lead and I will follow."

"Is that wise, do you think? You are more adept at this kind of thing than I."

Ulla laughed. "Exactly. And many here know that. I don't want them to feel I am scheming."

Torbal shook his head. "As you wish," he said, grinning. "Just kick me if I make a wrong turn."

"As *you* wish!"

The two of them stepped out from behind their table and slowly moved to the Tarakan table first. Ulla had advised this, reasoning nobody saw the plain dwellers as a threat and so any still holding suspicions would not perceive favour.

Torbal greeted the people of the Plains and once more gave his thanks for their help, acknowledging it had not been their fight. He was brief, allowing Ulla to use her powers of persuasion.

Charm them as you did me, my love.

While Ulla spoke to the Tarakans, Torbal moved over to the young lady from Fallowden, Emiren. She saw him approach and immediately stood up, almost knocking over her chair. Torbal gestured in a placating manner.

"Be at ease, young one. I think we can all let protocol slide today," he said, offering her a smile. She was a beautiful young woman and seemed alive with a pure energy Torbal wasn't sure he'd ever had.

"I am glad you made it through the many storms you were caught in, Emiren," he commented.

She took a deep breath and looked around. "It is hard to believe I am here in Gamle Hovestad now, my lord. A few months ago, Argol Forest and Fallowden were my world. And now, I have set foot in every corner of Ragnekai."

Torbal sighed. "It is easy for the lords of the realm to take it all for granted. Your words serve to remind me that Ragnekai is home to many people and different cultures. I hope the future will see the realm flow with new friendships."

Torbal then lowered his voice. "Tell me about the cure. Do you think it will work?"

"I think so," she whispered excitedly. "My mother remembers quite a bit of what was written, and I have been talking with my mentor about it. We believe a certain mix of herbs, some very rare, can unblock pathways within the mind."

She was already losing Torbal and he wished Cherin were here to help out.

"Is that what happened to those that turned? Their minds were blocked?"

Emiren scratched the back of her head and spoke her next words hesitantly. "I have a theory—just a theory, my lord—that the mind in all living things is like a flower."

Torbal nodded, glad she was keeping it simple.

"Some minds, like those in humans, are well watered and exposed to a great deal of sunshine, so they bloom. Our minds are like glorious tulips in spring, full of vibrant colour, loaded with thought."

She was grinning now and Torbal found her enthusiasm infectious.

"The fungus that Seolta used dried out this wonderful flower, starved it of sunlight, air, and water, and so those poor people lost their capacity for higher thinking. They wilted."

That makes sense.

"So, if we can give the flower, or mind, all that it needs, it might flourish again. My hope is that the minds of these poor souls are in a kind of hibernation, and have suffered no serious damage, my lord."

She looked at him with wide eyes and expectation.

"I am no expert with herb-lore," he said, "but what you have told me sounds reasonable. Indeed, the human body is a miraculous thing, healing all manner of wounds and sickness with a little help from medicine. It is not so strange to think the mind could be the same."

"Yes!" she cried and slapped his arm.

He stared at her. Her cheeks had turned a deep crimson.

"Forgive me, my lord. I sometimes get quite excited..."

Torbal chuckled. "May you keep that excitement alive for many years yet!"

He wanted to ask a few more questions about Emiren's theory, but he knew he should keep moving. He caught Ulla approaching out of the corner of his eye so bid Emiren a joyful evening. The young lady scampered off, no doubt embarrassed she had been so familiar with him.

"Charming the young ladies, my dear?" teased Ulla.

"Yes, as a matter of fact. She likes my beard apparently," he joked, stroking his white growth.

Ulla sighed. "Of course she does," she responded in a dry tone.

Torbal raised his elbow for her to link arms with him and they moved on. Torbal acquired a cup of wine from a passing attendant and the two of them carried on with their rounds.

"Do you think we can build a better realm?" he asked her.

"I believe we must. And so, we will."

He saw the determination in her face and felt his own nervous optimism rise above the doubts.

Yes, we will.

CHAPTER 2

SVARD

Two Months After The Storm Of Ragnekai

"Didn't see you at the feast, First Ranger?"

Svard turned on the cobbled street of the Hellag district, wincing in pain as he remembered his ankle was broken and sudden movements were a bad idea.

Kailen stood there with the same mocking expression he had seen a thousand times before the Dark Raven decided to shit all over the realm.

"I was on my way, truth be told, but can't move so quick these days. Are they still serving?" he asked as innocently as he could.

"Idiot!" She laughed. "You didn't miss much. Only Torbal and Ulla setting out their vision for the future of Ragnekai."

Svard shrugged and shifted his crutch under his arm. "Well, that's good. Glad I didn't miss anything of importance. Was worried I'd be in the dark about a rise in ale prices."

Kailen grinned and walked over to him, her body subtly swaying.

She knows exactly what she is doing but is very talented at hiding that fact.

"You going to kick my crutch away and rob me blind now?" he asked with a frown.

Kailen cocked her head left and right as if considering it. "Of course not," she said with a smile. "Was going to kick your crutch away and laugh."

Svard rolled his eyes. "I certainly missed your wit when I was stuck in the Holy Sepulchre with a horde of mindless beast-men." She opened her mouth to speak but he held up a finger. "And also when I was lying on the roof of that church tower in Bregustol, in agonising pain, waiting for the Valkyna to come and get me."

She gestured with her hands for him to hurry up and finish his complaining.

"And also, this morning when I spent Warrior knows how long getting dressed." He shook his head. "Yep, I really could have done with your singular wit in these times of hardship."

She came closer and he felt his heart beat a touch faster.

"It's so good to be wanted," she purred. "And let's not forget you only got down from that roof because Brax and I heard your pathetic moaning!" She grasped her own leg and put on a pained face. "Help, help, I've broken a toe-nail! First Warrior save me!"

Svard rolled his eyes. "I should have kept my mouth shut. Might have been saved by one of the many beauties I saw in Bregustol."

Kailen thrust out her chin. "Yeah?"

"Yeah."

She grinned and reached out a hand, taking his. She said nothing.

Now or never, you coward!

"So, erm, are you busy this evening?" he asked, his stomach rolling. Svard couldn't believe that with all he had been through, he was still scared of asking a simple question.

"Yes, I am a little busy actually," she replied, her hand slipping away.

Svard's heart fell, his courage crumbling and his hopes dashed.

You've been fooling yourself, you dumb ox!

Kailen brushed the hair from her eyes and casually continued, "I'm having dinner with someone."

Svard's gut tensed and a dull pain began to grow. It had just been one night for her, just a quick fling between the covers and a distant memory by morning. Svard tried to pull himself together.

"Oh… Well, that's nice. Anybody I know?" he asked and immediately regretted it.

"Strangely enough, you do know him," she replied with a wicked grin.

Raven's wings, what is this? Is she trying to hurt me?

Svard knew Kailen had a reputation for being cold-hearted with relationships, but to be on the receiving end gave him a whole new perspective of it. Who was her dinner companion? It was someone Svard knew.

Brax?! Please, First Warrior, don't let that be true…

He struggled to control himself, wanting to vent his frustration and tell her what he thought of women who teased men and gave them hope where there was none.

Kailen punched him lightly in the chest and he almost lost his crutch. He swiped it just as the wooden prop began to slip away from his body.

"Ow, what in…?!"

She sighed. "I'm having dinner with *you*, you numb-skull!"

Svard stared at her. His jaw dropped. Then she burst out laughing and he didn't know whether to punch her back or grab her for a kiss.

Kailen made the choice for him, grabbing his tunic and leaning up to him. She planted a kiss on his lips and then tutted.

"I thought you were the smart one out of you, Rorthal, and Brax."

Svard was still at a loss for words. He frowned.

"What will give you back the power of speech? Another kiss? Another punch?" She raised an eyebrow. "Or maybe a kick in the balls."

Svard instinctively hobbled backwards and closed his legs, which sent Kailen into another fit of laughter.

"First Warrior, help me! You are so easy to tease!"

Svard finally found his inner-calm and shook his head, trying his best to look sad. "No, I was just a bit surprised, that's all. I'm out with the Rangers tonight. Was wondering if you wanted to come. Cuyler asked me to bring you along. I think he rather likes you."

Kailen stopped laughing. Her face went grave, and she stared into his eyes.

There was a moment of silence. Then Svard's serious expression crumbled into a smirk.

"Raven's beak!" she cried. "I'll break your crutch if you're not careful, then the other ankle too!"

Svard held out his hand and she took it again. He pulled her in and kissed her with a fervour he hoped would send a message. She offered no resistance and he took that as a satisfactory answer.

"This is going to be fun, don't you think?" she murmured.

Svard shrugged, pulling her closer so their bodies were pressed against each other. And also so he could lean on her a bit, as his good leg was tiring.

"Either that, or one of us will be dead within the week."

He kissed her again and his chest heaved with a glorious feeling. She adopted a serious expression, placing a hand on her chin as if in deep thought.

"My money is on the Ranger. Heart gave out in the throes of ecstasy," she uttered, her voice now a sultry tone.

Svard twisted his body away, feeling himself harden and not wanting her to have the pleasure of that small victory. Kailen was not having it though and moved into him, grinding herself against his loins.

"Think you'll be able to wait till after dinner, First Ranger? Shall we take a quick nap at your place?"

Damn this woman. She is quite the siren.

Svard blew out a breath and bit his lip. "That might be a… Damn, no, sorry, I have to do something."

Her face darkened. "Are you playing with me?"

"No, really, Kailen. I'll meet you for dinner, but I must visit someone first."

Kailen studied him and then realisation dawned. "Your friend's family?"

Svard nodded. "Freda's looked in on them, but I haven't made the trip yet."

Kailen hugged him. "You're a good man, First Ranger."

"And you are a fine lady, Kailen. Meet me at The First Hammer around the evening bell?"

"The First Hammer. I'll be there." She kissed him again, then raised a hand to his face, her expression one of concern. "Do you want me to walk with you?"

Svard sighed. "I appreciate the offer, but I need to gather my thoughts. I can't walk quickly so I'll have time to sort my head out. You can walk me home after The First Hammer," he said with a grin.

"If you mind your manners, First Ranger."

She gave him one last kiss, then sauntered off. He watched her go and felt a whirl of emotion.

His closest friend Lorken was gone, killed because of schemes and treachery. Three of his captains were dead, victims of fanatics and sorcery. The realm had been ripped apart from within and the future was fragile.

Yet watching Kailen walking away, he felt a measure of optimism. At least he might get this right. Even if things didn't work out, he reckoned they would be good company for each other in the coming months. Kailen had left her position within the Helligan state, despite Lady Ulla begging her to continue in her role serving Gamle Hovestad. Svard knew though that Kailen could barely look Hulda in the eye and every day would be a torment to both of them.

Maybe it's better she takes a step back.

And he might still bear the title of First Ranger, but he was little more than a dead weight with his injuries. He was considering resigning his commission and encouraging Cuyler to take the leadership of the Rangers. Cuyler had seen much and was fortunate enough to have survived. He knew better than most that quick judgments were dangerous, and friends could be enemies, while enemies could become allies.

He'd be a good First.

Svard kept hobbling along, taking it slow. He looked at the houses and shops of Gamle Hovestad and mentally acknowledged how lucky the city was not to have suffered like Bregustol and Argyllan. And Meridia, he noted sourly.

Lorken, in a strange way, it may be that the future is brighter now for Darl, Torg, and Eira. Not in the way I had imagined back when Orben outlined his plan, but that is probably for the best.

He looked up at the deep summer blue of the sky.

Any advice for this new path I'm stepping onto here, old friend?

He grinned, knowing Lorken would be as surprised as himself that he was entering into some kind of relationship with a lady. A relationship that lasted more than a few days.

How did you keep Jenna happy? You never told me your secret, Lorken.

He found himself choking up, so he got back to the business of inching along the street, one foot raised, the crutch creaking with each step.

Best foot forward...

CHAPTER 3

WULFNER

Three Months After The Storm Of Ragnekai

"I really don't want to say goodbye to you two," said Wulfner, fighting back tears as they stood outside the gates of Fallowden. "You two troublemakers!"

To his left, Tacet chuckled.

Emiren and Lunyai both hugged him, and he felt love within him for the two young ladies. He'd lost his wife and daughter years ago but had found a new family in the midst of this terrible storm.

The Winds blow a merry dance…

Emiren pulled back. "Come back in the spring, Wulfner. Kall promised he'd brew more ale over the winter and Da has sworn he'll conjure up a new stew in the cold months."

Wulfner grinned. "How can I say no to that?"

"And tell Uncle Camran to visit us before he makes his journey to the Radiant Isles next month," she added.

He nodded.

Emiren then turned to Wulfner's companion. "Please sing again for us one day, Tacet."

The Meridian shot her a grin that fell away as he spoke. "I have been penning a rather long ballad about the events this year. Not sure people will be ready to hear it yet though. The memories are still too fresh," he finished, casting a sideways glance at Wulfner. The northerner knew there was more to that statement than Emiren and Lunyai might guess. The once Velox Rider of Lord Rencarro carried guilt along with his sorrow.

"And bring Balther with you to the Plains, Wulfner!" said Lunyai. "I would like to see him ride with the wind under hooves and Yaai shining on his back."

"Aye, I'll try to drag that big lunk down this way someday."

Emiren leaned up and kissed Wulfner on the cheek. "That's for Balther. Thank him again," she said, her voice croaking with emotion.

Lunyai pulled his head down and kissed the other cheek. "And tell him Lunyai will sing to him."

Wulfner couldn't speak. His eyes were blurring, and he felt a tear slip down his cheek.

"Come on, big man," said Tacet, slapping his back. "Let's get some miles behind us before midday."

Emiren had an arm around Lunyai's waist and the Tarakan had one arm draped over the Fallowden girl's shoulder. Both were crying silently.

Damn the Winds!

Wulfner managed to nod, then let Tacet pull him away. They began walking along the Forest Road that led to Argyllan. Each step felt heavy and Wulfner had to resist looking back.

"You know you've got to kiss Balther twice now, don't you?" commented Tacet flatly.

Wulfner snorted a laugh that was dangerously close to a sob. "Shut up, pretty boy! If you're not careful, Balther will give you a nice kiss with his fist. You didn't part on the best of terms, remember?"

"Hold on there. I am definitely not going to Ceapung. Westhealfe is my destination, thank you very much."

"Oh yeah?" said Wulfner with a wry smile. "Wonder why…"

Tacet put on a show of looking baffled. "No idea what you mean, my friend."

Friend? That is what we are now. We tried to kill each other that day...
I'm glad we were both inept in that endeavour.

Wulfner grinned and pulled on his beard. "I was actually thinking we could make a nice partnership, you and me."

Tacet turned to him. "Excuse me?"

"Wulfner the Trader and his minstrel friend, Rowan the Rhymer!" he cried out, throwing his arms to the sky. "You sing, I sell, and we split the profits down the middle. Travel the realm and see the sights!"

Tacet made a humming noise that Wulfner took to be him considering the idea.

"Your proposal has merit. Wouldn't mind seeing the sights..."

Wulfner had no doubt which *sights* Tacet had in mind. He gave in and turned to look back. Emiren and Lunyai hadn't moved and were watching them.

Wulfner waved one last time, then slapped Tacet on the shoulder. "Sing something, damn it, else I'll sob like a child."

Tacet cleared his throat rather dramatically.

"Far we shall roam on this blessed day
Where we go, I cannot say
Wulfner owes me an ale, yay
I reckon more than one, hey-hey!

"Those two ladies there said Don't you go!
But Tacet is thirsty, we all know
I'll take us to a place that I know
The bar-maid there's as pure as snow."

Wulfner stopped walking and turned to the Meridian. "I remember slightly different lyrics last time you sang this one."

Tacet shrugged. "I'm in need of an ale and a pretty smile."

Wulfner rolled his eyes. "Beginning to wonder if roaming the realm with you is a good idea," he huffed, then resumed his steps.

"How about letting me hear some of that ballad you wrote? There's only me to hear," he called over his shoulder.

Tacet hurried to match his stride and blew out a breath. "It's not finished yet. And needs work."

Wulfner knew Tacet was bursting to have an audience for his work-in-progress. "Just sing the bloody thing!"

Tacet made an even more dramatic show of clearing his throat. But when he let his voice soar, Wulfner was once again stunned by just how good a singer this man was. There was strength to his singing, coupled with an aching sorrow that hinted at a brighter past or future, but was awash with mystery.

"When I think of Ragnekai
I feel my heart, my heart it starts to ache so.
Ohh yea, oh yeyy, ohh yea.
My thoughts swirl, my memories curl
And I have to wonder just where it all began.
Ohh yea, oh yeyy, ohh yea."

It was a good start and Wulfner felt the tune was a skilled balance of the mournful and the hopeful.

"The wounds were old, so I was told
And they had never well and truly healed.
Mmm, hmm, mmm.
Mistrust and silence led to violence
We were blind, and the realm's fate was sealed.
Mmm, hmm, mmm.

Now remember those who're gone
See their face, hear their voice, remember how they shone
Never forget the words they said
Said to us all, Don't forget, oh keep them there
If you cry, look to the sky,
Your tears, your sigh

Never say good-bye.
They will forever be, so bright in our memory..."

Tacet stopped singing and coughed.

"I haven't got far yet, and what I just sang is jumbled."

Wulfner couldn't speak. It had been short, but the words and Tacet's voice had plunged deep within him and brought to the surface not just the recent past but years gone by.

Rowena, Sunniva, I see your faces, I hear your voices. And I remember so many words you said.

He saw Tacet look at him, but he couldn't respond yet. His friend kept his own silence and they carried on up the Forest Road, bird song the only sound other than their boots scuffing the ground.

That boy Anton, Loranna, Nerian, Corann, Lord Rencarro himself...so many lost to the darkness of vengeance.

Wulfner turned his mind to Emiren and Lunyai and found some comfort knowing they had survived the storm and were determined to help Ragnekai heal. There was so much to do. He hoped the wounds could heal properly this time.

"Let's pick up the pace," he grunted. "I want to have my dinner in Argyllan and sleep in a warm bed."

"I won't argue," replied the Meridian.

Wulfner shot him a sideways glance. "The song is good, my friend. Keep working on it."

CHAPTER 4

EMIREN

Four Months After The Storm Of Ragnekai

"It's so beautiful," murmured Emiren.

She sat with Lunyai upon a grassy cliff-top of the Plains, looking out over the Western Sea, the Tarakan settlement a few hundred yards away. Tarak was dozing beside them, tiny snorts and shudders making Emiren think he was dreaming. The sun was sinking and looked as if it was dipping gradually into the water on the horizon. The young lady from Fallowden imagined steam rising in great geysers, the fire of the sun meeting the cold of the depths.

"And the sea is so calm today," observed Lunyai. "I think we will soon have ships sailing this way again, bringing trade from the Radiant Isles."

"Will they stop here, at one of the coves down there you told me about?" asked Emiren, gesturing over the cliff.

"Maybe," said Lunyai with a smile. "I want to learn another of their shanties!"

Emiren laughed. She pulled Lunyai closer and placed a kiss lightly on her cheek.

"You charmed me so that night in Ceapung." Emiren raised a hand to Lunyai's cheek. "As Yaai sets out there, my sun sets with you, Lunyai."

Emiren looked into the Tarakan's eyes and there were tears there, balanced above a smile more glorious than the magnificent view before them.

"And while Tlenaii watches over us both in the night, I will sleep well with you beside me."

They kissed each other gently, then once more and held their lips together for longer, a gentle pressure moving to and fro between them. They broke away and leaned their foreheads together. Tarak slept on, his sleep undisturbed.

"I sometimes feel I am in a dream," whispered Emiren, stroking one of Tarak's ears. "All that happened. So many terrible things, so much sorrow crashed down upon this realm, and yet now I feel no fear. I worry I will wake up." She let out a mirthless chuckle.

Lunyai pulled her in. "If you wake up, I will be there. And then when you sleep again, I will be there." Lunyai paused and her breath shuddered. "I love you, Emiren, and I will never leave you."

Emiren felt a surge within her chest and she hugged Lunyai tightly.

"I love you too. And I would never leave you. I never could," she whispered into her ear.

They sat there in silence then as the sun continued to be swallowed by the vastness of the Western Sea. The sky before them became ablaze with simmering shades of orange and pink, a majestic sight that needed no words.

Emiren let thoughts about their future swirl in her head. They had agreed that they would not make a home in Fallowden or upon the Tarakan Plains, but travel the realm, returning every so often to be with their families. Emiren was eager to learn more about the incredible properties of plants and roots in the realm, and also to share what she knew already. Lunyai also felt a need to bring Tarakan knowledge and animal husbandry ways to the people who now lived in a new land with new laws, unified under the guidance of Lord

Torbal and Lady Ulla. In the spring they would visit the Lodge of Guardians and report to those who now resided within.

The future is brighter. We will make the realm a better place for all.

Emiren did lament the fact that both books had been lost though. So much could be learned from them and so much could be undone if the knowledge within were abused. Moryn had Cherin's book and nobody knew where he was now. Emiren felt a cold ache within her stomach as she thought about the deed he had committed in Lowenden.

Everything about him was a lie…

And Corann's daughter undoubtedly had the book High King Sedmund had hidden away. Idelisa also carried a frightening and deadly weapon. Nobody knew where she had gone either and that was a worrying thought. Lady Ulla had sent Helligan Rangers searching and Lord Eligius had dispatched Velox Riders, but as far as Emiren knew, there had been no sign of either Moryn or Idelisa's passing.

Maybe they left Ragnekai…

Lunyai nudged her. "Stop thinking about what might not be."

Emiren smiled. "Am I that easy to read?"

Lunyai rocked her head side to side. "Not that easy but your body does tense when you worry," she said, sticking a finger in Emiren's ribs.

Emiren snorted with laughter. She had always been ticklish.

She lowered herself into Lunyai's lap and let her head rest upon the Tarakan's arm. She breathed in the evening air and the scent of Lunyai.

The realm will heal.

Lunyai stroked her hair and began singing the Tarakalo.

All will be well.

EPILOGUE

"Now be polite, the both of you! Remember Freda fought alongside your father. She feels guilty she couldn't protect him, so do not ask what happened that day." Jenna took a deep breath to swallow the emotion rising. "All we should keep in mind is that she stood by him at the end and thanks to her, your father was not alone."

She rested a hand on a shoulder of each lad, Darl now a head taller than her, Torg's eyes the same level as hers. She smiled, wishing Lorken could see them now.

"Your father would be—"

A knock at the door interrupted her.

"That must be her now. Remember, best behaviour!"

Jenna went and opened the door to find Freda standing there. She couldn't help but gasp. The Helligan soldier had braided her hair into one length that hung forward past her left shoulder. The right side of her head was freshly shorn, and she had inked a delicate pattern there. A thin line of black accentuated her eyes and Jenna felt sure she had put some rouge upon her cheeks.

But if her hair and face were a surprise, her vestment was truly unexpected. Freda wore a dress, sleeveless but running down past her ankles.

"That bad, huh?" said Freda, shifting her weight side to side.

Jenna found her voice. "No, no. First Warrior, no! It seems you are beautiful no matter what the day."

Freda's face looked as surprised as Jenna had felt moments before. Lorken's widow ushered Freda in and couldn't help but hug her. Freda returned the embrace and whispered, "Lorken truly found a queen."

They parted and Jenna choked a laugh.

"I'd have been hard pressed to keep him if he saw you like this!"

Freda waved away the compliment and turned to the lads. "Nice to see you again, Darl. And pleasure to make your acquaintance, Torg."

Jenna chuckled. The pair were speechless.

"You like the dress, lads?" asked Freda, and she did a twirl, the linen flowing around her legs.

Jenna slapped her playfully on the arm. "Enough of your charm, Lady Ellepiger!"

She motioned to the table where food was laid out waiting.

"Freda, please sit here," said Jenna, gesturing to one end of the table. As soon as she had indicated where Freda was to be seated, Darl and Torg attempted to win the place next to her, both grabbing the chair. Their eyes locked and Jenna began to wonder if a quiet lunch, just her and Freda, would not have been a better idea.

"Darl, take my place there, and I'll sit at the opposite end to Freda," she told them, putting them equal distance from their apparently overly enchanting guest.

First Warrior, save me! Lorken, your sons are growing too quickly.

"Where's the little one?" enquired Freda, taking her seat.

Jenna sighed. "Off out somewhere as usual. I'm sorry, Freda, I did tell her we had a guest, but she seemed more agitated than usual this morning, so I didn't push the matter. Please forgive us."

Freda shook her head. "Not at all, Jenna. I'm sure I'll meet her one day. Maybe she is a roamer, needs to feel free like the wind."

Jenna smiled but inwardly wished she had been able to get through to Eira since Freda had last visited. If anything, she felt as if her daughter was becoming more distant as the days went by.

Lorken's widow took her place and started passing round the meal. She'd made a special effort and was delighted to see Freda beaming as her plate was piled up.

"Feels like I'm having dinner with Lady Ulla herself!" she exclaimed.

It didn't take long for the whole table to relax. Freda was relentless in her compliments toward Jenna's cooking and extremely adept at joking with the boys without straying into particularly bawdy humour.

"What is it like, out at sea?" asked Torg, his nervousness disappearing more quickly than his older brother's.

Freda grinned. "If you haven't got sea legs, it's one never-ending cycle of nausea, vomit, and thirst. But," she said, giving Jenna's son a wink, "if you can stomach it, it's like being a step closer to the First Warrior."

"How do you mean?" asked Darl. Jenna could see both her boys were fascinated.

"A storm on land is like the First Warrior's whisper in your ear. A storm out at sea is the First Warrior calling your name and making you feel His presence, sending rains that lash your face, winds that howl like a banshee, and waves so powerful even the bravest are cowed and pray to Him with everything they can muster."

Jenna smiled. Her two sons were wide-eyed and enthralled by this warrior who lived half her life an unlucky chance away from meeting the Dark Raven. She was fairly sure neither of her sons would suddenly leave home and join the Helligan navy, but she felt she should change the subject.

"Freda, the realm seems to be healing after the trouble to the north, but you said you were sent out to sea by Lady Ulla. To patrol the coasts in case of Xerinthian galleys coming this way…" She let it hang, inviting Freda to take up the story. Jenna was worried when Freda's face clouded.

"Not sure if it's good or bad news, but I don't think the Xerinthian Empire will be coming this way."

Jenna was confused. Surely this was welcome.

"Sounds like good news to me," said Darl, echoing her thoughts.

Freda knocked back her ale. Torg instantly grabbed her mug and hurried off to refill it from the keg.

The Helligan soldier grinned. "Could get used to this, Jenna. Two handsome boys bringing me beer, and delicious food cooked by your beautiful self."

Jenna rolled her eyes, then stopped as she saw Darl was blushing.

Torg set Freda's mug on the table, the froth perched to the brink of cascading down the side of the cup.

"Please tell us why that could be bad news," he said excitedly.

Freda's face lost its humour. "Well, the reason the Xerinthian Empire probably won't be coming here is that I'm not sure there is an empire anymore."

Jenna gasped.

"What happened?" whispered Darl.

"Rumour is that civil war has brought the empire down. Now I know that no Xerinthian Empire in the world sounds like a good thing, but you have to wonder what follows the end of an empire." Freda shrugged. "I'm not much good with history but my uncle seems to think a known enemy is better than chaos. *Better the demon whose voice you have heard than the shadow whose shape is unknown.* Not sure those are the exact words, but my uncle said something like that."

Jenna suddenly felt afraid for Eira, off playing somewhere. She always came back safely, but she was still such a little thing.

"Ragnekai is stronger now though," said Freda, looking across at Jenna. "Don't worry about it. Lady Ulla and the guardians are wise and determined. They'll protect the realm."

The Helligan warrior smiled and Jenna felt some of her fear dissipate. From what she had heard from friends and at the market, the future of Ragnekai seemed brighter. The chaos that had engulfed so much of the land seemed to have woken the lords and captains, opened their eyes to the foolishness of fighting each other. Jenna didn't know that much but she kept hearing words like *united* and *together*. It seemed Ragnekai was changing for the better.

The meal continued and Jenna found her jaw aching before long, so much had she laughed. Freda truly had a talent for pushing the clouds away and bringing brilliant sunshine and refreshing winds. Jenna wondered what her husband was like. She hoped he appreciated how lucky he was to have this beautiful force of nature as his wife.

"Jenna, I've had the best time ever today, but I should be taking the road home now," said Freda when they had finished their third round of Warrior's Fire, a sweet but potent liquor that the Helligan marine had brought with her.

Lorken's widow smiled, then almost burst into tears with the swell of emotion being further fuelled by the amount of alcohol swirling in her blood. They all stood and Jenna moved round the table, her steps a bit wobbly. She steadied herself and took Freda's hand.

"Thank you so much for coming, Freda. We've all had a wonderful time thanks to you."

Darl and Torg nodded enthusiastically.

Jenna wished from the depths of her heart that Lorken were with them now, making some silly remark and all of them having one last laugh before their guest left.

Jenna pulled Freda to her. She squeezed their new friend tightly, not caring if her sons saw that she was more than mildly inebriated.

"Please come again."

"Not even the First Warrior could stop me," she whispered.

They released each other from the embrace and turned to see Darl and Torg waiting. Waiting expectantly, it seemed to Jenna.

Freda must have seen it too, as she laughed, then grabbed them both and brought them in for a hug. Jenna couldn't help but laugh at the sight of her two strapping sons being manhandled by this fair warrior of the waves.

"Next time I hope to meet Eira too," she said, as she let them go. "And maybe next year, in the spring, we can all take a boat down the Mimir, go and look upon the Lodge of Guardians. Should be built by then."

They said their farewells and Freda left, leaving their home with a lingering feeling of joy and mirth. Jenna opened her arms and beckoned Darl and Torg to her. They let their mother hold them close. She rocked side to side on her feet, kissing their heads in turn.

"Your father is watching you now and I know he is smiling."

EIRA

Eira loved Bresden Forest. There were no loud voices, just the wonderful sounds of the trees and the creatures who lived beneath them or in them. She looked at the green leaves above her now, her eyes drawing imaginary lines from one to another, and forming patterns that made her tense with excitement.

She focused on a branch and asked it to move closer to its neighbour. It did so, shuddering in its movement until it touched its friend. Eira clapped, then let it go. The branch swung back and a handful of leaves fell. One landed upon her outstretched hand. She looked at it and thought how much nicer it was than all the things her brothers made.

I will bring them here soon and show them. They should shape their wood like these leaves.

She skipped along the forest path, jumping over roots and leaping up to brush her fingertips against anything that hung low. Eira laughed her silent laugh and felt as if her father was watching her. She knew he was gone forever from this world, but she felt certain he was waiting somewhere for her. Not in the place her brothers talked about, some great hall in the night sky, but in an autumn grove that was golden. She would meet him there and together they would walk into the snows of winter.

Little one…

Eira stopped. She looked around, searching for the source of the voice. She could see nobody in the trees. Eira grinned. Her friend was playing a game of hide-and-seek with her. Eira lets her eyes roam around the forest, then sent her thoughts to her friend. She probably wasn't very good at the game. Not like Eira, who was better than her brothers.

Lorken's daughter ran to a weeping willow, darting in under the canopy and waited.

Little one, I have come.

Eira felt she would burst with the fun of this game. But she calmed herself and crouched down. Had her friend truly come to her forest?

There was a rustle and she saw someone approaching, a figure carefully winding its way between the trees, not walking on the open path. It had to be her friend! Eira did not reveal herself as that would spoil the game. Instead she slid around the willow, keeping the trunk between her and her friend.

Little one, I know you are close. I saw these trees moments ago. Are you hiding?

Eira peeked out and saw her friend clearly now. She wore a long, dark robe, its colours the deepest shades of the forest. Eira's friend reached up and slid back the hood. Eira's eyes widened. Her friend had no hair, or very little hair. And she had painted her head. Eira emitted a noiseless giggle.

The willow...

Her friend turned and looked directly at the tree where she hid, her face lighting up with a smile.

Eira knew the game was up so she jumped out and sent a message to all the trees around them. They shook as she had asked. Her friend looked up and her mouth opened.

"How can you do this?" she said with a gasp.

Eira cocked her head. She didn't know why others couldn't make things happen. She remembered her father becoming angry with her and felt sadness heavy upon her.

You are a wonder!

The words were like a kind hand stroking her hair. Eira brightened immediately and skipped over to her new friend. She instantly reached up to touch her head. Her friend leaned down and let Eira run her fingers over the tiny buds of hair growing anew.

Eira jumped up and down with joy, her friend's head so warm yet full of texture like Bresden Forest. She wondered why her mother did not do this with her own hair. She didn't have to shave it all off. Eira had seen her mother's new friend come to the house that morning, watching her quietly from one of her many hiding places. That lady had only shaved one side and Eira now imagined her mother doing the same.

It will look wonderful!

Her new friend, the one standing here now, straightened and Eira's hand fell away. The lady smiled again and Eira saw something behind the smile. There was sadness there. Eira frowned and tried to peer inside her new friend's thoughts. She was stopped by a gate though, an old wooden gate that Eira felt was also unhappy.

Forgive me, little one. I do not want to show you all I have seen. There is too much pain.

Eira asked a question.

Yes, like you, little one, I have lost those I loved. One of them, I didn't know I loved till this very moment...

Eira felt tears come to her eyes.

And another, I had lost once before.

Eira leaned in and hugged her new friend. She felt the lady's body tense for a moment, then relax, and then a hand was gently stroking her own head.

You truly are a wonder...

Her friend leaned back from her hug, then knelt down so their eyes met. "My name is Siorraidh. What is yours?"

Eira cocked her head. Would her friend be with her forever? She let her thoughts flow.

"Eira. What a beautiful name!"

Siorraidh let out a sigh and looked at the forest around them. Eira asked the branches to reach down and they did. Siorraidh's eyes widened and she let out a small laugh.

The two of them then played together, running around the trees and kicking up leaves. Eira made the trees shake to bring more leaves tumbling down, showers of red and golden brown. Siorraidh twirled within the falling leaves, her smile so wonderful. Eira cart-wheeled over and grabbed her hand. Siorraidh looked down.

"If only we could be children for longer," she whispered, a tear slipping from the corner of one eye. Eira's hand darted up and caught it before it fell to the leaves below her feet. She rubbed the tear between her thumb and finger, then closed her eyes.

Why are there so many tears?

Her friend took a deep breath. Eira stared at her face and saw a new pain there. There was a struggle. Siorraidh was making a decision. Eira waited.

After a few moments, Siorraidh nodded, smiled, then took one of Eira's hands.

"I must go away for a time."

Eira pouted. Her friend had only just arrived.

"There are things I must do. Secrets I must discover."

Again, the pain in her eyes. Eira leaned in to hug her.

"Will you…"

Eira looked up once more.

"Will you wait for me? I will come back and we can play together again."

Eira pretended to be thinking about it, scrunching her face up.

"Little one?"

Eira sent her thoughts. Siorraidh smiled warmly.

"You are so kind. Such a wonder." She sighed. "And now I must say good-bye."

Siorraidh knelt down and hugged Eira. The young girl let herself be wrapped within the embrace. Her new friend was nice. She hoped Siorraidh would not be gone too long.

Eira asked Siorraidh where she was going.

A place that others can't see. I have to find something.

THE OLD WOUNDS TRILOGY

ENDS HERE.

BUT THERE IS MORE TO TELL.

SO MUCH MORE.

UPDATES AVAILABLE ON FACEBOOK:

BUCKMASTER BOOKS

NOTE OF THANKS TO READERS

Thank you, thank you, thank you so much for reading this trilogy! I sincerely hope you enjoyed it, and if so, please consider leaving a review on Goodreads or Amazon. The reviews help tremendously. And if you're ever in Yokohama, drop me a line and we'll go for a beer!

This trilogy is finished but as you can probably guess (and I wrote it in big letters anyway!), the world of Urami has more tales to tell. I have the basic outline of the next trilogy planned out. It will be set in a different realm, but it is set after the events of The Old Wounds trilogy, and those events will impact upon the story to some degree. But it will be a new story with new characters. End of 2020 with any luck!

Thank you again! I know there are so many books out there now and everyone is so busy, so for you to have given this trilogy your time is something I am very grateful for. Massive group hug!

WWW.BUCKMASTERBOOKS.COM

ACKNOWLEDGEMENTS

The third book was a joy to write but also extremely difficult, trying to bring all the threads together. As always, some wonderful people helped me to get it ready for print.

Stephanie Diaz knows my strengths and weaknesses well by now. She gave words of praise that lifted me, words of constructive criticism that pushed me, and words of wisdom that enlightened me! I am very grateful. (www.stephaniediazbooks.com)

Karin Wittig has created all three covers and I absolutely love them. There is a progression and a theme, and each one really embodies the story within that book. (karinwittig.com)

I have to apologise for Robert (www.fantasy-map.net) for not putting the latest map into the book but I felt I wasn't ready to show the wider world yet. The map will likely be in the first book of the next trilogy. Watch this space!

Once again, I could not have done this without the input of my good friend, Sarah Crabb. She gave up a lot of time over her summer to read the book, make corrections, offer suggestions and give me the reader's perspective. Thank you so massively much, matey!

Dad, Nick, Andrew, thank you for all the support!

Shout-out to Elle Lewis, a fellow newbie author, who has been a huge source of nerdy support and geeky humour! Check out her "Dark Touch" for some great supernatural urban fantasy!

And thank you Roger for reading & reviewing Winds and Moons, and then reading an ARC of Storms. Also, thanks to Hitomi, Kenta and Maria for their early support!

ABOUT THE AUTHOR

That's me! Born in Basingstoke, raised in Maidenhead and now in my twentieth year in Japan (with a couple of years in California thrown in for good measure when I was a kid).

I've loved books since I was a wee nipper and the same goes for writing stories. Pretty sure I wrote some epic stuff when I was ten years old!

I suffered from insomnia as a child and used to lie awake conjuring up stories, most of which had yours truly as the hero. When I was old enough to have a Walkman, the music would help shape the tales until I finally fell asleep (2-3 hrs after going to bed). And those stories were influenced by Fighting Fantasy Gamebooks (plus Out Of The Pit & Titan), Forgotten Realms (Avatar trilogy & Dark Elf trilogy), White Dwarf magazine and awesome 80s fantasy flicks (Red Sonja, Hawk the Slayer, Conan the Barbarian, Krull, Clash of the Titans, Time Bandits, The Beastmaster and Excalibur to name but a few – that was a Golden Age of fantasy cinema!).

Reality got busier (Booooo!) and my down-time to daydream faded away. Warwick University (good times!), then JET Programme (wonderful two years in Iwate), next bumped into my future wife on a train, got married, and began a life together in Yokohama. The next few years were work, work, and more work. Haruki and Tomoki entered the world, and it was happy-busy times. Then, in 2017, Tomoki started elementary school and I finally had the time to begin my quest to achieve that childhood dream of writing a book. So I did. Then two more. And I never want to stop! I just wish my Mum could be here. She wasn't a fantasy buff, but she would have read it and loved it, because she found something good in everything. I miss her greatly.

MUSIC THAT KEEPS ME GOING!

Here is a list of artists and music that I listen to in my daily life. All of them are incredible musicians and I am so grateful for their music.

- **Steeleye Span.** This group has been around for 50 years now! Sadly, I have never seen them live but listen to them a great deal. They remind me of England and also conjure up images of taverns, villagers and ales. My life is far more cheerful thanks to their music.
- **Loreena McKennitt.** An incredibly talented lady whose voice is one of pure strength and beauty.
- **Omnia.** Pagan folk at its best!
- **Les Miserables** soundtrack. Reminds me of my Mum and all the other musicals we went to see together.
- **The Cybertronic Spree.** A truly awesome group of nerdy musicians. I can't help but grin when I watch them on YouTube.
- **The HU.** A recent discovery, these guys are something special. Traditional Mongolian folk blended with modern metal.
- Honourable mentions go to Faun, Liliac, Miranda Kitchpanich, Led Zeppelin, Cream, Neil Diamond, Metallica, Slayer, White Zombie, Transvision Vamp, Belinda Carlisle!

And thank you to Shinichi Sekita and his Roundabout bar for introducing me to my British musical roots!

Made in the USA
Middletown, DE
13 October 2023

40762887R00298